FAIR WARNING

ALSO BY MICHAEL CONNELLY

THE HARRY BOSCH NOVELS

The Black Echo
The Black Ice
The Concrete Blonde
The Last Coyote
Trunk Music
Angels Flight
A Darkness More than Night
City of Bones
Lost Light
The Narrows
The Closers

Echo Park
The Overlook
Nine Dragons
The Drop
The Black Box
The Burning Room
The Crossing
The Wrong Side of Goodbye
Two Kinds of Truth
Dark Sacred Night
The Night Fire

THE LINCOLN LAWYER NOVELS

The Lincoln Lawyer
The Brass Verdict
The Reversal

The Fifth Witness
The Gods of Guilt
The Law of Innocence

OTHER NOVELS

The Poet
Blood Work
Void Moon
Chasing the Dime

The Scarecrow
The Late Show
Fair Warning

NONFICTION
Crime Beat

E-BOOKS

Suicide Run
Angle of Investigation
Mulholland Dive

The Safe Man
Switchblade

FAIR WARNING

MICHAEL CONNELLY

GRAND CENTRAL
PUBLISHING

NEW YORK BOSTON

Copyright © 2020 by Hieronymus, Inc.
Excerpt from *The Law of Innocence* copyright © 2020 by Hieronymus, Inc.

Grand Central Publishing
Hachette Book Group
1290 Avenue of the Americas, New York, NY 10104
grandcentralpublishing.com
twitter.com/grandcentralpub

Originally published in hardcover and ebook by Little, Brown & Company in May 2020
First trade paperback edition: February 2021

Grand Central Publishing is a division of Hachette Book Group, Inc. The Grand Central Publishing name and logo is a trademark of Hachette Book Group, Inc.

The publisher is not responsible for websites (or their content) that are not owned by the publisher.

The Hachette Speakers Bureau provides a wide range of authors for speaking events. To find out more, go to hachettespeakersbureau.com or call (866) 376-6591.

Library of Congress Control Number: 2020930361

ISBNs: 978-1-5387-3633-3 (trade paperback), 978-0-316-53943-2 (ebook)

Printed in the United States of America

LSC-H

Printing 1, 2020

To Tim Marcia, Detective
Many thanks for your service to the City of Angels

Who is not at once repulsed and attracted by a diabolical act?

—David Goldman,
Our Genes, Our Choices

FAIR WARNING

PROLOGUE

She liked his car. It was the first time she had been in an electric. All she could hear was the wind as they cut through the night.

"So quiet," she said.

Only two words and she had slurred them. The third Cosmo had done something to her tongue.

"It'll sneak up on you," the driver said. "That's for sure."

He looked over at her and smiled. But she thought he was just checking on her because she had messed up her words.

He then turned and nodded through the windshield.

"We're here," he said. "Is there parking?"

"You can park behind my car," she said. "I have two spaces in the garage but they're like...one behind the other. *Totem,* I think it's called."

"Tandem?"

"Oh, right, right. *Tandem.*"

She started to laugh at her mistake, a spiral laugh she couldn't get out of. The Cosmos again. And the drops from the green pharmacy she took before heading out in the Uber that night.

The man lowered his window and crisp evening air invaded the comfort of the car.

"Can you remember the combo?" he asked.

Tina pulled herself up in the seat so she could look around better and get her bearings. She recognized that they were already outside the garage gate at her apartment. That didn't seem right. She could not remember telling him where she lived.

"The combo?" he asked again.

The keypad was on the wall and within reach from the driver's window. She realized that she knew the combo that would open the gate but she could not remember the name of the man she had chosen to take home.

"4-6-8-2-5."

As he punched the numbers in she tried not to laugh again. Some guys really hated that.

They entered the garage and she pointed to the spot where he could pull in behind her Mini. Soon they were on the elevator and she pushed the correct button and then leaned into him for support. He put his arm around her and held her up.

"Do you have a nickname?" she asked.

"What do you mean?" he asked.

"Like, what do people call you? You know, for fun."

He shook his head.

"I guess they just call me by my name," he said.

No help there. She dropped it. She could figure out his name later, but the truth was she probably wouldn't need it. There would be no *later*. There almost never was.

The door opened on the third floor and she led him into the hallway. Her apartment was two doors down.

The sex was good but not extraordinary. The only thing unusual was that he didn't push back against her requirement of a condom. He had even brought his own. Kudos for that but she still thought he would be a one-timer. The search for that indescribable thing that would fill up the emptiness inside would go on.

After he flushed the condom he got back into bed with her. She was hoping for an excuse—early start in the morning, wife waiting at home, anything—but he wanted to get back in bed and cuddle. He roughly moved in behind her and turned her so her back was against his chest. He had shaved himself and she could feel the tiny spikes of returning hair pricking her back.

"You know..."

She got no further with the complaint. He pivoted his body and now she was on her back completely on top of him. His chest was like sandpaper. His arm came around from behind her and he bent it at the elbow into a V. He then used his free hand to push her neck into the V. He tightened his arms and she felt her air passages collapse. She could not yell for help. She had no air to make a sound. She struggled but her legs were tangled in the sheets and he was too strong. His hold on her neck was an iron vise.

Darkness began shading the edges of her vision. He raised his head off the bed and brought his mouth to her ear.

"People call me the Shrike," he whispered.

JACK

1

I had called the story "The King of Con Artists." At least that was my headline. I typed it up top but was pretty sure it would get changed because it would be overstepping my bounds as a reporter to turn in a story with a headline. The headlines and the decks below them were the purview of the editor and I could already hear Myron Levin chiding, "Does the editor rewrite your ledes or call up the subjects of your pieces to ask additional questions? No, he doesn't. He stays in his lane and that means you need to stay in yours."

Since Myron was that editor, it would be hard to come back with any sort of defense. But I sent in the story with the suggested headline anyway because it was perfect. The story was about the dark netherworld of the debt-collection business—$600 million a year of it siphoned off in scams—and the rule at *FairWarning* was to bring every fraud down to a face, either the predator's or the prey's, the victim's or the victimizer's. And this time it was the predator. Arthur Hathaway, the King of Con Artists, was the best of the best. At sixty-two years old, he had worked every con imaginable in a life of crime centered in Los Angeles, from selling fake gold bars to setting up phony disaster-relief websites. Right now, he ran a racket convincing people they owed money that they didn't really owe, and getting them to pay it. And he was so good at it that junior swindlers were paying him for lessons on Mondays and Wednesdays at a defunct acting studio in Van Nuys. I had infiltrated as one of his students and learned all I could. Now it was time to write the story and use Arthur to expose an industry that bilked millions each year from everybody from little old ladies with dwindling bank accounts to young professionals already deep in the red with college loans. They all fell victim and sent their money because Arthur Hathaway convinced them to send it. And now he was teaching eleven future con men and one undercover reporter how to do it for fifty bucks a head twice a week. The swindler school itself might be his greatest con of all. The guy was truly a king with a psychopath's complete lack of guilt. I also had reporting in the story on the victims whose bank accounts he had cleaned out and whose lives he had ruined.

Myron had already placed the story as a co-project with the *Los Angeles Times,* and that guaranteed it would be seen and the Los Angeles Police Department would have to take notice. King Arthur's reign would soon be over and his roundtable of junior con men would be rounded up as well.

I read the story a final time and sent it to Myron, copying William Marchand, the attorney who reviewed all *FairWarning* stories pro bono. We didn't put anything up on the website that was not legally bulletproof. *FairWarning* was a five-person operation if you counted the reporter in Washington, DC, who worked out of her home. One "wrong story" spawning a winning lawsuit or forced settlement would put us out of business, and then I'd be what I had been at least twice before in my career: a reporter with no place to go.

I got up from my cubby to tell Myron the story was finally in, but he was in his own cubicle talking on the phone, and I could tell as I approached that he was on a fundraising call. Myron was founder, editor, reporter, and chief fundraiser for *FairWarning*. It was an Internet news site with no paywall. There was a donate button at the bottom page of every story and sometimes at the top, but Myron was always looking for the great white whale who would sponsor us and turn us from beggars into choosers—at least for a while.

"There really is no entity doing what we're doing—tough watchdog journalism for the consumer," Myron told each prospective donor. "If you check out our site you'll see many stories in the archives that take on powerful kingpin industries including auto, pharmaceutical, wireless, and tobacco companies. And with the current administration's philosophy of deregulation and limiting oversight, there is nobody out there looking out for the little guy. Look, I get it, there are donations you could make that might give you a more visible bang for your buck. Twenty-five dollars a month keeps a kid fed and clothed in Appalachia. I get that. It makes you feel good. But you donate to *FairWarning,* and what you are supporting is a team of reporters dedicated to—"

I heard "the pitch" several times a day, day in and day out. I also attended the Sunday salons where Myron and board members spoke to potential white-hat donors, and I mingled with them afterward, mentioning the stories I was working on. I had some extra cachet at these gatherings as the author of two bestselling books, though it was never mentioned that it had been more than ten years since I had published anything. I knew the pitch was important and vital to my own paycheck—not that I was getting anywhere close to a living wage for Los Angeles—but I had heard it so many times in my four years at *FairWarning* that I could recite it in my sleep. Backward.

Myron stopped to listen to his potential investor and muted the phone before looking up at me.

"You in?" he asked.

"Just sent it," I said. "Also to Bill."

"Okay, I'll read it tonight and we can talk tomorrow if I have anything."

"It's good to go. Even has a great headline on it. You just need to write the deck."

"You better be—"

He took his phone off mute so he could respond to a question. I gave him a salute and headed toward the door, stopping by Emily Atwater's cubicle on my way out to say goodbye. She was the only other staffer in the office at the moment.

"Cheers," she said in her crisp British accent.

We worked out of an office in a typical two-story plaza in Studio City. The first level was all retail and food, while the second floor was walk-in businesses like car insurance, manicure/pedicure, yoga, and acupuncture. Except us. *FairWarning* wasn't a walk-in business, but the office came cheap because it was located above a marijuana dispensary and the venting in the building was such that it brought the aroma of fresh product inside our office 24/7. Myron took the place at a heavy discount.

The plaza was L-shaped and had an underground parking garage with five assigned spaces for *FairWarning* employees and visitors. That was a major perk. Parking in the city was always an issue. And sheltered parking was an even bigger perk for me because this was sunny California and I rarely put the top up on my Jeep.

I had bought the Wrangler new with the advance on my last book, and the odometer served as a reminder of how long it had been since I was buying new cars and riding bestseller lists. I checked it as I fired up the engine. I had strayed 162,172 miles from the path I had once been on.

2

I lived in Sherman Oaks on Woodman Avenue by the 101 freeway. It was a 1980s Cape Cod–style apartment building of twenty-four townhomes that formed a rectangle enclosing a courtyard with a community pool and barbecue area. It, too, had parking underneath.

Most of the apartment buildings on Woodman had names such as the Capri and Oak Crest and the like. My building stood nameless. I had moved in only a year and a half before, after selling the condo I had bought with that same book advance. The royalty checks had been getting smaller and smaller each year and I was in the midst of reordering my life to live within the paychecks from *FairWarning*. It was a difficult transition.

As I waited on the sloping driveway for the garage gate to lift, I noticed two men in suits standing at the call box at the pedestrian gate to the complex. One was white and middle fifties, the other a couple of decades younger and Asian. A little kick of wind opened the Asian man's jacket and I got a glimpse of the badge on his belt.

I drove down into the garage and kept my eyes on the rearview. They followed me down the slope and in. I pulled into my assigned space and killed the engine. By the time I grabbed my backpack and got out, they were behind the Jeep and waiting.

"Jack McEvoy?"

He had gotten the name right but had pronounced it wrong. *Mick-a-voy.*

"Yes, McEvoy," I said, correcting him. *Mack-a-voy.* "What's going on?"

"I'm Detective Mattson, LAPD," the older of the two said. "This is my partner, Detective Sakai. We need to ask you a few questions."

Mattson opened his jacket to show that he, too, had a badge, and the gun to go with it.

"Okay," I said. "About what?"

"Can we go up to your place?" Mattson asked. "Something more private than a garage?"

He gestured to the space around them as if there were people listening from all quarters, but the garage was empty.

"I guess so," I said. "Follow me. I usually take the stairs up but if you guys want the elevator, it's down at that end."

I pointed to the end of the garage. My Jeep was parked in the middle and right across from the stairs leading up to the center courtyard.

"Stairs are good," Mattson said.

I headed that way and the detectives followed. The whole way to my apartment door I was trying to think in terms of my work. What had I done that would draw the attention of the LAPD? While the reporters at *FairWarning* had a lot of freedom to pursue stories, there was a general division of labor, and criminal scams and schemes were part of my turf along with Internet-related reporting.

I began to wonder if my Arthur Hathaway story had run across a criminal investigation of the swindler and whether Mattson and Sakai were about to ask me to hold the story back. But as soon as I thought of that possibility, I dismissed it. If that were the case, they would have come to my office, not my home. And it probably would have started with a phone call, not an in-person show-up.

"What unit are you from?" I asked as we crossed the courtyard toward apartment 7 on the other side of the pool.

"We work downtown," Mattson said, being coy, while his partner stayed silent.

"What crime unit, I mean," I said.

"Robbery-Homicide Division," Mattson said.

I didn't write about the LAPD per se, but in the past I had. I knew that the elite squads worked out of the downtown head-quarters, and RHD, as it was called, was the elite of the elite.

"So then what are we talking about here?" I said. "Robbery or homicide?"

"Let's go inside before we start talking," Mattson said.

I got to my front door. His nonanswer seemed to push the answer toward homicide. My keys were in my hand. Before unlocking the door, I turned and looked at the two men standing behind me.

"My brother was a homicide detective," I said.

"Really?" Mattson said.

"LAPD?" Sakai asked, his first words.

"No," I said. "Out in Denver."

"Good on him," Mattson said. "He's retired?"

"Not exactly," I said. "He was killed in the line of duty."

"I'm sorry to hear that," Mattson said.

I nodded and turned back to the door to unlock it. I wasn't

sure why I had blurted that out about my brother. It was not something I usually shared. People who knew my books knew it, but I didn't mention it in day-to-day conversation. It had happened a long time ago in what seemed like another life.

I got the door open and we entered. I flicked on the light. I had one of the smallest units in the complex. The bottom floor was open-plan, with a living room flowing into a small dining area and then the kitchen beyond it, separated only by a counter with a sink. Along the right wall was a set of stairs leading up to a loft, which was my bedroom. There was a full bath up there and a half bath on the bottom floor beneath the stairs. Less than a thousand square feet in total. The place was neat and orderly but that was only because it was starkly furnished and featured little in the way of personal touches. I had turned the dining-room table into a work area. A printer sat at the head of the table. Everything was set for me to go to work on my next book—and it had been that way since I moved in.

"Nice place. You been here long?" Mattson asked.

"About a year and a half," I said. "Can I ask what this—"

"Why don't you have a seat on the couch there?"

Mattson pointed to the couch that was positioned for watching the flat screen on the wall over the gas fireplace I never used.

There were two other chairs across a coffee table, but like the couch they were threadbare and worn, having spent decades in my prior homes. The decline of my fortunes was reflected in my housing and transportation.

Mattson looked at the two chairs, chose the one that looked cleaner and sat down. Sakai, the stoic, remained standing.

"So, Jack," Mattson said. "We're working a homicide and your name came up in the investigation and that's why we're here. We have—"

"Who got killed?" I asked.

"A woman named Christina Portrero. You know that name?"

I spun it through all the circuits on high speed and came back with a blank.

"No, I don't think so. How did my name—"

"She went by *Tina* most of the time. Does that help?"

Once more through the circuits. The name hit. Hearing the full name coming from two homicide detectives had unnerved me and knocked the initial recognition out of my head.

"Oh, wait, yeah, I knew a Tina—Tina Portrero."

"But you just said you didn't know the name."

"I know. It just, you know, out of the blue it didn't connect. But yes, we met once and that was it."

Mattson didn't answer. He turned and nodded to his partner. Sakai moved forward and held his phone out to me. On the screen was a posed photo of a woman with dark hair and even darker eyes. She had a deep tan and looked mid-thirties but I knew she was closer to mid-forties. I nodded.

"That's her," I said.

"Good," Mattson said. "How'd you meet?"

"Down the street here. There's a restaurant called Mistral. I moved here from Hollywood, didn't really know anyone and was trying to get to know the neighborhood. I'd walk down there for a drink every now and then because I didn't have to worry about driving. I met her there."

"When was this?"

"I can't pinpoint the exact date but I think it was about six months after I moved in here. So about a year ago. Probably a Friday night. That's when I would usually go down there."

"Did you have sex with her?"

I should have anticipated the question but it hit me un-expectedly.

"That's none of your business," I said. "It was a year ago."

"I'll take that as a yes," Mattson said. "Did you come back here?"

I understood that Mattson and Sakai obviously knew more about the circumstances of Tina Portrero's murder than I did. But the questions about what happened between us a year ago seemed overly important to them.

"This is crazy," I said. "I was with her one time and nothing ever came of it afterward. Why are you asking me these questions?"

"Because we're investigating her murder," Mattson said. "We need to know everything we can about her and her activities. It doesn't matter how long ago. So I will ask you again: Was Tina Portrero ever in this apartment?"

I threw my hands up in a gesture of surrender.

"Yes," I said. "A year ago."

"She stay over?" Mattson asked.

"No, she stayed a couple hours, then she got an Uber."

Mattson didn't immediately ask a follow-up. He studied me for a long moment, as if trying to decide how to proceed.

"Would you have any of her property in this apartment?" he asked.

"No," I protested. "What property?"

He ignored my question and came back with his own.

"Where were you last Wednesday night?"

"You're kidding, right?"

"No, we're not."

"What time Wednesday night?"

"Let's say between ten and midnight."

I knew I had been at Arthur Hathaway's seminar on how to rip people off until the 10 p.m. start of that window. But I also knew that it was a seminar for con artists and therefore didn't really exist. If these detectives tried to check out that part of my alibi, they either would not be able to confirm the seminar even existed or would not be able to find anyone to confirm I was there, because that would be acknowledging that they were there. No one would want to do this. Especially after the story I just turned in was published.

"Uh, I was in my car from about ten to ten twenty and then after that I was here."

"Alone?"

"Yes. Look, this is crazy. I was with her one night a year ago and then neither of us kept in contact. It was a no-go for both of us. You understand?"

"You sure about that? Both of you?"

"I'm sure. I never called her, she never called me. And I never saw her at Mistral again."

"How'd that make you feel?"

I laughed uneasily.

"How did what make me feel?"

"Her not calling you back after?"

"Did you hear what I said? I didn't call her and she didn't call me. It was mutual. It just wasn't going to go anywhere."

"Was she drunk that night?"

"Drunk, no. We had a couple of drinks there. I paid the tab."

"What about back here? More drinks or right up to the loft?"

Mattson pointed upstairs.

"No more drinks here," I said.

"And everything was consensual?" Mattson said.

I stood up. I'd had enough.

"Look, I've answered your questions," I said. "And you're wasting your time."

"We'll decide if we're wasting our time," Mattson said. "We are almost finished here and I would appreciate it if you would sit back down, Mr. McEvoy."

He pronounced my name wrong again, probably intentionally. I sat back down.

"I'm a journalist, okay?" I said. "I've covered crime—I've written books about murderers. I know what you're doing, trying to knock me off my game so I'll make some kind of admission. But it's not going to happen, because I don't know anything about this. So could you please—"

"We know who you are," Mattson said. "You think we would come out here without knowing who we're dealing with? You're the *Velvet Coffin* guy, and just for the record, I worked with Rodney Fletcher. He was a friend and what happened to him was bullshit."

There it was. The cause of the enmity that was dripping off Mattson like sap off a tree.

"*Velvet Coffin* closed down four years ago," I said. "Mostly because of the Fletcher story—which was one hundred percent accurate. There was no way of knowing he would do what he did. Anyway, I work someplace else now and write consumer-protection stories. I'm not on the cop shop."

"Good for you. Can we get back to Tina Portrero?"

"There is nothing to get back to."

"How old are you?"

"You already know, I'm sure. And what's that got to do with anything?"

"You seem kind of old for her. For Tina."

"She was an attractive woman and older than she looked or

claimed to be. She told me she was thirty-nine when I met her that night."

"But that's the point, right? She was older than she looked. You, a guy in your fifties, moving in on a lady you thought was in her thirties. Kind of creepy, you ask me."

I felt my face turning red with embarrassment and indignation.

"For the record, I didn't 'move in on' her," I said. "She picked up her Cosmo and came down the bar to me. That's how it started."

"Good for you," Mattson said sarcastically. "Must've made your ego stand at attention. So let's go back to Wednesday. Where were you coming from during those twenty minutes you said you were in the car driving home that night?"

"It was a work meeting," I said.

"With people that we could talk to and verify if we need to?"

"If it comes to that. But you are—"

"Good. So tell us again about you and Tina."

I could tell what he was doing. Jumping around with his questions, trying to keep me off balance. I covered cops for almost two decades for two different newspapers and the *Velvet Coffin* blog. I knew how it worked. Any slight discrepancy in retelling the story and they would have what they needed.

"No, I already told you everything. You want any more information from me, then you have to give information."

The detectives were silent, apparently deciding whether to deal. I jumped in with the first question that came to mind.

"How did she die?" I asked.

"She had her neck snapped," Mattson said.

"Atlanto-occipital dislocation," Sakai said.

"What the hell does that mean?" I asked.

"Internal decapitation," Mattson said. "Somebody did a one-eighty on her neck. It was a bad way to go."

I felt a deep pressure begin to grow in my chest. I did not know Tina Portrero beyond the one evening I was with her, but I couldn't get the image of her—refreshed by the photo shown by Sakai—being killed in such a horrible manner out of my mind.

"It's like that movie *The Exorcist,*" Mattson said. "Remember that? With the possessed girl's head twisting around."

That didn't help things.

"Where was this?" I asked, trying to move on from the images.

"Landlord found her in the shower," Mattson continued. "Her body was covering the drain and it overflowed and he came to check it out. He found her, water still running. It was supposed to look like a slip-and-fall but we know better. You don't slip in the shower and break your neck. Not like that."

I nodded as though that was good information to know.

"Okay, look," I said. "I didn't have anything to do with this and can't help you with your investigation. So if there are no other questions, I would like—"

"There are more questions, Jack," Mattson said sternly. "We are only getting started with this investigation."

"Then what? What else do you want to know from me?"

"You being a reporter and all, do you know what 'digital stalking' is?"

"You mean like social media and tracking people through that?"

"I'm asking questions. You're supposed to answer them."

"You have to be more specific, then."

"Tina told a good friend of hers that she was being digitally stalked. When her friend asked what that meant, Tina said a guy she met in a bar knew things about her he should not have known. She said it was like he knew all about her before he even started talking to her."

"I met her in a bar a year ago. This whole thing is—wait a minute. How did you even know to come here to talk to me?"

"She had your name. In her contacts. And she had your books on the night table."

I couldn't remember whether I had discussed my books with Tina the night I met her. But since we had ended up at my apartment, it was likely that I had.

"And on the basis of that, you come here like I'm a suspect?"

"Calm down, Jack. You know how we work. We are conducting a thorough investigation. So let's go back to the stalking. For the record, was that you she was talking about with the stalking?"

"No, it wasn't me."

"Good to hear. Now, last question for now: Would you be willing to voluntarily give us a saliva sample for DNA analysis?"

The question startled me. I hesitated. I jumped to thinking about the law and my rights and totally skipped over the fact that I had committed no crime and therefore my DNA in any form from semen to skin residue could not be found at any crime scene from last Wednesday.

"Was she raped?" I asked. "Now you're accusing me of rape too?"

"Take it easy, Jack," Mattson said. "No sign of rape but let's just say we got some DNA from the suspect."

I realized that my DNA was my quickest way off their radar.

"Well, that wasn't me, so when do you want to take my saliva?"

"How about right now?"

Mattson looked at his partner. Sakai reached inside his suit jacket and pulled out two six-inch test tubes with red rubber caps each containing a long-ended cotton swab. I realized then that most likely the sole purpose of their visit was to get my DNA. They had the killer's DNA. They, too, knew that it would be the quickest way to determine whether I had any involvement in the murder.

That was fine with me. They were going to be disappointed by the results.

"Let's do it," I said.

"Good," Mattson said. "And there is one other thing we could do that would help us with the investigation."

I should have known. Open the door an inch and they push all the way through.

"What's that?" I said impatiently.

"You mind taking your shirt off?" Mattson said. "So we can check your arms and body?"

"Why would—"

I stopped myself. I knew what he wanted. He wanted to see if I had scratch marks or other wounds from a fight. The DNA in evidence had probably come from Tina Portrero's fingernails. She had put up a fight and taken a piece of her killer.

I started unbuttoning my shirt.

3

As soon as the detectives left, I pulled my laptop out of my backpack, went online, and searched the name *Christina Portrero*. I got two hits, both on the *Los Angeles Times* site. The first was just a mention on the newspaper's homicide blog, where every murder in the county was recorded. This report was early in the case and had few details other than the fact that Portrero was found dead in her apartment during a wellness check by the landlord after she did not show up for work and did not respond to calls or messaging through social media. The report said foul play was suspected but the cause of death had not yet been determined.

I was a religious reader of the blog and realized I had read the story and scanned through it without recognizing the name *Christina Portrero* as the Tina Portrero I had met one night the year before. I wondered what I would have done if I had recognized her as the woman I had met. Would I have called the police to mention my experience, my knowledge that on at least one occasion she had gone to a bar by herself and had picked me for a one-night stand?

The second hit in the *Times* was a fuller story that ran the same photo Detective Sakai had shown me. Dark hair, dark eyes, looking younger than she was. I had completely missed seeing this story, because I would have recognized the photo. The story said Portrero worked as a personal assistant to a film producer named Shane Sherzer. I thought this was interesting because when we had met a year earlier, she was doing something else in the film business: she was a freelance reader who provided "coverage" of scripts and books for a variety of producers and agents in Hollywood. I remembered her explaining that she read material submitted to her clients for possible development as films and TV shows. She then summarized the scripts and books and checked off on a form the kind of project they were: comedy, drama, young adult, historical, crime, etc.

She concluded each report with her personal take on the potential project, recommending a hard pass or further consideration by higher-ups in the client's company. I also remembered that she told me the job often required her to visit production companies located at the major studios in town—Paramount, Warner Brothers, Universal—and that it was very exciting because on occasion she saw major movie stars walking out in the open between the offices, stages, and the commissary.

The *Times* story included quotes from a woman named Lisa Hill, who was described as Portrero's best friend. She told the newspaper that Tina led an active social life and had recently straightened herself out after suffering from some addiction issues. Hill did not reveal what these issues were and probably wasn't even asked. It seemed to have little to do with who had killed Portrero by twisting her neck 180 degrees.

Neither of the *Times* posts mentioned the exact cause of death. The second, fuller story said only that Portrero had suffered a broken neck. Maybe *Times* editors had decided not to put the fuller details into the story, or maybe they had not been told. The information on the crime in both posts was attributed to the generic "police said." Neither Detective Mattson nor Detective Sakai was mentioned by name.

It took me a couple attempts to spell *atlanto-occipital dislocation* correctly so that I could search for it on Google. Several hits came up, most on medical sites that explained it was usually seen in traumatic vehicle accidents involving high-speed collisions.

The Wikipedia citation summed it up best:

Atlanto-occipital dislocation (AOD), orthopedic decapitation, or **internal decapitation** describes ligamentous separation of the spinal column from the skull base. It is possible for a human to survive such an injury; however, only 30% of cases do not result in immediate death. Common etiology for such injuries is sudden and severe deceleration leading to a whiplash-like mechanism.

The word *mechanism* in that description began to haunt me. Someone strong or with some kind of tool had powerfully twisted Tina Portrero's neck. I now wondered if there had been any markings on her head or body that indicated a tool had been used.

The Google search brought up a few citations of AOD as the cause of death in auto accidents. One in Atlanta and another in Dallas. The most recent in Seattle. All were deemed accident-related, and there was no reference to AOD being the cause of death in a murder case.

I needed to do a deeper dive. When I was working for the *Velvet Coffin,* I had once drawn an assignment to write a story about a convention of coroners from around the world. They had all met in downtown Los Angeles, and my editor wanted a feature on what coroners talk about at these events. The editor who assigned me the piece wanted war stories and the gallows humor exhibited by people who deal in death and dead bodies day in and day out. I wrote the story and in reporting it learned of a website primarily used by medical examiners as a resource for posing questions to other coroners when faced with unusual circumstances involving a death.

The site was called causesofdeath.net and it was password protected, but because it was available to coroners around the world, the password was mentioned in much of the literature handed out at the convention. I had visited the site a few times over the years since attending the convention just to poke around and see what was of current interest on the discussion board. But I had never posted anything until now. I worded my post so that I was not falsely portraying myself as a medical examiner, but I wasn't exactly saying that I wasn't, either.

Hey all. We have a homicide case here at LA with atlanto-occipital dislocation—female victim, 44 yoa. Anybody seen AOD before in homicide? Looking for etiology, tool marks, derma marks, etc. Any help is welcome. Hope to see all at next IAME con. Have not been since it was here in the City of Angels. Cheers, @MELA

The shorthand in my post suggested expertise. *YOA* for *years of age, AOD* the abbreviation for *atlanto-occipital dislocation*. The mention of the International Association of Medical Examiners convention was legit because I was there. But it would also help readers of the post believe I was a working coroner. I knew it skirted ethical considerations but I wasn't acting on this as a reporter. At least not yet. I was acting as an interested party. The cops had all but said I was a suspect. They had come and collected my DNA and studied my arms and upper torso. I needed information and this was one means of getting it. I knew it was a shot in the dark but it was one worth taking. I would check the site in a day or two to see if I had any responses.

Next on my list was Lisa Hill. She was quoted in the *Times* story as a close friend of Portrero's. For her, I switched hats — from potential suspect to journalist. After the routine efforts to get a phone number for her turned up nothing, I reached out to her — or at least who I thought was her — with private messages to her Facebook page, which appeared dormant, and to her Instagram account as well.

> Hi, I am a journalist working on something on the Tina Portrero case. I saw your name in the *Times* story. I am sorry for your loss. I would like to talk to you. Are you willing to talk about your friend?

I included my name and cell number on each message but also knew that Hill could reach back to me through those social-media outlets as well. Like the message on the IAME board, it would be a waiting game.

Before shutting down my efforts, I checked back on causes ofdeath.net to see if my fishing expedition had attracted any bites. It had not. I then went back into Google and started reading up on digital stalking (or *cyberstalking,* as it was more commonly called). Most of what was out there didn't jibe with what Mattson had described. Cyberstalking most often involved victims being harassed by someone they knew in at least a peripheral way. But Mattson had specifically said that Tina Portrero had complained to a friend — most likely Lisa Hill — that she had randomly met a man in a bar who seemed to know things about her he shouldn't have known.

With that in mind, I set out to learn all I could about Tina Portrero. I quickly realized I might already have an advantage over the mystery man who had set off alarms with her. When I went down the usual checklist of social-media apps, I remembered that I was already her friend on Facebook and a follower on Instagram. We had exchanged these connections the night we met. Then afterward, when no second date grew out of the initial meeting, neither of us had bothered to unfriend or block the other. This I had to admit was vanity—everybody likes to pad their numbers, not subtract from them.

Tina's Facebook page had not been very active and appeared to be used primarily to keep in touch with family. I remembered that when we had met she said her family was from Chicago. There were several posts spread over the last year from people with her last name. These were routine messages and photos. There were also several cat and dog videos posted by her or to her.

I moved on to Instagram and saw that Tina was far more active there, routinely posting photos of herself engaged in various activities with friends or alone. Many had captions that identified the locations and people in the shot. I went back through the feed several months. Tina had been to Maui once and Las Vegas twice during that time. There were shots of her with various men and women, and multiple photos of her at clubs, bars, and house parties. It was clear from these that her drink of choice was a Cosmo. I remembered that that was the drink she held in her hand when she came down the bar to me at Mistral the night we met.

I have to admit that even though I knew she was dead, I felt envious as I reviewed photos of her recent life and saw how full and active it was. My life was not nearly as exciting in comparison and I fell into morbid thoughts about her upcoming funeral, where invariably her friends and others would say she had lived life to the fullest. The same could not be said about me.

I tried to shake off the feelings of inadequacy, reminding myself that social media was not a reflection of real life. It was life exaggerated. I moved on and the only post I found of real interest was a photo and caption from four months earlier that showed Tina and another woman about the same age or slightly older. They had their arms around each other. The caption Tina had written said: "Finally tracked down my half sis Taylor. She's a blast and a half!!!!!"

It was hard to tell from the post whether Taylor was a half sister who had fallen out of touch and therefore had to be tracked down, or whether Taylor had been previously unknown to Tina. What was clear was that the two women definitely looked related. Both had the same high forehead and high cheekbones, dark eyes, and dark hair.

I searched to see if there was a *Taylor Portrero* on Instagram or Facebook but drew a blank. It appeared that if Tina and Taylor were half sisters, they had different last names.

After my survey of social media ended, I went into full reporter mode and used a variety of search engines to look for other references to Christina Portrero. I was soon able to find the side of her not celebrated on social media. She had a DUI arrest on her record as well as an arrest for possession of a controlled substance—that being MDMA, more commonly referred to as Ecstasy or Molly, a party drug with mood-elevating effects. The arrests resulted in two stints in court-ordered rehab and probation, which she completed in order to have the judge expunge her record of convictions. Both arrests had occurred more than five years before.

I was still online, looking for more details about the dead woman, when my phone buzzed and the screen showed a blocked number.

I took the call.

"This is Lisa Hill."

"Oh, good. Thank you for calling me."

"You said you wanted to do a story. For who?"

"Well, I work for an online publication called *FairWarning*. You might not have heard of it but our stories are often picked up by newspapers like the *Washington Post* and the *L.A. Times*. We have a first-look agreement with NBC News as well."

I heard her typing on a keyboard and knew she was going to the site. It made me think she was smart and nobody's fool. There was silence for a moment as I guessed she was looking at the *FairWarning* home page.

"And you're on here?" she finally said.

"Yes," I said. "You can click on the link where it says OUR STAFF in that black header and it will take you to our profiles. I'm the last one. The most recent hire."

I heard the click while I was giving directions. More silence followed.

"How old are you?" she asked. "You look older than every-body but the owner."

"You mean the editor," I said. "Well, I worked with him at the *L.A. Times* and then joined him here after he set it up."

"And you're here in L.A.?"

"Yes, we are based here. Studio City."

"I don't get it. Why does a site like this for consumers care about Tina getting murdered?"

That was the question I was ready for.

"Part of my beat is cybersecurity," I said. "And I have sources in the LAPD and they know I'm interested in cyberstalking because that gets into the area of consumer security. That's how I heard about Tina. I talked to the detectives on the case—Mattson and Sakai—and they told me that she had complained to friends that she felt some guy she had dated or met was *digitally stalking* her—that was the phrase the detectives used."

"They gave you my name?" Hill asked.

"No, they wouldn't give out a witness's name. I—"

"I'm not a witness. I didn't see anything."

"Sorry, I didn't mean it that way. From the investigation standpoint, they consider anybody they talk to in the case a witness. I know you don't have any immediate knowledge of the case. I saw your name in the *Times* story and that's why I reached out."

I heard more typing before she responded. I wondered if she was checking on me further by typing an email to Myron, who was at the top of the *FairWarning* staff page and listed as founder and executive director.

"Did you use to work for something called *Velvet Coffin?*" she asked.

"Yes, before I came to *FairWarning*," I said. "It was locally based investigative reporting."

"It says you went to jail for sixty-three days."

"I was protecting a source. The federal government wanted it, but I wouldn't give up the name."

"What happened?"

"After two months the source came forward on her own and I was released because the feds got what they wanted."

"What happened to her?"

"She was fired for leaking information to me."

"Oh, man."

"Yeah. Can I ask you a question?"

"Yes."

"I'm curious. How did the *Times* find you?"

"I once dated someone who works there in the Sports section. He's on my Instagram and saw the photo I posted after Tina died, and he told the reporter that he knew somebody who knew the dead girl."

Sometimes it takes a break like that. I'd had more than a few of those in my career.

"Got it," I said. "So, can I ask you, then, are you the one who told the detectives about the cyberstalking?"

"They asked me about anything unusual with her lately and I couldn't really think of anything except some asshole she hooked up with in a bar a few months ago seemed like he knew too much about her, you know? It freaked her out a little bit."

"Knew too much how?"

"Well, she didn't really say a lot. She just said she met this guy at a bar and it was supposed to be some rando hookup but that it felt like a setup. Like they were having drinks and he said stuff that made her realize he already knew who she was and things about her and it was really fucking creepy and she just got the hell out of there."

I was having trouble tracking the steps of the story so I tried to break it down into pieces.

"Okay, so what was the name of the place where they met?" I asked.

"I don't know but she liked to go to places up in the Valley," Hill said. "Places on Ventura. She said the men up there weren't so pushy. And I think it had something to do with her age."

"How so?"

"She was getting older. The guys in the clubs in Hollywood, West Hollywood, they're all younger or looking for younger."

"Right. Did you tell the police about her preferring the Valley?"

"Yeah."

I had met Tina in a restaurant bar on Ventura. I was beginning to understand Mattson and Sakai's interest in me.

"She lived near the Sunset Strip, right?" I asked.

"Yes," Hill said. "Just up the hill. Near the old Spago's."

"So would she drive over the hill to the Valley?"

"No, never. She got a DUI a while back and she stopped driving when she went out. She used Uber and Lyft."

I assumed that Mattson and Sakai had gotten Tina's Uber and Lyft records. They would help identify the bars she frequented and determine her other movements.

"And so, getting back to the stalking thing," I said. "She just went to the club on her own and met this guy, or was it prearranged like through a dating app or something?"

"No, she was doing her thing," Hill said. "She just went there to get a buzz on and hear music, maybe meet a guy. Then she sort of bumped into this guy at the bar. From her standpoint it was random, or it was supposed to be."

It seemed that what had happened between Tina and me wasn't a one-off. Tina had a habit of going alone to bars to maybe meet a guy. I held no old-fashioned beliefs about women. They were free to go wherever and do whatever they wanted, and I did not believe that a victim was responsible for what happens to her. But along with the DUI and prior drug possession, I did have an angle on Tina now as a risk-taker. Going to bars where men were less pushy was not enough of a safety edge. Not by a long shot.

"Okay, so they meet at the place and start talking and having drinks at the bar," I said. "And she had never seen him before?"

"Exactly," Hill said.

"And did she tell you what he specifically said that creeped her out?"

"Not really. She just said, 'He knew me. He knew me.' It was like he somehow let something slip and it wasn't random at all."

"Did she say whether he was already there when she got to the club or came in after?"

"She didn't say. Hold on, I have another call."

She didn't wait for my response. She clicked over to the other call and I waited, thinking about the incident in the club. When Hill came back on the line her tone and words were completely different. She was harsh and angry.

"You motherfucker. You scumbag. You're the guy."

"What? What are you—"

"That was Detective Mattson. I emailed him. He said you're not working a story and I should stay away from you. You knew her. You knew Tina and now you're a suspect. You fucking asshole."

"No, wait. I'm not a suspect and I am working on a story. Yes, I met Tina once but I'm not the guy from the—"

"Don't fucking come near me!"

She disconnected the call.

"Shit!"

I felt like I had been punched in the gut, and my face burned with humiliation over the subterfuge I had used. I had lied to Lisa Hill. I wasn't even sure why, or what I was doing. The visit from the detectives had tipped me into a rabbit hole and I wasn't sure of my motives. Was it about Christina Portrero and me, or was it about the case and the story I might write about it?

Christina and I were one and done. That night she had

ordered a car and left. I had asked for another date and she had said no.

"I think you're too straight for me," she said.

"What does that mean?" I asked.

"That it wouldn't work."

"Why?"

"Nothing personal. I just don't think you're my type. Tonight was great, but for the long haul, I mean."

"Well, then, what is your type?"

It was such a lame response. She just smiled and said her car was arriving. She went out the door and I never saw her again.

Now she was dead and I couldn't leave it alone. My life had somehow changed since the moment the two detectives had approached me in the garage. I was down the rabbit hole now and I sensed that what was ahead of me in this place was only darkness and trouble. But I also sensed that it was a story. A good story. My kind of story.

Four years ago I had lost everything because of a story. My job and the woman I loved. I had blown it. I had not taken care of the most precious thing I had. I had put myself and the story ahead of everything else. True, I had come through dark waters. I had killed a man once and nearly been killed. I had ended up in jail because of a commitment to my job and its principles, and because deep down I knew the woman would sacrifice herself to save me. When it all fell apart, my self-imposed penance was to leave everything behind and turn myself in a different direction. For a long time before, I had said death was my beat. Now, with Christina Portrero, I knew it still was.

4

Myron was waiting for me when I came into the office the next morning. The newsroom where we worked followed an egalitarian open-floor design — individual cubicles in a cluster. Everybody from editor in chief to most recent hire (me) had the same amount of work space. Up-lighting bounced off the ceiling tiles and came down gently on each of our spaces. Our desktop computers had silent-touch keyboards. Some days the place was as silent as a church on Monday, unless somebody was working the phones, and even then they might move into the conference room at the back of the office so as not to disturb anyone. It was nothing like the newsrooms I had worked in earlier in my career, where the cacophony of clacking keyboards alone could make you lose focus on what you were doing.

The conference room, with a window looking out at the newsroom, was also used for walk-in interviews and employee conferences. That was where Myron took me, closing the door behind him after we entered. We took seats across an oval table from each other. Myron had a printout of what I assumed was my "King of Con Artists" story that he put down on the table.

He was old school. He edited with a red pen on paper, then he had our office assistant, Tally Galvin, enter the changes digitally in the story.

"So, you didn't like my headline," I said.

"No, the headline has to be about what the story means to the consumer, not the personality—good or bad, tragic or inspirational—that you tell the story through," Myron said. "But that's not what I want to talk about here."

"Then what, you didn't like the story either?"

"The story's fine. It's more than fine. Some of your best work. But what I want to talk about is an email I got last night. A complaint."

I laughed uneasily. I instinctively knew what this was about but I played innocent.

"A complaint about what?"

"This woman—Lisa Hill—says you misrepresented yourself in an interview about a murder that *you* are a suspect in. Now normally I would have deleted this or put it up on the wall with the rest of the crazies."

There was a corkboard in the break room where people posted printouts of the most outrageous and bizarre responses to stories we publish. Often they came from the companies and people who were behind the consumer dangers in our stories. We called the board the wall of shame.

"But then," Myron said, "I got a call first thing this morning from the LAPD that backs this woman's email and now we have an LAPD complaint as well."

"That's complete bullshit," I said.

"Well, tell me what's going on because the cop who called wasn't friendly."

"Was his name Mattson?"

Myron looked down at the printout and some of the notations he had made by hand on it. He nodded.

"That's him."

"Okay, this whole thing started last night when I drove home from work."

I proceeded to walk Myron step-by-step through what happened the night before, from Mattson and Sakai following me into the garage at my apartment complex to Lisa Hill's call in response to my messages and her angry misunderstanding and hang-up. Myron, always the old-school reporter, took notes while I told the story. When I was finished, he reviewed his notes before speaking.

"Okay," he finally said. "But what I don't get is why you thought a story about a murder would be something we would put on *FairWarning*. So—"

"But don't you—"

"Let me finish. So it makes me think you were using *FairWarning* and your legitimate standing here as a reporter to investigate something else, the death of this woman you knew. You see what I'm getting at? It doesn't feel right."

"Okay, look, whether or not Lisa Hill emailed you or the cops called you, I was going to come in here today and tell you this is my next story."

"It can't be your story. You have a conflict of interest."

"What, because I knew a woman who was murdered a year later?"

"No, because you're a person of interest in the case."

"That's bullshit. It's pretty clear from what Lisa Hill told me before she hung up and my review of the victim's social media that she dated a lot of guys. No judgment there, but all of them, including me, are persons of interest. That's just the cops throwing out a big net. They have DNA from the crime scene because they took a sample from me and—"

"You conveniently left that out of your story just now."

"I didn't think it was important because it's not. The point is I voluntarily gave it because I know that once it gets analyzed I will be in the clear. And free to write this story."

"What story, Jack? We are a consumer watchdog, not the *L.A. Times* murder blog."

"The story is not the murder. I mean, it is, but the real story is the cyberstalking and that gets us into the arena of consumer protection. Everybody has social media. This is a story about how vulnerable we are to cyber predators. How privacy is a thing of the past."

Myron shook his head.

"That's an old story," he said. "It's been done by every paper in the country. That's not a story we can partner on and I can't let you go off chasing it. We need stories that break new ground and draw a lot of eyes."

"I guarantee it will be one of those stories."

Myron shook his head. This was going sideways.

"What could you possibly bring to this that's new?" he said.

"Well, I have to spend some time on it before I can fully answer that but—"

"Look, you are a great reporter who has a history with this kind of story. But it's not what we do here, Jack. We have certain objectives in our reporting that need to be followed and fulfilled."

I could tell Myron was extremely uncomfortable because we were peers. He wasn't dressing down a kid fresh out of J-school.

"We have followers and we have a base," he continued. "Our

readers come to our site looking for what it says on our mission statement: tough watchdog reporting."

"You're saying that our readers and financial supporters determine what stories we pursue?" I asked.

"Look, don't even go there. I didn't mention our donors and you know that isn't true. We are completely independent."

"I'm not trying to start a fight. But you can't go into every story knowing what the end result is. The best reporting starts out with a question. From who would break into the Democrats' national headquarters to who killed my brother. Did cyberstalking get Christina Portrero killed? That's my question. If the answer is yes, then that *is* a *FairWarning* story."

Myron looked at his notes before answering.

"That's a big 'if,'" he finally said.

"I know," I said. "But that doesn't mean you don't try to answer the question."

"I still don't like that you are knee-deep in this story. The cops took your DNA, for Chrissake!"

"Yeah, I gave it to them. I volunteered it. And do you think if I had anything to do with this I would say, *Sure, guys, take my DNA. I don't need a lawyer. I don't need to hesitate.* No, Myron, I wouldn't. And I didn't. I will be cleared of this, but if we wait for the police lab on it, we lose the momentum and we lose the story."

Myron kept his eyes on his notes. I knew I was close.

"Look, let me just run with this for a few days. I'll either find something or I won't. If I don't I'll come back and work on whatever you put me on. Killer cribs, dangerous car seats—I'll take over the whole baby beat, if you want."

"Hey, don't knock it. The baby-beat stuff gets more eyes than almost anything else we do."

"I know. Because babies need protection."

"All right, what are the next steps…*if* I let you run with this?"

I felt I had won the battle. Myron was going to give in.

"Her parents," I said. "I want to see what she told them about being stalked. She also posted something on Instagram about finding her half sister. I don't know what that means and want to find out."

"Where are the parents?" Myron asked.

"Not sure yet. She told me she was from Chicago."

"You're not going to Chicago. We don't have the funds for—"

"I know. I wasn't asking to go to Chicago. There's a thing, they call it the phone, Myron. I'm asking you for time. I'm not asking to spend money."

Before Myron could respond, the door opened and Tally Galvin stuck her head in.

"Myron," she said. "The police are here."

I leaned back in my chair and looked out the window into the newsroom. I saw Mattson and Sakai standing at Tally's desk at the public entrance to the office.

"Well," Myron said. "Send them back."

Tally went to get the two detectives and Myron looked across the table at me. He spoke in a low voice.

"Let me handle this," he said. "You don't say anything."

Before I could protest, the conference-room door opened and Mattson and Sakai entered.

"Detectives," Myron said. "I'm Myron Levin, founder and executive director of *FairWarning*. I believe I spoke to one of you this morning."

"That was me," Mattson said. "I'm Mattson and this is Detective Sakai."

"Have a seat. What can we do for you?"

Sakai started to pull one of the chairs away from the table.

"We don't need to sit down," Mattson said.

Sakai froze, his hand still on the chair.

"What we need is for you to stand down," Mattson continued. "We are conducting a murder investigation and the last thing we need is a couple of half-assed reporters poking around and screwing things up. *Stand. Down.*"

"Half-assed reporters, Detective?" Myron said. "What does that mean?"

"It means you aren't even the real thing and you've got this guy running around, talking to our witnesses and intimidating them."

He gestured to me. I was 'this guy.'

"That's bullshit," I said. "All I—"

Myron put his hand out to cut me off.

"Detective, my reporter was pursuing a story. And as far as you thinking we are half-assed anything, you should know we are a fully recognized and legitimate member of the media and enjoy all the freedoms of the press. We are not going to be intimidated while pursuing a valid news story."

I was amazed by Myron's calm demeanor and strong words. Five minutes earlier he was questioning my motives and the story I wanted to pursue. But now we had closed ranks and were standing strong. This was why I went to work for Myron in the first place.

"You won't have much of a story if your reporter ends up in jail," Mattson said. "How will that look to all your media brethren out there?"

"You are saying that if we continue to look into this story, you will jail our reporter?" Myron asked.

"I'm saying he could go from reporter to prime suspect

pretty quick and then freedom of the press won't matter much, will it?"

"Detective, if you arrest my reporter, I guarantee you it will be a story of widespread interest. It will make news across the country. Just as it will do when you are forced to release him and admit publicly that you and your department were wrong and trumped up a case against a reporter because you were afraid he might find the answers you could not."

Mattson seemed to hesitate in responding. Finally he spoke, looking directly at me since he now understood that Myron was a solid wall. But he no longer had the hard edge in his words.

"I'm telling you for the last time to stay away from this," he said. "Stay away from Lisa Hill and stay away from the case."

"You don't have anything, do you?" I said.

I expected Myron's hand to come up to signal me to silence again. But this time he did nothing. He looked intently at Mattson, awaiting a reply.

"I have your DNA, buddy boy," Mattson said. "And you better hope it comes back clean."

"Then that confirms it," I said. "You've got nothing and you're wasting time trying to intimidate people and make sure nobody finds out."

Mattson snickered like I was a fool who didn't know what I was talking about. He then reached out and hit Silent Sakai on the arm.

"Let's go," he said.

Mattson turned and led Sakai out. Myron and I watched through the window as they swaggered through the newsroom toward the door. I felt good. I felt supported and protected. It was not a good time to be a journalist. It was the era of fake news and reporters being labeled by those in power as enemies of the people. Newspapers were folding right and left and some said the industry was in a death spiral. Meanwhile, there was a rise in biased and unchecked reporting and media sites, the line increasingly blurring between impartial and agenda-based journalism. But in the way Myron had handled Mattson I saw a throwback to the days when the media was undaunted, unprejudiced, and therefore could not be intimidated. I suddenly knew for the first time in a long time that I was in the right place.

Myron Levin had to raise money and run the website. Those were his priorities and he didn't get to be a reporter as much as he wanted to be. But when he put on that hat he was as relentless as any I had ever known. There was a famous story about Myron from his days as a consumer reporter at the *Los Angeles Times*. This was before he took a buyout, left the paper, and used the money to initially fund *FairWarning*. In reporting circles there is no better feeling than to expose a scoundrel, to write the story that reveals the con man and shuts him down. Most often the charlatan claims innocence and damage. He sues for millions and then quietly slips out of town to start over somewhere else. The legend about Myron is that he exposed a grifter who was running an earthquake-repair con after the Northridge quake in '94. Once outed on the front page of the *Times,* the grifter claimed innocence and filed a defamation-and-slander suit seeking $10 million in damages. In the filing documents, the grifter stated that Myron's story had caused him so much humiliation and anguish that the damages went beyond reputation and earnings to his health. He said that Myron's article had caused him bleeding from the rectum. And that was what cemented Myron's legendary status as a reporter. He had written a story that allegedly made a man bleed from the ass. No reporter would ever be able to best that, no matter how many millions they were sued for.

"Thanks, Myron," I said. "You had my back."

"Of course," Myron said. "Now go get the story."

I nodded as we watched the two detectives go through the office door.

"And you better watch yourself on this," Myron said. "Those assholes don't like you."

"I know," I replied.

5

With my editor and publisher's approval I was officially on the story. And on my very first official move, I got lucky. I went back on Tina Portrero's social media, used her Facebook tagging history to identify her mother, Regina Portrero, and reached out to her through her own Facebook page. I assumed that if Regina reached back from her home in Chicago we would set up a phone call. Phone calls with the bereaved were safest— I still have a scar on my face from asking the wrong question of a woman grieving the sudden death of her fiancé. But things can get lost or missed in a phone call: nuances of conversation, expressions, emotion.

But that is where the luck came in. Within an hour of sending my private message, Regina contacted me and said she was in town to make arrangements to take her daughter home. She said she was staying at a hotel called the London West Hollywood and expected to leave Los Angeles the next morning, Tina's body in the cargo hold of the jet. She invited me to come to the hotel to talk about Tina.

I couldn't make an invitation like that wait, especially when I knew that Mattson and Sakai might take it upon themselves to warn Regina about me. I told her I would be in the lobby of the hotel in an hour. I told Myron where I was going and headed off in the Jeep, taking Coldwater Canyon south over the Santa Monica Mountains and down into Beverly Hills. I then went east on Sunset Boulevard toward the Sunset Strip. The London West Hollywood was located right in the middle of it.

Regina Portrero was a small woman in her mid-sixties, which indicated she had Tina early in her life. I could see the resemblance most in the same dark brown eyes and hair. She met me in the lobby of the hotel, which was just a half block south of Sunset on San Vicente. It was her daughter's neighborhood. She had lived just a few blocks away.

We sat in an alcove that was probably meant for people waiting for their rooms to be ready. But there was no one there at the moment and we had privacy. I took out my notebook and put it on my thigh so I could write notes and be as inconspicuous about it as possible.

"What is your interest in Tina?" she asked.

Regina's first question threw me because she had not asked it during the initial communication. Now she wanted to know what I was doing and I knew that if I answered it fully and honestly it would probably end the interview before it got started.

"Well, first of all, I am very sorry for your loss," I said. "I can't imagine what you are going through and I hate so much to be an intruder. But what the police on this case told me makes it different and makes what happened to Tina something that the public should possibly know about."

"I don't understand. Are you talking about what happened to her neck?"

"Oh, no."

I was mortified that my clumsy answer to her first question had conjured in her mind the horrible manner in which her daughter had been killed. In many ways I would have preferred a backhand across the face, the diamond of an engagement ring raking across my skin and leaving another scar.

"Uh…," I stammered. "What I meant was…the police, they told me that she might have been the victim of cyberstalking, and so far, as far as I know, there is no evidence that the two are connected but…"

"They didn't tell me that," Regina said. "They said they didn't have any leads."

"Well, I don't want to speak for them and maybe they don't want to tell you anything until they're sure. But I understand that she told friends—like Lisa Hill—that she felt she was being stalked. And to be honest, that is what is of interest to me. That is a consumer thing—it's about privacy—and if there is a…problem then that's what I'm going to write about."

"How was she stalked? This is all news to me."

I knew I was in trouble here. I was telling her things she didn't know, so the first thing she was going to do after I left was call Mattson about it. Then Mattson would learn that I was still actively pursuing the case, and Regina would in turn learn that my reporter's interest in Tina and her death was compromised by my having known her briefly but intimately. This meant that this was the one and only time I would get to talk to Tina's mother. She would be turned against me in the same way Lisa Hill had been.

"I don't know exactly how she was stalked," I said. "That is only what the police said. I talked to her friend Lisa and she said Tina apparently met a man in a bar but that it felt like he was there waiting for her or something. That it wasn't a random encounter."

"I told her to stay out of the bars," Regina said. "But she couldn't keep away—even after the arrests and rehab."

It was an incongruous response. I was talking about her daughter being stalked and she fixated on her daughter's drug and alcohol issues.

"I am not saying one thing had anything to do with the other," I said. "I don't think the police know yet either. But I know she had arrests and had been to rehab. Is that what you mean about her going to bars?"

"She was always going out, meeting strangers...," Regina said. "All the way back to high school. Her father told her it could end this way—he warned her—but she didn't listen. She didn't seem to care. She was boy crazy from the start."

Regina seemed to stare off into the distance when she spoke. *Boy crazy* seemed like an innocent term but, clearly, she was seeing a memory of her daughter as a young woman. An unpleasant memory in which there was upset and rancor.

"Was Tina ever married?" I asked.

"No, never," Regina said. "She said she never wanted to be tied down by one man. My husband used to joke that she saved him a bundle by never getting married. But she was our only child and I always wished I had gotten to plan her wedding. It never happened. She was always looking for something she felt no man she met could provide.... What that was, I never knew."

I remembered the post I had seen on Tina's social media.

"I saw on her Instagram that she said she found her sister," I said. "A half sister. But she's not your daughter?"

Regina's face changed and I knew I had hit on something bad in her life.

"I don't want to talk about that," Regina said.

"I'm sorry, did I say something wrong?" I asked. "What happened?"

"All these people, they are so interested in that stuff. Where they come from. Are they Swedish, are they Indian. They don't know what they're playing with. It's like that privacy thing you mentioned. Some secrets are meant to stay secret."

"The half sister was a secret?"

"Tina sent her DNA in and then next thing she does is tell us she's got a half sister out in Naperville. She…I shouldn't be telling you this."

"You can tell me off the record. It will never go into a story but if it helps me understand your daughter and what she was interested in, it could be important. Do you know why she sent her DNA in for analysis? Was she look—"

"Who knows? That's what people do, right? It's quick. It's cheap. She had friends that were doing it, finding their heritage."

I had not submitted my DNA to any of the genetic-analytics sites but I knew people who had and therefore knew generally how it worked. Your DNA went through a genetic data bank that returned matches to other customers of the site, along with the percentage of shared DNA. Higher percentages meant a closer relationship—from distant cousins to direct siblings.

"She found her half sister. I saw the photo of them. Naperville—that's near Chicago, right?"

I needed to keep her talking about something she didn't want to talk about. Easy questions got easy answers and kept the words coming.

"Yes," Regina said. "I grew up there. Went to high school there."

She paused and looked at me and I realized she needed me to tell the story. It was always amazing to me when people opened up. I was a stranger but they knew I was a reporter, a recorder of history. I had found many times when reporting tragedies that those left behind wanted to reach out through their grief to talk and set down some sort of record of the lost loved one. Women more than men. They had a sense of duty to the lost one. Sometimes they needed only a little prodding.

"You had a baby," I said.

She nodded.

"And Tina didn't know," I said.

"Nobody knew," she said. "It was a girl. I gave her up. I was too young. And then later I met my husband and we started a family. Tina. And then she grew up and sent her DNA in to one of those places. And she had done it, too. The girl. She knew she was adopted and was looking for connections. They connected through the DNA site and that's what destroyed our family."

"Tina's father didn't know…"

"I didn't tell him at first and then it was too late. It was supposed to be my secret. But then the world changes and your own DNA can unlock everything and secrets aren't secrets anymore."

I once had an editor named Foley who said that sometimes the best question is the one not asked. I waited. I didn't feel I had to ask the next question.

"My husband left," Regina said. "It wasn't that I'd had the baby. It was that I didn't tell him. He said our marriage was built on a lie. That was four months ago. Christina didn't know. Her father and I agreed not to put that guilt on her. She would have blamed herself."

Regina had been holding a clot of tissues in her hands and now used them to dry her eyes and wipe her nose.

"Tina went back to Chicago to meet her half sister," I said, hoping to spark more revelations from the broken woman.

"Tina was such a sweet girl," Regina said. "She wanted to re-unite us. She thought it was a good thing. She didn't know what was going on with her father and me. But I told her no, I couldn't see the girl. Not now. And she was very upset with me."

She shook her head and continued.

"Funny how life is," she said. "Everything's good, everything's fine. You think your secrets are safe. Then something comes along and it all just goes away. Everything changes."

It would only be a detail in the story but I asked what genetics site Christina had submitted her DNA to.

"It was GT23," Regina said. "I remember because it only cost twenty-three dollars. So much grief for just twenty-three dollars."

I knew about GT23. It was one of the more recent entries into the DNA testing-and-analytics business. The upstart company was attempting to take control of the billion-dollar industry by dramatically undercutting the pricing of the competition. It had an advertising campaign based on the promise of DNA analytics accessible to the masses. Its slogan was *DNA You Can Afford!* The *23* in its name stood for the twenty-three pairs of chromosomes in a human cell as well as the price of its basic kit: a full DNA and heredity report for twenty-three dollars.

Regina started to cry full-on then. Her knot of tissues was falling apart. I told her I would get her more and got up. I started looking for a restroom.

Something told me that while the emergence of the half sister in Tina's life was important, this was not the angle of the story that led to the cyberstalking. This was just one spoke in the wheel of Tina's life, although it was one that brought about profound changes to those close to her. But the stalking had to have come from another angle and I was guessing that was her lifestyle.

I found a restroom, pulled open a steel container holding a

cardboard box of tissues, and took the whole thing back out to the lobby alcove.

Regina was gone.

I looked around and she was nowhere to be seen. I checked the couch where she had been sitting. No purse, no wad of tissue.

"Sorry, I had to go to the bathroom."

I turned around and it was her. She returned to the couch. She looked like she had washed her face. I put the box of tissues down next to her and returned to the chair I had been sitting in to her left.

"I'm sorry to make you go through all of this," I said. "I didn't know when I asked the question that it would bring up this difficult stuff."

"No, it's okay," Regina said. "It's kind of therapeutic in a way. To talk about it, get it out. You know?"

"Maybe. I think so."

I wanted to move in a different direction now.

"So," I asked. "Did Tina ever talk to you about any of the men she dated?"

"No, she knew my feelings about that and her lifestyle," Regina said. "Also, what could I say? I met my husband at a blues club in South Side Chicago. I was only twenty years old."

"Do you know if she did any online dating, that sort of thing?"

"I would guess that she did but I don't know about it. The police asked me the same thing and I said that Tina didn't tell me about the specifics of her life here. I knew about the arrests and the rehab—because she needed money. But that was all. The one thing I always told her was that I wished she'd come back home and be close. I told her that every time we talked."

I nodded. I wrote the lines down.

"And now it's too late," she added.

She started to cry again and I wrote that last line down as well.

I should have ended the interview there and not pushed the woman further. But I knew that once she interacted with Mattson again he would tell her to steer clear of me. It was now or never and I had to roll with it.

"Have you been to her apartment?" I asked.

"Not yet," she said. "The police said it's still sealed because it was the crime scene."

I was hoping to get a look inside Tina's home myself.

"Did they say when you could go in and get her things?"

"Not yet. I'll have to come back for that. After the funeral, maybe."

"Where exactly was her place?"

"Do you know where the Tower Records used to be?"

"Yes, across from the bookstore."

"She lived right above it. Sunset Place Apartments."

Regina pulled fresh tissues out of the box and dabbed at her eyes.

"Cute place," she said.

I nodded.

"She was beautiful and kind," Regina said. "Why did someone have to kill her?"

She buried her face and her sobs in the tissues. I just watched her. She had asked a question only a mother could ask and only the killer could answer. But it was a good line and I memorized it to write down later. For the moment I just nodded sympathetically.

6

I got back to the office by lunchtime and everyone was in their cubicles eating sandwiches from Art's Deli. Most days we ordered in food but no one had thought to text me for my order. That was okay because at the moment I didn't need food. I was fueled by the momentum of the story. I was in that early stage where I knew I had something but wasn't sure what it was or what the next step should be. I started by opening up a Word file on my laptop and typing up my handwritten notes from the interview with Regina Portrero. I was halfway through the process when I realized my problem. The next step was to go back to Lisa Hill to ask more questions about Tina and her stalker, but Lisa Hill thought I was not only a scumbag but a suspect in her friend's murder.

I put transcribing my notes aside and checked my phone to see if Hill had gotten around to blocking me on Instagram. She had not, but my guess was that this was just an oversight and she would do so as soon as she checked her followers and was reminded of my previous deception.

I spent the next half hour composing a private message to her that I hoped would give me a second chance.

Lisa, I apologize. I should've been up-front with you. But the cops are wrong about me and they know it. They just don't want you talking to a reporter. It would be embarrassing if I got to the real suspect ahead of them. I liked Tina a lot. I wished she had wanted to meet again. But that's it, nothing else. I am going to find out who stalked her and may have hurt her. I need your help. Please call me again so I can explain further and tell you what I know that the cops don't. Thank you.

I put my phone number on the end of the message and sent it, hoping for the best but knowing it was a long shot, and that I couldn't just wait for Lisa Hill to change her mind about me. I next checked the causes-of-death website where I had posted my request for information on atlanto-occipital dislocation. And this was where my luck and the story changed dramatically. There were already five messages waiting for me.

The first message had been posted at 7 a.m. L.A. time but 10 a.m. Florida time, where the posting had come from the Broward County Medical Examiner's Office. A pathologist named Frank Garcia cited an AOD case from the previous year that had been ruled a homicide.

Have an open homicide. Female, 32, came in last year as single-car traffic fatal with COD orthopedic decapitation (AOD) but TA investigator said impact not enough. Scene was staged. TA injuries postmortem. Victim name: Mallory Yates. I/O Ray Gonzalez FLPD.

I could decipher most of the shorthand. *COD* was cause of death and *TA* meant traffic accident, while *I/O* meant investigating officer. And I thought *FLPD* meant Florida Police

Department until I googled it and came up with Fort Lauderdale Police Department, which was located within Broward County. I copied the message and transferred it to the story file I had created on my computer.

The next message was from Dallas and it was similar to the first in that the victim was a woman of similar age—thirty-four-year-old Jamie Flynn—who had died in what appeared to be a single-car accident with AOD listed as cause of death. This was not classified as a homicide but as a suspicious death because all of Flynn's toxicity reports came back clean, so there was no clear explanation as to why she drove off a road and down an embankment into a tree. Flynn's death had occurred ten months earlier and the case was still open because of the suspicious circumstances.

The third message was a follow-up from Frank Garcia at the Broward County Medical Examiner's Office.

Checked with Gonzalez at FLPD. Case still open, no suspects, no leads at this time.

The fourth post on the message board was about another case, which had occurred three months before. This one came from Brian Schmidt, who was an investigator with the Santa Barbara County Coroner's Office.

Charlotte Taggart, 22 yoa, fell from cliff at Hendry's Beach, found DOA next morning. AOD and other injuries, accidental. BAT .09 and fall occurred 03:00 in full darkness.

I knew that *BAT* meant blood-alcohol toxicity and that the limit for driving in California was .08, indicating Taggart was at least slightly inebriated when she walked to the edge of a cliff in darkness and fell to her death.

The fifth message was posted most recently. It was the shortest message but it froze me.

Who is this?

It had been posted only twenty minutes earlier by Dr. Adhira Larkspar, who I knew was the chief medical examiner of Los Angeles County. It meant I was in danger of discovery. When no one volunteered to identify themselves to their boss, Larkspar might check to see if her office did indeed have a recent AOD case, and this inquiry would undoubtedly lead her to Mattson and Sakai, who would undoubtedly conclude that I had been the one to initially post on the message board.

I tried to push thoughts of another visit from the detectives aside and to focus on the information I had in front of me. Three cases of AOD in the last year and a half, with Tina Portrero making a fourth. The victims were women ranging in age from twenty-two to forty-four. So far, two of the cases had been ruled homicides, one was suspicious, and one—the most recent before Portrero—was classified as an accident.

I did not know enough about human physiology to be sure whether the fact that all four cases involved females was significant. Since men are generally larger and more muscled than women, it was possible that AOD happened more to women because their bodies were more fragile.

Or it could be that they are stalked and become the targets of predators more often than men.

I knew that I had to add more to the profiles of these four women if I were to make any informed judgment based on the information I had. I decided to work backward and start with the most recent case first. Using basic search engines I found very little on Charlotte Taggart other than a paid obituary that had run in the *East Bay Times* and an accompanying online memorial book where friends and family could sign their names and make comments about the deceased loved one.

The obituary said Charlotte Taggart grew up in Berkeley, California, and attended UC–Santa Barbara. She was in her senior year when she passed. She was interred at Sunset View Cemetery in Berkeley. She was survived by both parents, two younger brothers, and many close and distant relatives she had discovered in the past year.

The end of the last line drew my focus. Charlotte Taggart had discovered new relatives in the last year of her life. That said to me that she most likely discovered these people through a heritage-analysis company. My guess was she had submitted her DNA just as Christina Portrero had done.

This connection didn't necessarily mean anything—millions of people did what these two young women had. It was not uncommon at all and at this stage it appeared to be a coincidence.

I scanned the comments in the online memorial book and found it to be full of heartfelt but routine messages of love and loss, many written directly to Charlotte as though she would be reading them from the great hereafter.

After entering what I knew about Charlotte Taggart's life and death into the story file, I moved on to the Dallas case, where Jamie Flynn's death was labeled suspicious because there was no explanation for her driving down an embankment into a tree.

This time I found a short story about the death in the *Fort Worth Star-Telegram.* Jamie was from a prominent family that ran a well-known boot-and-saddlery business in Fort Worth.

Flynn was a graduate assistant at Southern Methodist University in Dallas while working on a doctorate in psychology. She lived on a horse ranch in Fort Worth owned by her parents and commuted because she liked to be close to her horses. It was her life's goal to open a counseling practice that incorporated riding as therapy. The story contained an interview with Flynn's father, who lamented that his daughter had battled depression and alcoholism before straightening her life out and returning to school. He seemed proud of the fact that she had not had a relapse and that her blood screens in the autopsy were clean.

The story also quoted a traffic-accident investigator from the Dallas Police Department. Todd Whitney said he wouldn't close the case until he was confident the death of Jamie Flynn was an accident.

"A young healthy woman with a lot going for her doesn't just go off the road and down into a ravine and get her neck broken," he said. "It may be purely an accident. She could have seen a deer or something and swerved. But there are no skid marks and no animal tracks. I wish I could tell her parents I have the answers, but I don't. Not yet."

I noted that there was nothing in the story about whether Jamie Flynn might have driven off the road on purpose in an attempt to disguise a suicide as an accident. It was not an uncommon occurrence. But if it had been considered, it was not publicly reported. There was such a stigma attached to suicide that most newspapers avoided it like the plague. It was only when public figures offed themselves that suicide stories were written.

I moved on for the moment from Jamie Flynn. I wanted to keep my momentum. I was certain that I was closing in on something and did not want to be delayed.

7

The last case I reviewed was the first mentioned on the causes-of-death message board. It had been posted with a short case summary. The death of thirty-two-year-old Mallory Yates in Fort Lauderdale was open and being treated as a homicide because, like the case in Dallas, there were incongruities about the supposed traffic accident that took her life. Histamine levels in some of the wounds to her body suggested that the injuries were postmortem and the accident was staged. But moving on from the post, I found no funeral notice or news story about the case. A second-tier search brought up a Facebook page that was publicly accessible and had been turned into a memorial page for Yates. There were dozens of messages posted by friends and family in the sixteen months since her death. I scrolled through them quickly, picking up bits and pieces of the dead woman's history and updates on her case.

I learned that Mallory had grown up in Fort Lauderdale, had attended Catholic schools and gone to work in her family's boat-rental business operating out of a marina called Bahia Mar. She had apparently not attended college after high school and, like Jamie Flynn in Fort Worth, lived alone in a home owned by her father. Her mother was deceased. Several of the Facebook posts were messages of condolence directed to her father in regard to losing both his wife and daughter in the space of two years.

A message posted three weeks after Mallory's death caught my eye and brought my casual scroll through the page to a dead stop. Someone named Ed Yeagers posted a message of sympathy that identified Mallory as his third cousin and lamented that they were just getting acquainted when she was taken away. He said, "I was just getting to know you and wish there was more time. Profoundly sad to find family and then lose family in the same month."

That sentiment could have come from the obituary for Charlotte Taggart. Finding family in this day and age usually meant DNA. There were heredity-analytics companies that used online data to search for family connections but DNA was the shortcut. I was now convinced that both Charlotte Taggart and Mallory Yates had been searching for connections through DNA heritage analysis. And so had Christina Portrero. The coincidence extended to three of the women and might include all four.

I spent the next twenty minutes running down social-media links to relatives and friends of Mallory Yates and Charlotte Taggart. I sent every one of them the same message asking if their loved one had submitted DNA to an analytics company and, if so, which one. Even before I finished I got an email response from Ed Yeagers.

Met her through GT23. It was only 6 weeks before she died so never got the chance to meet in person. Seemed like a really good girl. What a shame.

My adrenaline hit the floodgates. I had two confirmed cases that shared a rare cause of death and submission of DNA to GT23. I quickly went back to the story about Jamie Flynn in the

Fort Worth paper and got the name of her father and the family business he ran, selling boots, belts, and equestrian products like saddles and reins. I googled the business, got a phone number for the main office, and called it. A woman answered and I asked for Walter Flynn.

"Can I ask what this is regarding?" she asked.

"His daughter Jamie," I said.

Nobody likes to cause someone more grief than they already carry. I knew that I would do that with this phone call. But I also knew that if I was right about my instincts I might eventually be able to lessen that grief with answers.

A man picked up the call after a very brief hold.

"Walt Flynn, what can I do for you?"

He had a no-nonsense Texas drawl that I guessed went back generations. In my head I pictured the Marlboro Man in a white Stetson sitting on a horse, his chiseled features set in a frown. I chose my words carefully, not wanting him to dismiss me or grow angry.

"Mr. Flynn, I'm sorry to disturb you. I'm a reporter calling from Los Angeles and I'm working on a story about the unexplained deaths of several women."

I waited. The bait had been thrown out. He would either bite or hang up on me.

"And this is about my daughter?" he asked.

"Yes, sir, it could be," I said.

I didn't fill the silence that followed. I started to hear a background noise, like running water.

"I'm listening," he said.

"Sir, I don't want to cause you any more grief than you're already going through," I said. "I am so sorry about the loss of your daughter. But can I speak frankly to you?"

"I'm still on the phone."

"And off the record?"

"Isn't that what I say to you?"

"What I mean is, I don't want you to turn around and share this conversation with anyone apart from your wife. Is that okay?"

"It's fine for now."

"Okay, well, then I'll just lay it out for you, sir. I'm looking at — I'm sorry, do we have a bad connection? I hear this back —"

"It's raining. I stepped outside for privacy. I'll put it on mute while you talk."

The line went silent.

"Uh, okay, that's fine," I said. "So, I'm looking at four deaths of women aged twenty-two to forty-four across the country in the last year and a half where the cause of death was determined to be atlanto-occipital dislocation — AOD, as they call it. Two of the deaths, one here and one in Florida, have been classified as homicides. One is listed as accidental but I find it suspicious. And then the fourth, which is your daughter's case, is officially classified as suspicious."

Flynn took it off mute and I heard the rain before he spoke.

"And you're saying these four are somehow linked?"

I could hear the disbelief creeping into his voice. I was going to lose him pretty quickly if I didn't change that.

"I'm not sure," I said. "I'm looking for commonalities in the cases and the women. You could help if I could ask you a few questions. That is why I'm calling."

He didn't respond at first. I thought I heard the low rumble of thunder providing a bass line for the rain. Flynn finally replied.

"Ask your questions."

"Okay. Before her death, had Jamie submitted her DNA to a genetic-analytics lab, whether for hereditary or health analysis?"

Flynn had muted the call. There was only silence in reply. After a few moments I wondered if he had disconnected the call.

"Mr. Flynn?"

The rain came back.

"I'm here. The answer is she was just getting into that sort of stuff. But as far as I know, she had not gotten anything back. She said she wanted to incorporate it into her doctoral program somehow. She said that she was having everyone in one of her classes at the university do it. How does this connect to her death?"

"I don't know yet. Do you happen to know what company your daughter submitted DNA to?"

"Some of the kids in her class, they're scholarship kids. Money is tight. They went with the cheapest one. The one that charges twenty-three bucks for the test."

"GT23."

"That's it. What does all of this mean?"

I almost didn't hear his question. I could hear my pulse pounding in my ears. I now had a third confirmation. What were the odds that these three women who suffered the same kind of death had all sent their DNA to GT23?

"I don't really know what it means yet, Mr. Flynn," I said.

I had to guard against Flynn getting as excited over the connection in the cases as I was. I didn't want him running to the Texas Rangers or the FBI with my story.

"Do the authorities know about this?" he asked.

"There is nothing to know about yet," I said quickly. "When and if I have a solid link between the cases, I'll go to them."

"What about this DNA stuff you just asked about? Is that the connection?"

"I don't know. It's not confirmed yet. I don't have enough to take to the authorities. It's just one of a few things I'm looking at."

I closed my eyes and listened to the rain. I knew it would come to this. Flynn's daughter was dead and he had no answers, no explanations.

"I understand what you're feeling, Mr. Flynn," I said. "But we need to wait until—"

"How could you understand?" he said. "Do you have a daughter? Was she taken from you?"

A flashback memory hit me. A hand swinging at my face, me turning to deflect the blow. The diamond raking across my cheek.

"You're right, sir, I shouldn't have said that. I have no idea what kind of pain you carry. I just need a little bit more time to get further into this. I promise you I will stay in touch and keep you informed. If I come up with something solid you will be the first person I call. After that, we'll go to the police, the FBI, everybody. Can you do that? Can you give me that time?"

"How long?"

"I don't know. I can't—we can't—go to the FBI or anybody if we don't have this nailed down. You don't yell *fire* unless there's a fire. You know what I mean?"

"How long?"

"A week, maybe."

"And you'll call me?"

"I'll call you. That's a promise."

We exchanged cell numbers and he needed to hear my name

again because he had missed it the first time. We then disconnected, with Flynn promising to sit tight until he heard from me at the end of a week.

My phone rang as soon as I put it back in its cradle. It was a woman named Kinsey Russell. She had been one of the posters in Charlotte Taggart's online memorial book. I had found her on Instagram and sent her a private note.

"What kind of story are you doing?" she asked.

"To be honest, I'm not quite sure yet," I said. "I know that your friend Charlotte's death was listed as an accident but there are three other similar deaths of women that are not. I'm writing about those three and just want to check out Charlotte's death to make sure something wasn't missed."

"I think it was murder. I've said that from the beginning."

"Why do you say that?"

"Because she wouldn't have gone out to those cliffs at night. And definitely not alone. But the police aren't interested in finding out the truth. An accident looks better for them and the school than a murder."

I had little knowledge of who Kinsey Russell was. She had written one of the messages directly to her dead friend.

"How did you know Charlotte?"

"From school. We had classes together."

"So this was like a school party."

"Yes, kids from school."

"So how do you jump from her disappearing at the party to it being a murder at the cliffs?"

"Because I know she wouldn't have gone out there by herself. She wouldn't have gone out there at all. She was scared of heights. She always talked about all the bridges they have up there where she was from and being too scared even to drive over the Bay Bridge or the Golden Gate. She almost never went into San Francisco because of the bridges."

I wasn't sure that was convincing enough to declare the death a murder.

"Well…I'm going to look into it," I said. "I've already started. Can I ask you a few other questions?"

"Sure," she said. "I'll help you any way I can because this isn't right. I know something happened out there."

"The obituary that ran in the paper up in Berkeley said she was survived by her family and several distant relatives she had discovered in the last year. Do you know what that meant, the part about distant relatives?"

"Yes, she did the DNA thing. We both did, except she was really into it and was tracing her family back to Ireland and Sweden."

"You both did it. Which company did you use?"

"It's called GT23. It's not as well-known as the big ones, but it's cheaper."

There it was. I was four for four. Four AOD deaths, four victims who had turned their DNA over to GT23. There had to be a connection.

I asked Kinsey Russell a few follow-up questions but didn't register their answers. I was moving on. I had momentum. I wanted to get off the phone and get to work. Finally, I thanked her for her help, said I would stay in touch, and ended the call.

I looked up after putting the phone down and saw Myron Levin looking over the half-wall of my cubicle. He was holding a mug of coffee with the *FairWarning* logo on it. The *A* in *Warning* was a red triangle with a lightning bolt through it. I was feeling the power of that bolt right now.

"Did you hear all of that?"

"Some of it. You have something?"

"Yeah, I got something big. I think."

"Let's go to the conference room."

He pointed his cup toward the room.

"Not yet," I said. "I need to make a few more calls, maybe go see somebody, then I'll be ready to talk. You're going to like it."

"Okay," Myron said. "Ready when you are."

8

I pulled up everything I could on GT23 and immersed myself in the business of DNA analytics.

The piece that was most informative was a 2019 profile of the company published in *Stanford Magazine* as GT23 turned two years old and had just gone public, making its five founders extremely wealthy. It was an offshoot of an older company called GenoType23, which was founded two decades earlier by a group of Stanford University chemistry professors who pooled money to open a secure lab catering to law-enforcement agencies too small to fund their own labs to conduct forensic DNA analysis in criminal cases. The first company was initially successful and grew to have more than fifty court-certified technicians working and testifying in criminal cases across the western United States. But DNA became the panacea. It was increasingly being used around the world to solve crimes old and new, as well as to clear those wrongfully accused and convicted. As more and more police departments and law-enforcement agencies caught up technologically and opened their own forensic DNA labs or funded joint and regional labs, GenoType23 faced declining business and revenues and had to lay off staff.

As the company declined, a new area of social analytics

emerged in the DNA field following the completion of the human-genome project. Millions of people began seeking their ancestral and health histories. The founders retooled and opened GT23, a budget DNA analytics firm. There was a catch to the low cost, however. While the large forerunners in the field asked customers to volunteer their DNA anonymously for research, GT23 didn't offer a choice. The low cost of analysis needed to be offset by making the collected samples and data available—still anonymously—to research facilities and biotech firms willing to pay for it.

The move was not without controversy, but the whole field was awash in privacy-and-security concerns. GT23's founders weathered the questions with the basic explanation that submitting DNA to them was in fact volunteering it for research, and they proceeded to market. And the market responded. So much so that little more than a year later the founders decided to take their company public. The five founders rang the bell on the New York Stock Exchange as trading in their company opened—ironically or perhaps coincidentally—at twenty-three dollars a share. The founders became rich overnight.

I next came across a more recent article in *Scientific American* that carried the headline "Who Is Buying GT23's DNA?" The article was a sidebar to a larger story that explored the ethical and privacy concerns in the freewheeling world of DNA analysis. The writer of the article had found a source inside GT23 and obtained a list of universities and biotech research facilities that bought DNA data from the company. These ranged from labs at Cambridge University in England to a biologist at MIT to a small private research lab in Irvine, California. The article said that DNA from GT23 participants—the company did not use the word *customers*—was being used in studies involving the genetics behind a variety of diseases and ailments, including alcoholism, obesity, insomnia, Parkinson's, asthma, and many others.

The variety of studies that the data from GT23 contributed to and the good that might come from it—not to mention the potential profits to universities, Big Pharma, and companies producing wellness products—were staggering. The article identified a study at UCLA that dealt with appetite satiation and the genetic roots of obesity. A cosmetic company was using GT23 participants to study aging and skin wrinkling. A pharmaceutical company was researching why some people produce more earwax than others, while the lab in Irvine was studying the connection between genes and risky behaviors such as smoking, use of drugs, sex addiction, and even speeding while driving. All these studies aimed at understanding the causes of human maladies and developing drug and behavioral therapies that would treat or cure them.

It all seemed good and it was all profitable—at least to the founders of GT23.

But the main article that ran with the sidebar threw a shadow over all the good news. It reported that regulatory enforcement of the billion-dollar genetic-analytics industry fell to the U.S. Food and Drug Administration, which until recently had taken a complete pass on those responsibilities. The article quoted a recent report from the National Human Genome Research Institute:

Until recent years, FDA chose to apply "enforcement discretion" to the vast majority of genetic tests. FDA can use such discretion when it has the authority to regulate tests but chooses not to.

The article went on to report that the FDA was only now in the process of formulating rules and regulations that would eventually be presented to Congress for adoption. Only then would any kind of enforcement begin.

Due to the rapid growth of direct-to-consumer genomic testing, and FDA's mounting concern that unregulated tests pose a public health threat, FDA is modifying its approach. To this end, FDA has drafted new guidance to describe how it intends to regulate genetic testing. FDA "guidance" is different from laws and regulation in that it represents only FDA's "current thinking" on a topic and is not legally binding for FDA or the parties it regulates.

I was stunned. The report concluded that there was virtually no government oversight and regulation in the burgeoning field of genetic analytics. The government was far behind the curve.

I printed a copy of the story for Myron to read and then went to GT23's website to look for any acknowledgment that the services the company provided and the security it promised were not backed by government regulation. I found none. But I did stumble across a page that outlined how researchers could go about requesting anonymized data and biological samples and the fields of study the company supported:

Cancer
Nutrition
Social Behaviors
Risky Behaviors
Addiction
Insomnia

Autism

Mental Disorders (bipolar disorder, schizophrenia, schizo-
affective disorder)

On the website the recipients of data and bio samples were
called *collaborators*. It was all presented in a cheery, change-the-
world-for-the-better pitch that I was sure was crafted to allay
any potential participant's concerns about anonymously putting
their DNA into the great unknown of genetic analysis and
storage.

Another section of the website contained a four-page privacy-
and-informed-consent statement that outlined the anonymity
guaranteed with the submission of one's DNA in a GT23
home-sampling kit. This was the boring fine print but I read
every word of it. The company promised participants multiple layers of security in the handling of their DNA and
required all collaborators to meet the same levels of physical
and technical protection of data. No biological sample would
be transferred to a collaborator with any participant's identity
attached.

The consent statement clearly said that the low cost to
participants for DNA analytics, matching, and health reporting was underwritten by the collaborating companies and labs
that paid for the anonymized data. As such, the participant
was agreeing to field requests from collaborators funneled
through GT23 to maintain anonymity. The requests could
range from additional information on personal habits to sur-
veys in the specific field of study or even additional DNA
samples. It was then up to the participant to decide whether
to respond. Direct participation with collaborators was not
required.

After three pages of outlining self-imposed security measures and promises, the last page contained the bottom line:

We cannot guarantee that a breach will never happen.

It was the lead sentence of the last paragraph and was followed by a list of worst-case scenarios that were "highly unlikely." These ran from collaborator security breaches to the theft or destruction of DNA samples while in transit to labs sponsored by collaborators. There was one line in the disclaimer paragraph I read over and over, trying to understand it:

It may be possible, but unlikely, that a third party could identify you if they are able to combine your genetic data with other information available to them through other means.

I copied this off the screen and put it at the top of a notes document. Below it I typed: *WTF?*

I now had my first follow-up question. But before I pursued it I clicked on a tab labeled LAW ENFORCEMENT on the menu. This page revealed GT23's statement of support and cooperation with the FBI and police agencies in using its genetic data in criminal investigations. This had become a hot-button topic in recent years as police used genetic-analytics providers to help solve cases through linkage of familial DNA. In California, most notably, the alleged Golden State Killer was captured decades after a murder-and-rape spree when DNA from a rape kit was uploaded on GEDmatch and investigators were provided with matches to several relatives of the alleged killer. A family tree was constructed and soon a suspect was identified and then confirmed through further DNA analysis. Many other lesser-known murders were also solved similarly. GT23 made no bones about cooperating with law enforcement when asked.

I was now finished with my review of GT23's website and I had one question on my notes page. I wasn't sure what I had or what I was doing. I had a connection among the deaths of four young women. They were connected by their gender, the cause of their deaths, and their participation in GT23. I assumed that GT23 had millions of participants so was unsure if this last connection was a valid common denominator.

I sat up and looked over the wall of my cubicle. I could only see the top of Myron's head in his cubby. I thought about going to him and saying now was the time to talk. But I quickly dismissed the idea. I didn't like going to my editor, my boss, and saying I didn't know what to do next. An editor wants confidence. He wants to hear a plan that will lead to a story. A story that would draw attention to *FairWarning* and what we were doing.

I stalled the decision by googling a contact number for GT23 and calling the corporate office in Palo Alto. I asked for Media Relations and soon was talking to a media specialist named Mark Bolender.

"I work for a consumer news site called *FairWarning* and I'm doing a piece on consumer privacy in the area of DNA analytics," I said.

Bolender did not respond at first but I heard him typing.

"Got it," he finally said. "Looking at your website right now. I was not familiar with it."

"We usually partner on stories with more recognizable media outlets," I said. "*L.A. Times, Washington Post,* NBC, and so on."

"Who is your partner on this one?"

"No partner at the moment. I'm doing some preliminary work and—"

"Gathering string, huh?"

It was an old newspaper phrase. It told me Bolender was a former news guy who had crossed to the other side. He was handling media now, rather than being media.

"Only a reporter would say that," I said. "Where'd you work?"

"Oh, here and there," Bolender said. "My last gig was twelve years at the *Merc* as a tech reporter and then I took a buyout, ended up here."

The *San Jose Mercury News* was a very good newspaper. If Bolender had been a tech reporter in the breadbasket of technology then I knew I wasn't dealing with a public-relations hack. I now had to worry that he would figure out what I was really up to and find a way to block me.

"So what can I do for you and *FairWarning*?" Bolender asked.

"Well, right now I need some general information about security," I said. "I was on the GT23 website and it says there are multiple layers of security established for handling participant genetic data and material, and I was hoping you could walk me through that."

"I wish I could, Jack. But you are asking about proprietary matters that we don't talk about. Suffice it to say, anyone who submits a genetic sample to GT23 can expect the highest level of security in the industry. Way beyond government requirements."

It was a stock answer and I noted that going beyond government requirements when there were no such requirements meant nothing. But I didn't want to jump on Bolender and position myself as an adversary so early in the conversation. Instead, I typed his words into the file because I would need to use them in the story—if a story was published.

"Okay, I understand that," I said. "But on your website you clearly say you can't guarantee that there will never be a breach. How do you reconcile that with what you just said?"

"What is on the website is what the lawyers tell us to put on the website," Bolender said, an edge sharpening in his voice. "Nothing in life is one hundred percent guaranteed, so we need to make that advisement. But as I said, our safety measures are beyond question second to none. Do you have another question?"

"Yes, hold on."

I finished typing in his answer.

"Uh, could you explain what this means?" I asked. "It's from your website: *It may be possible, but unlikely, that a third party could identify you if they are able to combine your genetic data with other information available to them through other means.*"

"It means exactly what it says," Bolender said. "It's possible but unlikely. Again, it's legal speak. We are required to provide it in our consent form."

"Do you want to expand on that? For example, what does 'other information available to them' mean?"

"It could mean a lot of things but we are not going to go past the disclaimer on that, Jack."

"Has there ever been a breach of participant data at GT23?"

There was a pause before Bolender answered. Just long enough for me to be suspicious of his answer.

"Of course not," Bolender said. "If there had been it would have been reported to the Food and Drug Administration, the agency that regulates the industry. You can check with them and you will find no report because it has never happened."

"Okay."

I was typing.

"Are you putting this into a story?" Bolender asked.

"I'm not sure," I said. "Like you said, I'm just gathering string. We'll see."

"Are you talking to the others? Twenty-Three and Me, Ancestry?"

"I will, yes."

"Well, I would appreciate it if you would circle back to me if you're going to publish a story. I would like to review my quotes to make sure I'm quoted accurately."

"Uh…you didn't make that request at the top of the call, Mark. It's not something I usually do."

"Well, I didn't know at the top what the call was about. Now I'm concerned about being quoted accurately and in context."

"You don't have to worry about that. I've been doing this a long time and I don't make up quotes or use them out of context."

"Then I guess this conversation is over."

"Look, Mark, I don't get why you're upset. You were a reporter, you now deal with reporters, you know how it works. You don't lay down rules after the interview. What's upsetting you?"

"Well, for one, I pulled up your bio and now see who you are."

"I told you who I was."

"But you didn't mention the books you wrote about those killers."

"Those are old, old stories that have nothing to—"

"Both were about advances in technology being used by bad people. The Poet? The Scarecrow? Serial killers so bad they had media names. So I don't think you called up here to do a reassuring piece on our security. There is something else going on."

He wasn't wrong but he wasn't right either. I still didn't know what I had but his evasiveness was only increasing my feeling that there might be something here.

"There is nothing going on," I said. "I am truly interested in knowing about the security of the DNA that is submitted to your company. But I will do this for you: if you want me to read back your quotes to you now, I will do that. You will see that I have them down accurately."

There was silence and then Bolender responded in a clipped tone that told me the conversation was over — unless I found a way to keep it going.

"So, if we're done here, Jack—"

"I'd like to ask a couple more questions. I was reading about how GT23 has grown so quickly into one of the largest providers of DNA analytics."

"That's true. What's your question?"

"Well, does GT23 still do all of the lab work or has it gotten so big so fast that it subcontracts lab work?"

"Uh, I believe there is some contracting out of work to other labs. I know your last question is whether they operate with the same safety-and-privacy measures and the answer is yes, absolutely. Same standards right down the line. Well beyond government requirements. There is no story here and I need to go now."

"Last question. You mentioned that the company and its contractors go beyond federal regulations and requirements in terms of security, reporting of any privacy breaches, and so forth. Are you aware that there aren't any regulations and requirements and that any reporting on these issues would have to be self-reporting?"

"I, uh…Jack, I think you have bad information there. The FDA regulates DNA."

"True, it falls under FDA purview, but the FDA has chosen, up till now, at least, not to regulate. So when you say that GT23 goes beyond govern—"

"I think what I'm saying is that we're done here, Jack. Have a nice day."

Bolender disconnected and I put the phone back in its cradle. I made a fist and silently bounced it on the desk like a hammer. My torching of Bolender with his own words aside, I was feeling the groundswell building around me. Bolender had great reason to be upset. Beyond his efforts to protect the reputation of the company that employed him, he had to know that the larger secret of the industry as a whole was in danger of being exposed. Genetic testing was a self-regulating industry with very few if any government eyes upon it.

And that was a news story.

9

I printed out all of my notes from the research and interviews. After retrieving the pages from the communal printer, I left the office, passing by Myron while he was on the phone making a pitch to another potential donor. This was a break. I would not have to explain what I was doing or where I was going. I got out the door without hearing my name called.

It took me forty-five minutes to drive downtown and find parking. I knew I was risking about two hours of wasted time by not calling ahead but I also knew that calling ahead risked that Rachel Walling would be conveniently out of her office when I got there.

Her office was in the elegant old Mercantile Bank at 4th and Main. It was on the historic registry, which guaranteed that the front of the structure still looked like a bank. But the once-grand interior had been renovated and chopped up into private offices and creative spaces primarily leased by lawyers, lobbyists, and others with business in the nearby civic center. Rachel had a two-room office with a secretary.

On the door it said RAW DATA SERVICES. *RAW* as in *Rachel Anne Walling*. Her secretary was named Thomas Rivette. He was sitting behind his desk, staring at his computer screen. He handled much of the computer work involved in the background investigations that were the mainstay of the business.

"Hey, Jack," Thomas said. "Didn't expect you today."

"Wasn't expecting it myself," I said. "Rachel back there?"

"She is. Let me just check if it's clear. She might have client stuff spread out."

He picked up the desk phone and called the room six feet behind him.

"Rachel? Jack McEvoy is here."

I noted the use of my full name. It made me wonder whether there was another Jack in Rachel's life and Thomas had to be clear about which one was waiting to see her.

He hung up the phone and looked up at me with a smile.

"It's all clear. You can go back."

"Thank you, Thomas."

I walked around his desk and through the door centered on the wall behind him. Rachel had a long, rectangular office with a small seating area in front and then an L-shaped desk with large monitors on each side so she could work different jobs simultaneously on separate computers with separate IP addresses.

She looked away from one of the screens and at me as I entered and closed the door behind me. It had been at least a year since I had seen her and that was only at the crowded open house in these offices when she announced that RAW Data was in business. There had been random texts and emails in the meantime but I realized as I smiled at her that I had probably not been alone with her for two years.

"Jack," she said.

Nothing else. No *What are you doing here?* No *You can't just show up here anytime you feel like it.* No *You need to make an appointment before coming here.*

"Rachel," I said.

I stepped up to her desk.

"Got a minute?" I asked.

"Of course. Sit down. How are you, Jack?"

I wanted to go around behind the desk and pull her up out of her chair into an embrace. She still had that power. I got the urge every time I saw her. It didn't matter how long it had been.

"I'm good," I said as I sat down. "You know, same old same old. What about you? How's business?"

"It's good," she said. "Real good. Nobody trusts anybody anymore. That means business for me. We've got more than we can handle."

"We?"

"Thomas and me. I made him a partner. He deserved it."

I nodded when I couldn't find my voice. Ten years ago we shared a dream of working side by side as private investigators. We put it off because Rachel wanted to wait until she was fully vested in her FBI pension. So she stayed with the bureau and I worked for the *Velvet Coffin*. Then the Rodney Fletcher case came up and I put the story ahead of what we had and what we planned. Rachel was two years shy of full vesting when they fired her. And our relationship fell apart. Now she did background searches and private investigations without me. And I did tough watchdog reporting for the consumer.

This was not the way it was supposed to be.

I finally found my voice.

"You going to put his name on the door?"

"I don't think so. We've already done the branding with *RAW Data* and it works. So...what brings you here?"

"Well, I was hoping maybe I could pick your brain and get some advice on a story I'm working on."

"Let's move over here."

She gestured toward the seating area and we shifted there, me sitting on the couch and Rachel taking the armchair across a coffee table from me. The wall behind her was hung with photos from her time with the bureau. I knew it was a selling tool.

"So," she said when we were seated.

"I have a story," I said. "I mean, I think. I wanted to run it by you, see if anything pops for you."

As quickly as I could I told the story of Tina Portrero's murder, the connection to three other deaths of women across the country, and the rabbit hole it had led me down. I pulled the printouts from my back pocket and read her passages from the GT23 informed-consent pages and some of the quotes from Bolender and Tina's mother.

"It feels like there's something there," I concluded. "But I don't know what the next steps would be."

"First question," Rachel said. "Is there any indication that the LAPD is going the same way with this? Do they know what you know?"

"I don't know but I doubt they've come up with the three other cases."

"How did you find out about this in the first place? It doesn't feel like the new you. The consumer reporter."

I had conveniently left out the part about the LAPD coming to me because I had spent a night with Tina Portrero the previous year. Now there was no way around it.

"Well, I sort of knew Tina Portrero—briefly—so they came to me."

"You mean you're a suspect, Jack?"

"No, more of a person of interest, but that will get cleared up soon. I gave them my DNA and it will clear me."

"But then you have a big conflict of interest here. Your editor is letting you run with this?"

"Same thing. Once the DNA clears me there is no conflict. Yes, I knew Tina, but that doesn't preclude me from writing about the case. It's been done before. I wrote about my brother and before that I knew an assistant city manager who got murdered. I wrote about the case."

"Yeah, but did you fuck her too?"

That was harsh and it led me to realize that Rachel had a conflict of interest herself when it came to me. Though our decision to part three years before was mutual, I don't think either of us had gotten over the other and possibly never would.

"No, I didn't fuck the assistant city manager," I said. "She was just a source."

I realized as soon as I said the last line that it had been a mistake. Rachel and I had had a secret relationship that blew up publicly when she revealed that she was my source on the series of stories exposing Rodney Fletcher's misdeeds.

"Sorry," I said quickly. "I didn't mean—"

"It's okay, Jack," Rachel said. "Water under the bridge. I think you're right about this DNA stuff. There is something there and I would pursue it."

"Yeah, but how?"

"You said it's a self-regulating industry. Remember when it came out that Boeing was essentially self-regulating and self-reporting when they had those airliner crashes? You could be onto something just as big here. I don't care what it is—a government, a bureaucracy, a business. When there are no rules then corruption sets in like rust. That's your angle. You have to find out if GT23 or any of them has ever been breached. If it has, then game over."

"Easier said than done."

"You need to ask yourself where the vulnerability is. That part you read to me: *We cannot guarantee that a breach will never happen.* That's important. If they can't guarantee that, then they know something. Find the vulnerabilities. Don't expect the media flack to just give them to you."

I understood what she was saying but I was on the outside looking in. The weaknesses of any system are always hidden from the outside.

"I know that," I said. "But GT23 is like a fortress."

"Weren't you the one who told me once that no place is a fortress to a good reporter? There is always a way in. Former employees, current employees with grievances. Who have they fired? Who have they mistreated? Competitors, jealous colleagues—there's always a way in."

"Okay, I'll check all of that—"

"The collaborators. That's another vulnerability. Look at what GT23 is doing, Jack. They are handing off data—they're selling it. That is the point where they lose control of it. They don't control it physically anymore and they don't control what's done with it. They do their due diligence on the research application and then trust that that is the research that is actually conducted. But do they ever double back and check that it is? That's the direction you have to take this. What did the mother say?"

"What?"

"The mother of the victim. You read me her quotes. She said Tina was never married, never wanted to be tied down to one man, was *boy crazy* from the start. What is all of that? It's a nice way of saying she was promiscuous. In current society, that is considered a behavioral problem in females. Right?"

I was seeing all of her profiling instincts come into play. I might have had ulterior motives in coming to see Rachel Walling again, but now she was using her skills to give direction to my reporting and it was beautiful.

"Uh, right, I guess."

"It's the classic profile. A man pursues sex with multiple partners, no big deal. A woman? She's loose. She's a whore. Well, is it genetic?"

I nodded, remembering.

"Sex addiction. At least one of the GT23 collaborators is studying risky behaviors and their genetic origin. I saw that in a story. There might be others."

Rachel pointed at me.

"Bingo," she said. "Sex addiction. Who is studying the genetic relation to sex addiction?"

"Wow," I said.

"Man, I wish we had this stuff when I was working bureau cases," Rachel said. "It would have been a huge part of both victimology and suspect profiling."

She said it wistfully, remembering her past work for the bureau. I could tell that what I had brought to her excited her but also served as a reminder about what she once had and once was. I almost felt bad about my motives for coming.

"Uh, this is all fantastic, Rachel," I said. "Great stuff. You've given me a lot of angles to look at."

"All of which I think a seasoned reporter like you already knew," she said.

I looked at her. So much for my motives. She had read me the way she used to read crime scenes and killers.

"What did you really come here for, Jack?" she asked.

I nodded.

"Well, that's just it," I said. "You just read me like an open book. And that's what I came for. I thought maybe you'd want to take a shot at this, maybe profile the killer, profile the victims. I have a lot of victimology and on the killer I've got times, locations, how he staged things—I've got a lot."

She was shaking her head before I finished.

"I've got too much going on," she said. "This week we're backgrounding candidates for the Mulholland Corridor Planning Board for the city, and I have the usual backlog from our steady clients."

"Well, I guess all that pays the bills," I said.

"Besides…I really don't want to go down that path. That was the past, Jack."

"But you were good at it, Rachel."

"I was. But doing it this way…I think it will be too much of a reminder of that past. It's taken a long time, but I've let it go."

I looked at her, trying to get a read now myself. But she had always been a hard nut to crack. I was left to take her at her word but I wondered if the past she didn't want to return to was more about me than the job she had left behind.

"Okay," I said. "I guess I should let you get back to it, then."

I stood up and so did she. The shin-high coffee table was between us and I leaned across to engage in an awkward hug.

"Thanks, Rachel."

"Anytime, Jack."

I left the office and checked my phone as I walked down Main Street to the lot where I had left the Jeep. I had silenced it before going in to see Rachel and now saw that I had missed two calls from unknown numbers and had two new messages.

The first was from Lisa Hill.

"Stop harassing me."

Short and simple, followed by the hang-up. This message led

me to accurately guess who the second message was from before playing it. Detective Mattson used a few more words than Hill.

"McEvoy, if you want me to put together a harassment case against you, all you have to do is keep bothering Lisa Hill. Leave. Her. Alone."

I erased both messages, my face burning with both indignation and humiliation. I was just doing my job, but it bothered me that neither Hill nor Mattson viewed it that way. To them I was some kind of intruder.

It made me all the more determined to find out what had happened to Tina Portrero and the three other women. Rachel Walling said she didn't want to venture into the past. But I did. For the first time in a long time I had a story that had my blood moving with an addictive momentum. It was good to have that feeling back.

10

*F*air*Warning* did not have the budget for such niceties as the LexisNexis legal search engine. But William Marchand, the lawyer who was on the board of directors and reviewed all *Fair-Warning* stories for legal pitfalls, did have the service and offered it to our staff as just one of the many things he did for us gratis. His office, where he served most of his paying clients, was located on Victory Boulevard near the Van Nuys Civic Center and the side-by-side courthouses where he most often appeared on their behalf. I made my first stop there after leaving downtown.

Marchand was in court but his legal assistant, Sacha Nelson, was there and allowed me to sit next to her at her computer while she conducted a LexisNexis search to see if GT23 or its parent company and founding partners had ever been the subject of a lawsuit. I came across one pending action against the company and another that had been filed and dismissed when a settlement had been reached.

The pending case was a wrongful-termination claim filed by someone named Jason Hwang. The cause-of-action summary on the first page of the lawsuit stated that Hwang was a regulatory-affairs specialist who was fired when another employee claimed that he had fondled him during an encounter in the coffee room.

Hwang denied the accusation and claimed to have been fired without the due process of a full internal investigation. The lawsuit stated that the sexual-harassment complaint was trumped up as a means of getting rid of Hwang because he had demanded strict adherence to company protocols regarding DNA testing and research. The lawsuit also stated that the alleged victim of the unwanted sexual contact was promoted to Hwang's position after he was fired, a clear indication that the termination was unlawful.

What stood out to me in the filing was that Hwang did not work directly for GT23 at the company's Palo Alto lab. He was technically an employee of Woodland Bio, an independent lab located in the Woodland Hills section of Los Angeles. Woodland Bio was described in the lawsuit as a GT23 subcontractor, a lab that handled some of the overflow demands of the mother company's genetic testing. Hwang was suing the mother company because they had ultimate control over personnel decisions and that was also where the money was. Hwang was seeking $1.2 million in damages, saying his reputation had been ruined in the industry by the false accusation and no other company would hire him.

I asked Sacha to print out the lawsuit, which included a notifications page with the name and contact information for Hwang's attorney, who was a partner in a downtown L.A. law firm. Sacha sensed my excitement.

"Good stuff?" she asked.

"Maybe," I said. "If the plaintiff or his lawyer will talk to me, it could lead to something."

"Should we pull up the other case?"

"Yes, sure."

I was sitting on a roller chair next to Sacha's as she worked the keyboard. She was in her early forties, had been with Marchand for a long time, and I knew from previous conversations that she was going to law school at night while working in the office by day. She was attractive in a bookish, determined sort of way— pretty face and eyes hidden behind eyeglasses, never lipstick or any sign that she spent much time in front of a makeup mirror. She wore no rings or earrings and had an unconscious habit of hooking her short auburn hair behind her ears as she stared at the computer screen.

It turned out that there had been six Stanford men who had originally founded GenoType23 to cater to the burgeoning law-enforcement need for DNA lab work. But Jenson Fitzgerald had been bought out early by the five other partners. When years later GT23 was founded, he filed a lawsuit claiming that he was owed a piece of the GT23 action because of his standing as an original founder of the mother company. The initial response to the lawsuit said Fitzgerald had no claim to the riches generated by the new company because they were separate entities. But the LexisNexis file ended with a joint notice of dismissal, meaning the two parties had come to an agreement and the dispute was settled. The details of the settlement were kept confidential.

I asked Sacha to print out the documents that were available even though I did not see much in the way of follow-up on that case. I believed that the Hwang case could be far more fruitful.

After finding no other legal action regarding the company, I had Sacha enter the names of the five remaining founders one by one to see if there was ever a legal action personally filed by them or against them. She found only a divorce case involving one of the founders, a man named Charles Breyer. His marriage of twenty-four years came to an end in a divorce petition filed two years earlier by his wife, Anita, who made claims of intolerable cruelty and called her husband a serial philanderer. She settled the divorce for a lump-sum payment of $2 million and the home they had shared in Palo Alto, which was valued at $3.2 million.

"Another happy loving couple," Sacha said. "Print it?"

"Yeah, might as well print it," I said. "You sound pretty cynical about it."

"Money," she said. "It's the root of all troubles. Men get rich, they think they're king of the world, then they act like it."

"Is that from personal experience?" I asked.

"No, but you see it a lot when you work in a law office."

"You mean with the cases?"

"Yes, the cases. Definitely not the boss."

She got up and went to the printer, where all the pages I had asked for were waiting. She tapped them together and then put a clip on the stack before handing it to me. I stood up and moved around from behind her desk.

"How is law school?" I asked.

"All good," she said. "Two years down, one to go."

"Think you'll work here with Bill, or strike out on your own?"

"I'm hoping I'll be right here, working with you and *FairWarning* and our other clients."

I nodded.

"Cool," I said. "Well, as always, thanks for your help. Tell Bill thanks as well. You two really take good care of us."

"We're happy to," she said. "Good luck with the story."

When I got back to the office, Myron Levin was closed up in the conference room. Through the glass I could see him talking to a man and woman but they didn't look like cops, so I assumed it had nothing to do with my pursuits. I looked over at Emily Atwater in her cubby, caught her attention, and pointed at the conference-room door.

"Donors," Emily said.

I nodded, sat down in my cubicle, and started the search for Jason Hwang. I found no phone number or social-media footprint. He wasn't on Facebook, Twitter, or Instagram. I got up and walked over to Emily. I knew she was on LinkedIn, the professional networking site, and I wasn't.

"I'm looking for a guy," I said. "Can you do a quick check on LinkedIn?"

"Let me finish this line," she said.

She kept typing. I checked on Myron through the glass and saw that the woman was writing a check.

"Looks like we'll get paid this week," I said.

Emily stopped typing and glanced at the conference-room window.

"She's writing a check," I explained.

"Six figures, I hope," Emily said.

I knew *FairWarning*'s biggest financial support came from individuals and family foundations. Sometimes there were one-to-one matching grants from journalism foundations.

"Okay, what's the name?" Emily asked.

"Jason Hwang," I said, and spelled it.

Emily typed. She had a habit of leaning forward when she typed, as though she was diving headfirst into whatever she was writing. With powder-blue eyes, pale skin, and white-blond hair, she seemed just a few genetic ticks away from being full albino. She was also tall—not just for a woman but for anyone, at least six feet in flats. She chose to accentuate this signature feature by always wearing heels. On top of that she was a damn good reporter, having been a war correspondent, followed by stints in New York and Washington, DC, before heading west to California, where she eventually landed at *FairWarning*. Her two separate postings in Afghanistan had left her tough and unflappable, great attributes for a reporter.

"Who is he?" she asked.

"He worked for a lab that subcontracted for the company I'm looking at," I said. "Then he got fired and sued them."

"GT23?"

"How do you know that?"

"Myron. He said you might need help on it."

"I just need to find this guy."

She nodded.

"Well, there's four here," she said.

I remembered how Hwang was described in the lawsuit.

"Lives in L.A.," I said. "He's got a master's in life sciences from UCLA."

She started looking at the pedigrees of the four Jason Hwangs, shaking her head and saying "Nope" each time.

"Strike four, and you're out. None of these are even from L.A."

"Okay, thanks for looking."

"You could try LexisNexis."

"I did."

I went back to my desk. Of course, I had not run Hwang's name through LexisNexis as I should have. I now called the law office and quietly asked Sacha Nelson to do the search. I heard her type it in.

"Hmm, only the lawsuit comes back up," she said. "Sorry."

"That's okay," I said. "I have a few other tricks up my sleeve."

After hanging up I continued the search for Jason Hwang. I knew I could simply call the attorney who had filed the lawsuit on Hwang's behalf but my hope was to get to Hwang without his lawyer sitting on his shoulder and trying to control the flow of information. The attorney was useful, however, in that he had listed Hwang's credentials and experience in the claim, noting his receiving the master's degree from UCLA in 2012 before being recruited by Woodland Bio. That told me that Hwang was a young man, most likely in his early thirties. He had started at Woodland as a lab technician before being promoted to regulatory-affairs specialist just a year before he was fired.

I conducted a search for professional organizations in the DNA field and came up with a group called the National Society of Professional Geneticists. Its website menu had a page labeled *Looking for a Lab,* which I took to be a help-wanted section. Hwang claimed in his still-pending lawsuit that he had become a pariah in the genetics industry because of the accusation made against him. In the #MeToo era, just an accusation was enough to end a career. I thought maybe there was a chance Hwang had posted his résumé and contact information in an effort to land an interview somewhere. He could have even been instructed to do so by his lawyer to help prove his inability to get work in the field.

The résumés were listed in alphabetical order and I quickly found Jason Hwang's curriculum vitae as the last entry under the letter *H.* It was the jackpot. It included an email address, phone number, and mailing address. The work-experience section revealed the responsibilities of his GT23 job as a quality control specialist and liaison between the company and any regulatory agencies that kept watch on the various aspects of DNA analysis. The primary agencies were the Food and Drug Administration, the Department of Health and Human Services, and the Federal Trade Commission. I noticed Hwang had also listed several references. Most were personal or academic supporters but one was a man named Gordon Webster, who was described as an investigator with the Federal Trade Commission. I wrote the name down, thinking that Webster might be useful to interview.

I wrote Hwang's details down as well. I was in business and keeping my momentum. If Hwang's mailing address was his home, he lived just over the hill in West Hollywood. I checked the time and realized that if I left the office now I could probably get through Laurel Canyon before it became clogged with rush-hour traffic.

I put a fresh notebook and batteries for my tape recorder into my backpack before heading to the door.

11

The winding two-lane snake that was Laurel Canyon Boule-vard took nearly a half hour to pass. I relearned another object lesson about Los Angeles: there was no rush hour because every hour was rush hour.

The address on Jason Hwang's CV corresponded to a home on Willoughby Avenue in a neighborhood of expensive homes with high hedges. It seemed too nice for an out-of-work biologist in his early thirties. I parked and walked through an archway cut into a six-foot-thick hedge and knocked on the aquamarine door of a two-story white cube. After knocking I rang the doorbell, when I should have done just one or the other. But following the doorbell I heard a dog start to bark inside and then the sound was quickly cut off by someone yelling the dog's name: *Tipsy*.

The door opened and a man stood there cradling a toy poodle under one arm. The dog was as white as the house. The man was Asian and very small. Not just short but small in all dimensions.

"Hi, I'm looking for Jason Hwang," I said.

"Who are you?" he said. "Why are you looking for him?"

"I'm a reporter. I'm working on a story about GT23 and I would like to talk to him about it."

"What kind of story?"

"Are you Jason Hwang? I'll tell him what kind of story."

"I'm Jason. What is this story?"

"I'd rather not talk about it standing out here. Is there a place we can go to sit down and talk? Maybe inside or somewhere nearby?"

It was a tip my editor Foley had given me when I started out in the business. Never do an interview at the door. People can shut the door if they don't like what you ask.

"Do you have a card or some sort of ID?" Hwang asked.

"Sure," I said.

I dug a business card out of my wallet and handed it to him. I also showed him a press pass issued six years earlier by the Sheriff's Department when I was regularly writing crime stories for the *Velvet Coffin*.

Hwang studied both but didn't mention that the press pass was dated 2013 or that the man in the photo looked a lot younger than me.

"Okay," Hwang said, handing me back the card. "You can come in."

He stepped back to allow me entrance. "Thank you," I said.

He led me through the entryway to a living room decorated in white and aqua furnishings. He gestured toward the couch—that was for me—while he sat on a matching stuffed chair. He put the dog down next to him on the chair. He was wearing white pants and a sea-foam-green golf shirt. He blended in perfectly with the house's design and decor, and I didn't think that was by happenstance.

"Do you live here alone?" I asked.

"No," Hwang said.

He offered no further details.

"Well, as I said at the door, I'm doing a story about GT23 and I came across your lawsuit. It's still pending, correct?"

"It's pending—we don't have a trial date yet," he said. "But I can't talk to you because the case is still active."

"Well, your case is not really what I'm writing about. If I steer clear of the lawsuit, can I ask you a few questions?"

"No, impossible. My lawyer said I could not speak at all when the other journalist called. I wanted to, but he wouldn't let me."

I was suddenly gripped by a reporter's greatest fear—being scooped. Another journalist might be following the same trail as me.

"Who was the other journalist?" I asked.

"I don't remember," Hwang said. "My lawyer told him no."

"Well, was it recent? Or are you talking about when you filed the lawsuit?"

"Yes, when I filed."

I felt a wave of relief. The lawsuit had been filed almost a year ago. It was probably a routine call from a reporter—probably from the *L.A. Times*—who had noticed the lawsuit on the courthouse docket and called for a comment.

"What if we talk off the record?" I said. "I don't quote you or use your name."

"I don't know," Hwang said. "It still sounds risky. I don't even know you and you want me to trust you."

This was a dance I had engaged in many times before. People often said they couldn't or didn't want to talk. The trick was to leverage their anger and give them a safe outlet for it. Then they would talk.

"All I can say is that I would protect you from being identified," I said. "My own credibility is at stake. I burn a source and no source will ever trust me. I went to jail once for sixty-three days because I wouldn't give up the name of a source."

Hwang looked horrified. Mentioning that experience often worked with people on the fence about talking to me.

"What happened?" Hwang asked.

"The judge finally let me go," I said. "He knew I wasn't going to give up the name."

All of that was true, but I left out the part about my source—Rachel Walling—coming forward and revealing herself. After that there was no point in continuing the contempt order and the judge released me.

"The thing is, if I talk they'll know it came from me," Hwang said. "They'll read the story and say, *Who else could it come from?*"

"Your information would be for background only. I won't record. I don't even have to take notes. I'm just trying to understand how all of this works."

Hwang paused and then made a decision.

"Ask your questions and if I don't like them, I won't answer."

"Fair enough."

I had not really thought about how I would explain myself should Hwang agree to talk to me—on or off the record. Now it was time. Like a good police detective, I didn't want to give the subject of my interview all my information. I didn't know him and didn't know who he might pass it on to. He was worried about trusting me but I also had to worry about trusting him.

"Let me start by explaining who I am and what I'm doing," I began. "I work for a news site called *FairWarning*. It's consumer-protection reporting. You know, watching out for the little guy. And I've been assigned to look at the security of the personal information and biological material in the genetic-analytics field."

Hwang immediately scoffed.

"What security?" he said.

I wanted to write the line down because I instinctively saw it as possibly the first quote in a story. It was provocative and would pull the reader in. But I couldn't. I had made a deal with Hwang.

"It sounds like you were not impressed by the security at GT23," I said.

The question was deliberately open-ended. He could run with it if he wished.

"Not the lab," Hwang said. "I ran a tight lab. We adhered to all protocols and I will prove that in court. It was what happened afterward."

"Afterward?" I prompted.

"The places the data went. The company wanted the money. They didn't care where it went as long as they were getting paid."

"When you say 'They,' you're talking about GT23?"

"Yes, of course. They went public and needed more revenue to support the stock. So they were wide open for business. They lowered the bar."

"Give me an example."

"Too many to list. We were shipping DNA all over the world. Thousands of samples. The company needed the money and no one was turned away as long as it was a lab registered with the FDA or the equivalent in other countries."

"So then they had to be legit. It wasn't like somebody drives up and says, *I need DNA*. I'm not understanding your concern."

"It's the Wild West right now. There are so many directions to go with genetic research. It's really in its infancy. And we— meaning the company—don't control what happens with the bio and how it's used once it goes out the door. That's the FDA's problem, not ours—that was the attitude. And let me tell you, the FDA didn't do jack."

"Okay, I get that and I'm not saying that's a good thing, but wasn't there the safety that it was all anonymous? I mean, these researchers were given the DNA but not the identities of the participants, right?"

"Of course, but that's not the point. You're thinking in the present. What about the future? This science is very young. We haven't even had the whole genome for twenty years. New things are discovered about it every day. Will what is anonymous now stay that way in twenty years? In ten years? Or will usernames and passwords not matter? What if your DNA is your identifier and you've already given it away?"

Hwang raised his hand and pointed a finger at the ceiling.

"Even the military," he said. "Did you know that this year the Pentagon told all members of the military not to do DNA kits because of the security issues they pose?"

I had not seen that report but I did grasp Hwang's point.

"Were you warning GT23 about this?" I asked.

"Of course I was," Hwang said. "Every day. I was the only one."

"I read the lawsuit."

"I can't talk about that. Even off the record. My lawyer—"

"I'm not asking you to. But the lawsuit, it says the employee who filed the complaint against you—David Shanley—set you up to get your job and that it was not investigated by the company."

"It was all lies."

"I know. I get that. But the motive. You don't think it could have been to shut you up about this—about the lack of controls or concern over where the DNA was going?"

"All I know is that Shanley got my job. He lies about me and gets my fucking job."

"That could have been his reward for getting you out of the company. They were afraid you would be a whistleblower."

"My lawyer has subpoenaed company documents. Emails. If it's there, we'll find it."

"Let's go back to what you were saying about the DNA being sold by the company. Can you remember any names of labs or biotechs that were sold samples?"

"There were too many to remember. We put bio-packs together almost every single day."

"Who was the biggest buyer of DNA? Do you remember?"

"Not really. Why don't you tell me what it is you're looking for?"

I looked at him for a long moment. I was the seeker of facts and information. I was supposed to hold them close to the vest and not share them until it was time to put them into a story. But I felt that Hwang knew more than he was saying, even if he didn't yet realize it. I felt that I needed to break my own rule and give in order to get.

"Okay, I'll tell you why I'm really here."

"Please."

"A young woman was murdered last week in L.A.—her neck broken. I was looking into it and came up with three other women in California, Texas, and Florida who were killed in exactly the same way."

"I don't understand. What does it have to do with—"

"Maybe nothing. Maybe it's all coincidence. But all four of the women were GT23 participants. They didn't know each other but they had all sent in their DNA. Four women killed in the same way, four women who were participants. To me, that moves beyond coincidence and that's why I'm here."

Hwang said nothing. He seemed to be contemplating the possibilities of what I was telling him.

"There's more," I said. "I haven't done a lot of work on this yet but there may be another commonality."

"Which is what?" Hwang asked.

"Some sort of addictive behavior. The L.A. woman had been treated for alcoholism and drugs. She was sort of a party girl— went out to a lot of clubs, met men in bars."

"Dirty four."

"What?"

"*Dirty four.* It's what some geneticists call the DRD4 gene."

"Why?"

"It has been identified in relation to at-risk behavior and addiction, including sex addiction."

"Is it in the female genome?"

"Both male and female."

"Take a woman who frequently goes to bars by herself to pick up men for sex—are you saying it's because she has the DRD4 gene?"

"Possibly. But the science is in its infancy and everybody is individual. I don't think you can say for sure."

"As far as you know, are any of GT23's collaborators studying the dirty-four gene?"

"It's possible, but that's what I'm saying is wrong. We can sell DNA for one purpose, but who's to stop them from using it for another purpose? What stops them from selling it again to a third party?"

"I saw a story about the company. It listed some of the places the DNA was going. It mentioned a study of addiction and risky behavior at a lab down in Irvine."

"Yes. Orange Nano."

"That's the lab?"

"That's the lab. Big buyers."

"Who runs it?"

"A bio guy named William Orton."

"Is it part of UC–Irvine?"

"No, privately funded. Probably Big Pharma. You see, GT23 liked to sell to the private labs better than to universities. The private labs paid more and there wasn't a public record of transactions."

"Did you deal with Orton?"

"A few times on the phone. That was it."

"Why were you on the phone with him?"

"Because he would call me and ask about a bio-pack. You know, checking to see if it had shipped or maybe to add to an existing order."

"He ordered more than once?"

"Sure. Many times."

"Like every week? Or what?"

"No, like once a month or sometimes longer."

"And what would an order be? How much?"

"A bio-pack contains one hundred samples."

"Why would he need to keep ordering bio-packs?"

"For continuing-research purposes. They all do that."

"Did Orton ever talk about his lab's research?"

"Sometimes."

"What did he say?"

"Not much. Just that that was his field of study. Addiction in many forms. Alcohol, drugs, sex. He wanted to isolate those genes and develop therapies. But that's how I know about dirty four. From him."

"He used the phrase 'dirty four'?"

"Yes."

"Had anybody else used it with you before?"

"Not that I remember."

"Have you ever been down to Orange Nano?"

"No, never. My only contact was by phone and email."

I nodded. I knew at that moment that I would be going down to Irvine to visit Orange Nano.

12

I decided that the best use of my time would not be to get into the crush of cars waiting to go over the mountain to the Valley through one of the choked-off freeways or mountain roads. That could take ninety minutes at this time of day. One of the things that made the City of Angels so beautiful also created one of its greatest hardships. The Santa Monica Mountains cut through the middle of the city, leaving the San Fernando Valley—where I lived and worked—on the north side and the rest of the city, including Hollywood and the Westside, to the south. There were two freeways that cut through the big passes and several two-lane winders. Take your pick but at five o'clock on a weekday you weren't going anywhere. I drove over to Cofax Coffee and set up with a cappuccino and my laptop at a table beneath the display of bobbleheads and other Dodger paraphernalia.

I first sent Myron Levin an email briefly summarizing my interview with Jason Hwang and the leads I had picked up regarding Orange Nano. Next, I opened a file and tried to recall everything Hwang had told me, writing a detailed summary of the interview from memory. I was halfway through my second cappuccino when I took a call from Myron.

"Where are you?"

"Other side of the hill. I'm at a coffee shop on Fairfax writing up notes and waiting out the traffic."

"It's six now. When do you think you're coming back?"

"I'm almost finished with my notes, then I'll wade into the traffic."

"So, by seven, you think?"

"Hopefully before."

"Okay, I'll wait for you. I want to talk about this story."

"Well, do you want to just talk now? Did you get my email? I just had a killer interview over here."

"I got the email but let's talk it out when you get here."

"Okay. I'm going to try Nichols Canyon. Maybe I get lucky."

"I'll see you when I see you."

After the call I wondered why Myron wanted to talk face-to-face. My guess was that he might not be as convinced as I was that there was something here. He had not commented on my email and it seemed as though I would need to sell him on the story all over again.

Nichols Canyon was a charmed route. The traffic flowed smoothly through the hillside neighborhoods above Hollywood until the unavoidable bottleneck at Mulholland Drive. But once I got through, it was clear sailing again down into the Valley. I walked into the office at 6:40 and considered it an accomplishment.

Myron was in the conference room with Emily Atwater. I put my backpack down on my desk and gave him a wave through the window. Since I had gotten back earlier than expected, I figured he was probably in a story conference with her.

But he waved me in and made no move to dismiss Emily when I entered.

"Jack," he said, "I want to bring Emily in to help out with your story."

I looked at him a long moment before responding. He had done a smart thing. He had kept Emily in the room because that would make it harder for me to push back against his plan. Still, I couldn't just accept the encroachment without protest.

"How come?" I asked. "I mean, I think I have it covered."

"This Orange Nano angle you mentioned in your email looks promising," Myron said. "I don't know if you know Emily's pedigree but she covered higher ed for the *Orange County Register* before coming to *FairWarning*. She still has contacts down there and I think it would be good for you two to partner up."

"Partner up? But it's my story."

"Of course it is, but sometimes stories get bigger and need more hands—more experienced hands. Like I said, she knows people down there. You also have the police situation to deal with."

"What police situation?"

"As far as I know, you're still on their person-of-interest list. Have you talked to them lately? Have they processed your DNA?"

"I haven't talked to them today. But that's not a situation. As soon as they run the DNA I'll be off the list. I was planning on going down to Orange Nano first thing tomorrow."

"That sounds good but that's what I mean. I don't want you going there without preparation. Have you done any back-grounding on the lab or its people?"

"Not yet, but I will. That's why I came back to the office, to do some research."

"Well, talk to Emily. She's already done some work and maybe you two can come up with a plan of action."

I didn't say anything. I just looked down at the table. I knew

I wasn't going to change his mind, and maybe also knew—grudgingly—that he was right. Two reporters were better than one. Besides, having half the staff on the story would make Myron more invested in it.

"Okay," Myron said. "Then I'll let you two get after it. Keep me in the loop."

Myron got up and left the room, closing the door behind him. Before I could speak, Emily did.

"Sorry, Jack," she said. "I didn't go asking to be part of this. He pulled me in."

"Don't worry," I said. "I'm not blaming you. I just thought I had things in hand, you know?"

"Yes. But while we were waiting for you I did do a preliminary workup on William Orton, the guy who runs Orange Nano."

"And?"

"I think there's something there. Orton left UC-Irvine to start Orange Nano."

"So?"

"So, you don't just leave a UC job where you're tenured and have a full lab at your disposal and unlimited doctoral candidates at your beck and call. You can start an outside company or lab but the university is your anchor. You keep that affiliation because it works for you. It's easier to get grants, professional exposure, everything."

"So something happened."

"Right, something happened. And we're going to find out what it is."

"How?"

"Well, I'm going to work UCI—I still have a few sources there—and you do what you said, you work Orange Nano. I don't want to step on your toes but I think I can help here."

"Okay."

"Good, then."

"This is how I think we should work it…"

Over the next hour I shared everything I knew so far about the deaths of the four women and GT23. Emily asked many questions and together we made an action plan that had us attacking the story from two angles. I went from being reluctant to being glad she was on board. She was not as experienced as I was but she was impressive, and I knew she had probably broken the most important stories *FairWarning* had put out in the last couple of years. I left the office that night believing Myron had made a good move putting us together.

It was eight o'clock when I got back to my Jeep and drove home. After parking in the garage I walked to the front of the apartment building to check my mail. It had been a week since I checked the box and this was primarily to empty it of all the junk mail I received.

The building's management provided a trash can next to the bank of mailboxes so junk mail could be quickly transferred to its final destination. I was going through my stack, dropping one piece after the other into the bin, when I heard steps coming from behind me and then a voice I recognized.

"Mr. McEvoy. Just who we were looking for."

It was Mattson and Sakai. Mattson was back to saying my name wrong. He was carrying a folded document and held it out to me as he approached in the dimming light of the day.

"What's this?" I asked.

"This is a warrant," Mattson said. "All signed, sealed, and delivered by the City Attorney's Office. You're under arrest."

"What? Arrest for what?"

"That would be section 148 of the California Penal Code.

Obstructing a police officer in the discharge of his duty. That officer would be me and the investigation of the murder of Christina Portrero. We told you to back off, McEvoy, but no—you kept harassing our witnesses and lying your ass off."

"What are you talking about? I didn't obstruct you or anybody. I'm a reporter working a story and—"

"No, you're a person of interest and I told you to back off. You didn't, so now you're fucked. Put your hands up on that wall."

"This is crazy. You're going to create a major embarrassment for your department, do you know that? You ever heard of a thing called freedom of the press?"

"Tell it to the judge. Now turn around and put your hands up there. I'm going to search you for weapons."

"Jesus, Mattson, this makes no sense. Is it because you don't have jack shit on Portrero and you want a distraction?"

Mattson said nothing. I did what I was told and moved to the wall, not wanting to add resisting arrest to the bogus charge of obstruction. Mattson quickly searched me and emptied my pockets, giving my phone, wallet, and keys to Sakai. I turned my head enough to check out Sakai and he didn't look like a man who was fully on board with this move.

"Detective Sakai, did you try to talk him out of this?" I asked. "This is a mistake and you're going to go down with him when the shit hits the fan."

"It would be best if you kept quiet," Sakai said.

"I'm not going to keep quiet," I threw back at him. "The whole world is going to hear about this. This is bullshit."

One by one Mattson pulled my hands off the wall and cuffed my wrists behind my back. He led me to their car, which was parked against the curb.

As I was about to be placed in the back seat I saw a neighbor from the building come up the sidewalk with her dog on a leash and stare silently at my humiliation while her dog yipped at me. I looked away, then Mattson put his hand on the top of my head and pushed me down into the back seat.

HAMMOND

13

Hammond was in the lab at his station, spreading nitrocellulose over a gel tray he had just retrieved from the cooker. He felt his watch vibrate against the inside of his wrist. He knew it was one of his flags. He had gotten an alert.

But the process could not be interrupted. He continued his work, next blotting the gel tray with paper towels, making sure to keep uniform pressure on the gel across the entire tray. When he was finished blotting he knew he could take a break from the work. He checked his watch and read the text.

Hey Hammer, wanna grab some beers?

This was a cover text emanating from a cellular relay coded as Max. Of course, Max didn't exist but anybody who happened to see the message pop up on his watch, even worn on the inside of his wrist, would not be suspicious, though the message came in at 3:14 a.m. and all the bars were closed.

Hammond went to his lab table and pulled his laptop from his backpack. He checked the other stations in the lab and saw that nobody was watching him. Only three other technicians were working graveyard anyway, and there were empty stations

separating all of them. It was a budgetary thing. The wait time on
rape kits and some cold-case homicides was still months where
it should be weeks if not days, but the city's budget masters had
cut back on the lab's third shift. Hammond expected that soon
he would be working days again.

He opened the laptop and used his thumb to authenticate. He
went to the surveillance software and pulled up the alert. He
saw that one of the detectives he was monitoring had just made
an arrest and put someone in jail. His filing the arrest report
had triggered the alert. Hammond's partner, Roger Vogel, had
hacked the internal LAPD network and set the whole alert
system up. He had master skills.

Hammond checked the other techs and then looked back at
his screen. He called up the report filed by Detective David Mattson. He had arrested a man named Jack McEvoy and booked
him at the jail at LAPD's Van Nuys Division. Hammond read
the details of the arrest, then reached into the backpack for the
phone he carried in an inside zippered pocket. The phone for
emergency contact.

He turned the phone on and waited for it to boot up. Meantime, he closed out the arrest report and went to the public-access
page for the city's jail system. He put in the name *Jack McEvoy*
and was soon looking at a mug shot of the man. He looked angry
and defiant as he stared at the camera. There was a scar on his
upper left cheek. It looked like it could have been easily erased
by plastic surgery. But McEvoy kept it. Hammond thought it
might be some sort of badge of honor with the reporter.

The phone was ready. Hammond called the single number
stored in its memory. Vogel answered with sleep in his voice.

"This better be good."

"I think we have a problem."

"What?"

"Mattson arrested somebody tonight."

"That's not a problem. That's good."

"No, not for the murder. It was a journalist. He was arrested for obstructing the investigation."

"You woke me for that?"

"It means he may be onto this."

"How could that be? The police aren't even—"

"Call it a hunch—whatever."

Hammond looked at the mug shot again. Angry and determined. McEvoy knew something.

"I think we have to watch him," he said.

"All right, whatever," Vogel said. "Text the details and I'll see what's out there. When did this happen?"

"They booked him last night. I got flagged on the software you set up."

"Glad it worked. You know, this could be a good thing for us."

"How?"

"I don't know yet. A couple of ways. Let me go to work on it. You want to meet in the morning? In daylight?"

"Can't."

"You fucking vampire. Sleep later."

"No, I have court first thing. Testifying today."

"What case? Maybe I'll come watch."

"A cold case. Guy killed a girl thirty years ago. He kept the knife, thought washing it off would be okay."

"Dumbass. Where?"

"Up in the hills. Threw her off an overlook on Mulholland."

"I mean where's the courtroom?"

"Oh."

Hammond realized he didn't know himself.

"Hold on."

He dug into the backpack and pulled out the notice to appear.

"Downtown criminal courts. Department 108, Judge Riley. I have to be there at nine to go on first."

"Well, maybe I'll see you there. Meantime, I'm on this reporter. Does he work at the *Times*?"

"The arrest report didn't say. It said occupation journalist and the summary said he was obstructing the investigation by harassing witnesses, not revealing he was an acquaintance of the victim."

"Holy shit, Hammer, you left the key part out. He knew the victim?"

"That's what it says. On the report."

"Okay, I'm on it. Maybe I see you in court."

"Okay."

Vogel disconnected. Hammond turned off his phone and dropped it back into his backpack. He stood there thinking about things.

"Hammer?"

He whipped around. Cassandra Nash was standing there. His supervisor. She had come out of her office without him noticing.

"Uh, yes, what's up?"

"Where are you with that batch? It looks like you're just standing there."

"No. Uh, I mean I was just taking a second. I'm blotting and was just giving it a minute, then I'll start hybridization."

"Good, so you'll get that done before end of shift?"

"Of course. Absolutely."

"And you've got court in the morning, right?"

"Yes, all set on that, too."

"Good. Then I'll leave you to it."

"You hear anything about the next deployment?"

"As far as I know, we're still on third shift. I'll let you know what I know when I know it."

Hammond nodded and watched her go check on the other techs, doing her supervising thing. He hated Cassandra Nash. Not because she was his boss. It was because she was aloof and fake. She spent her money on designer handbags and shoes. She talked about fancy restaurants she and her douchebag husband went to for chef tastings. In his mind Hammond had conflated her named to Cash because he believed she was wholly motivated by money and possessions the way all women were. *Fuck them,* he thought as he watched Nash talk to one of the other technicians.

He went back to the gel he was prepping.

14

At 9 a.m. Hammond sat on a marble bench in the hallway of the ninth floor of the Criminal Courts Building. He had been told to wait there until it was time for him to testify. On the bench next to him were his notes and charts regarding the case and a cup of black coffee from the snack bar near the elevator alcove. The coffee was terrible. Not the designer stuff he was used to. He needed it because he was dragging after a full eight hours on the graveyard shift, but he was having a hard time stomaching the harsh brew and feared it would give him stomach issues that might haunt him on the witness stand. He stopped drinking it.

At 9:20, Detective Kleber finally stepped halfway out of the courtroom and waved Hammond over. Kleber was the lead detective on the case.

"Sorry, they had to argue a motion before bringing the jury in," he explained. "But now we're ready."

"Me too," Hammond said.

He had testified many times before and it was now a routine. All except for his satisfaction in knowing that he was the Hammer. His testimony always sealed the deal and from the witness stand he had the best angle on "the moment"—the second when even the defendant was convinced by Hammond's testimony and the hope went out of his eyes.

He stood in front of the witness stand, raised his hand, and took the oath to tell the truth. He spelled his first and last names—Marshall Hammond—and then stepped up and took the witness seat that was between Judge Vincent Riley and the jury. He looked at the jurors and smiled, ready for the first question.

The prosecutor was named Gaines Walsh. He handled many of the LAPD's cold cases and so Hammond had testified on direct examination from him many times before. He practically knew the questions before they were asked but acted as though each one was a new one to consider. Hammond was a slightly built man—never played sports while growing up—with a professorial goatee whose reddish whiskers contrasted with his dark brown hair. His skin was paper white after nearly a year on the midnight shift. Vogel's teasing on the phone call had been on point. He looked like a vampire caught in daylight.

"Mr. Hammond, can you tell the jury what you do for a living?" Walsh asked.

"I'm a DNA technician," Hammond said. "I work in the Los Angeles Police Department's bio-forensics lab located at Cal State L.A."

"How long have you had that position?"

"Twenty-one months with the LAPD. Before that I worked for eight years in the bio-forensics lab for the Orange County Sheriff's Department."

"Can you tell the ladies and gentlemen of the jury what your duties are in the LAPD lab?"

"My responsibilities include processing forensic cases that require DNA analysis, generating reports based on the conclusions of that analysis, and then testifying about those conclusions in court."

"Can you tell us a little bit about your background education in the field of DNA and genetics?"

"Yes, I have a bachelor of arts degree in biochemistry from the University of Southern California and a master's in life sciences with a specialty in genetics from the University of California at Irvine."

Walsh fake-smiled, as he did at this point in every trial.

"Life sciences," he said. "Is that what we older folks used to call plain old *biology*?"

Hammond fake-smiled back, as he did at every trial.

"Yes, it is," he said.

"Can you describe what DNA is and what it does in layman's terms?" Walsh asked.

"I can try," Hammond said. "DNA is short for *deoxyribonucleic acid*. It is a molecule composed of two strands that twist around each other, forming a double helix that carries the genetic code of a living thing. By *code* I really mean instructions for the development of that organism. In human beings DNA contains all our hereditary information and therefore determines everything about us, from the color of our eyes to the function of our brains. Ninety-nine percent of the DNA in all human beings is identical. That last one percent and the myriad combinations within it is what makes each of us completely unique."

Hammond gave the answer like a high school biology teacher. He spoke slowly and recited the information with a tone of awe. Walsh then moved on and led him quickly through the basics of his assignment to the case. This part was so routine Hammond was able to go on autopilot and glance a few times at the defendant. It was the first time he had seen him in person. Robert Earl

Dykes, a fifty-nine-year-old plumber, had long been suspected of killing his ex-fiancée, Wilma Fournette, in 1990, stabbing her to death, then throwing her body down a hillside off Mulholland Drive. Now he was finally brought to justice.

He sat at the defense table in an ill-fitting suit his lawyer had given him. He had a yellow legal pad in front of him in case he came up with a genius question to pass to the lawyer next to him. But Hammond could see it was blank. There would be no question from him or his lawyer that could undo the damage Hammond would inflict. He was the Hammer and it was about to come down.

"Is this the knife that you tested for blood and DNA?" Walsh asked.

He was holding up a clear evidence bag containing an opened switchblade.

"Yes, it is," Hammond said.

"Can you tell us how it came to you?"

"Yes, it had been sealed in evidence from the case since the original 1990 investigation. Detective Kleber reopened the case and brought it to me."

"Why you?"

"I should have said he brought it to the DNA unit and it was assigned to me on rotation."

"What did you do with it?"

"I opened the package and examined the knife visually for blood and then under magnification. The knife appeared to be clean but I could see that there was a spring-loaded mechanism in the handle, so I asked for a knife expert from the toolmark unit to come to the lab to disassemble the weapon."

"Who was that?"

"Gerald Lattis."

"And he opened the knife for you?"

"He took it apart and then I examined the spring mechanism under a lab magnifier. I saw what I believed to be a minute amount of dried blood on the coil of the spring. I then began a DNA-extraction protocol."

Walsh walked Hammond through the science. This was the boring technical part where the danger was that the jurors' thoughts could wander off. Walsh wanted them keenly interested in the DNA findings and asked quick, short questions that required quick, short answers.

The provenance of the knife would have already been testified to by Kleber. The knife was confiscated from Dykes when he was originally questioned in the investigation. The original detectives had it examined for blood by a lab using archaic methods and materials and were told it was clean. When Kleber decided to reopen the case at the urging of the victim's sister, he took another look at the knife and brought it to the DNA lab.

Finally, Walsh arrived at the point where Hammond provided his findings that the DNA extracted from the minute amount of blood on the spring of the switchblade mechanism matched the DNA of the victim, Wilma Fournette.

"The DNA profile developed from the material on the knife does match the profile from the victim's blood obtained during the autopsy," Hammond said.

"How close is the match?" Walsh asked.

"It is a unique match. A perfect match."

"Can you tell the jurors if there is a statistic associated with that perfect match?"

"Yes, we generate statistics based on the human population of Earth to give a weight to that match. In this case the victim was African-American. In the African-American database, the frequency of this DNA profile is one in thirteen quadrillion unrelated individuals."

"When you say one in thirteen quadrillion, how many zeros are we talking about?"

"That would be a thirteen with fifteen zeros behind it."

"Is there a layman's way of explaining the significance of this frequency?"

"Yes. The current population of Planet Earth is roughly seven billion. That number is significantly eclipsed by thirteen quadrillion. That tells us there is no one else on Earth or in the last one hundred years on Earth who could have that DNA. Only the victim in this case. Only Wilma Fournette."

Hammond stole a glance at Dykes. The killer sat unmoving, his eyes downcast and focused on the blank yellow page in front of him. It was the moment. The Hammer had come down and Dykes knew that it was over.

Hammond was pleased with the part he had played in the legal play. He was the star witness. But it also pained him to see another man go down for what Hammond did not consider to be much of a crime. He had no doubt that Dykes had done what he had to do, and his ex-fiancée had gotten what she had coming.

He still had to sit for cross-examination but he knew as well as the defense attorney that he was bulletproof. The science didn't lie. The science was the hammer.

He looked out into the rows of the gallery and saw a woman weeping. It was the sister who had urged Kleber to reopen the case after nearly three decades. Hammond was her hero now. Her superman. With an S on his chest for *Science,* he had taken down the villain. It was too bad that her tears didn't touch him. He felt no sympathy for her or her long-held pain. Hammond believed women deserved all the pain they got.

Then, two rows behind the weeping woman, Hammond saw Vogel. He had slipped into court unnoticed. Now Hammond was reminded of the greater villain who was out there. The Shrike. And that everything Hammond and Vogel had worked for was at risk.

15

Vogel was waiting in the hallway after Hammond finished answering the weak cross-examination from the defense attorney and was finally dismissed as a witness. Vogel was the same age but not the same demeanor. Hammond was the scientist, the white hat, and Vogel was the hacker, the black hat. Vogel was a guy who only had blue jeans and T-shirts in his closet. And that hadn't changed since they were college roommates.

"Way to go, Hammer!" Vogel said. "That guy's going down!"

"Not so loud," Hammond cautioned. "What are you doing here?"

"I wanted to see you kick ass in there."

"Bullshit."

"Okay, come with me."

"Where?"

"We're not even going to leave the building."

Hammond followed Vogel down the hall to the elevator alcove. Vogel pushed the down button and turned to Hammond.

"He's here," Vogel said.

"Who's here?" Hammond asked.

"The guy. The reporter."

"McEvoy? What do you mean he's here?"

"He's getting arraigned. Hopefully, we didn't miss it."

They took the elevator down to the third floor and entered the large and busy arraignment court where Judge Adam Crower was presiding. They took seats on one of the crowded benches of the gallery. Hammond had never seen this part of the system in which he played a part. There were several lawyers standing and sitting while waiting for the names of their clients to be called. There was a wood-and-glass corral where defendants were brought in eight at a time to confer through narrow windows with their lawyers, or with the judge when their case was called. It looked like organized chaos, a place you would not want to be unless you had no choice or were paid to be there.

"What are we doing?" Hammond whispered.

"We're going to see if McEvoy has been arraigned," Vogel whispered back.

"How will we know?"

"Just watch the people they're bringing out. Maybe we'll see him."

"Okay, but what's the point? I don't get why we're looking for this guy."

"Because we might need him."

"How?"

"As you know, Detective Mattson filed his reports on the case in the department's online case archives. I took a look. You're right, the reporter knew Portrero, the victim. The detectives interviewed him and he voluntarily gave his DNA to prove he's not the guy."

"So?" Hammond asked.

"So, that DNA is somewhere in your lab. And you know what to do."

"What are you talking about?"

Hammond realized he had said it too loud. People on the benches in front of them turned to look back. What Vogel was suggesting was beyond anything they had even thought of before.

"First of all," he whispered. "If it's not assigned to me I can't get near it—different procedures than Orange County. Second, we both know he isn't the Shrike. I would never frame an innocent man."

"Come on, isn't it just like what you did in Orange County?" Vogel whispered back.

"What? That was completely different. I kept somebody from going to jail for what should not even be a crime. I didn't send him there. And this is murder we're talking about here."

"It was a crime in the eyes of the law."

"Have you ever heard the saying that it's better that a hundred guilty men escape than one innocent suffer? Benjamin fucking Franklin."

"Whatever. All I'm saying is, we could use this guy to buy us time. Time to find the Shrike."

"And then do what? Say *Never mind, I cooked the DNA*? That might work for you but not me. We need to shut it all down. Everything. Now."

"Not yet. We need it open in order to find the guy."

The dread that had been growing in Hammond's chest was in full bloom now. He knew his hatred and greed had led him to this. It was a nightmare he saw no way out of.

"Hey," Vogel whispered. "I think that's him."

Vogel surreptitiously pointed his chin at the corral at the front of the courtroom. A fresh line of arrestees had been led in by the courtroom deputies. Hammond thought that the third man looked like the mug shot he had seen the night before. It looked like the reporter, Jack McEvoy. He looked weary and worn down from his night in jail.

JACK

16

The courtroom was the crowded port of entry to the criminal justice system, a place where those swept up in the maw of the legal machinery stood before a judge for the first time for a reading of the charges against them. Then their initial court date would be scheduled, the first step in their long and twisting pathway through the morass that would leave them at least bowed and bloodied, if not convicted and incarcerated.

I saw Bill Marchand rise from a seat in the row running along the front rail of the courtroom and start making his way toward me. It had been a night without sleep, and every muscle in my body seemed to hurt from the hours I had spent clenched like a fist and fearful in the communal holding tank. I had been in jail before and knew that danger could come from any quarter. It was a place where men felt betrayed by their lives and the world, and that made them desperate and dangerous, ready to attack anybody and anything that appeared vulnerable.

When Marchand got to the slot through which we would be able to talk, I opened with the five most urgent words in the world to me.

"Get me out of here."

The lawyer nodded.

"That's the plan," he said. "I already talked to the prosecutor and explained to her the hornet's nest her detectives have kicked over, and she's going to nolle pros this one. We'll get you out of here in a couple hours tops."

"The DA's just going to drop the charge?" I asked.

"Actually, it's the city attorney because it's a misdemeanor charge. But they've got nothing to support it. You were doing your job with full First Amendment protections. Myron's here and ready to go to war. I told the prosecutor, you arraign this reporter on that charge and that man over there will hold a press conference outside the courthouse within the hour. And it won't be the kind of press her office wants."

"Where's Myron now?"

I scanned the crowded rows of the gallery. I didn't see Myron but motion caught my eye and I thought I saw someone duck behind another person as though bending down to pick something up. When the man came back up, he looked at me and then shifted behind the person sitting in front of him. He was balding and wore glasses. It wasn't Myron.

"He's around somewhere," Marchand said.

At that moment I heard my name as Judge Crower called my case. Marchand turned to the bench and identified himself as counsel for the defense. A woman stood up at the crowded prosecution table and identified herself as Deputy City Attorney Jocelyn Rose.

"Your Honor, we move to drop the charge against the defendant at this time," she said.

"You are sure?" Crower asked.

"Yes, Your Honor."

"Very well. Case dismissed. Mr. McEvoy, you're free to go."

Only I wasn't. I wasn't free to go until after a two-hour wait to be bussed back to the county jail, where my property was returned and I was processed out. The morning was gone, I had missed both breakfast and lunch at the jail, and I had no transportation home.

But when I stepped through the jail exit I found Myron Levin waiting for me.

"Sorry, Myron. How long were you waiting?"

"It's okay. I had my phone. You all right?"

"I am now."

"You hungry? Or you want to go home?"

"Both. But I'm starving."

"Let's go eat."

"Thanks for coming for me, Myron."

To get to the food quicker we went just over to Chinatown and ordered po'boy sandwiches at Little Jewel. We grabbed a table and waited for them to be made.

"So, what are you going to do?" I asked.

"About what?" Myron asked.

"The LAPD's flagrant violation of the First Amendment. Mattson can't get away with this shit. You should hold a press conference anyway. I bet the *Times* will be all over this. The *New York Times,* I'm talking about."

"It's not that simple."

"It's very simple. I was on a story, Mattson didn't like it. So he falsely arrests me. It's not only First Amendment, it's the Fourth as well. They had no probable cause to detain me. I was doing my job."

"I know all of that but the charges were dropped and you're back on the story. No harm, no foul."

"What? I spent a night in jail where I was backed into a corner with my eyes open all night."

"But nothing happened. You're okay."

"No, I'm not okay, Myron. You try it sometime."

"Look, I'm sorry for what happened, but I think we should roll with it, not inflame things any further, and get back on the story. Speaking of which, I got a text from Emily. She says she got some good stuff from UC–Irvine."

I looked across the table at Myron for a long moment, trying to read him.

"Don't deflect the conversation," I said. "What is it really? The donors?"

"No, Jack, I told you before, the donors have nothing to do with this," Myron said. "I would no sooner let donors dictate what we do and what we cover than I would let Big Tobacco or the auto industry dictate to us."

"Then why are we sitting on our hands on this? That guy Mattson needs to be raked over the coals."

"Okay, if you want to know the truth, I think if we make a stink about this it could come back on us."

"Why would that happen?"

"Because of you. And me. You are a person of interest in this case until we know otherwise. And I'm the editor who didn't yank you off it when I should have. If we go to war that's all going to come out and it's not going to look that great, Jack."

I leaned back and shook my head in impotent protest. I knew he was right. Maybe Mattson had known he could do what he did because we were compromised.

"Shit," I said.

Myron's name was called because he had paid for lunch. He got up and got our sandwiches. When he returned I was too hungry to keep talking about the issue. I had to eat. I mowed through half of my po'boy before saying another word. By then, without the edge of hunger in my anger, my desire for a constitutional battle with the LAPD had waned.

"It's just that I feel like this is where we've come to," I said. "Fake news, enemy of the people, the president canceling subscriptions to the *Washington Post* and *New York Times*. The LAPD thinks nothing of just throwing a reporter in jail. At what point do we take a stand?"

"Well, this would not be the time," Myron said. "If we're going to take that stand then we have to do it when we are one hundred percent clean, so there are no comebacks from the police or the politicians who love seeing journalists thrown in jail."

I shook my head and dropped the argument. I couldn't win and the truth was I wanted to get back to the story more than I wanted to take on the LAPD.

"All right, fuck it," I said. "What did Emily say she has?"

"She didn't," Myron said. "She just said she got good stuff and was heading up to the office. I figure that after we finish here we'll go meet with her."

"Can you drop me at my apartment first? My car's there and I want to take a shower before I do anything else."

"You got it."

My phone, wallet, and keys had been confiscated during the booking process. When they had been returned upon my departure I stuffed them back into my pockets in a hurry because I wanted to get out of that place as soon as I could. It became clear that I should have looked more carefully at the key chain when Myron dropped me off in front of my building on Woodman. The key to the front gate was on the ring, as well as the key to the Jeep, a storage locker in the garage, and a bike lock. But the key to my apartment was missing.

It was only after I rousted the live-in property manager from a post-lunch nap and borrowed the management copy of the key that I got into the apartment. Once in, I found a copy of a search-warrant receipt on the kitchen counter. While I was in a jail cell the night before, Mattson and Sakai were searching my apartment. They had most likely used my trumped-up obstruction case as part of the probable cause for the search. I realized that was probably their goal all along. They knew the case would get kicked but they used it with a judge to get into my home.

My anger quickly returned and again I took their action as a direct assault on my rights. I pulled my phone and called the LAPD's Robbery-Homicide Division and asked for Mattson. I was transferred.

"Detective Mattson, how can I help you?"

"Mattson, you better hope I don't solve this before you because I will make you look like the piece of shit you are."

"McEvoy? I heard they turned you loose. Why are you so mad?"

"Because I know what you did. You booked me so you could search my place, because you are so far up your ass on this case you wanted to see what I had."

Looking at the search-warrant receipt I saw that they did not list a single item being taken.

"I want my key back," I said. "And whatever you took from here."

"We didn't take anything," Mattson said. "And I have your key right here. You are welcome to come by anytime and pick it up."

I suddenly froze. I wasn't sure where my laptop was. Had Mattson taken it? I quickly reviewed the evening before and realized I had left my backpack in the Jeep when I decided to go up to the front curb to check my mailbox. I'd been intercepted there by Mattson and Sakai.

I grabbed the search-warrant receipt and quickly checked to see if the search was authorized for my home and vehicle. My laptop was fingerprint- and password-protected but I assumed it would be easy for Mattson to go to the cyber unit and have someone hack their way in.

If Mattson got into my laptop he would have everything I had and know everything I knew about the investigation.

The search warrant was only for the apartment. I would find out in the next thirty seconds if there was a second warrant waiting in my car.

"McEvoy, you there?"

I didn't bother responding. I disconnected the call and headed for the door. I went down the concrete steps to the garage and quickly crossed to my Jeep.

My backpack was on the passenger seat where I remembered putting it the day before. I returned to my apartment with the backpack and dumped its contents on the kitchen counter. The laptop was there and it appeared that Mattson had not gotten to it or the case notes. The rest of the contents of the backpack seemed to have been untouched as well.

The relief that came from not having my work and my emails rifled through by the police came with a wave of exhaustion, no doubt due to my sleepless night in jail. I decided to stretch out on the couch and catch a half-hour nap before going into the office to meet with Myron and Emily. I set a timer and was asleep within a few minutes, my last waking thought about the men I had been bussed to the courthouse with that morning, all of them most likely back in their cells now in a place where just closing your eyes made you vulnerable.

17

I was disoriented when I woke. I had been stirred from a deep sleep by the sound of a leaf blower outside. I checked my phone for the time but it was dead, having spent the night in a jail property room rather than on a charger. I had no doubt slept through my allotted thirty minutes. I didn't wear a watch since I usually carried the time on my phone. I got up and stumbled into the kitchenette, where I saw it was 4:17 on the oven. I had been out more than two hours.

I had to plug my phone in and wait for it to get enough charge for the screen to activate. I then texted Myron and Emily on a group text and explained my delay. I asked if it was too late to meet and the response was immediate: *Come to the office.*

Twenty-five minutes later we met.

The text Emily had sent Myron earlier was correct. She had gotten good stuff on William Orton down at UC–Irvine. We met in the *FairWarning* conference room and she laid out what she had found.

"First of all, none of this is on the record," she said. "If we want to use it we need to find independent verification—which I think will exist at the Anaheim Police Department, if we can find a source there."

"How good is your source at the school?" Myron asked.

"She's an assistant dean now," Emily said. "But four years ago when all of this went down she was the assistant to the coordinator of the Title IX unit. Do you know what Title IX is, Jack?"

"Yes," I said. "That's the sexual violence and harassment protocol for all schools that get federal money."

"Correct," Emily said. "So my source told me off the record and on deep background that William Orton was suspected of being a serial abuser of his students, but they never got the goods on him. Victims got intimidated, witnesses recanted. They never got a solid case against him until Jane Doe came along."

"Jane Doe?" I asked.

"She was a student—a biology major—who took classes from Orton and claimed he had roofied her and then raped her after a chance encounter at a bar in Anaheim. She came to naked in a motel room and the last thing she remembered was the drink with him."

"What a creep," Myron said.

"You mean what a criminal," Emily said.

"That too," Myron said. "What happened? Jane Doe change her mind?"

"No, not at all," Emily said. "She was solid. And smart. She called the police that night and they got a rape kit and took blood. Orton used a condom during the assault but they got saliva off her nipples. They were building a solid case against this guy. The tox on Jane came back with flunitrazepam, better known as Rohypnol, the date-rape drug. They had a solid witness in the victim and they were good to go with a case. They were just waiting on the DNA."

"What happened?" I asked.

"The DNA typing was done by the Orange County Sheriff's Lab," Emily said. "The saliva came back as no match to Orton."

"You're kidding," Myron said.

"I wish," Emily said. "It killed the case. It cast doubt on her story because she had said under questioning that she had not been with another man for six days. An investigator with the District Attorney's Office down there then dug up a number of prior sex partners Jane Doe had been involved with. It all added up to the DA passing. They wouldn't touch it without the direct DNA link."

I thought about what Jason Hwang had said about the DRD4 gene. The Orange County DA had dismissed Jane Doe as promiscuous and therefore not believable enough to support the case at trial.

"You said it was a chance encounter," I said. "Was there any more on that? How did they know it was a chance encounter?"

"I didn't ask that," Emily said. "They just said it was random, you know. They ran into each other in a bar."

"Did the saliva match anybody else?" I asked.

"Unknown donor," Emily said. "There was a rumor going around at the time that Orton, being a DNA researcher, had somehow altered his own DNA to prevent the match."

"Sounds like science fiction," Myron said.

"It does," said Emily. "According to my source, they ran the test at the sheriff's lab a second time and it came back again as a negative match."

"What about tampering?" Myron asked.

"It was suggested, but the Sheriff's Department stood by the lab," Emily said. "I think any indication that there was an evidence-integrity problem would endanger every conviction that relied on that lab for evidence analysis, and they weren't going to go down that road."

"And Orton walked away," I said.

"To a degree," Emily said. "There was no criminal case, but there was enough smoke because of Jane Doe's unwavering story, even in the face of the DNA, for the school to go after Orton under the employee-conduct policies. Their mandate wasn't criminal. They needed to protect other students at the school. So they quietly negotiated his exit. He kept his pension and a cloak of silence was dropped over the whole thing."

"And what happened to Jane Doe?" I asked.

"That I don't know," Emily said. "I asked my source whom she dealt with at Anaheim PD and she could only remember that the detective who handled it had a perfect name for a detective: *Dig.*"

"First or last?" I asked.

"She said first," Emily said. "She described him as Latino so I am assuming the first name is Digoberto or a variation of that. It shouldn't be too hard to figure out."

I nodded.

"So," Myron said. "Orton gets shown the door at UC–Irvine and just sets up shop in a private lab down the road. He got off easy."

"He did," Emily said. "But like my source told me, their big concern was getting him out of the school."

"What about that rumor about changing his DNA?" I asked. "Is that even possible?"

"I did a little bit of research while waiting for you to show up," Emily said. "Gene-editing technologies are advancing every day but they are not at the point—and certainly not four years ago when this happened—where you can change your entire code. What happened with the Jane Doe case is a mystery. According to my source, Jane Doe had a lawyer ready to sue Orton and the school. His office conducted its own testing on the sample and got the same result. No lawsuit was ever filed."

All three of us were silent for a moment before Myron spoke.

"So what's next?" he asked.

It was my story and I wanted to be protective of it, but I had to acknowledge that Emily Atwater had moved it along in a big way.

"Well, one thing we have to remember is that William Orton is a shady figure, but what Jack is pursuing does not touch him—yet," Emily said. "It bears further reporting but let's look at where we are. The four victims we know about were GT23 participants. It is possible but not yet proved that their DNA could have been sold to Orton's lab for his research purposes. Now add in that Orton appears to be a sexual predator and it all gets more interesting. But we have nothing concrete that connects one with the other."

"Exactly," Myron said. "I'm wondering how far we go with this without a stronger connection."

Myron looked at me, which I took as a good sign. It was still my story and he wanted to hear from me.

"I think it's part of throwing out the net," I said. "We have to see what comes up. I think the thing to do is try to get inside Orange Nano and talk to Orton. Maybe get a feel for him from a direct contact. I'm not sure how to do that, though. I don't think we should call up and say we're looking into the murders of four women. We need another way in."

"I was thinking about that," Emily said. "Again, waiting for Jack today I was looking around for anything I could find on

Orton and I found one listing for him in an annual report for the Rexford Corporation. He's a member of the board."

"What's Rexford do?" I asked.

"Primarily, it's hair products for men," Emily said. "With an emphasis on alopecia — hair loss. It is on the rise in both genders and within five years is expected to be a four-billion-dollar industry."

"Orton's trying to cure it," I said.

"My guess, too," Emily said. "If he can discover or create the genetic therapy that cures it or even slows it down, then just think what that would be worth. He's on the Rexford board because the company is funding his research and that could be our way in."

"We say we're looking into hair loss?" I asked.

"We follow the money," Emily said. "Billions are being spent each year but there is no cure — not now. We go in with the consumer angle: How many of these treatments are worthless and where are we on the genetic cure? We play to Orton's ego, say we heard that if anybody is going to make the breakthrough, it's you."

It was a good plan, only marred by my wish that I had thought of it first. I said nothing and Myron looked at me.

"What do you think, Jack?" he asked.

"Well, this alopecia research is new to me," I said. "Jason Hwang told me that Orton was studying addiction and risky behaviors. Going bald is not connected with either — as far as I know."

"That's how these researchers work," Emily said. "They get a ride on a Big Pharma ticket to do research in one arena and it funds their other research, the stuff that really holds their interest. Rexford is paying for the research they want but funding the research Orton wants."

I nodded.

"Then I think it's a good idea," I said. "That's our way in. Maybe we go through Rexford first. Get their corporate PR people to set it up, make it harder for Orton to say no—especially if he's got something hinky going on down there."

"That's a good idea," Emily said. "I—"

"I'll call first thing in the morning," I said. "Try to get it set."

"Tell them there will be two of you on the interview," Myron said.

"What do you mean?" I asked.

"I want you both to go down there," Myron said.

"I think I can handle it," I said.

"I'm sure you can," Myron said. "But for security reasons I want you both to go. Emily, take the Canon and you can take photos."

"I'm not a photographer," Emily protested.

"Just take the camera," Myron said.

"What about Anaheim PD?" Emily asked. "You want us to tag-team that too?"

"I was going to go down there tomorrow," I said. "I'll find Detective Dig."

Emily said nothing. I was expecting a protest, with her claiming it was her lead, but she didn't make one.

"Okay, fine, you go, Jack," Myron said. "But listen, I don't want this to be a competition. Work together. I'm devoting half our staff to this. We can't waste time. Find out if there is something there and if not, get out and move on to the next story."

"Got it," Emily said.

"Okay," I said.

The meeting broke up after that and we returned to our respective work stations. The first thing I did was call the Anaheim

Police Department and try to get a line on Dig. This turned out to be easy. I asked for the detective bureau and asked the woman who answered, "Can I speak to Dig?"

"I'm sorry, Detective Ruiz is gone for the day. Can I take a message?"

"No, that's okay. Will he be working tomorrow?"

"He is, but he's signed out to court all day. Do you want to leave a message?"

"No, I guess I'll see him at the courthouse. That's the rape case?"

This was an educated guess based on Ruiz working the Jane Doe/Orton case.

"Yes, Isaiah Gamble. Who can I tell him called?"

"That's okay. I'll see him there tomorrow. Thank you."

After disconnecting, I pulled up the Orange County District Attorney's Office website and plugged the name *Isaiah Gamble* into the search window. This led me to an extract on the case—abduction and forcible rape—and the courtroom it was assigned to in the courthouse in Santa Ana. I would be good to go in the morning.

I was writing the information down in a notebook when I was interrupted by a text from Rachel Walling.

You want to get a drink tonight?

It came out of the blue. I drop in on her unannounced for the first time in more than a year and the next day she wants to have a drink. I didn't wait long to reply.

Sure. Where? What time?

I waited but there was no immediate reply. I started packing up for the day, shoving into my backpack everything I might need in Orange County the next day. I was about to get up and leave when I got the return message from Rachel.

I'm in the Valley. I could meet now or later. How about that place you met Christina? I want to see it.

I stared at my phone's screen. I knew that she meant Mistral. That seemed a bit weird but maybe there was going to be more to the meeting than a drink. Maybe Rachel had changed her mind about my proposal to her. I texted back with the name and address and told her I was on my way.

I went by Emily Atwater's cubicle on my way out. She looked up from her screen.

"I located Dig," I said. "His last name is Ruiz. He's going to be in court tomorrow on another case."

"That's perfect," Emily said. "You should be able to get to him there."

"Yeah, that's what I thought. And also, I wanted to say sorry if it seems like I'm being a dick."

"No, you aren't. It was your story. I get it."

I nodded.

"Thanks for understanding," I said. "So if you want to go down with me to find Ruiz that would be fine. It was your lead."

"No, I'm fine to stay up here, actually," she said. "I was thinking that while you do that, I'll see what I can come up with through the feds. I'll start with the FDA."

"They're not doing anything on this," I said. "They're still in the 'thinking about it' enforcement stage."

"Yes, but we need to get that on the record and ask why it

is and when it's going to change. The government is behind the curve and that's a big part of the story."

"Right."

"So, I'll do that and you go down to Orange County."

"I'll try to set something up with Orton through Rexford PR. I'll let you know."

She smiled. Somehow it made me think that I was still being a dick about things.

"So we're good?" I asked.

"Sure," she said. "Let's see where things are tomorrow."

I nodded and she spoke as I turned to leave.

"I would never apologize for being protective about my story, Jack."

I looked back at her.

"You saw something and went after it," she said. "You have every right to keep it."

"Okay," I said.

"See you tomorrow," she said.

18

Rachel was already at the bar at Mistral when I got there, her martini glass half full. She didn't see me enter and so I stood back and looked at her for a few moments. She had her eyes down on the bar, reading a document. She reached for the stem of the martini glass without looking and then took a small sip. My interactions with her had spanned nearly twenty-five years and had been hot and cold, intense and distant, intimate and strictly professional, and ultimately heartbreaking. From the beginning, she had left a hole in my heart that could never quite heal. I could go years without seeing her but I could never stop thinking about her. Thinking about where she was, what she was doing, who she was with.

I knew the moment I decided to visit her the day before that I was buying myself another round of hope and hurt. But some people are fated this way, fated to play the same music over and over like a scratched record.

The moment was ruined when the bartender saw me standing by the door and called out her version of my name.

"Jacques, what are you doing?" she said. "Come in, come in."

Elle, whose last name I did not know, spoke with a French accent. She knew me as a regular, though she put a French twist on my name. Still, it was close enough that it caused Rachel to look up and see me. And my moment of reverie and hope ended.

I walked to the bar and sat next to Rachel.

"Hey, been here long?" I asked.

"No, just ahead of you," Rachel said.

Elle came down the bar to take my order.

"The usual, Jacques?" she asked.

"Sure," I said.

Elle went back down the bar to where the bottle of Ketel One was and started preparing my drink.

"*Ze use-you-well, Jacques?*" Rachel whispered mockingly. "You know that accent is fake, right?"

"She's an actress," I said. "The place is French."

"Only in L.A."

"Or maybe Paris. So, what brings you over the hill to the Valley?"

"Trying to hook up a new client and today we had the dog-and-pony show."

"Background searching?"

"Our meat and potatoes."

"So you go in there, flash the former-FBI credentials, and tell them what you can do and they give you their business?"

"That's a little simplistic but, yeah, that's how it works."

Elle brought my martini over and put it down on a cocktail napkin.

"*Voilà,*" she said.

"*Merci,*" I said.

Elle moved back down the bar, smart enough to give us space.

"And this is your hang?" Rachel said. "The bartender with the phony French accent?"

"I only live a couple blocks away," I said. "I can walk home if I get into trouble."

"Or you get lucky. Gotta get them home before they change their minds, right?"

"That's a low blow, and I wish I hadn't even told you that yesterday. That is the one and only time that ever happened to me here."

"I'm sure."

"It's true, but it's beginning to sound like you're jealous."

"That'll be the day."

We broke off the conversation there for a few moments and I had the feeling we were both reviewing memories of our checkered history. It always seemed to be me who blew it. Once during the Poet investigation when my own insecurities caused me to doubt her in a relationship-stunting way, and the last time when I put my work ahead of our relationship and put her into an intolerable position.

Now we were left to meet at a bar and trade coy remarks. What could have been was killing me.

"I have to say I am jealous about one thing," Rachel said.

"That I live in the Valley now?" I said.

I still couldn't get away from the coy remark. *Jesus.*

"No, that you're on a case," she said. "A real case."

"What are you talking about?" I asked. "You have your own business."

"Which is ninety percent sitting at a computer and doing background searches. I haven't worked a real...I'm not using my skills, Jack. And if you don't use them you lose them. You coming in yesterday just reminded me of what I don't do anymore."

"I'm sorry. I know it's all on me. Your badge, everything.

I fucked everything up for a story. I was so blind and I'm so sorry."

"Jack, I didn't come because I need your apology. The past is past."

"Then what, Rachel?"

"I don't know. I just…"

She didn't finish. But I knew this wasn't going to be a quick drink and goodbye. I held two fingers up to Elle at the other end of the bar: *two more.*

"Did you do anything with what we talked about yesterday?" Rachel asked.

"I did," I said. "I got some really good stuff and would have continued today but then I ended up staying all night in jail."

"What? Why?"

"Because the LAPD guy on the case is scared. Scared I'm ahead of him on this, so he grabbed me on a trumped-up obstruction thing last night and I spent all night in Metro and then half the day in court and riding jail buses back and forth."

I finished my martini just as Elle delivered a new one.

"Je vous en prie," she said.

"Merci," I said.

"Gracias," Rachel said.

Elle went away.

"Hey, we forgot," I said.

I held my fresh drink up.

"To the single-bullet theory?" I asked.

Maybe that was going too far, but Rachel did not balk. She held up her glass and nodded. It was a reference to something she had told me years before: that she believed everybody had somebody out there in the world who could pierce their heart like a bullet. Not everybody had the good fortune of meeting that person, and not everybody could hold on to that person if they did meet.

To me there had never been any doubt. Rachel was the one. Her name was on the bullet that pierced me.

We clinked glasses. But then Rachel moved on before any more could be said on that subject.

"Were you charged?" she asked.

"The deputy city attorney kicked the case as soon as she saw it," I said. "It's just a new form of harassment in the era where reporters are viewed by some as lower than scum. These cops think they can get away with everything."

"You really think you're out in front of them on this case?"

"I do. Have you changed your mind about—"

"What have you gotten?"

I spent the next twenty minutes telling her about Jason Hwang, William Orton, and how my partner on the story, Emily Atwater, had made further strides with a source at UC–Irvine. Rachel asked several questions and offered bits of advice here and there. It was clear that she felt I was onto something that was right in her ten ring. She had once hunted serial killers with the FBI; now she was doing background searches on job candidates. We drank another round of martinis and when the talking ended there was a decision to be made.

"You just leave your car here?" Rachel asked.

"The valets know me here," I said. "If I'm walking home because I've had one too many, they'll give back my keys. Then I just walk back up in the morning and get my car."

"Well, I shouldn't drive either."

"You can walk with me to my place. We can come back for your car when you're ready to drive."

There it was. A half-assed invitation. She gave it a half-smile in return.

"And what if that is not until the morning?" she asked.

"Three martinis…I think it's going to take at least that long," I said.

I paid the tab with a platinum American Express card. Rachel saw it.

"You still getting royalties, Jack?"

"Some. Less every year but the books are still in print."

"I heard that every time they catch a new serial, he has a copy of *The Poet* somewhere in his possessions. It's also a popular book in every prison I've ever been in."

"Good to know. Maybe I should've had a book signing in Metro last night."

She laughed loudly and I knew she'd overdone it with the martinis. She was usually too much in control to laugh out loud like that.

"Let's go before we both pass out," I said.

We slid off our stools and headed for the door.

The alcohol continued to loosen her tongue as we walked the two blocks.

"I just want you to know that the maid at my place has been on vacation for about a year," I said.

She laughed again.

"I would expect nothing less," she said. "I remember some of your places. Heavy on the bachelor."

"Yeah, well, I guess some things never change," I said.

"I want in," she said.

I took a few unsteady steps without responding. I wondered if she was talking about our relationship or my story. She made it clear without my asking.

"I'm making tons of money but I'm not...doing anything," she said. "I used to...I had a skill, Jack. Now..."

"That's why I came to see you yesterday," I said. "I thought you would be—"

"You know what I did today? I presented to a company that makes plastic furniture. They want to make sure they don't hire any illegals, so they come to me and guess what? I'll take their money if they want to give it to me."

"Well, that's what the business is about. You knew that when—"

"Jack, I want to do something. I want to help. I can help you with your story."

"Uh...yeah, I thought maybe you'd want to profile this guy—whoever's doing this. Also, the victims. We need—"

"No, I want more than that. I want to be out there on this. Like with the Scarecrow."

I nodded. We had worked hand in hand on that.

"Well, this is a little different. You were an agent back then and I already have a partner on—"

"But I can really help you on this. I still have connections in the federal government. I can get things. Find out things you can't."

"What things?"

"I don't know yet. I would have to see but I still know people in all the agencies because I worked with them."

I nodded. We had gotten to my building. I couldn't tell how much of what she was saying was the alcohol talking but she seemed to be talking from the heart. I fumbled with the keys to open the gate.

"Let's go in and sit down," I said. "We'll talk more about it."

"I don't want to talk anymore tonight, Jack," she said.

19

I had never been to the courthouse in Santa Ana, nor had I ever driven from the San Fernando Valley down to Orange County on a weekday morning. I left at seven to make sure I got there before nine. That was after I walked up the street twice to Mistral to retrieve my Jeep and then Rachel's BMW. I parked hers in front of the building, in the same spot Mattson and Sakai had used to arrest me. I then returned her key to the table next to the bed where she slept. I wrote a note asking her to call me when she woke up and left it with two Advils on the bed table.

Rachel might find waking to an empty apartment upsetting, but I wanted to get to Detective Digoberto Ruiz before the trial started.

Best-laid plans. After tie-ups on both the 101 and 5 freeways, I rolled into the parking garage at the Criminal Courts Building in Santa Ana at 9:20. Proceedings in the trial of Isaiah Gamble were already underway. I slipped into the back row of the gallery and watched. I was in luck. It took me only a few minutes to realize that Detective Ruiz was the man on the witness stand giving testimony.

The gallery of the courtroom was empty except for me and a woman in the front row on the prosecution side of the room. The case apparently had drawn no attention from the local populace or media. The prosecutor was a woman who stood at a lectern between the prosecution and defense tables. The jury was to her left: twelve jurors and two alternates, still alert and paying attention in the first hour of the day.

The defendant, Isaiah Gamble, sat at a table next to another woman. I knew that it was part of the sexual-predator playbook to go to trial with a female lawyer. It forces the jury to ask: If this man really did what they say he did, would a woman represent him?

Ruiz looked close to retirement. He had a gray fringe of hair circling a bald dome and permanently sad eyes. He had seen too much on his job. He was recounting just one episode of many.

"I met with the victim at the hospital," he said. "She was being treated for her injuries and evidence was being collected."

"And was she able to provide you with other evidence or information?" the prosecutor asked.

"Yes, she had memorized a license plate that was in the trunk of the car with her."

"It wasn't on the car?"

"No, it had been removed."

"Why was it removed?"

"Probably to help the suspect avoid being identified in case someone saw the abduction."

The defense attorney objected to the detective's answer, saying it was conjecture. The judge ruled that Ruiz had more than enough experience in rape cases to form the opinion he had voiced and allowed the answer to stand. It also emboldened the prosecutor to take the question further.

"You have seen this before in cases?" she asked. "The removal of the license plate."

"Yes," Ruiz said.

"As an experienced detective, what does that indicate to you?"

"Premeditation. That he had a plan and went out hunting."

"Hunting?"

"Looking for a victim. For prey."

"So going back to the victim being in the trunk, wasn't it too dark in the trunk to see the plate?"

"It was dark but every time the kidnapper hit the brakes the taillights lit up part of the trunk and she could see. She memorized the plate that way."

"And what did you do with that information?"

"I ran the plate on the computer and got the registered owner's name."

"Who was it registered to?"

"Isaiah Gamble."

"The defendant."

"Yes."

"What did you do next, Detective Ruiz?"

"I pulled Gamble's photo from his driver's license, put it in a six-pack, and showed it to the victim."

"Please tell the jury what a six-pack is."

"It's a photo lineup. I put together six photos, including the shot of Isaiah Gamble and five other men of the same race and similar age, build, hair, and complexion. I then showed it to the victim and asked if any of the men in the photos was the man who abducted and raped her."

"And did she identify any of the men in the photo lineup?"

"Without hesitation she identified the photo of Isaiah Gamble as that of the man who had abducted, raped, and beaten her."

"Did you have her sign her name under the photo of the man she identified?"

"Yes, I did."

"And did you bring that six-pack with you to court today?"

"I did."

The prosecutor went through the steps of introducing the six-pack as a state's exhibit and the judge accepted it.

Twenty minutes later Ruiz had completed his direct testimony and the judge took the morning break before the defense's cross-examination would start. He told the jurors and all parties to be back in fifteen minutes.

I watched Ruiz intently to see if he would leave the courtroom for a restroom or coffee break, but at first he stayed seated in the witness box and small-talked with the courtroom clerk. But then the clerk took a phone call and turned her attention away from the detective. After another minute Ruiz stood up and told the prosecutor he was going to the restroom and would be right back.

I watched Ruiz walk out the door and then followed him. I gave him a one-minute lead time in the restroom before I entered. He was at the sink washing his hands. I went to a sink two down and started doing the same. We saw each other in the mirror over the sink between us and both nodded.

"That must feel good," I said.

"What's that?" Ruiz asked.

"Putting sexual predators away for a long time."

Ruiz looked at me strangely.

"I was in the courtroom," I said. "I saw you testify."

"Oh," Ruiz said. "You're not on the jury, are you? I can't have any contact with—"

"No, I'm not. I'm a reporter, actually. Down from L.A."

"For this case?"

"No, not this one. Another case you handled. My name's Jack McEvoy."

I threw the paper towel I was drying my hands with into the trash can and offered my hand. Ruiz took it tentatively. I didn't know if that was because of what I had said or the general awkwardness that comes with holding out a hand in a restroom.

"What other case?" Ruiz asked.

"I guess it's the one who got away," I said. "William Orton."

I watched his face for a reaction and thought I caught a glimpse of anger flare before his face turned to stone.

"How do you know about that case?" he asked.

"Sources," I said. "I know what he did at UCI. You didn't put him in jail but at least you got him away from the students there."

"Look, I can't talk to you about that case. I need to get back to court now."

"Can't or won't?"

Ruiz opened the door and looked back at me.

"You're doing a story about Orton?" he asked.

"Yes," I said. "Whether you talk to me or not. I'd rather it be after we've talked and you can explain why he was never charged."

"What do you think you know about him or that case?"

"I know he may still be a predator. That enough?"

"I have to go back to court. If you're still here after I'm finished, then maybe we can talk."

"I'll—"

He was gone and the door slowly closed.

After I returned to the courtroom, I watched the defense lawyer cross-examine Ruiz, but she scored no points that I could tally and made one large misstep in asking a question that allowed Ruiz to state that DNA collected at the hospital after the abduction and rape was matched to her client. This, of course, would come out anyway, or may have already come out through an earlier prosecution witness, but it's never a good thing for the defense to reference the state's key piece of evidence against your client.

After twenty minutes of questions gained little traction for her client's cause she gave up and the detective was dismissed as a witness.

I left the courtroom and sat on a bench in the hallway. If Ruiz was going to talk to me he would come out. But when he did it was to collect the next witness, who was waiting in the hall on the next bench down. I heard Ruiz call her Dr. Sloan and tell her she was up. He walked her to the courtroom and when he opened the door for her he looked back at me and nodded. I took it to mean he would be back for me.

Another ten minutes passed and Ruiz finally came out of the courtroom again and sat on the bench next to me.

"I should be in there," he said. "The prosecutor doesn't know the case like I do."

"That doctor, is she the DNA expert?" I asked.

"No, she runs the rape-treatment center at the hospital. She collected the evidence. The DNA expert comes next."

"How long will the trial last?"

"We'll finish tomorrow morning, then it will be whatever the defense puts on—which doesn't look like much."

"If it was such a lost cause, why didn't he plead, get a deal?"

"Because a guy like that, we don't give him a deal. Why are you here?"

"I'm working on a story and it's taken me to Orton. We found out about the UCI case and I wondered why it never went anywhere."

"Short answer: the DNA didn't match. We had the victim's ID, witness corroboration of checkable facts, but the DNA knocked our legs out. The DA passed. How is Orton related to what you're working on?"

I could see what Ruiz was doing. He was trading. He'd give up information to get information. But so far he hadn't told me anything I didn't already know.

"I'm looking at the murder of a woman," I said. "No direct link in the case to Orton but I think her DNA went through his lab."

"At UCI?" Ruiz asked.

"No, this is after he left. His current lab, Orange Nano."

"I don't get the connection."

"My victim was killed by a sexual predator. From what I've found out about Orton, he's one too."

"I can't make that statement. We never charged him with a crime."

"But you wanted to. It was the DA who wouldn't go forward."

"With good reason. DNA works both ways. It convicts and it clears."

I pulled out my notebook to write down that line. It freaked Ruiz out.

"You can't use anything from me. I don't want to be sued by him. There was no case. The DNA cleared him."

"But you had the victim's story."

"Doesn't matter. The DNA threw a wrench into things. Made the case untenable. We didn't proceed. End of story. Is this—do you work for the *Times* up there?"

"I work for a website that partners with the *Times* on occasion. How surprised were you when the DNA came back and it wasn't a match to William Orton?"

"Off the record: very. On the record: no comment."

I put my notebook down on the bench so he would not perceive it as a threat.

"Any theories on the DNA and where it came from?" I asked.

"Nope," Ruiz said. "I just know it killed the case. It didn't matter how credible our victim seemed. DNA from another man on her body killed the case."

"What about the possibility of tampering?"

"I don't see where. I took the sample from Orton with a court order. I delivered it to the lab. You accusing me of something?"

"Not at all. Just asking. There's also the second sample Orton's was compared to. Was there any kind of internal investigation of that?"

"Not beyond doing the test over and getting the same result. You are talking about a very sensitive subject. You know what the criminal defense lawyers in this courthouse would do with something like that? We'd get buried with appeals of every conviction that ever came out of that lab."

I nodded. It was a case of looking into the matter but not looking too hard.

"How did the victim take it when you told her?" I asked.

"She was more surprised than me, I'll tell you that," Ruiz said. "She insisted then and still does that there was no other man. Just Orton."

"Did you ever talk to him? Interview him, I mean. Maybe when you took his swab?"

"Not really. We started to get into it but then he lawyered up and that was it. You know, you were right about this one. What you said."

"What did I say?"

"About him being the one who got away. The motherfucker's a rapist. I know it. And the DNA doesn't change that. That's off the record, too."

Ruiz stood up.

"I need to go back in," he said.

"Two more quick questions," I said.

He gestured for me to go ahead. I stood up.

"Jane Doe's lawyer, who was that?"

"Hervé Gaspar—I recommended him to her."

"What is Jane Doe's real name?"

"You should be able to get that from your source at the school."

"Okay, then what about the lab report on the DNA? Where can I get that?"

"You can't. All that got destroyed when the case wasn't filed. The lab report, the records. His arrest was expunged after his lawyer got a court order."

"Shit."

"You're telling me."

Ruiz turned toward the courtroom door and took a few steps, but then stopped and came back to me.

"Do you have a card or something? In case."

"Sure."

I opened a zipper on my backpack, dug out a business card, and handed it to him.

"Call anytime," I said. "And good luck with this one."

"Thanks," he said. "But with this one we don't need luck. He's going down."

I watched him go back into the courtroom to take care of business.

20

When I turned my phone on after leaving the courthouse, I had a message from Randall Sachs, head of public relations for the Rexford Corporation. With the two-hour time difference in Indianapolis working in my favor, I had called him on my drive down. It was early my time but he was well into his day and I told him that I needed to get into Orange Nano and interview William Orton. I made it clear that if he turned down my request, I would wonder what they were hiding at Rexford, a publicly traded company, when I could not speak to a board member and top researcher. I told him that I would be in the vicinity of Orange Nano later in the day and would love to make the visit then.

The message was that my photographer and I had a two-o'clock interview with Orton that came with a hard stop at three. I immediately called Sachs back to confirm and he gave me the lowdown on who I should ask for on arrival and reminded me that the interview would last no more than an hour. He implied that Orton was against the interview but he, Sachs, had been able to make him see the light.

"We are a transparent company," Sachs assured me.

I thanked him, disconnected, and immediately called Emily Atwater.

"How fast can you get down here?" I asked. "We have a two o'clock with Orton."

"I'll leave right now and should make it in time for us to work out a script," she said.

"Okay, good. Don't forget the camera. You're the photographer and I'm the interviewer."

"Don't be a dick. I know what I'm supposed to be."

"Sorry. You get anything out of the feds?"

"The FTC was good. I'll tell you about it when I'm down there."

"Now who's being a dick?"

"Touché. Leaving now."

She disconnected.

I had time to kill so I went for an early lunch at Taco María in Costa Mesa. While I ate *arrachera* tacos I thought about the best approach to Orton. I knew that it might be the one and only time to get an audience with him. Would Emily and I maintain the cover of the story we had told Rexford PR we were doing, or would we confront him?

Based on what I had heard from Detective Ruiz, I was pretty sure that Orton would not bend if confronted. It was likely that a direct approach would only get us shown the door. Still, it might be useful to see how he would react and possibly defend himself against the accusations leveled against him while he was a professor at UCI. Or what he would say if we asked if the DNA from the four dead women at the center of our story had ended up in the lab at Orange Nano.

The tacos were excellent and I was finished with ninety minutes to go before the appointment with Orton.

As I was walking through the parking lot my phone buzzed. It was Rachel.

"Did you just get up?" I said.

"No, I'm at work, thank you," she said.

"Well, I thought you'd call sooner. Did you see my note?"

"Yes, I saw it. I just wanted to get to work and start my day. Are you down in Orange County?"

"Yeah, I'm here. I talked to the detective who handled the Orton case."

"What did he say?"

"Not much, but I think he wanted to talk. He asked for my card and that usually doesn't happen. So we'll see."

"Now what?"

"I meet Orton at two. His corporate sponsor set it up."

"I wish I was there. I could give you a good read on him."

"Well, the other reporter is coming down. Three would be a crowd, and I'm not sure how I would explain who—"

"I was just saying, Jack. I know it's not my story or case."

"Oh, well, you could always give me a secondhand read tonight."

"Mistral?"

"Or I could come over the hill to you."

"No, I like Mistral. I'll be there. After work."

"Good. I'll see you then."

I got in my car and just sat there for a long moment thinking. Though the feelings and senses of the night before had been fogged by alcohol, they were nonetheless wonderful to me. I was with Rachel again and there was no better place in the world to be. But it was always hope and hurt. Hope and hurt. With her, there had never been one without the other, and I had to prepare myself for the same cycle again. I was riding on the high now but history and the laws of physics were clear. What goes up always comes down.

I put the address of the lab into my GPS app and drove by Orange Nano a few times before pulling over on MacArthur Boulevard and using the cell to look up and call the offices of Hervé Gaspar, the lawyer who had represented Jane Doe. I identified myself as a reporter who needed to talk to the attorney for a story that would be posted by the end of the day. Most lawyers wanted their names in the media. It was free advertising. As expected, I was transferred to his cell phone and could tell I had caught him in a restaurant, eating.

"This is Hervé Gaspar. What can I do for you?"

"My name's Jack McEvoy. I'm a reporter for *FairWarning* up in L.A."

"What the hell is a *FairWarning*?"

"Good question. It's a consumer-protection news site. We watch out for the little guy."

"Never heard of it."

"That's okay. There are many who have, especially the charlatans we expose on a regular basis."

"What's it got to do with me?"

I decided to jump over all the buildup.

"Mr. Gaspar, sounds like you're eating so I'll get to the point."

"Taco María, ever been here?"

"Yeah, about twenty minutes ago."

"Really?"

"Really. And now I have a two-o'clock interview with William Orton. If you were me, what would you ask him?"

There was a long silence before Gaspar responded.

"I would ask him how many lives he's ruined. You know about Orton?"

"I know about the case involving your client."

"How?"

"Sources. What can you tell me about it?"

"Nothing. It was settled and everybody signed NDAs."

Nondisclosure agreements, the bane of a reporter's life.

"I thought no lawsuit was filed," I said.

"There wasn't, because we reached a settlement."

"And you can't share the details of it."

"No, I can't."

"Is there anyplace where this settlement would be recorded?"

"No."

"Can you tell me your client's name?"

"Not without her permission. But she can't talk to you either."

"I know that, but can you ask her?"

"I can but I know the answer will be no. You'll be at this number?"

"Yes, it's my cell. Look, I'm not looking to put her name out there publicly. It would just help me to know it. I'm interviewing Orton today. It makes it hard to go at him on this if I don't even know the victim's name."

"I understand and I will ask her."

"Thank you. Going back to my first question. You said you would ask how many lives he has ruined. You think there were more than just your client?"

"Put it this way, the case I handled was not an aberration. And that's off the record. I can't talk about the case or him at all."

"Well, if we're off the record, what did you think about the DNA report? Detective Ruiz said he was pretty shocked by that."

"You talked to Ruiz, huh? Yeah, it was a big fucking shock."

"How'd Orton get around it?"

"When you find out, let me know."

"Did you try to find out?"

"Of course, but I got nowhere."

"Was tampering involved?"

"Who knows?"

"Can someone change their DNA?"

Gaspar started laughing.

"That's a good one."

"I didn't mean it as a joke."

"Well, put it this way, if Orton invented a way to change his DNA, he'd be the richest asshole in California, because a lot of people would pay big bucks for that. You could start with the Golden State Killer and work your way down from there."

"Last question," I said. "Does the NDA you and your client signed cover the records of your investigation, or could I look at what you've got in your files?"

He laughed again.

"Nice try."

"What I thought. Mr. Gaspar, I would appreciate it anyway if you would give my name and number to your client. She can talk to me in confidence. I will promise her that."

"I'll tell her. But I will also advise her that she risks breaking the agreement if she does."

"I understand."

I disconnected and sat in my car thinking. So far my trip down to Orange County had produced nothing that pushed the needle or made any connection between the four deaths that I was ostensibly investigating and William Orton or Orange Nano.

My phone buzzed and it was Emily.

"I just got off the 405. Where are you?"

I gave her directions to where I was parked and she said she'd be there in five minutes. I got a text before she arrived. It was from the 714 area code—Orange County.

Jessica Kelley

I assumed that the name had come from Gaspar and he had used a burner phone that could not be traced back to him. This told me a number of things. First, that he was concerned enough about Orton to break the NDA, but to do it in a way that gave him protection. It also said he was the kind of lawyer who used burner phones, and that could be useful down the line.

I texted a thank-you and added that I would be in touch. No reply came. I added the number to my contact list, assigning it the name Deep Throat. I was a reporter because of Woodward and Bernstein, the *Washington Post* duo who took down a president with the help of a confidential source they had given that nickname.

I saw Emily's car pull to the curb in front of me. It was a small Jaguar SUV and it was nicer than my Jeep. I got out with my backpack and got into the passenger seat of her car. I checked my phone and saw we still had time to kill.

"So," I said. "Tell me about the feds."

"I talked to a guy I had worked with on other stories," Emily said. "He's with Federal Trade Commission enforcement, which used to have oversight of the DNA industry until it got too big and the FTC turned it over to the FDA."

"Which basically does nothing."

"Exactly. But my guy can still dip into the licensing records and the database."

"And?"

"And basically these DNA labs have to be licensed, but as you know there is no oversight or enforcement after that. However, the FDA does have to accept complaints, and my guy told me there was a flag on Orton."

"Is that on the record?"

"On the record but not for attribution."

"Where did the flag come from?"

"He could not get that, but my guess is that it was from UCI and what happened there."

That seemed most likely to me.

"All right," I said. "Anything else?"

"One other thing," Emily said. "Orange Nano's license has an amendment allowing it to share anonymized data with other licensed research facilities. So the data it gets from GT23 can pass through the lab and Orange Nano and go somewhere else."

"Is any approval required of such transactions?"

"Not at this time. It's apparently going to be part of the rules and regs the FDA is taking its sweet time with."

"We need to find out who they give DNA to," I said. "We can ask Orton when we see him, but I kind of doubt that will go anywhere."

"We'll see soon enough. What about Jason Hwang, disgruntled ex-employee of the mothership? Maybe he knows something and will share."

"Maybe. But he would be a transaction removed. He sent DNA to Orange Nano. He would have no control and probably no knowledge of where it went afterward. What about your FTC guy?"

"I'll try him, but the FTC washed its hands of the DNA industry when the FDA took over. Whatever he can get will be at least two years old or more."

"Well, it's worth a shot."

"I'll call him later. What did you get from the cop on the UCI case?" she asked.

"I talked to him in court and then I called the lawyer who represented the UCI victim."

"Jane Doe."

"Actually, it's Jessica Kelley."

"Who gave you that?"

"I think Gaspar, the lawyer."

I explained the text I had gotten.

"Good stuff," Emily said. "If she's still around we can find her."

"She signed an NDA, so that may be a dead end. But having the name will help us with Orton, if the case comes up."

"Oh, I think it's going to come up. Are we ready?"

"We are."

21

Orange Nano was in a clean industrial park off MacArthur and not far from UCI. It was a single-level precast concrete building with no windows and no sign out front identifying it. The front door led to a small reception area where we found Edna Fortunato, the woman I had been told by Rexford PR would get us to William Orton.

She escorted us into an office where two men sat waiting, one directly behind a large desk and the other to his left side. The office was basic: a desk cluttered with files and paperwork, diplomas framed on one wall, shelves of medical-research books on another, and finally a six-foot-tall sculpture in a corner that was an abstract double helix made of polished brass.

The man behind the desk was obviously Orton. He was about fifty with a tall and slim build. He stood up and easily reached across the wide desk to shake our hands. Though ostensibly looking for the cure to baldness, he had a full head of brown hair slicked back and held in place with heavy product. His bushy, unkempt eyebrows gave him the inquisitive look of a researcher. He wore the requisite white lab coat—his name stitched above the breast pocket—and pale green scrubs.

The other man was the mystery. Dressed in a crisp suit, he remained seated. Orton quickly solved the mystery.

"I am Dr. Orton," he said. "And this is my attorney, Giles Barnett."

"Are we interrupting something you two need to finish?" I asked.

"No, I asked Giles to join us," Orton said.

"Why is that?" I asked. "This is just a general interview."

There was a nervousness about Orton that I had seen before in people unaccustomed to dealing directly with the media. And he had the added burden of worrying about his secret discharge from UCI. It seemed that he had brought his lawyer to make sure the interview didn't stray into an area Emily and I surely intended to take it.

"I need to tell you at the outset that I don't want this intrusion," Orton said. "I rely on Rexford Corporation to sponsor my work and so I cooperate with their demands. This is one of them. But as I say, I don't like it, and I am more comfortable with my attorney present."

I looked over at Emily. It was clear our planning for the interview had been for naught. The scheme to slowly lead Orton down a path toward a discussion of his past troubles would now clearly be stopped by Giles Barnett. The attorney had a tight collar and the thick body of an offensive lineman. In my glance at Emily I tried to get a read on whether she thought we should abandon ship or press on. She spoke before I could make a determination.

"Could we start in the lab?" she said to Orton. "We wanted some photos of you in your element. We could get that out of the way and then do the interview."

She was proceeding with the plan: get photos first because the interview was going to lead to a confrontation. It's hard to get photos after you've been ordered to leave the premises.

"You can't go into the lab," Orton said. "There are contamination concerns and a strict protocol. There are, however, viewing windows in the hallway. You can take your photos from there."

"That'll work," Emily said.

"Which lab?" Orton said.

"Uh, you tell us," I said. "What labs are there?"

"We have an extraction lab," he said. "We have a PCR lab, and we have an analysis lab."

"PCR?" I asked.

"Polymerase Chain Reaction," Orton said. "It is where samples are amplified. We can make millions of copies of a single DNA molecule in a matter of hours."

"I like that," Emily said. "Maybe some shots with you involved in that process."

"Very well," Orton said.

He stood up and signaled us through the door into a hallway that led to the far reaches of the building. Emily hung back so that Orton was several feet ahead of us, his lab coat flowing behind him like a cape. She took photos as we walked.

I walked next to Barnett and asked him for a card. He reached behind the pocket square in the breast pocket of his suit coat and handed me an embossed business card. I glanced at it before putting it in my pocket.

"I know what you're going to ask," Barnett said. "Why does he need a criminal defense attorney? The answer is that it's only one of my specialties. I handle all Dr. Orton's legal work. That's why I'm here."

"Got it," I said.

We turned down a forty-foot hallway with several large windows running along both sides. Orton stopped at the first set of windows.

"Over here to my left is PCR," he said. "To the right is the STR analysis lab."

"STR?" I asked.

"Short Tandem Repeat analysis is the evaluation of specific loci," he said. "This is where we hunt. Where we look for the commonalities in identity, behavior, hereditary attributes."

"Like balding?" I asked.

"That is certainly one of them," Orton said. "And one of our main points of study."

He pointed through the window at a device that looked like a countertop dishwasher with a rack containing dozens of test tubes. Emily snapped another photo.

"Where does the DNA for your studies come from?" I asked.

"We buy it, of course," Orton said.

"From who?" I asked. "You must need a lot."

"Our primary source is a company called GT23. I'm sure you've heard of it."

Nodding, I pulled a notebook out of my back pocket and wrote down his direct quote. While I was doing so, Emily continued her role as photographer.

"Dr. Orton, I know we can't go into the lab," she said. "But could you go in and sort of interact with what you see in there so I can take a few shots?"

Orton looked at Barnett for approval and the attorney nodded.

"I can do that," Orton said.

"And I don't see anybody in the labs," Emily added. "Don't you have staff that helps with your research?"

"Of course I do," Orton said, an irritated tone in his voice.

"They preferred not to be photographed, so they have the hour off."

"Forty minutes now," Barnett added helpfully.

Orton used a key to unlock the STR-lab door. He stepped into a mantrap where an exhaust fan roared to life and then died. He used the key to open the next door and enter the lab.

Emily walked up to the glass and tracked Orton through the lens of her camera. Barnett took the moment to move next to me.

"What are you doing here?" he asked.

"Excuse me?" I responded.

"I want to know what is behind this charade."

"I'm doing a story. It's about DNA and how it gets used and protected and who's out there on the frontier of the science."

"That's bullshit. What are you really here for?"

"Look, I didn't come here to talk to you. If Dr. Orton wants to accuse me of something, let him do it. Call him out here and we'll all talk about it."

"Not until I know —"

Before he could finish, he was interrupted by the roar of the fan in the mantrap. We both turned to see Orton stepping out. Concern was written on his face, as he had either heard the confrontation or seen the pointed discussion through the lab's window.

"Is there a problem?" he asked.

"Yes," I said before Barnett could respond. "Your lawyer doesn't want me to interview you."

"Not until I know what the interview is really about," Barnett said.

All at once I knew the plan for a subtle lead-up was out the window. It was now or never.

"I want to know about Jessica Kelley," I said. "I want to know how you fixed the DNA."

Orton stared hard at me.

"Who gave you that name?" Barnett demanded.

"A source I won't give up," I said.

"I want you both out of here," Orton said. "Right now."

Emily turned the camera on Orton and me and started firing off shots.

"No pictures!" Barnett yelled. "Put that away *right now*!"

His voice was so tight with anger that I thought he might lunge at Emily. I slid into the space between them and tried to salvage an unrecoverable situation. Over Barnett's shoulder I saw Orton pointing toward the door we had come through from the office.

"Get out of here," he said, his voice rising with each word. "Get out!"

I knew my questions were not going to be answered by Orton or his lawyer, but I wanted them on the record.

"How'd you do it?" I asked. "Whose DNA was it?"

Orton didn't answer. He kept his hand raised and pointing toward the door. Barnett started pushing me that way.

"What's really going on here?" I yelled. "Tell me about dirty four, Dr. Orton."

Barnett shoved me harder then, and I hit the door with my back. But I saw that the impact of my words hit Orton harder. *Dirty four* had registered with him and for a moment I saw the facade of anger slip. Behind it was…trepidation? Dread? Fear? There was something there.

Barnett shoved me into the hallway and I had to turn to keep my balance.

"Jack!" Emily cried.

"Don't fucking touch me, Barnett," I said.

"Then get the hell out of here," the lawyer said.

I felt Emily's hand on my arm as she walked by me.

"Jack, come on," she said. "We have to go."

"You heard her," Barnett said. "Time to go."

I followed Emily down the hall in the direction we had come from. The lawyer followed to make sure we kept going.

"And I can tell you something right now," he said. "If you print one word about Dr. Orton or one photograph, we will sue you and your website into bankruptcy. You understand that? We will own you."

Twenty seconds later we were getting into Emily's car and slamming the doors. Barnett stood in the main entrance of the building and watched. I saw him looking down at the front license plate of Emily's car. Once we were in, he turned and disappeared inside.

"Jesus Christ, Jack!" Emily yelled.

Her hands were shaking as she pushed the button to start the engine.

"I know, I know," I said. "I blew it."

"That's not what I'm talking about," she said. "You didn't blow anything, because they fucking knew why we were coming. We were never going to get anything. They cleared everybody out of there, then started the phony dog-and-pony show. They were trying to extract information, not give it."

"Well, we got something. Did you see his face when I said *dirty four*?"

"No, I was too busy trying to not get thrown into a wall."

"Well, it hit him. I think it scared him that we know about it."

"But what do we actually know?"

I shook my head. It was a good question. I had another.

"How'd they know what we were there for? I had it set up through corporate PR."

"Somebody we talked to."

Emily pulled out of the industrial park and headed back toward my Jeep.

"No," I said. "No way. The two guys I talked to today, the detective and the lawyer, they hate Orton's guts. And one of them gave me the name. You don't do that and then turn around and warn Orton about why we're coming."

"Well, they knew," Emily insisted.

"What about your FTC guy?"

"I don't know. I don't see it. I didn't say anything about us coming down here."

"Maybe he just tipped them off, said a reporter was sniffing around. Then Orton gets word from corporate in Indianapolis to let me in. He calls his lawyer guard dog and is waiting for us."

"If it was him, I'll find out. Then I'll burn his ass at the stake."

The tension from the confrontation turned to relief now that we were in the car and away from Orange Nano. I involuntarily started to laugh.

"That was crazy," I said. "I thought for a moment the lawyer was going to go after you."

Emily started shaking her head and smiling, casting off tension herself.

"I thought he was too," she said. "But that was nice of you, Jack, to step in there between us."

"It would have been pretty bad if something I said got you attacked," I said.

A City of Irvine patrol car went streaking past us, its lights flashing but no siren engaged.

"You think that's for us?" Emily asked.

"Who knows?" I said. "Maybe."

22

Myron Levin frowned and told us that he needed to pull us off the story.

"What?" I said. "Why?"

We were sitting in the conference room—Emily, Myron, and me—after Emily's and my long, separate rides back to L.A. We had just spent thirty minutes reviewing the events in Orange County.

"Because it actually isn't a story," Myron said. "And I can't afford to have you chasing after something for this long with no results."

"We'll get results," I promised.

"Not with what happened today," Myron said. "Orton and his lawyer were ready for you and they shut that whole avenue down. Where do you go from there?"

"We keep pushing," I said. "The four deaths are connected. I know they are. You should have seen Orton's face when I said *dirty four.* There is something there. We just need a little more time to pull it all together."

"Look," Myron said. "I know there's smoke, and where there is smoke there's fire. But right now, we can't see through the smoke and we're hitting dead ends. I let you two run with this but I need you back on your beats producing stories. I was never convinced this was a *FairWarning* story in the first place."

"Of course it is," I insisted. "That guy down there has something to do with these deaths. I know it. I feel it. And we are obligated to—"

"We are obligated to our readers and our mission—consumer-watchdog reporting," Myron said. "You can always take your suspicions and what you've found so far to the police, and that would take care of any other obligation you think you have."

"They won't believe me," I said. "They think I did it."

"Not once your DNA comes back," Myron said. "Talk to them then. Meantime, go back to your stations, refresh your story lists, and let's meet individually in the morning to sequence."

"Damn it," I said. "What about if Emily goes back to her beat and I stay on Orton? Then you don't have half the staff on this."

"Way to throw me under the bus, asshole," Emily said.

I spread my hands.

"It's my story," I said. "What's the alternative? You stay on it and I go back to the beat? That's not happening."

"And neither is your scenario," Myron said. "You're both back on the beats. Story lists in the morning. I have to go make calls."

Myron stood up and exited the conference room, leaving Emily and me staring at each other across the table.

"That was really uncool," she said.

"I know," I said. "I think we were getting close."

"No, I'm talking about you throwing me under. I'm the one keeping the story going and you were the one who fucked it up with that lawyer."

"Look, I admit I messed up with the lawyer and Orton, but

you said yourself it wasn't going to go anywhere. And it was probably your FTC contact who tipped him off. But this thing about you being the one keeping the story going, that's bullshit. We both had moves in play and were pushing it forward."

"Whatever. I guess it doesn't matter now."

She got up and left the room.

"Shit," I said.

I contemplated things for a few moments and then pulled out my phone and composed a text to the contact I had labeled *Deep Throat.*

> I'm not sure who you are but if you have anything else that can help me, now is the time. I just got pulled from the story for lack of progress. Orton was a bust. He was waiting and ready. In fact, there is no story. I need your help. I know some bad shit is going down out there and Orton is the key. Please respond.

I read it twice and wondered if it sounded like I was whining. Finally, I cut the last two words and sent it. I then got up and went back to my cubicle, passing Emily's on the way. I felt bad about what I'd said and the way things ended with her in the conference room.

At my desk I opened my laptop and went into a few folders labeled with stories I had been working on before Mattson and Sakai first showed up at my apartment. Top of the list was the "King of Con Artists" story, which had already been written and turned in but not yet posted because there had been no time for me to sit down with Myron and go over his edit. That would be the first priority. After that, I looked at my futures list, but nothing excited me after being on the recent adrenaline-charged story chase.

I next looked at my follow-up file. It contained stories that had already been posted but that I knew I should circle back on to see if anything had changed—whether the companies or government agencies had fixed the problems my stories had put the spotlight on. Though any reporter at *FairWarning* could pursue a story of their own interest in any industry, I had informally been given the auto-industry beat. For it, I had posted several pieces about sudden-acceleration issues, faulty electronic-control chips, dangerous gas tanks, and substandard parts, from outsourced integral assemblies to unregulated foreign manufacturers. The U.S. was an auto-based society and these stories hit hard and drew attention. They ran in several newspapers, and I had put on a jacket and tie to appear on the *Today* show as well as CNN, Fox, and several local news channels including L.A., Detroit, and Boston—with *FairWarning* getting credit all the way. It was a general rule that if you wrote a negative story about a Japanese car manufacturer, you would get on TV in Detroit.

I knew that I could now piggyback on any one of these stories and probably get a solid nothing-has-changed piece. That might please Myron and help ease me away from the DNA story.

I had a physical file in a desk drawer with all the documentation and contact information I had accumulated while originally reporting the auto-industry stories. I now pulled it and slid it into my backpack so I could refresh my thoughts while taking my morning coffee.

But I was done for the day. I couldn't simply transition from the unfinished story of Christina Portrero and William Orton to something wholly different and uninspiring. I needed time and now I was going to take it.

But I was still bothered by how things had just gone with

Emily. I zipped up the backpack and got up and moved down the aisle to her cubicle.

"Hey," I said.

"Hey what?" she replied curtly.

"I made the wrong move in there. I shouldn't have thrown you under the bus, okay? If anything happens, we're both on it together. I just sent a text to my Deep Throat source and told him the story is on fumes and he needs to come through. We'll see. I probably sounded like a whiny asshole."

"Probably."

But she looked up and smiled at me after saying it. I smiled back.

"Well, thanks for being so agreeable about my deficiencies."

"Anytime. So…"

She turned her screen so I could see it.

"Look what I just got."

On her screen was what looked like a document with the Federal Trade Commission seal on it.

"What is it?" I asked.

"Well, I sent my FTC guy an email directly asking if he tipped off Orton," she said. "I exaggerated and said that if he did he almost got me killed."

"And?"

"And he denied it. He even called me to deny it. And then he sent me this as some kind of gesture of good faith. It's the last list Orange Nano turned over to the FTC of labs it redistributed DNA to. It's almost three years old but these might be worth checking out—I mean, if we were still on the story."

Because it was a photo of a document, the writing was small and difficult to read from my angle.

"Well, anything jump out right away?" I asked.

"Not really," Emily said. "There's only five companies and all were registered with the FTC back then. I need to pull their profiles to get names, locations, things like that."

"And you're going to do that when?"

"Soon."

She glanced over the top of her cubicle in the direction of Myron's pod. We could only see the top of his head, but the arch of his headphone crossed over his hair. He was on the phone and the coast was clear. Emily corrected herself.

"Now," she said.

"Can I help?" I asked. "I was about to leave but I can stay."

"No, that will be too obvious. You go. I'll do this from home. I'll call if anything pops."

I hesitated before walking away. I didn't like the ball being in her court. Emily read me.

"I promise to call you, okay?" she said. "And you call me if Deep Throat comes through."

"That's a deal," I said.

23

I got to Mistral early and grabbed the same stool where I had sat the evening before. I put my backpack on the stool next to me to save it for Rachel and after an exchange of *bonsoirs* with Elle, I ordered a Stella, deciding to go with a lower octane this night. I put my phone on the bar and saw that I had just gotten a pair of texts from Deep Throat. I opened them up and found two attachments. One was marked "DNA" and the other "Transcript."

I opened the first and saw that my secret source had sent photos of the pages of a document. I quickly determined that it was the four-year-old DNA analysis report from the Orange County Sheriff's Department forensics lab that found no match between William Orton's DNA sample and the DNA collected from Jessica Kelley. I scanned the report and realized that I would need a geneticist to translate what the bar chart, percentages, and abbreviations all meant. But the summary was clear: the saliva sample swabbed from the victim's nipples after her assault did not belong to William Orton.

The attachment that came in the second text was a transcript of a very short interview with Orton conducted by Detective Digoberto Ruiz. It was five pages long and once again the attachment was composed of photos of the hard-copy pages.

I forwarded both attachments to myself on email, then pulled out my laptop so I could download them and see them on a bigger screen. Mistral didn't offer its customers Wi-Fi service, so I had to use my cell as a hotspot connection. While I waited for everything to boot up and connect I thought about the sender of the texts. I had asked Ruiz for the DNA report, not the attorney Hervé Gaspar. I was shifting my suspicions about Deep Throat and now was thinking it was the police detective. Of course, Gaspar could have acquired the DNA report and interview transcript in the course of preparing a lawsuit against Orton, but the fact that the attachments were photographs of documents led me in the direction of Ruiz. Sending photographs instead of scans or real documents gave him an extra measure of protection against being identified as my source should there ever be an internal investigation. Office scanners and copiers kept digital memories.

My conclusion was further muddled when I was finally able to open the interview transcript on my laptop. I noticed that the document had several short redactions and was able to determine from context that the victim's name had been removed. This was puzzling since Deep Throat had already provided me with the victim's name. Had he forgotten?

Putting the question aside, I proceeded to read the entire interview. It was essentially five pages of denial from Orton. He did not assault the victim, he did not know the victim outside the one class he had with her, and he had not been with the victim. When Ruiz started walking him through the night in question in detail, Orton shut it down and asked for a lawyer. The transcript ended there.

I closed my computer and put it away. I thought about the transcript. Aside from the redactions, there were also sections of Orton's answers highlighted in yellow. Wanting to keep the digital conversation with Deep Throat going, I used this as a reason to text him again and ask what the highlights meant. His response came quickly but indicated that Deep Throat was not as interested in conversation as I was.

Checkable facts

That was all he said, but it was enough to further convince me that my source was Detective Ruiz. *Checkable facts* was a detective's term. An interview with a suspect in a crime is choreographed to draw answers that can be confirmed or disputed through witnesses, video, digital trails, cell-phone triangulations, GPS navigation systems, and other means. This interview was no different, and someone—presumably Ruiz—had highlighted the things Orton had said that could be proved or disproved.

Of course, I had not gotten the follow-up reports on these checkable facts, so the interview transcript only served to intrigue me. I wanted more. Had Ruiz proved or disproved Orton's claim to have been somewhere else entirely on the night Jessica Kelley was assaulted? Had he proved or disproved his claim that he was the victim of a smear campaign at UCI organized by another professor who was vindictive because of a dispute over tenure?

I was about to compose another text to Deep Throat saying I needed more information when Rachel slipped onto the stool next to me, not the one I'd been saving with my backpack.

"What's that?" she asked by way of a greeting.

"I've been getting texts from somebody I think is the cop on the Orton case," I said. "I talked to him today and he wouldn't tell me anything. But then I started getting these tips. This is a transcript of a short interview he had with Orton before he lawyered up. He denied everything but put a few things on record that they could check. I was about to text and ask if he did."

"A transcript? That sounds like a lawyer."

"Well, it could be. I talked to the victim's lawyer too. He said he and his client couldn't talk because of an NDA. But I think it's the cop. He also sent the DNA-analysis report that cleared Orton. I don't know if anybody would have had that but Ruiz."

"The prosecutor who dropped the case probably had it. And he or she could have given it to the victim's lawyer."

"True. Maybe I should just ask Deep Throat point-blank who he is."

"*Deep Throat.* Cute."

I looked away from my phone to Rachel.

"By the way, hello," I said.

"Hello," she replied.

Starting the meeting with a discussion about my source had eclipsed the fact that we had spent the night together—and would again this night if intentions didn't change. I leaned over and kissed her on the cheek. She accepted the kiss and gave no indication of any tremor in the Force.

"So, were you up here again or did you have to trek over the mountain?" I asked.

"I was here, just closing the deal from yesterday. I timed it to meet you."

"Congratulations! Or not?"

"I know I was whining yesterday. I was getting drunk. And it wasn't the only thing I said that was wrong."

There *was* a tremor.

"Really?" I said. "Like what else?"

Rachel was saved from answering immediately by the approach of Elle, the faux-French bartender.

"*Bonsoir,*" she said. "Would you like a drink?"

"Ketel One martini straight up," she said. "*S'il vous plaît.*"

"*Bien sûr.* Coming up."

Elle moved down the bar to make the cocktail.

"That accent is terrible," Rachel said.

"You said that yesterday," I said. "Going with the hair of the dog, huh?"

"Why not? I signed a new client today. I can celebrate."

"So, what else did you say wrong yesterday?"

"Oh, nothing. Never mind."

"No, I want to know."

"I didn't mean to say that. Don't read anything into it."

The night before, this woman had whispered four words to me in the dark of the bedroom that rocked my world. *I still love you.* And I had returned them without hesitation. Now I had to wonder if she was trying to walk them back.

Elle approached and put Rachel's drink down on a napkin. The martini glass was filled to the brim and she had placed it too far from Rachel on the bar top for her to lean in and sip the level down before trying to lift it. Anything but a rock-steady hand would spill it when it was moved. I knew then that Elle had heard what Rachel had said about her accent and this was bartender payback. Elle retreated, throwing a wink at me that Rachel didn't see. A man took a stool in the middle of the bar and Elle approached him with her bad accent.

My cell's screen lit as a call came in. I saw it was Emily Atwater.

"I'd better take this," I said.

"Sure," Rachel said. "Your girlfriend?"

"My colleague."

"Take it."

In one steady motion Rachel lifted her glass, brought it across the bar top to her lips, and sipped. I never saw a drop spill.

"I'm going outside so I can hear."

"I'll be here."

I grabbed the phone off the bar and connected.

"Emily, hold on."

I took a notebook out of my backpack, then walked through the bar and out the front door, where the music wouldn't intrude on the call.

"Okay," I said. "You get something?"

"Maybe," she said.

"Tell me."

"So, first, you remember that what the FTC has is all over two years old. From before the FDA takeover?"

"Right."

"So, prior to the switch to the FDA, there is a record of Orange Nano selling DNA code and biological samples to five other labs. Three look like one-time transactions and the other two were repeat customers, so I think we can assume that business continues."

"Okay. Who were the two repeat customers?"

"First, I think we should keep clear lines. Orange Nano conducted these transactions, not Orton in particular. Yes, it's his lab, but he has employees and they made these transactions. His name is not on a single document I looked at."

"Okay. So did you see anything suspicious?"

"Suspicious? Not really. More like curious. The two repeat customers are nearby—Los Angeles and Ventura. The others were a little farther-flung."

"Which one are you curious about?"

"The L.A. lab."

I heard papers rustling.

"There were three things that popped for me on this one," Emily said. "First of all, I google-mapped it and it's not a commercial address. It's a residence. In Glendale, actually. I think this guy has a lab in his garage or something."

"Okay, that's a little weird," I said. "What else?"

"The business is registered with the FTC as Dodger DNA Services and I think the owner is a DNA tech with the LAPD's forensics lab. I googled him and his name came up in an *L.A. Times* story from last year about a murder trial where he testified about matching DNA taken from a gun to the defendant."

"So what's his side business?"

"The mission statement with the FTC says…"

More paper rustling. I waited.

"Here it is," Emily said. "'Testing applications of DNA in criminal forensics.' That's it."

"Okay, that's not that suspicious," I said. "It's his lifework. He's probably trying to invent an instrument or something that will make his job easier and make him a million dollars."

"Maybe. Until you get to my third point of curiosity."

"Which is?"

"He only bought female DNA from Orange Nano."

"Okay, yeah. What's this guy's name?"

"Marshall Hammond."

"Let me write that down."

I spelled the name out loud as I wrote it down, the phone held in the crook of my neck. Emily confirmed.

"We need to background him," I said.

"I tried but nothing came up," Emily said. "I was thinking you might try some of your old LAPD sources, see if you can get a take on him."

"Yeah, not a problem. I'll make some calls. Are you still at the office?"

"No, I went home. I didn't want Myron to see this stuff on my desk."

"Right."

"You get anything from Deep Throat?"

"Yes. He texted me the transcript of the interview with Orton and the DNA report that cleared him. I think Deep Throat is Detective Ruiz."

"I'd like to read that interview."

"I'll send it when we get off."

"Where are you?"

"Meeting a friend for a drink."

"Okay, see you tomorrow."

"Let's take one more run at Myron with all of this stuff. See if we can get a couple more days."

"I'm there."

"Okay, see you then."

I went back into the bar and saw that Rachel had finished her drink. I slipped back onto the stool.

"Ready for another?" I asked.

"No, I want to keep my wits about me tonight. Finish yours and let's go to your place."

"Yeah? What about dinner?"

"We can order in."

THE SHRIKE

24

He waited until it was dark.

He loved the silence of the Tesla. The car was like him. It moved swiftly and stealthily. Nobody heard him coming. He pulled to the curb a block from the house on Capistrano and got out, silently closing the door behind him. He pulled the hood of the black nylon runner's shell up over his head. He already wore a clear plastic mask that distorted his facial features to better guard against identification should there be a camera in the neighborhood that picked him up. Everybody had motion-activated cameras around their homes these days. It made his work difficult.

He carefully moved down the street, staying tucked into the shadows and out of the circles of illumination created by the streetlights. He had a small black duffel bag he kept tight against his body and under his arm. He finally reached the side yard of the target house and slipped into its backyard through an unlocked gate.

The house was dark but the oval-shaped pool was lighted — most likely on a timer — and cast a shimmering glow into the house through a row of sliding glass doors. There were no curtains. He checked each of the sliders and found them locked.

He then used a small pry bar from the duffel on the bottom of the center door to raise it up and out of its track. He carefully lifted it out and onto the concrete patio surface. This created a slight popping sound. He remained still, squatting next to the door and waiting to see if the disturbance had triggered an alarm or alerted anyone.

No lights came on. No one checked the living room. He got up and slid the door open along the rough concrete surface, then entered the house.

No one was home. A room-by-room search of the house determined that there were three bedrooms where no one was sleeping. Thinking it possible that he had indeed awakened someone by popping the slider and that they were hiding some-where sent him through the house in a more thorough search that again produced no occupants, hiding or otherwise.

But the second search led him to the garage, which he found had been converted into a laboratory. He realized that what he had found here was the lab support for Dirty4. He set to work examining the equipment and the notebooks left on a worktable, as well as data marked on hanging whiteboards and a calendar.

There was also a desktop computer. When he pressed the space bar, he learned that it was thumbprint protected.

He reached into his duffel for the roll of clear duct tape he kept among his tools and bindings. Leaving the garage, he walked through a TV room and found a powder room—the closest bathroom to the lab. He flicked on the light and peeled two three-inch segments of tape off the roll. He put one down on the sink counter with the sticky side up, then carefully and lightly applied the second to the top of the toilet's plastic flush handle. Raising the tape, he looked at it from an oblique angle.

He had lifted a print. He could tell it was big enough to be a thumb.

He put the tape down on top of the other segment, locking the print between the plastic. He then returned to the lab and sat at the computer. He took off a rubber glove and wrapped the plastic containing the captured print against his own thumb. He pressed it down on the desktop's reader square and the computer's screen activated. He was in.

He put his glove back on and began moving through the files on the desktop. He had no idea where the homeowner was but there was plenty on the computer for him to look through and attempt to understand. His study went on for hours and only ended after dawn, when he heard a car pull into the driveway on the other side of the garage door.

He was alerted but did not bother to hide. He quickly prepared for the homeowner, then turned off the lights in the lab and waited.

Soon he heard footsteps in the house and then the rattle of a set of keys being dropped on a table or counter. He noted this sound, thinking that he might need those keys and the car that was parked outside. He hated to part with the Tesla but he might not be able to risk returning to it through the neighborhood in daylight. He had not planned to be in the house past dawn and now the quick escape might be the best escape.

The overhead lights in the lab came on and a man took five steps into the room before stopping short when he noticed the intruder sitting at the lab table.

"Who the fuck are you?" he said. "What do you want?"

The seated man pointed at him.

"You're the one who calls himself the Hammer, aren't you?" he asked.

"Listen to me," Hammond said. "I work for the LAPD and I don't know how you got in here but you need to get the fuck out right now."

Hammond pulled a cell phone from his pocket.

"I'm calling the police," he said.

"You do and they will know all about your little side business of selling female data on the dark web," the intruder said. "Particular female data. You don't want that, do you?"

Hammond put his phone back into his pocket.

"Who are you?" he asked again.

"You sent me an email," the intruder said. "An archaic method of communication. It was fair warning about a reporter from *FairWarning*. Jack McEvoy?"

Hammond's face had started to turn pale as he understood his situation.

"You're the Shrike," he said.

"Yes, and we need to talk," the intruder said. "I want you to sit in that chair there."

He pointed to a chair he had prepared for Hammond. It was a wooden chair he had taken from one end of a table in the kitchen. He chose it because it had armrests to which he had attached zip ties, each with a very wide loop.

Hammond didn't move.

"Please," the intruder said. "I won't ask you again."

Hammond tentatively went to the chair and sat down.

"Put your hands through the plastic loops and then pull the tabs tight around your wrists," the intruder said.

"I'm not going to do that," Hammond said. "You want to talk, we can talk—I'm on your side here. We sent you that email to alert you. As a warning. But I'm not going to tie myself up in my own house."

The Shrike smiled at Hammond's resistance and spoke in a tone that suggested that Hammond was being a bit of a nuisance.

"You're going to do it or I'm going to go over there and snap your neck like a twig," he said.

Hammond looked at him, blinked once, and then started putting his left hand through the loop on the armchair.

"Now pull the tab tight."

Hammond pulled the loop closed around his wrist, not even having to be told to make it tighter.

"Now the other."

Hammond put his right hand through the loop.

"How do I tighten this one? I can't reach it."

"Bend down and use your teeth."

Hammond did as he was told and then looked up at his captor. He waved his hands to show he was securely locked to the arms of the chair.

"Okay, now what?"

"Do you think I would bind you if I meant to harm you?"

"I don't know what you would do."

"Think about it. If I wanted to hurt you it would have already been done. But now we can comfortably talk."

"I'm not comfortable at all."

"Well, I am. And so now we can talk."

"Talk about what?"

"The email you sent about this reporter—how did you know to send it to me?"

"See, that's the thing. This is why you don't have to worry about me. I don't know who you are. We just have the email you used when you joined the site. That's it. No way of knowing who you are, so this—"

He shook his arms against the plastic bindings.

"—is completely unnecessary. Really. I mean it."

The Shrike stared at him for a long moment, then got up and went to a printer that was on a table in the corner. He pulled a stack of documents out of the printer tray. He had been printing things through the night that had caught his interest on the lab's computer.

He returned to his seat and held the stack on his lap.

"You miss the point," he said without looking up from the documents. "How did you arrive at the decision to send me an email?"

"Well," Hammond said. "You were the only one who down-loaded the ones who died."

"At Dirty4."

"Yes, at the site."

"That is a problem. Your site promises full anonymity, but now you are saying you identified me through my interactions on the site. That is disappointing."

"No, wait, we did not identify you. That's what I'm saying. Right now I could not tell you your name to save my life. We looked for anybody who had downloaded details about those whores who got killed. There was only one client. You. We sent the email in good faith. To warn you because you have a reporter on your trail. That's it."

The Shrike nodded as if accepting the explanation. He had noticed that Hammond was becoming more animated as his fear grew, and that was a problem because his wrists would chafe against the plastic bindings and that would leave marks.

"I'm curious about something," he said conversationally.

"What?" Hammond asked.

"Your operation is magnificent. How are you able to take

the DRD4 samples and link them back to each woman's ID? I understand just about everything else but that—and that's the beauty of this whole thing."

Hammond nodded in agreement.

"Well, that's proprietary but I'll tell you. We totally own GT23's database, only they don't know it. We got inside. Complete access."

"How?"

"We actually encrypted a DNA sample with a Trojan-horse virus and sent it in like everybody else does. Once in, the sample was reduced to code and it activated and we were in their mainframe. Complete backdoor access to their data. I'm a second-tier buyer of their DNA. I buy it, isolate the DRD4 carriers we want, and match the serial number that comes on every sample to the flesh-and-blood bitch we then list on the site."

"That's genius."

"We think so."

"Who is 'we,' by the way?"

Hammond hesitated, but for only a second.

"Uh, I have a partner. I'm DNA and he's digital. He runs the site. I give him what he needs. We split the cash that comes in."

"Sounds like a perfect partnership. What's his name?"

"Uh, he doesn't want to—"

"Roger Vogel, correct?"

"How do you know that name?"

"I know a lot because I've been here all night. Your records are not encrypted. Your computer security is a joke."

Hammond did not answer.

"So where can I find Roger Vogel to ask him for more details of your operation?"

"I don't know. He sort of comes and goes. He's a private guy and we sort of lead separate lives. We were roommates once. In college. But since then we don't see each other in person too much. In fact, I don't even know where the guy lives."

The Shrike nodded. Hammond's refusal to give up his partner was admirable but hardly a problem. During the night he had read numerous deleted emails still in the desktop's memory. Posing as Hammond, he had then sent a message to Vogel setting up a meeting for later in the day. Vogel had responded and agreed.

It was now time to end this. He got up and started to walk toward Hammond. He saw his captive's arms tense and push against the bindings on his wrists.

The Shrike held up a hand to calm him as he approached.

"Just relax," he said. "Nothing to worry about. Not anymore."

He walked behind Hammond, wondering how different this would be. He had never actually done this to a man. He quickly leaned down and wrapped his powerful arms around Hammond's head and neck, his left hand coming around and over his mouth so there would be no noise.

Hammond's muffled cries of *"No!"* died in his hand and soon there was the deeply fulfilling snap of bone, cartilage, and muscle twisting to the extreme limit. Hammond's last breath flowed hotly through his fingers.

JACK

25

I got up early but stayed in bed watching Rachel sleep, not wanting to disturb her. I pulled my laptop off the bedside table and checked emails, finding the only one of note from Emily At- water. It had been sent late the night before, asking me where the Deep Throat documents were that I had promised to send after our call. She then suggested that I had intentionally held them back.

I quickly wrote a return email apologizing for the delay and pulled up the documents to attach. I first gave each one a quick read so their contents would be fresh in my mind when Emily called later to discuss them. As I scanned the DNA report from the Orange County Sheriff's Lab I saw a name I recognized.

"Holy shit!"

Rachel stirred and opened her eyes. I had jumped out of bed and gone to my backpack to retrieve the notebook I had used the night before while on the call with Emily. I came back to the bed with it and quickly opened it to the page where I had written down a name. It was a match.

Marshall Hammond

"What is it, Jack?" Rachel asked.

"It's Elvis in the box," I said.

"What?"

"Old newspaper phrase. It means the thing, the nuts, the photo everybody wants. Only this is not a photo. It's a name."

"You're not making sense."

"Look at this."

I turned the laptop's screen so she could see it.

"This is the DNA report from the Orange County Sheriff's Office that cleared Orton in the rape case down there. Remember, Deep Throat sent it to me? Now look down here where it says the name of the DNA tech who compared Orton's DNA to the sample taken off the victim."

"Okay. *M. Hammond.* What does it mean?"

"Marshall Hammond now works up here for LAPD's crime lab and lives in Glendale. My partner on the story ran down the second-tier labs that have bought DNA from Orton's lab. And this guy, Hammond, is one of them. And get this, he buys only female DNA."

"I'm not sure I'm following you. I need my coffee."

"No, listen, this is big. This guy Hammond cleared Orton, said the DNA was not a match. Now four years later he's in business with him. On the FTC paperwork he says he's researching forensic applications of DNA, but he only buys female DNA from Orton. Why only female if he's looking at forensic applications? You see? Emily and I were already zeroed in on this guy and now I found out he was Orton's ticket to freedom. That is no coincidence."

I got up from the bed again and started getting dressed.

"What are you going to do?" Rachel asked.

"I'm going to go to his house and his so-called lab and check it out," I said.

"You shouldn't do that alone, Jack."

"I won't. I'll call Emily."

"No, take me. I want to go."

I looked at her.

"Uh…"

"I can help you get a read on this guy if he's there."

I knew that she could. But bringing her directly into the story would not go over well with Emily Atwater. Or Myron Levin.

"Come on, Jack," Rachel said. "We've done this before."

I nodded.

"Then get dressed," I said. "Let's catch this guy before he goes to work. We can grab coffee after."

26

Forty minutes later we were on the street Hammond had listed with the FTC as the location of his lab. It was a residential street, as Emily Atwater had determined on Google Maps.

"Let's do a drive-by first," I said. "Get the lay of the land a little bit."

We cruised by a nondescript, two-story house with a two-car garage and a BMW SUV parked in the driveway.

"A little odd that the BMW is not in the garage," Rachel said.

"At least it means somebody's probably home," I said.

"Wait, Jack, I think the front door was open."

"Maybe he's about to leave. Turning around."

I used a neighbor's driveway to make the maneuver and then drove back to Hammond's house. I pulled into the driveway behind the BMW. It was a reporter's trick. It would make it hard for Hammond to jump into his car and get away when I hit him with the hard questions.

We got out and I saw Rachel put her hand on the BMW's front hood as she passed by it.

"Still warm," she said.

We approached the front door, which had been partially

hidden from the street by a small front porch with leafy potted plants standing sentinel on either side of the entry portal.

Rachel's observation was quickly confirmed. The door stood a foot open. The entry room beyond it was dark.

On the frame of the door was a lighted button for a door-bell. I stepped up and pushed it and a loud solitary gong echoed through the house. We waited but no one came. Rachel pulled a sleeve down over her hand and gently pushed the door open further. She then crossed behind me as she changed her angle of view into the house. There was a small entry area with a wall directly in front of us and arched entries to hallways to the left and right.

"Hello?" I called loudly. "Mr. Hammond? Anybody home?"

"There's something wrong," Rachel whispered.

"How do you know?"

"I feel it."

I rang the doorbell again, this time pushing it repeatedly, but only the solitary gong sounded. I looked back at Rachel.

"What do we do?" I asked.

"We go in," Rachel said. "Something's wrong. The car engine's warm, the door's open, nobody's answering."

"Yeah, but we're not cops. We should call the cops."

"I'm fine with that, if that's how you want to play it. But say goodbye to your story if the cops lock this place down."

I nodded. Good point. I stalled by yelling loudly into the house once more.

No one answered, no one came.

"Something's wrong," Rachel repeated. "We need to check it out. Maybe somebody needs help."

This last part was said for my benefit, giving me the excuse I could use later if things went sideways once we entered.

"Okay," I said. "Lead the way."

She moved past me before I was finished speaking.

"Put your hands in your pockets," she said.

"What?" I asked.

"No prints."

"Got it."

I followed her into the hallway to the right. It led to a living room that was furnished in contemporary styles, with a Warhol print of a Volkswagen Beetle over a fireplace protected by a freestanding glass panel. There was a thick book called *The Broad Collection* on the table between the maroon couch and two matching chairs. There was no sign of disturbance or anything wrong. It looked like a room that never got used.

"Are we in the right house?" Rachel asked.

"Yeah, I checked the address," I said. "Why?"

"The LAPD must pay its DNA techs a lot better than I thought."

"Plus, buying DNA from Orange Nano can't be cheap."

Next we moved through a modern kitchen with an island counter that divided the space from a large TV room that looked out onto a pool. Nothing seemed amiss. Held by a magnet to the refrigerator was a color photo printed on cheap copy paper that depicted a naked woman with a ball gag in her mouth.

"Nice fridge art," I said.

"We need to check upstairs," Rachel said.

We found the stairs by retracing our steps and going down the other hallway. Upstairs there were three bedrooms, but only one that appeared to be in use—the bed was unmade and there were dirty clothes in a pile next to it. A quick sweep of these rooms produced no people and no sign of trouble.

We went back down the stairs. There were two closed

doors at this end of the hallway. Rachel opened these with her sleeve-covered hand. The first was to a laundry room. Nothing there. The second was to the garage, and that's where we found Hammond's lab.

And where we found Hammond hanging from a noose fashioned from an orange industrial power cord.

"Shit," I said.

"Don't touch anything," Rachel said.

"Hands in pockets. I got that."

"Good."

But I pulled one of my hands out of its pocket with my cell phone. I pulled up the keyboard and tapped in 9-1-1.

"What are you doing?" Rachel asked.

"Calling it in," I said.

"No, not yet."

"What do you mean? We need to call the police."

"Just hold your horses for a minute. Let's see what we've got here."

"We got a dead guy hanging from the crossbeam."

"I know, I know."

She offered nothing else as she moved in closer to the body. There was a wooden chair kicked over on its side below the body, which I assumed was that of Marshall Hammond.

The body was suspended completely motionless in front of Rachel.

"Record this," she said.

I moved from the phone app on my cell to the camera app and started a recording.

"Recording," I said. "Go."

She circled completely around the body once before speaking.

"I'm assuming the car out front is his," she said. "So we are to assume that he went somewhere, came home, and then just came in here and threw that extension cord over the beam."

The garage had an open ceiling where there was some cross-planking for storage up above. The center support beam had been used as Hammond's gallows.

The body was suspended about two feet above the concrete floor of the garage lab. Rachel continued to slowly move around it without touching it.

"No damage to the fingernails," she said.

"Why would there be?" I asked.

"Second thoughts. Often people change their mind at the last second and claw at the noose. They break their fingernails."

"Got it. I think I knew that."

"But there is slight chafing on both wrists. I think he was bound either at the time of death or shortly before."

She looked around and saw a cardboard dispenser that held rubber gloves, most likely used by Hammond during DNA processing. She put on one glove and then used that hand to right the chair that had been knocked over during the hanging. She stepped up onto it so she could get a closer view of the noose and the dead man's neck. She studied it for a long moment before telling me to put on gloves from the dispenser.

"Uh, why?"

"Because I want you to steady the chair."

"Why?"

"Just do it, Jack."

I put my phone down on a table, then put on the gloves. I came back to the chair and held it steady as Rachel stepped up onto the armrests so she could get a downward view of the noose and the knot behind the dead man's head.

"This doesn't work," she said.

"You want me to look around for a ladder?" I asked.

"No, I'm not talking about that. I think his neck is broken and that doesn't really work."

"What do you mean doesn't work? I thought that's what happens when you hang yourself."

"No, not often with suicide by hanging."

She put her ungloved hand on the top of my head to steady herself as she climbed off the arms of the chair. She stepped down off the chair, turned it on its side, and positioned it as it had been when we entered the garage.

"You need a big drop to break the neck. Most hanging suicides basically die from strangulation. It was the execution hangings back in the day where you'd get the broken neck. Because you drop through a trap door, fall ten or fifteen feet, and then the impact snaps the neck, causing instant death. You ever heard that phrase *Build my gallows high*? I think it was a book or a movie or something. Whoever said that wanted to get it over with quick."

I raised my hand, pointing at the dead man.

"Okay, then how did he get a broken neck?"

"Well, that's the thing. I think he was dead first and then hung up like that to make it look like a suicide."

"So somebody broke his neck and then hoisted…"

It hit me then: *Somebody broke his neck just like the four AOD victims.*

"Oh, man," I said. "What is going on here?"

"I don't know but there has to be something in this lab that helps explain things. Look around. We have to hurry."

We searched but found nothing. There was a desktop computer but it was thumbprint protected. There were no hard files or lab books. Two whiteboards mounted on the walls had been erased. It became pretty clear that whoever had hung Hammond from the rafters—if the dead man was Hammond—had made sure that whatever the lab tech was doing with the female DNA he bought from Orange Nano was wiped clean as well.

There was a refrigerator that had racks of test tubes presumably holding DNA samples. I pulled one tube out of its slot and read the printing on the tape over the rubber seal at the top.

"This stuff is from GT23," I said. "Says it right here on the tube."

"Not a surprise," Rachel said.

"There's nothing else here," I said. "Just a dead guy and that's it."

"We still have the rest of the house to check," Rachel said.

"We don't have time. We have to get out of here. Whoever did this probably spent all night searching the place. Whatever was here is gone and probably so is my story."

"It's not about your story anymore, Jack. This is bigger than your story. Check the printer."

She pointed behind me. I turned and went to the printer in the corner. The tray was empty.

"Nothing here," I said.

"We can print the last job," Rachel said.

She stepped over and looked at the printer. Still wearing a single glove, she pressed the menu button on the printer's control screen.

"Little-known fact," she said. "Almost all modern printers print from memory. You send the job from your computer, it goes into printer-buffer memory, and then it starts to print. It means the last job is in memory until a new job comes in."

She clicked on the "Device Options" tab and chose the "Print

Memory" option. The machine immediately started humming and was soon printing pages.

We both stood there watching. The last job was a big one. Many pages were sliding into the tray.

"The question is who printed this," Rachel said. "This guy or his killer?"

Finally the printing stopped. There were at least fifty pages in the tray. I made no move to grab the stack.

"What's wrong?" Rachel asked. "Take the printouts."

"No, I need you to take them," I said.

"What are you talking about?"

"I'm a reporter. I can't just come into some dead guy's house and take printouts from his computer. But you can. You don't have to live by the same standards I do."

"Either way it's a criminal act and that trumps your journalistic ethics."

"Maybe. But just the same, you can take the pages and then give them to me as my source. Then I can use them—stolen or not—in a story."

"You mean like we did before and it cost me my job?"

"Look, can you just take the pages, and we can talk about this later? I want to either call the police or get the hell out of here."

"All right, all right, but this buys me into the case."

She scooped the thick sheaf of documents out of the tray.

"It's not a case," I said. "It's a story."

"I told you, it's more than that now," she said. "And I'm totally in."

"Fine. Split or call it in?"

"Your car's been sitting out there for at least a half hour. It was most likely seen by a neighbor and if not, there are probably cameras on every house. Too risky. I say we secure the documents and call it in."

"And we tell them everything?"

"We don't know everything. This is going to be Burbank PD, not L.A., so they won't connect the dots to the other murders. Not at first. I think you run your original cover story about researching DNA data protections and say you followed the bouncing ball to this guy and this lab and here you are."

"And what about you?"

"I'm your girlfriend and I just came along for the ride."

"Really? My girlfriend?"

"We can discuss that later too. We need to find a place to hide the printouts. If they're good, they'll search your car."

"You're kidding."

"I would if it was my call."

"Yeah, but you're better than everybody. I have so many files and other junk in the back of my Jeep they won't know what it is if they look."

"Suit yourself."

She handed me the stack of documents.

"Then, as your source," she said, "I am officially giving these to you."

I took the stack.

"Thank you, source," I said.

"But that means they're mine and I want them back," she said.

27

After camouflaging the printouts in the paperwork debris that monopolized the back seat of my Jeep, I dialed 9-1-1 on my cell and reported finding the body to the Burbank Police. Ten minutes later a patrol car arrived followed by a rescue ambulance. I left Rachel in the Jeep and got out. After showing my driver's license and press pass to an officer named Kenyon, I assured him that the RA and its EMTs were not necessary.

"They respond on all death calls," Kenyon said. "Just in case. Did you go inside the house?"

"Yes, I told the dispatcher that," I said. "The door was open and something seemed wrong. I called out, rang the doorbell, nobody answered. So I went in, looked around, continued to call out Hammond's name, and eventually found the body."

"Who is Hammond?"

"Marshall Hammond. He lives here. Or lived here. You have to ID the body, of course, but I'm pretty sure that's him."

"What about the woman in the Jeep? Did she go in?"

"Yes."

"We're going to have to talk to her."

"I know. She knows."

"We'll let the detectives handle that."

"What detectives?"

"They also roll on all death cases."

"How long you think I'll have to wait?"

"They'll be here any minute. Let's run down your story. Why were you here?"

I gave him the clean version: I was working on a story on the security of DNA samples submitted to genetic-analysis companies and it led me to want to talk to Marshall Hammond because he ran a private lab and also had a foot in law enforcement. This was not a lie. It just wasn't a full explanation. Kenyon wrote down some notes while I spoke. I glanced back at the Jeep casually to see if Rachel could see me talking to him. Rachel had her eyes down like she was reading something.

An unmarked police car arrived on scene and two men in suits emerged. The detectives. They spoke briefly to each other and then one headed toward the front door of the house while the other came toward me. He was mid-forties, white, with a military bearing. He introduced himself as Detective Simpson, no first name. He told Kenyon that he would take it from here and to file his paperwork on the call before EOW—which I was pretty sure meant end of watch. He waited for Kenyon to walk away before addressing me.

"Jack McEvoy—why do I know that name?" he asked.

"Not sure," I said. "I haven't done much in Burbank before."

"It'll come to me. Why don't we start with you telling me what brought you here today to discover this body inside the house."

"I just told Officer Kenyon all of that."

"I know, and now you have to tell me."

I gave him the exact same story, but Simpson stopped the narrative often to ask detailed questions about what I did and what I saw. I believed I handled it well but there was a reason he was a detective and Kenyon was a patrol officer. Simpson knew what to ask and soon I found myself lying to the police. Not a good thing for a reporter—or anybody, for that matter.

"Did you take anything from the house?" he asked.

"No, why would I do that?" I said.

"You tell me. This story you say you're working on, were you looking at any sort of impropriety involving Marshall Hammond?"

"I don't think I have to reveal all the details of the story, but I want to cooperate. So I'll tell you the answer is no. I knew very little about Hammond other than that he was a second-tier buyer of DNA samples and data and that made him of interest to me."

I gestured toward the house.

"I mean, the guy ran a DNA lab out of his garage," I said. "That was pretty curious to me."

Simpson did what all good detectives do: he asked his questions in a nonlinear fashion so the conversation was disjointed and seemed to be all over the place. But in reality, he was trying to keep me from relaxing. He wanted to see if I might slip up or contradict myself in my answers.

"What about your sidepiece?" he asked.

"'Sidepiece'?" I said.

"The woman in your car. What's she doing here?"

"Well, she's a private detective who helps me with my work sometimes. She's also sort of my girlfriend."

"Sort of?"

"Well, you know, I'm...not sure about things, but it doesn't have anything—"

"What did you take from the house?"

"I told you, nothing. We found the body and then I called the police. That's it."

"'We' found the body? So your girlfriend went in with you from the start?"

"Yes, I said that."

"No, you indicated you called her in after finding the body."

"If I did that, I was wrong. We went in together."

"Okay, why don't you stay right here and I'll go talk to her."

"Fine. Go ahead."

"Mind if I look around in your vehicle?"

"No, go ahead if you have to."

"So, you are giving me permission to search your vehicle?"

"You said 'look around.' That's fine. If searching means impounding it, then no. I need my car to get around."

"Why would we want to impound it?"

"I don't know. There's nothing in there. You're really making me regret calling you guys. You do the right thing and you get this."

"What is 'this'?"

"The third degree. I didn't do anything wrong here. You haven't even been in the house and you're acting like I did something wrong."

"Just stay here while I go talk to your 'sort of' girlfriend."

"See, that's what I mean. Your tone is bullshit."

"Sir, when we are finished here, I'll explain how you can make a complaint to the department about my tone."

"I don't want to make a complaint. I just want to finish here so I can go back to work."

He left me there and I stood on the street watching him interview Rachel, who had stepped out of the Jeep. They were too far away for me to hear the exchange and confirm that she was telling him the same story I had. But my pulse kicked up a notch when I saw she was holding the stack of printouts from Hammond's lab in her hand while talking to Simpson. At one point she even gestured toward the house with the stack and I had to wonder if she was telling the detective where she had found the paperwork.

But the conversation between Simpson and Rachel ended when the other detective came out the front door of the house and signaled his partner over for a huddle. Simpson broke away from Rachel and spoke to his partner in hushed tones. I nonchalantly walked over to Rachel.

"What the hell, Rachel? Are you going to just give that stuff to them?"

"No, but I could tell you were going to give him permission to search the car. I have certain protections for my clients, so I was prepared to say it was work material I had with me and not part of any search they might conduct. Luckily, he never asked."

I was not convinced it was the best way to protect the cache of paperwork from the lab.

"We need to get out of here," I said.

"Well, we're going to find out right now if we can," she said.

I turned and saw Simpson walking toward us. I was ready for him to say that the case was now a murder investigation, that my vehicle would be impounded, and that Rachel and I would be taken to the station for further questioning.

But he didn't.

"Okay, folks, we appreciate the cooperation," Simpson said. "We have your contact information and will be in touch should we need anything else."

"So, we can go?" I asked.

"You can go," Simpson said.

"What about the body?" Rachel asked. "Is it suicide?"

"It looks that way, yes," Simpson said. "My partner confirmed it. We appreciate your calling it in."

"All right, then," I said.

I turned to head to the Jeep. Rachel did as well.

"I remember who you are now," Simpson said.

I turned back to him.

"Excuse me?" I asked.

"I remember who you are now," he repeated. "I read about the Scarecrow a few years back. Or maybe it was one of those *Dateline* shows. Hell of a story."

"Thanks," I said.

Rachel and I got into the Jeep and drove away.

"That guy didn't believe a word I said to him," I said.

"Well, he may get a second shot at you," Rachel said.

"What do you mean?"

"First, his partner is an idiot for signing off on that as suicide. But the coroner will probably set them straight and it may change to a murder case. They'll come back to us then."

That added a layer of dread to the moment. I looked down and saw that Rachel had the printouts on her lap. I remembered glancing back at her in the Jeep while I was being interviewed and seeing her eyes down. She had been reading.

"Anything good in there?" I asked.

"I think so," Rachel said. "I think the picture is getting clear. But I need to keep reading. Let's go get that coffee you promised me."

28

I sat in the conference room with Myron Levin and Emily Atwater. Through the window to the newsroom I could see Rachel sitting at my pod and waiting to be called in. She had asked to use my computer so I knew she was still digging, even as I was attempting to keep her involved in the story. I thought it best that I explain things to Myron and Emily before Rachel came into the meeting.

"If you've read my books or know anything about me, you know who Rachel is," I said. "She has helped me on the biggest stories of my career. She put herself on the line and protected me when I was at the *Velvet Coffin,* and it cost her her job as an FBI agent."

"I think it also got the *Coffin* shut down," Myron said.

"That's a bit of an oversimplification but, yeah, that happened then too," I said. "She had nothing to do with that."

"And you want to bring her in on the story," Emily said. "Our story."

"When you hear what she has, you will see we have no choice," I said. "And remember, it was *my* story before it was *our* story."

"Oh, wow, a day doesn't go by that you don't throw that in my face, does it?" Emily responded.

"Emily," Myron said, trying to keep the peace.

"No, it's true," she said. "I've made some major gains on this story but he wants to take what I bring and go off on his own with it."

"No, I don't," I insisted. "It's still our story. Like I said, Rachel isn't going to write it. She's not part of the byline. She's a source, Emily. She has information about Marshall Hammond that we need to have."

"Why can't we get it direct from Marshall Hammond ourselves?" Emily asked. "I mean, I was under the impression that we actually were reporters."

"We can't because he's dead," I said. "He got murdered this morning...and Rachel and I found the body."

"Are you fucking kidding me?" Emily said.

"What?" Myron exclaimed.

"If we had gotten to his place a little earlier we probably would have run into the killer ourselves," I said.

"Way to bury the lede," Myron said. "Why didn't you tell me this from the start?"

"Because I'm telling you now so you will understand why Rachel is so important to this. Let us tell you what happened and then she'll explain what she's found out and where we're at."

"Go get her," Myron said. "Bring her in."

I got up, left the room, and walked to my pod.

"Okay, Rachel, they're ready," I said. "Let's just go in and tell them what we've got."

"That's the plan."

She stood up and started gathering the papers she had spread out on the desk. She carried the paperwork under my open laptop, an indication she had something on the screen she planned to show us.

"You found something?" I asked.

"I found a lot," she said. "I just feel like I should be presenting this to the police or the bureau, not the editor of a website."

"I told you, not yet," I said. "Once we publish, you can give it to whoever you want."

I turned and looked at her as I opened the door to the conference room.

"Showtime," I whispered.

Myron had moved to a chair next to Emily on one side of the table. Rachel and I sat across from them.

"This is Rachel Walling," I said. "Rachel, this is Myron Levin and Emily Atwater. So let's start with what happened this morning."

I proceeded to tell them how I had stumbled across the connection between William Orton and Marshall Hammond, and how we had gone to Hammond's home and found him hanging from the crossbeam in his garage lab.

"And it's a suicide?" Myron asked.

"Well, it was pretty clear the police think that," I said. "But Rachel thinks otherwise."

"His neck was broken," Rachel said. "But I estimated that his drop was no more than a foot. He was not a large or heavy man. I don't think that kind of drop breaks the neck, and since that is the recurring circumstance in the cases you're looking at here, I would term the death suspicious at the very least."

"Did you share this with the police when they said it was suicide?" Myron asked.

"No," I said. "They weren't interested in what we thought."

I looked at Rachel. I wanted to move on from the details of the death. She got the message.

"His broken neck is not the only reason to be suspicious," she said.

"What else is there?" Myron asked.

"Documents recovered from the lab reveal—"

"'Recovered'? What exactly does that mean?"

"I believe the killer spent time in Hammond's lab either before or after he killed him. He hacked the desktop that contained records of much of the lab's work. He printed out the records. But the printer memory kept the last fifty-three pages he printed. I printed those pages and that's what I've been studying. We now have a good amount of documentation from the lab."

"You stole it?"

"I took it. If that was stealing, then I would argue that I stole it from the killer. He was the one who printed it."

"Yeah, but you don't know for sure that that's what happened. You can't do that."

I knew going into the meeting that this would be the place where ethical questions clashed with potentially the best and most important story of my career.

"Myron, you need to know what we've been able to learn from the printout," I said.

"No, I don't," Myron said. "I can't let my reporters steal documents, no matter how important they are to the story."

"Your reporter didn't steal them," I said. "I got them from a source. Her."

I pointed to Rachel.

"That doesn't work," Myron said.

"It worked for the *New York Times* when they published the

Pentagon Papers," I said. "They were stolen documents given to the *Times* by a source."

"That was the Pentagon Papers," Myron said. "We're talking about a totally different kind of story."

"Not if you ask me," I said.

I knew it was a weak rejoinder. I gave it another shot.

"Look, we have a duty to report on this," I said. "The documents reveal that there is a killer out there using DNA to identify and acquire victims. Unsuspecting women who thought their DNA and identities were safe. This has never been seen before and the public needs to know."

That created a moment of silence, until Emily bailed me out.

"I agree," she said. "The transfer of the documents is clean. She's a source and we need to go public with what she knows—even if she came into possession of the documents in...an unsavory way."

I looked at her and nodded, even though *unsavory* was not the word I would have used.

"I'm not agreeing to anything yet," Myron said. "But let's hear or see what you've got."

I turned and nodded to Rachel.

"I haven't even gotten through everything in the printouts," Rachel said. "But there is a lot there. First off, Hammond was a very angry man. In fact, he was an incel. Does everybody know what that is?"

"Involuntarily celibate," Emily said. "Women haters. Real creeps."

Rachel nodded.

"He was part of a network, and that anger and that hate led him to create this," Rachel said.

She turned my laptop so it was facing Emily and Myron. She

reached around the screen so she could manipulate the keyboard. On the screen was a red log-in page.

Dirty4

The page had fields for entering a username and password.

"Based on what I read in the pages I was able to figure out Hammond's keywords," Rachel said. "His online name was *The Hammer*—that was easy—and for the password I started feeding keywords from an online incel glossary into the log-in. His password was *Lubitz.*"

"'You bitch'?" Emily asked.

"No, Lubitz," Rachel said. "It's the name of a hero in the incel movement. A German airline pilot who intentionally crashed a plane he said was full of sluts and slayers."

"Slayers?" Myron said.

"What incels call normal men who have normal sex lives. They hate them almost as much as they hate women. Anyway, there is a whole vocabulary within the incel movement, most of it misogynistic, and it's traded in online forums like Dirty4."

Rachel typed in Hammond's username and password and entered the site.

"We're in the dark web here," she said. "And this is an invitation-only site that identifies women with a specific genetic pattern called DRD4, or dirty four."

"What is it?" Myron said. "What does it determine?"

"It is a genetic sequence generally believed to be associated with addictive and risky behaviors," Rachel said. "Sex addiction being among them."

"Hammond was buying only female DNA from Orange Nano," Emily said. "He must have been identifying women with DRD4 in his lab. Women who had sent their DNA into GT23, never realizing it would be sold down the line to someone like him."

"Exactly," Rachel said.

"But wasn't it anonymous?" Myron asked.

"It was supposed to be," Rachel said. "But once samples were identified as having the DRD4 sequence, he had some means of reversing the anonymity. He was able to identify the women and put their identities, details, and locations on the Dirty4 website. Some of the profiles have cell numbers, home addresses, photos—everything. He sold them to his customers, who could search for women by location. If you are one of these creeps in Dallas then you search for women in Dallas."

"And then what?" Myron asked. "They go out and find these women? I don't—"

"Exactly," I said. "Christine Portrero complained to her friend that she met some creepy guy in a bar and he knew things about her he shouldn't have known. She thought she was being digitally stalked."

"Dirty4 gave its members an edge," Rachel said. "The women identified through DNA analysis by Hammond had the genetic makeup believed to be linked to promiscuity, as well as drug use, alcohol abuse, and other risky behaviors."

"Easy marks," Emily said. "He was telling his customers exactly who they were and where to find them. And one of those customers is a killer."

"Exactly," Rachel said.

"And we think that same customer is the one who killed Hammond," I added.

"It appears from the printouts that Hammond had a partner in this," Rachel said. "And they somehow became aware that women listed on the Dirty4 site were dying—were being killed. I think they looked at their subscriber base and figured out that there was at least one who had bought and downloaded the details of all the dead women. All of this is conjecture at the moment, but I think they warned him or told him to stop."

"And that's what got Hammond killed?" Myron asked.

"Possibly," Rachel said.

"Who was the customer?" Myron asked.

"The Shrike," Rachel said.

"What?" Myron asked.

"It's the dark web," Rachel said. "People use alternate names, IDs. If you are going to download names off a site like this, you don't give your real name and you don't pay with a credit card. You use an alias and you trade in cryptocurrency. The customer they identified as having downloaded the names of all four of the dead women went by the alias 'the Shrike.'"

"Any idea what it means?" Myron asked.

"It's a bird," Emily said. "My father was a birder. I remember him talking about shrikes."

Rachel nodded.

"I looked it up," she said. "It silently stalks and attacks from behind, gripping its victim's neck in its beak and viciously snapping it. It is considered one of nature's most formidable predators."

"All the women had broken necks," Myron said. "And this guy Hammond."

"And there's something else," Rachel said. "We think he may have hacked Hammond's computer or made him open it before he was murdered. He then started printing. We repeated the last job he sent to the printer. It was a file that had the IDs of all the women."

"How many names?" Myron asked.

"I didn't count," Rachel said. "But it looks like a hundred or so."

"Did you check to see if the four victims we know about are on the printout?" I asked.

"I did but they're not on there," Rachel said. "They could have been removed when it was determined they were dead."

"So he kills Hammond and gets away with what?" Myron asked. "A hundred names of potential victims?"

That brought a long pause to the discussion.

"Why would he print the names if he's already a customer and can access the same names through the site?" Myron asked.

"I think he's probably anticipating that the site is going to get closed down," Rachel said. "He may know about Jack and Emily or he might think law enforcement is closing in."

"That puts a clock on things," Emily said. "We can't sit on this and put those women at risk. We have to publish."

"We don't even have the whole story yet," I said.

"Doesn't matter," Rachel said. "You people write your story while I take it to the bureau."

"No," I said. "I told you that had to—"

"And I agreed," Rachel said. "But that was before I saw what was in the printouts. I have to go to the bureau and the bureau has to go to the police. This killer has all the names. They have to be protected. We can't wait."

"She's right," Myron said.

"It works, Jack," Emily said. "We can say the FBI is investigating, give the story immediate credibility. The FBI gets us past go."

I realized all three of them were right and that I had just come off rather badly, putting the story ahead of the safety of dozens of women. I saw the disappointment in both Rachel's and Emily's eyes.

"Okay," I said. "But two things. We make it clear to the bureau, the cops, any agency involved that they can do what they need to do but no press conferences or announcements until after we publish."

"How long will that be?" Rachel asked.

I looked at Myron and said the first number that popped into my head.

"Forty-eight hours," I said.

Rachel thought about it and nodded.

"I can try to make that work," she said. "Realistically, it will probably take them that long to confirm what we give them."

"Myron, you good with that?" I asked. "Emily?"

They both nodded their approval and I looked at Rachel.

"We're good," I said.

THE SHRIKE

29

He waited on the food-court level at a table against the railing. It gave him a view directly down onto the second-level stores on the north side of the mall. There was a circular banquette designed as a spot for husbands to sit while waiting for their wives to shop. He did not know what Vogel looked like. Hammond's partner had managed to keep his images and locations off the web. Kudos for that. But the hacker was of a type. The man who called himself the Shrike hoped to be able to identify him among the weekday shoppers in the mall.

The Shrike had picked the spot, putting out the mall location with the excuse that he—as Hammond—already planned to be there. It wasn't the best location for what he intended but he didn't want to raise any suspicions in Vogel. The priority was to get him to come.

He had a full tray of takeout food in front of him as camouflage. On the chair across the table from him was a shopping bag containing two gift-wrapped boxes that were empty. He was making a high-risk move and blending in was key.

He didn't touch any of the food because after he ordered it he thought it all smelled disgusting. He also thought it might draw attention to him if someone noticed he was wearing gloves. So he kept his hands down in his lap.

He checked below and saw that a woman was now seated on the banquette. She was watching one of the children in the nearby Kiddie Korner playground. No sign of anyone who might be Vogel.

"Can I clear anything here?"

He turned to see a table cleaner standing at his side.

"No, thank you," he said. "I'm still working on it."

He waited until the cleaner walked away before checking down below. Now the woman was gone and a man had taken her place. He looked like he was in his early thirties. He had on jeans and a lightweight sweater. He seemed to be checking his surroundings in a casual but purposeful way. He wore sunglasses inside and that was the final giveaway. It was Vogel. He was a bit early but that was okay. It meant he might grow tired of waiting sooner and would leave when he believed the rendezvous was not happening.

That was when the Shrike would follow him out.

JACK

30

On any story reported by a team there always comes the awkward decision of who writes it and who feeds the facts to the writer. Writing together never works. You can't sit side by side at the computer. The one who writes generally controls the tone of the story and the way the information is delivered, and usually gets the lead byline too. This was my story and it was my call, but I was smart enough to know that Emily Atwater was the better writer and I was the better digger. She had a way with words that I did not. I would be the first to admit that the two books I had published were heavily edited to the point of being reorganized and rewritten. All kudos to my editors but the royalty checks still went to me.

Emily was a lean writer, a follower of the less-is-more school. Short sentences gave her stories momentum and I was not blind to this. I also knew that putting her name first in the byline would not reflect badly on me. It would look like we had equal billing because it would be in alphabetical order: Atwater and McEvoy. I told her she could write the story. She was at first floored and then thankful. I could tell she believed it was the right call. She was just surprised I had made it. I thought the moment helped me make up for some of my missteps with her lately.

This decision to put her in the writer's chair freed me up to do more digging and to review what I had already reported.

It also gave me time to notify people who had been helpful on the story and whom I had promised to alert. Christina Portrero's mother and Jamie Flynn's father were high on this list.

I tried to make these notifications by phone, and the calls were more emotional than I had anticipated. Walter Flynn in Fort Worth burst into tears when I told him the FBI had now officially linked his daughter's death to a serial killer who was still at large.

After the calls were out of the way, I started pulling together my notes and making a list of other people I needed to call for the first time or to check back with for any new information. We essentially had twenty-four hours even though we had told Rachel Walling we needed twice that. It was a journalist's trick to always say a story would take longer to report than it really did, or would be published later than it actually would. It gave us an edge against the investigation's being leaked and our being scooped on our own story. I wasn't naive. Rachel was taking the story into the FBI's Los Angeles Field Office. There probably wasn't an agent in the building who didn't have an I'll-scratch-your-back-you-scratch-mine deal with a reporter somewhere. I had been burned by the FBI on more than one occasion and still had the scars.

Topping the list of who I needed to find and talk to was Hammond's unknown partner. There were emails scattered throughout the printouts from Hammond's house that indicated that he had a partner on Dirty4 who handled the digital aspects of the dark-web venture while he handled the lab work. The partner's email identified him only as *RogueVogueDRD4* and he used a Gmail account. The same alias was listed on the DRD4 site as the administrator. Rachel had said before leaving that she was confident the FBI could run it down, but I wasn't sure about that and didn't want to wait for the FBI. I contemplated directly reaching out to RogueVogue in a message. And after discussing it with Emily I did just that.

> Hello. My name is Jack. I need to talk to you about Marshall Hammond. It wasn't suicide and you could be in danger. We need to talk. I can help.

I hit the send button and let it fly. It was a long shot but a shot I had to take. Next, I started organizing what I would transfer to Emily for the story. She had not started writing and I could hear her on the phone in her cubicle making calls to watchdog agencies and observers of the genetic-analytics industry for general comments on what this sort of breach could mean. Every story had to have a lead quote—a line from a credible source that summed up the outrage, or tragedy, or irony of the story. It underscored the greater implications of the report. This story was going to trade in all of those elements and we needed to come up with one quote that said it all: that no one was safe from this kind of intrusion and horror. It would give the story a deeper resonance than a basic murder story and would get it picked up by the networks and cable. Myron would be better able to place the story with one of the big media guns like the *Washington Post* or the *New York Times*.

I heard Emily briefly summarize what we had found and what we would publish. As in her writing, she had a way of keeping it short and to the point. Still, I was getting nervous listening to her. My story paranoia was kicking in. We had to be careful when we solicited these comments because every one of those experts and industry observers could turn around and tip off a reporter they had a source relationship with. The trick was to give them enough information to respond with a usable quote without giving them enough to pass to another reporter.

I tried to tune her out and go about my work, reviewing the early stages of my investigation before I knew what I had stumbled into. I thought about calling the LAPD detectives and asking if I had been cleared yet through DNA analysis and if they had made any headway on the case. But I concluded that would be a waste of time as I was persona non grata with Mattson and Sakai.

Next I thought about causesofdeath.net and realized I had not checked the website since I saw the initial flurry of responses to my query. It had been a great starting point for me in connecting the cases linked—I believed—to the Shrike, and now I checked for more.

I went to the message chain I had started with the inquiry about atlanto-occipital dislocation and saw that three messages had been posted since I last checked. The first was a follow-up by Dr. Adhira Larkspar to her first post, in which the chief medical examiner had asked the original poster—me—to identify himself.

This is a reminder that this forum is open to medical examiners and coroners' investigators only.

The warning did not stop two others from posting. A day earlier a medical examiner in Tucson, Arizona, reported that they had an AOD case with a female victim that was attributed to a motorcycle accident. The case was six months old and no other details were offered.

I copied the posting and shot it over to Emily in an email alerting her that we might have a fifth case to look into. Her response came quickly.

That can be a follow-up. Right now we have to go with what we have confirmed and get the story out.

I didn't respond. The latest message on the forum chain had drawn my full attention. It had been posted only twenty minutes earlier.

Wow, we just caught two of these in the same day! A hanging in Burbank and a fall in Northridge. Coincidence? I don't think so—GTO

I was stunned by the message and read it several times before taking another breath. Obviously, the hanging in Burbank had to be Hammond, and I noted that GTO had not called it a suicide. I had no doubt that Rachel's take on Hammond's death had been on the money. Maybe the coroner's office was onto it as well.

The second death was what had my full attention. A fatal fall in Northridge. Calling a death a fatal fall did not rule out the possibility of murder. I needed to get more details. Northridge was a Valley neighborhood. I called the LAPD's Valley Bureau, identified myself as a journalist, and asked for the lieutenant. I wasn't connected for nearly five minutes but refused to hang up, being better at waiting games than most of the people who didn't want to talk to me.

Finally, I was connected.

"Lieutenant Harper, how can I help you?"

"Lieutenant, this is Jack McEvoy. I work at a consumer-watchdog website called *FairWarning* and—"

"How can I help you?"

"Okay, well, I'm looking for information on the fatal fall up in Northridge today. Like I said, we are a consumer watchdog and we pay attention to workplace injuries and accidents, et cetera. I was hoping you could tell me what happened."

"A guy fell off the roof of a parking structure. That's it."

"What parking structure? Where?"

"He was in the mall up there and when he left he went to his car and then jumped or fell off the roof of the garage. We're not sure which yet."

"Did you identify the victim yet?"

"Yes, but we're not putting that out. We haven't found next of kin. You'll have to get the name from the coroner."

"Okay. What about age?"

"He was thirty-one, I think my guys told me."

The same age as Hammond, I noted.

"There wasn't a note or anything?"

"Not that we've found. I need to—"

"Just a couple last questions, Lieutenant. Were there any cameras that showed the fall and could shed light on what happened?"

"We do a camera canvass on these sorts of things and we haven't found anything yet."

"Who is the investigator assigned to this?"

"That would be Lefferts. He's lead."

"Thank you, L-T."

"You got it."

A five-minute wait for less than a minute of information. I next went to the website of the county medical examiner's office and pulled down the staff menu. I was trying to find out who GTO might be. None of the medical examiners fit the bill, but when I looked at the list of coroner's investigators, I zeroed in on Gonzalo Ortiz. My guess was that his middle name began with *T*.

Sometimes a phone was the best way to get what you needed—like when you are trying to penetrate the LAPD. But for the coroner's office I wanted to go in person. I wanted a face-to-face with GTO because I sensed from the message on the causesofdeath board that he might be a guy who would talk. Maybe it was a long shot, but I wanted to take it. I shut down my computer and walked over to Emily's pod. She was typing up notes from one of her calls.

"I think I found Hammond's partner."

She immediately stopped typing and looked up at me.

"Who is he?"

"I don't know. I didn't get a name yet."

"Then where is he?"

"The coroner's office. He fell off a parking garage a couple hours ago, broke his neck. I'm going to go down there to see the investigator, see if he'll talk."

"You mean broke his neck like we're seeing here?"

She pointed to her screen, meaning the whole case. I nodded.

"There's a coroner's investigator who I think has put two and two together. He posted to me on the message board less than an hour ago. I want to go see if he'll talk. The LAPD won't tell me shit."

"But doesn't he think you're a coroner after the way you first posted?"

"I don't know. The head medical examiner sort of outed me but he still posted."

"Well, don't dawdle. We have a lot to do."

"Dawdle? Not my style. I'll call you after I get there."

31

It was my first time to the coroner's office in at least four years. It had been a regular stop for me when I covered crime for the *Times* and later the *Coffin*. But at *FairWarning* death had not been my beat until now.

The death complex, as I termed it, was on Mission Road near the County–USC Medical Center in Boyle Heights. The two medical centers—one for the dead, the other for the living—were attached by a long tunnel that once facilitated the movement of bodies from one side to the other. The original office sat close to the street, a forbidding brick structure that was nearly a hundred years old and now was mostly used as a souvenir shop and for meeting rooms. They did big business selling toe tags, coroner's blankets, and other morbid items to the tourist trade.

Behind the old structure was the new modern structure with clean lines and soothing beige tones. There was a glass-doored entrance that I used to get to the reception desk. I asked for Investigator Gonzalo Ortiz. The receptionist asked what my visit was in reference to.

"Uh, the police told me to talk to the coroner's office to get information about a death," I said. "It happened today up in the Valley."

It was a carefully crafted answer that did not contain a false-hood but didn't exactly tell the whole truth. I hoped that the answer plus my somber demeanor would lead her to believe I was there as next of kin to someone awaiting autopsy. I didn't want her calling back to the investigations department and announcing that a reporter was in the lobby. If GTO refused to talk to me, I wanted him to tell me so to my face.

The receptionist asked my name and then made a call. She spoke briefly to someone and then looked up at me.

"What's the name of the deceased?" she asked.

Now I was cornered. But I had an out. Burbank was considered part of the Valley so I could still answer without lying.

"Marshall Hammond."

The receptionist repeated the name and then listened. She hung up without another word.

"He's in a meeting and will be out as soon as it ends," she said. "There is a family room down that hall to the right."

She pointed behind me.

"Okay, thanks."

I walked down the hall, hoping there would be no one in the "family" room, but had no such luck. This was Los Angeles, where more than ten million people lived. And died. Some un-expectedly, some by accident, and some by murder. I knew that the county coroner's office had a whole fleet of pale blue vans with racks in the back for making multiple-body pickups. There was not a chance the family room would ever be empty.

In fact, the place was almost full with small groups of grieving people huddled in silence or in tears, probably hoping there had been a mistake and it wasn't their loved one they had been asked to come identify or to arrange for transfer and burial.

I didn't mind skirting the truth with the receptionist but here

I felt like an intruder, an impostor they assumed was among them in loss and grief. I had been in their place once, with my brother, and I had knocked on the doors of homes where loved ones had been taken by violence, but something about this room was sacred. I felt awful and thought about making a U-turn and just waiting for Gonzalo Ortiz in the hallway outside the door. But instead I took the first seat near the door. The last thing I wanted was to interact with someone in the throes of their own pain hoping to assuage mine with a smile of understanding. That would be like stealing.

The wait felt like an hour as I listened to murmured pleas, and one woman began to wail. But the truth was that no more than five minutes after my arrival I was rescued from the family room when a Latino man in his fifties, dark-skinned with a salt-and-pepper mustache, stepped in and asked if I was Mr. McEvoy. I was up and out of my seat faster than I could say *yes*. I led him out into the hallway and then hesitated when I realized he had to lead.

"Let's take a shortcut," he said.

He waved me down the hall in the opposite direction from Reception. I followed.

"Are you Investigator Ortiz?" I asked.

"Yes, I am," he said. "And I have a private meeting room set up."

I decided to wait till we got to the private room before explaining who I was and what I wanted. Ortiz used a card key to swipe the lock on a door marked AUTHORIZED PERSONNEL ONLY, and we were admitted to the pathology wing of the complex. I knew this because of the odor that engulfed me as we entered. It was the smell of death cut with industrial-strength disinfectant, a sweet and decidedly sour smell that I knew would stay in my nasal passages long after I left the premises. It prompted me to remember the last time I had been in this place. It was four years earlier, when the chief medical examiner had gone public with complaints about health and safety issues in the complex coupled with budgetary issues that affected staffing and crippled service. He reported autopsies being backed up by fifty bodies at a time and toxicology testing taking months instead of weeks. It was a move to persuade the county commissioners to give him the budget he had requested, but it only resulted in the chief's being forced out of his job.

I doubted much had changed since then and was thinking of bringing up the issue with Ortiz as a way of breaking the ice when I informed him I was a journalist. I could mention the stories I wrote about the deficiencies for the *Velvet Coffin* in hopes that it would help convince him to talk to me about the atlanto-occipital-dislocation cases.

But as it turned out, I wasn't going to have to tell him I was a journalist or worry about breaking the ice. It had already been broken. Ortiz led me to a door marked MEETING ROOM B. He knocked once and opened the door, holding his arm out to usher me in first. As I entered I saw a rectangular table with six chairs in the middle of the room. Sitting at the far end of the table were Detectives Mattson and Sakai.

I probably revealed my surprise with a slight hesitation in my step but then I regained speed and entered the room. I did my best to recover with a half-smile.

"Well, well, LAPD's finest," I said.

"Have a seat, Jack," Mattson said.

He hadn't bothered intentionally mispronouncing my last name. I took that as a sign that maybe he had learned something from the stunt he had pulled arresting me. My surprise slipped into bafflement. Were they following me? How did they know I was coming to the coroner's office?

I took a chair directly across from Mattson, and Ortiz took the seat beside me. I put my backpack on the floor next to me. There was a momentary pause as we all stared at one another. I decided to start out incendiary and see what it got me.

"You guys here to arrest me again?" I asked.

"Not at all," Mattson said. "Let's put that behind us. Let's try to help each other here."

"Really?" I said. "That's different."

"Are you the one who made the post on causesofdeath?" Ortiz said.

I nodded.

"Yeah, that was me," I said. "And I guess you're GTO."

"That's right," Ortiz said.

"Jack, I admit it, you put this thing together," Mattson said. "That's why I think we can help each—"

"Last we spoke, I was a murder suspect," I said. "Now you want to work together."

"Jack, you're cleared," Mattson said. "The DNA was clean."

"Thanks for letting me know," I said.

"You *did* know," Mattson said. "You knew all along. I didn't think you were waiting for me."

"How about this: Did you tell Christina Portrero's friend that I wasn't the creep you told her I was?" I said.

"It's at the top of my list," Mattson said.

I shook my head.

"Look, Mr. McEvoy," Sakai said, pronouncing my name perfectly. "We can sit here and potshot each other about mistakes made in the past. Or we can work together. You get your story and we get the guy out there who is killing people."

I looked at Sakai. He was obviously assigned the role of peacemaker—the man who was above all the skirmishes with only the truth in his sights.

"Whatever," I said. "You're about to get bigfooted by the FBI. You'll be turning this over by tomorrow morning."

Mattson looked stunned.

"Jesus Christ, you went to the bureau with this?" he exclaimed.

"Why wouldn't I?" I asked. "I went to you people and you put me in jail."

"Look, can I just say something?" Ortiz said, holding his hands up in a calming gesture. "We really need—"

"No," Mattson said. "Who did you go to over there?"

"I don't know," I said. "Another person I'm working on this with went there while I went here."

"Call them off," Mattson said. "It's not their case."

"It's not your case either," I said. "There are killings from here to Florida and up the coast to Santa Barbara."

"See? I told you he was the one who connected all of this," Ortiz said, looking at Mattson.

"So why am I here?" I asked. "You want to know what I know? Then it's got to be an even trade and it's got to be ironclad exclusive or I am out of here. I'll take my chances with the FBI."

Nobody said anything. After a few seconds I started to get up.

"Okay, then," I said.

"Just hold your horses," Mattson said. "Sit down and let's cool down. Let's not forget that there's a sick fuck out there killing people."

"Yeah, let's not," I said.

Mattson turned slightly to check with his partner. Some sort of nonverbal message was communicated, then he looked back at me.

"All right, we trade," he said. "Info for info, intel for intel."

"Fine," I said. "You first."

Mattson spread his hands.

"What do you want to know?" he said.

"How'd you get here?" I asked. "Were you following me?"

"I invited them," Ortiz said. "I saw the post."

"Coincidence, Jack," Mattson said. "We were here, meeting with Gonzo, when you showed up."

"Tell me why," I said.

"Simple," Mattson said. "Gonzo started looking around after your post and started connecting cases, same as you. He knew Sakai and I had Portrero, so when two of these AOD cases came up in one day he called us and said they might all be connected. Here we are."

I realized that I was light-years ahead of them on the investigation. I could share some of what I knew and blow their minds—and still keep some details for myself and my story. I also had the printouts from Hammond's lab that I had to be careful about revealing.

"Your turn," Mattson said.

"Not yet," I said. "You haven't told me anything I don't already know."

"Then what do you want?" Mattson said.

"The guy who fell off the parking garage today, who is he?" I asked.

"Gonzo?" Mattson prompted.

"Guy's name is Sanford Tolan," Ortiz said. "Thirty-one years old, lived in North Hollywood and worked at a liquor store."

That was not what I was expecting.

"A liquor store?" I asked. "Where?"

"Up in Sunland off Sherman Way," Ortiz said.

"How does that fit with Hammond?" I asked.

"As far as we can tell, it doesn't," Mattson said.

"So, you're saying it's a coincidence?" I asked. "The two deaths are unrelated?"

"No, we're not saying that," Mattson countered. "Not yet. We're just getting into this thing."

He looked at Ortiz as if throwing the ball to him.

"Autopsy has not been scheduled yet," Ortiz said. "But the preliminary notes from the field indicate he was already dead when he fell."

"How can they tell that?" I asked.

"We have witnesses," Ortiz said. "He didn't yell and he didn't attempt to break his fall—which we would have seen in the injuries. Plus, you don't see AOD in falls like this. A broken neck is common, but not AOD. There is no twisting of the neck in a fall like that."

"You said he worked in a liquor store," I said. "You mean, like behind the counter?"

"Correct," Ortiz said.

"What else do you know?" I pressed.

"We know he had a criminal record," Ortiz said.

Ortiz looked at Mattson as if for permission.

"The whole deal's off if you hold back on me," I said.

Mattson nodded.

"He was a pedophile," Ortiz said. "Did four years in Corcoran for raping his stepson."

Again, the information didn't fit. I was expecting an Internet cipher, some sort of expert who handled the dark-web part of Dirty4. A woman-hating incel. Pedophile was not part of the profile that was emerging.

"Okay," Mattson said. "Now it's your turn to give. Tell us something we don't know, Jack."

I nodded and to buy some time I reached down to my backpack, unzipped it, and pulled out the notebook in which I had written the facts of the story. I flipped through the pages for show and then looked up at Mattson.

"The man you're looking for calls himself the Shrike," I said.

32

I sat in my Jeep in the parking lot of the coroner's office and made calls. I didn't want to be driving during these conversations. I also wanted to watch for Mattson and Sakai. They had stayed behind with Ortiz after our meeting and I was curious to see how long it would be before they left. I didn't know what I would get from that but I wanted to know anyway.

The first call was to Emily Atwater to check on her status.

"I've started writing," she reported. "So far so good. We've got a lot so I'm playing with the balance. What to move up, what to move down. As you know, Myron doesn't like sidebars. So it's got to be one story and follow-ups in the days after. What about you?"

"I was wrong about the second case being Hammond's partner," I said. "They think the Shrike might have made a mistake and killed the wrong guy. So we have to keep looking for him."

"'They'?"

"Yeah, the police were here. Mattson and Sakai. With the help of a smart coroner's investigator they've put the cases together."

"Shit."

"Well, I made a deal with them. Traded information on the basis of exclusivity."

"Can we trust them?"

"Not at all. I don't trust them and I don't trust the FBI not to leak. So I held back. I gave them Dirty4 but didn't mention GT23 or Orange Nano or Hammond's connection to the Orton case. I think they have a lot of catching up to do before we have to worry about them leaking."

I saw a man and woman leaving the coroner's office, arms wrapped around each other, heads down. I recognized them from the family room earlier. The man had tears on his face. The woman didn't. She was supporting him more than he was supporting her. She walked him to the passenger side of a car and helped him get in before going around to get in behind the wheel. I saw a man in another car watching them as well.

"Jack, you there?"

"Yeah."

"Why do they think the Shrike killed the wrong guy?"

"Because he was the wrong profile. Guy worked in a liquor store and was a convicted pedophile. Not the right fit. We are just guessing here but they think the Shrike tried to lure RogueVogue to a meeting at the Northridge Mall and somehow thought this guy—his name was Sanford Tolan—was RogueVogue. Tolan was there by himself, probably sitting around watching children in the mall. The Shrike followed him out to his car, broke his neck, and threw him over the edge."

"That's horrible. Do you think the Shrike knows he made a mistake?"

"You mean like he realized this is not the right guy but killed him anyway? Maybe. Hard to say. The whole idea of setting up the meeting is a guess."

"What about the FBI? Have you heard from Rachel?"

"My next call. I wanted to check in with you first."

"All right, then I'm going to get back to it. Let me know what you know."

"You got it."

Before calling Rachel I pulled up my email account to check for new messages. My pulse jumped when I saw I had received a reply from RogueVogue to the message I had sent earlier.

> I don't understand this. Who are you? Why did you send this to me?

I checked the time on the message and saw that it was sent well after the lifeless body of Sanford Tolan had dropped from the fourth floor of the mall parking garage. It was further proof that the Shrike had killed the wrong man. The message was short and simple and most of all innocent. No acknowledgment, no admission, just tell me more.

I considered how to answer in a way that would not scare him off: I can safeguard you . . . I can tell your story . . . I can be your go-between . . .

I decided on a direct approach that laid the reality of his situation on the line. Looking up every few seconds or so to check for the detectives, I composed an email that I hoped would lead RogueVogue to trust me with his story and safety.

> I am a writer. I have written books about killers like the Poet and the Scarecrow. I am writing now about the Shrike. You are in danger. He killed Hammond and he killed a man he thought was you. I can help you. I can get you to safety and I can tell your story. I know you and Hammond had nothing to do with the Shrike. You never planned on that. I'm including my number here. Call me and we can help each other.

I read it twice and typed my cell number at the bottom before sending it. My hope was that RogueVogue would read and react to it right away.

I checked the parking lot and the front of the coroner's office once more but saw no sign of the LAPD detectives. I realized that they might have parked over at USC Medical Center and taken the tunnel through to the coroner's office. I may have missed them. But I decided to call Rachel while maintaining my vigil. She answered in a whisper.

"Jack, are you okay?"

"I'm fine. I was just checking in. Did you meet with anybody yet?"

"Yes, we're in the middle of it. I just stepped out to take the call."

"And?"

"Well, they're working on it. They're looking for other cases and trying to run down Hammond's partner. I should have something on that soon."

"There might be a case in Tucson. But more importantly at the moment, there was another killing today here in L.A. I thought it was Hammond's partner but it's not. It looks like a mistake. Like the Shrike thought it was Hammond's partner."

"How did you find that out?"

I filled her in on how a check of the causesofdeath website led me to the coroner's office. I told her that the bureau now had competition in the form of the LAPD connecting the same cases the *FairWarning* team had. I suggested that maybe the FBI should join forces with the LAPD rather than have the agencies run parallel investigations.

"I'll suggest it but don't hold your breath," Rachel said. "That never worked well when I was here and I doubt attitudes have changed much."

"Well, it won't look that great when the story comes out and it says they're running different investigations," I said.

"Jack, that's another thing."

"What is?"

"They don't want you to publish yet."

"Jesus, I knew it would come to that. You can tell them to forget it. It's our story. We brought it to them as a courtesy. We're going with it."

"They feel—and I agree—that it would be better if this guy doesn't know they're coming. You go with the story, he'll probably drop from sight and then we'll never get him."

"'We'? You're back with them now?"

"You know what I mean. As soon as this guy knows we're on to him he'll disappear and change his pattern."

"And if we don't publish and warn the public about this guy, he just goes on killing until maybe he is caught."

"I know that's the argument but—"

"He killed two people today alone. And this was him covering his tracks. He must already know that something is up, that people are on to him."

"But not the FBI, Jack."

"Look, I'll talk to Myron and Emily about it but I will vote to publish. The world needs to know this guy is out there and what he's doing and how these victims are identified and stalked."

"And you have to make sure you don't get scooped."

"Look, I'm not denying that. I'm a reporter and this is my story, and yes, I want to be sure I'm first out with it. But now with both the FBI and LAPD aware of it, it's only a matter of time before some asshole leaks it to some reporter he's trying to leverage. That alone makes me want to publish, but the more important reason is to alert the public to the very dangerous thing going on out there."

"Okay, Jack, I'll tell them. How long can I say they have before it goes out?"

I looked through the windshield and saw Mattson and Sakai walking along the sidewalk that fronted the parking lot. I put my phone on speaker so I could use it to take a photo of them. Myron liked to put photos into the body of long stories as visual breaks. As long as they were somehow connected to the story, that was all that mattered.

The detectives went down either side of an unmarked car and got in.

"A day," I said. "We'll try to get it out by tomorrow night."

"Can't you push it back at least twenty-four hours, Jack? There is not much they can do by tomorrow night."

"What if he kills somebody on that extra day? You want that on you, Rachel? I don't."

I got the call-waiting buzz in my ear and looked at my phone's screen. An *Unknown Caller* was reaching out to me.

"Rachel, I've got a call I have to take," I said quickly. "It might be him."

"Who?" Rachel said.

"RogueVogue. I'll call you back."

"Jack—"

I disconnected and accepted the other call.

"This is Jack McEvoy."

Nothing. Just an open line. I watched Mattson and Sakai drive out of the parking lot and turn right on Mission Road.

"Hello? This is Jack."

"You sent me a message…"

The voice came through a digital modulator that turned it into the voice of a robot.

"Yes…I did. You're in danger. I would like to help you."

"How can you help me?"

I quietly unzipped my backpack and grabbed a notebook and pen so I could write his words down.

"For one thing, I can get your side of the story out. When this thing hits, there are going to be victims and villains. You want to get your story out there before other people put it out there for you. People who don't know you."

"Who are you?"

"I told you. I'm a writer. I track killers. I'm tracking the Shrike."

"How do you know about him?"

"He killed someone I knew. He got her name and details from Dirty4."

There was a silence and I began to think I'd lost him. I wanted to persuade him to talk. But I wasn't willing to dance around what he and Hammond had wrought with their scheme. As far as I was concerned, RogueVogue was firmly on the villain side of the ledger. He was not as culpable as the Shrike but pretty damn close.

"This wasn't supposed to happen."

I wrote the line down verbatim before responding. I knew it would go high up in the story.

"What *was* supposed to happen?"

"We…it was just supposed to make money. We saw a niche."

"What was that niche?"

"You know, helping guys…some guys have trouble meeting girls. It wasn't that different from Tinder and some of those others."

"Except the women whose profiles you were selling didn't know, right?"

I said it in a non-accusatory tone but it brought silence. I threw a softball question out before I lost him.

"How did you and Marshall Hammond meet?"

After a pause he answered.

"College roommates."

"Where was that?"

"UC–Irvine."

A little piece of the puzzle clicked into place.

"You knew William Orton there?"

"Marshall did."

I threw a curveball at him. A possibility that had been growing in the back of my mind.

"Is he the Shrike?"

"No."

"How do you know that?"

"Because I know. What happened to Marshall?"

"The Shrike broke his neck, then tried to make it look like he hanged himself in his home lab. How do you know Orton is not the Shrike? Do you know who the Shrike is?"

"I figured it out."

I wrote it down. I knew my next words to him might be the most important part of the conversation.

"Okay, listen. There is a way for you to help your situation— if you want to."

"How?"

"Tell me who the Shrike is. The FBI needs to stop him."

"The FBI?"

I immediately realized I had misspoken. He didn't know that this had come to the attention of the FBI. I sensed that I had to keep him on the phone by going in another direction. I blurted out a question.

"How do you think the Shrike found Marshall?"

There was a pause but then he finally spoke again.

"He made contact."

"Who did? Marshall?"

"Yes. We knew about the ones who died. Clients told us that we had—that some of our profiles were…defunct. Marshall looked into it. He checked the downloads and found the link between them. It was him. Marshall reached out. He told him he had to stop."

That was all the explanation he gave, but again it helped me put more pieces of the story together.

"And that's how the Shrike found him? He traced the contact?"

"Somehow. We took precautions but somehow he found him."

"'We'?"

"We agreed to send the note. Marshall sent it."

"Let's go back to Orton. Marshall fixed his case, right? The DNA."

"I'm not talking about that."

"Then Orton owed him. He gave you the DNA."

"I told you, I—"

"Okay, okay, forget it. What about the Shrike? You said you know who he is. Give me a name. You do that and you won't be a villain in this. You'll be somebody trying to stop it. Like you said, this wasn't supposed to happen."

"And then you give the name to the FBI?"

"I can or you can. Doesn't matter as long as you are the one who gives it."

"I'll think about that. It's all I have."

I guessed he meant that the Shrike's ID was all he had to trade in exchange for not being prosecuted.

"Well, don't think too long," I said. "If you found it, the FBI will eventually find it and then you've got nothing to give."

He didn't respond. I realized I was asking for the Shrike's ID when I didn't even have my source's real name.

"What about you? Can you give me your name so I know who I'm talking to?"

"Rogue."

"No, your real name. You know my name—why don't you tell me yours?"

I waited. Then I heard the connection go dead.

"Hello?"

He was gone.

"Shit."

The interview was over.

THE SHRIKE

33

He watched the reporter across the parking lot. He seemed to be going from one call to the next. And he had snuck a photo of the two men leaving the coroner's office. They were obviously cops—homicide detectives, since this was where they brought dead people. The whole thing was curious. How much did the reporter know? How much did the police know?

He had followed him from the office, making the identification off the photo on the *FairWarning* website. The reporter had been in a hurry then, running through yellow lights and driving in the carpool lane on the freeway even though he was clearly alone. Now he had slowed down and was just sitting in the Jeep making calls. The Shrike wondered what he had learned inside the coroner's office.

He drummed his fingers on the center console. He was agitated. Things had gone wrong and were spinning out of his control. He was still frustrated and angry about Vogel. Once he had started interrogating the man from the mall, he quickly learned he was not Vogel but had to finish the kill. He now wondered who had warned Vogel or how he had known it was a trap. Maybe it was Vogel who had trapped him.

Finally, the reporter pulled out of his parking space and

headed to the exit. The Shrike had backed in so he could also make an easy exit and not lose his quarry. From the coroner's office he turned left on Mission and then took the next left on Marengo. The Shrike stayed with him and followed the reporter as he drove onto the northbound 5 freeway.

For the next thirty minutes he followed the reporter on freeways going north and then west into the San Fernando Valley. He finally realized that he was heading toward the mall where the Shrike had been just that morning.

Again, he seemed to know things.

The reporter pulled into the parking garage and then continued up the ramps to the top level. He parked and walked to the spot, crossing without hesitation under the yellow tape the police had left in place. He looked down over the concrete balustrade. He used his phone to take photos. He backed away from the edge and took more.

The Shrike realized several things. The killing of the man here had already been identified as his work. The reporter knew about it, indicating he had sources inside the police department and medical examiner's office. The questions that remained were about Vogel. What did he know and who had he shared it with? Was he talking to the police or was he talking to the reporter?

Final conclusion: eliminating the reporter now would be a mistake when he might be the best chance of getting to Vogel.

The Shrike changed his plans, deciding to let the reporter live. For now.

JACK

34

I got back to the office in the late afternoon and started feeding the new quotes and information from RogueVogue to Emily. She had already put together a fifteen-hundred-word story, which was generally considered the line at *FairWarning* when reader exhaustion starts to set in. But the new stuff was vital. RogueVogue was one of the two men who created Dirty4 and had set a killer down the path of death and destruction.

"I'm just going to have to tighten up other parts," she said.

"We can also keep some of the minor stuff for the follow-up stories," I said. "I'm sure there will be many."

We were sitting together in her pod.

"True," she said. "But if we have good stuff now, there's no reason not to try to get it in."

"You think Myron's going to throw a flag because we only have his online name?"

"Probably. Are we one hundred percent sure he's the guy?"

I thought about it for a moment and nodded.

"He responded to the email I sent to the address that clearly belonged to Hammond's partner. And he expressed enough knowledge about the site and what was happening to verify who he was. So, we don't have his name, but it's him. For sure."

Emily didn't nod in agreement or say anything. This told me she was still uncomfortable with putting her name on a story that contained information she wasn't completely sure of.

"All right," I said. "I was hoping to avoid having to do this but I will call Rachel and see if the bureau has made any headway in identifying the guy."

"Why are you avoiding calling her?" Emily asked.

I realized I had just talked myself into a jam. I would have to reveal to Emily the rift that had opened between Rachel and me.

"She has taken the bureau's side on something," I said.

"What is it?" Emily asked. "We need her, Jack. She's our in with the bureau. Once this breaks, we will really need that."

"The issue is that the FBI don't want us to publish because it will alert this guy that they're on to him. They're afraid he'll disappear. My side of it is that we are called *FairWarning* for a reason, and we have to warn the public about this guy. He has killed two people today alone and he has the list of women identified by Dirty4."

Emily nodded.

"I agree with you," she said. "We have to go now. Should we run it by Myron before he leaves?"

"Let me see if I can get Rachel on the line first," I said. "Then we'll be completely up-to-date with what we've got."

"So...what happened between you two back in the day?"

"We just...I screwed up and she paid for it is what happened."

"How so?"

I had to decide whether I wanted to get into this. I thought maybe talking about it would exorcise it. But we were in the middle of chasing a story.

"It might help me to know," Emily said. "Since she's become part of this."

I nodded. I got that.

"I was working for the *Velvet Coffin,*" I said. "And Rachel and I were together. It was a secret. We kept our separate places but that was for show. And I was working on this story about an LAPD cop I heard the feds were looking at for corruption. I had a source who said the guy had been indicted by a federal grand jury but then nothing happened. It got quashed because the target had dirt on the sitting U.S. Attorney."

"You asked Rachel for help?" Emily asked.

"I did. She got me the grand-jury transcripts and we published. The U.S. Attorney sued and the chief judge got mad and I got pulled into court. I wouldn't name my source and the judge put me in jail for contempt. Meantime, the cop this was all about offs himself and leaves a note saying he was an innocent man bullied by the media—meaning me. That didn't win me any sympathy, and after two months I was still in lockup."

"Rachel came forward."

"She did. She admitted she was the source. I was freed and she lost her job. End of story and end of us."

"Wow. That's rough."

"She used to chase serial killers and terrorists. Now, she mostly runs background checks for corporations. And it's all on me."

"It wasn't like you forced her to do it."

"Doesn't matter. I knew what could happen if I took the transcripts. I took them anyway."

Emily was silent after that. And so was I. I got up, rolled my chair back to my pod, and called Rachel's cell. She answered right away. I could tell she was in a moving car.

"Jack."

"Hey."

"Where are you?"

"At the office, working on the story. You left the bureau?"

"Yes. I was about to call you."

"Going home?"

"No, not yet. What's up?"

"I was wondering if you and your FBI friends got anywhere with identifying Rogue."

"Uh, not really. They're still working on it."

I suddenly grew suspicious.

"Rachel, you're not moving in on him right now, are you?"

"No, not at all. I would tell you that, Jack."

"Then what's going on? I haven't heard from you all afternoon and now you're going somewhere but not telling me where."

"I told you, I was just about to call. Thanks for trusting me."

"I'm sorry but you know me. I get suspicious about what I don't know. What were you going to call about?"

"I told you they're trying to determine if there were other victims, right? All you had were cases people mentioned on that coroner's website. The bureau is doing a deeper dive than that."

"Okay, that's good. Are they finding anything?"

"Yes. There are more cases, more women with broken necks. But they aren't going to share with you if you publish the story before they're ready. They're going to come to you tomorrow and try to make a trade. You hold back and they'll give you more cases."

"Shit. How many are we talking about?"

"At least three other deceased victims—including the Tucson case you mentioned today."

Now I paused. What did that mean?

"Are you saying there are non-deceased victims?"

"Well, there may be one. That's where I'm going now. They

identified an assault where a woman's neck was broken in similar fashion to the others. But she didn't die. She's a quadriplegic."

"Oh god. Where is she?"

"It's a Pasadena case. We pulled the file and it seems to match up. There's a composite sketch and she met the guy in a bar."

"What happened? How did they find her?"

"He had to have thought she was dead. He dumped her down a set of stairs in the hills. Have you ever heard of the Secret Stairs in Pasadena?"

"No."

"I guess there are stairs that run up and down all through this neighborhood. After he broke her neck he took her body to the stairs and threw her down so it would look like an accident. But some guy running the stairs at dawn found her body and she still had a pulse."

"Does this mean he knew Pasadena? Maybe the location is a big clue."

"Well, they are called the Secret Stairs but they aren't really that secret. There are Yelp reviews and photos all over the Internet. All the Shrike had to do was search *Pasadena Stairs* online and he'd have found them."

"What about DNA? Did she go to GT23?"

"I don't know. It wasn't part of the case file. That's why I'm going now to try to interview her."

"Alone?"

"Yes, alone. The agents on this won't get around to it until tomorrow. Too much else going on."

I remembered my early research on atlanto-occipital dislocation. It wasn't always fatal.

"Where?" I asked. "I'm going to meet you."

"I don't know if that's best, Jack," Rachel said. "I'm going as an investigator. She might not want to talk to a reporter—if she can talk at all."

"I don't care. You can do the interview but I want to be there. Where are you going?"

There was a pause and I felt that everything about the fragile relationship I had with her was on the line.

"Altadena Rehab," Rachel finally said. "Google the address. Her name is Gwyneth Rice. She's only twenty-nine."

"I'm on my way," I said. "Wait for me."

I disconnected and went back to Emily's pod to inform her that there were more victims and that I was going to see one who was still alive. I told her about the FBI's plan to float a deal: information on other victims in exchange for delaying publication.

"What do you think?" she asked.

"I don't know," I said. "We have till tomorrow to think about it. Why don't you talk to Myron about that while I try to get this interview?"

"Sounds good."

"By the way. They have a composite drawing of the Shrike."

"Is that part of the deal?"

"We'll make it part of it."

I left the office then, grabbing my keys off my desk and hurrying out.

35

Rachel was waiting for me in the lobby of Altadena Rehab. She was all business. No hug, no hello, just "It took you long enough."

She turned and headed toward a set of elevators and I had to catch up.

"Her father agreed to meet me," she said after we entered an elevator and she hit the 3 button. "He's with her now. Brace yourself."

"For what?" I asked.

"This is not going to be a good scene. Happened four months ago and the victim—Gwyneth—is not doing well physically or mentally. She's on a ventilator."

"Okay."

"And let me handle the introductions. They don't know about you yet. Don't be obvious."

"About what?"

"That you're there for a story. Maybe it would be better if I took notes."

"I could just record it."

"There is nothing to record. She can't speak."

I nodded. The elevator moved slowly. There were only four levels.

"I'm here for more than the story," I said to set the record straight.

"Really?" Rachel said. "When we talked earlier today it felt like that's all you cared about."

The elevator door opened and she exited before I could defend myself on that.

We walked down a hallway and Rachel gently knocked on the door to room 309. We waited and a man opened the door and emerged into the hallway. He looked to be about sixty years old with a worn expression on his face. He pulled the door closed behind him.

"Mr. Rice?" Rachel asked.

"Yes, that's me," he said. "You're Rachel?"

"Yes, we spoke on the phone. Thank you for allowing me to visit. As I said, I am FBI retired but still—"

"You look too young to be retired."

"Well, I still keep my hand in and work with the bureau on occasion. Like with this case. And I wanted to introduce you to Jack McEvoy. He works for *FairWarning* and is the journalist who first connected all the cases and brought the investigation to the bureau."

I put my hand out and Mr. Rice and I shook.

"Good to meet you, Jack," Rice said. "I wish somebody like you was there four months ago and could have warned Gwynnie about this guy. Anyway, come on in. I told her she was having company and finally something is being done. I have to warn you, this is going to go slow. She has a screen and something called a mouth-stick stylus that allows her to communicate."

"No problem," I said.

"It's kind of amazing," Rice said. "It turns her teeth and the roof of her mouth into a keyboard. And each day she gets more proficient at it. Anyway, she does get tired and she'll shut down at some point. But let's see what we can get."

"Thank you," Rachel said.

"One more thing," Rice said. "This kid has been through hell and back. This is not going to be easy. I told her she didn't have to do it but she wants to. She wants to get this evil man and she's hoping you can do it. But at the same time she's fragile. Go easy is what I'm saying, okay?"

"We understand," Rachel said.

"Of course," I added.

With that, Rice opened the door and went back inside the room. I looked at Rachel and nodded her in first as we followed.

The room was dimly lit by a soft spotlight over a hospital bed with railings. Gwyneth Rice was raised at a 45-degree angle on the bed and flanked by equipment and tubes that monitored her, breathed for her, fed her, and took her bodily wastes away. Her head was held steady by a framework that looked like scaffolding and appeared to be screwed into her skull in at least two points. Altogether it was a horrible tableau and my first instinct was to look away, but I knew that she might register my reflex for what it was and refuse the interview before it started. So I looked at her straight on and smiled and nodded as I entered the room.

There was a metal arm that was attached to the headboard and extended around and in front of Gwyneth at eye level. Attached to it were two small back-to-back flat screens that allowed her to see one, and her audience the other.

The first thing that Gwyneth's father did was take a folded paper towel off a bedside table and dab the corners of her mouth where saliva had accrued. I could see a very thin glassine wire extending from the right side of her mouth, down her cheek, and into the nest of wires and tubes attached to the electronic assembly.

Her father put the paper towel aside and introduced us.

"Gwynnie, this is Rachel Walling, who I told you about," he said. "She's the one working with the FBI on your case and on those other girls. And this is Jack. Jack's the writer who discovered this whole thing and called Rachel and the FBI. They have some questions about the man who did this, and you answer what you want, okay? No pressure at all."

I could see Gwyneth work her jaw and tongue inside her mouth. Then the letters *OK* appeared on the screen facing us.

This is how it would work.

Rachel moved to the side of the bed and Mr. Rice brought her a chair to sit down on.

"Gwyneth, I know this may be very difficult for you and we really appreciate your willingness to help," she began. "I think it's best if the questions just come from me and you try to answer them as best as you can. And if there is anything I ask that you just don't want to answer, that's absolutely okay."

OK

This left me as a spectator on my own story but I was willing to let Rachel start out. If I thought there was something that needed to be asked, I would tap her on the shoulder and we could conference outside the room.

"I want to start by saying we are very sorry for what you've been through," Rachel said. "The man who did this is evil and we are doing everything we can to find and stop him. Your help will be extremely valuable. The Pasadena Police seemed to deal with this when it happened as an isolated case. We now believe one man has hurt several women like you and so what I want to do today is concentrate on him. Who he is, how he chose you, things of that nature. It will help us build a profile of him that will identify him. So, some of my questions might seem odd to you. But there is a purpose to them. Is that okay, Gwyneth?"

YES

Rachel nodded and then glanced back at me and Mr. Rice to see if we had anything to add. We didn't. She turned back to Gwyneth.

"Okay, then let's start. It's very important that we learn how this offender chose his victims. We have one theory and I want to ask about that now. Have you in the past done any sort of DNA hereditary or medical analysis?"

I saw Gwyneth's jaw start moving. It almost looked like she was eating something. The letters always came out in all caps and as the interview progressed the only punctuation seemed to come through automatic spell-check.

YES

I saw Mr. Rice raise his head in surprise. He didn't know about his daughter's looking into her DNA. I wondered if it would have been a sore subject within the family.

"Which company did you use?" Rachel asked.

GT23

To me that all but confirmed her as a victim of the Shrike. But she had somehow lived to tell about it, even if it was a life now severely circumscribed by her injuries.

"Okay, so let's go to the night this happened," Rachel said. "You were still in extremely critical condition when the initial investigation was carried out. The detectives were mostly trying to work with some grainy video footage from outside the bar. Once you were able to communicate, another detective was on the case who didn't appear to ask you very many questions about who—"

HE WAS AFRAID

"'He was afraid,'" Rachel read off the screen. "Who was afraid? You mean the detective?"

YES. HE DIDN'T WANT TO BE HERE TO SEE ME

"Well, we're not afraid, Gwyneth," Rachel said. "I assure you of that. We are going to find the man who did this to you and he will pay for his crimes."

DON'T TAKE HIM ALIVE

Rachel paused when the message printed on the screen. There was a dark shine in Gwyneth's brown eyes. The moment felt sacred to me.

"I'll say this, Gwyneth," Rachel said. "I understand your feelings and you should know that we are going to find this guy and justice is going to be carried out. Now, I know this is tiring for you, so let's get back to the questions. Has any of your memory of that night come back to you?"

BITS AND PIECES LIKE NIGHTMARES

"Can you talk about them? What do you remember?"

HE BOUGHT ME A DRINK I THOUGHT HE WAS NICE

"Okay, do you remember anything in particular about the way he talked?"

NO

"Did he tell you about himself at all?"

ALL LIES, RIGHT?

"Not necessarily. It is harder to sustain a conversation based on lies than one that is close to the truth. It could be a mix of both. Did he tell you, for example, what he did for a living?"

SAID HE WROTE CODE

"Okay, that fits with what we already know about this man. So, that could be the truth and that could be very helpful, Gwyneth. Did he say where he worked?"

DON'T REMEMBER

"Were you a regular at that bar?"

PRETTY MUCH

"Had you ever seen him in there before?"

NO HE SAID HE WAS NEW IN TOWN
HE WAS LOOKING FOR AN APARTMENT

I admired how Rachel was conducting the interview. Her voice was soothing and she was establishing rapport. I read it in Gwyneth's eyes. She wanted to please Rachel by giving her information she didn't have. I felt no need to jump in with a question. I felt confident Rachel would get to all the relevant questions — as long as Gwyneth didn't tire.

It went on like this for another fifteen minutes, with Rachel drawing out little details of the behavior and character of the man who had hurt Gwyneth so badly. And then Rachel looked back over her shoulder at Gwyneth's father.

"Mr. Rice, I'm going to ask Gwyneth some personal questions now," she said. "I think it might be better if you and Jack went out into the hall for a few minutes."

"What kind of questions?" Rice asked. "I don't want her upset."

"Don't worry. I won't let that happen. I just think she will be better able to answer if it's just between us girls, so to speak."

Rice looked down at his daughter.

"You okay, honey?" he asked.

I'M FINE DAD YOU CAN GO

And then,

I WANT TO DO THIS

I didn't like getting the boot myself but saw the logic in it. Rachel would get more doing the questioning one-on-one. I moved toward the door and Rice followed me. In the hallway I asked if there was a cafeteria but he said there was just a coffee vending machine in an alcove down the hall.

We went that way and I treated us each to a terrible cup of coffee. We stood there sipping the liquid levels down in our cups before attempting to walk back down the hall. I decided to do what Rachel was doing: work a subject one-on-one.

"This must be unbelievably hard for you, seeing your daughter like that," I said.

"I couldn't even begin to tell you," Rice said. "It's a nightmare. But I'm there for her. Whatever she needs and whatever will help catch the bastard who did this to her."

I nodded.

"Do you have work?" I asked. "Or is this—"

"I was an engineer at Lockheed," Rice said. "I retired early so I could just be here for her. She's all that matters to me."

"Is her mother in the picture?"

"My wife passed six years ago. We adopted Gwynnie from an orphanage in Kentucky. I think her doing that DNA stuff was her attempt to find her birth mother and family. If you're saying that had something to do with this, then...Jesus Christ."

"It's an angle we're looking at."

I started walking back down the hallway. We talked no further until we reached the door of 309.

"Are there any treatments out there that might help your daughter's situation?" I asked.

"I'm on the Internet every morning searching," Rice said. "I've contacted doctors, researchers, the Miami Project to Cure Paralysis, you name it. If it's out there, we'll find it. The main thing right now is to get her off the respirator and breathing and talking on her own. And that's not as far-fetched as you might think. This kid—somehow—stayed alive. He thought she was dead and just dumped her down the stairs. But she was alive and whatever it was that kept her going and kept her breathing, that's still there."

I could only nod. I was completely out of my element here.

"I'm an engineer," Rice said. "I've always looked at problems like an engineer. Identify the problem, fix it. But with this, identifying the—"

The door to the room opened and Rachel stepped out. She looked at Rice.

"She's getting tired and we're almost finished," she said. "But I want to show her something that I held to the end because it might upset her."

"What is it?" Rice asked.

"It's a composite drawing of the suspect that was put together with the help of people who were in the bar that night and saw your daughter with him. I need her to tell us if it's accurate to her memory."

Rice paused for a moment as he thought about his daughter's possible reaction to the drawing. Then he nodded.

"I'll be here for her," he said. "Let's show it to her."

I realized that I had not seen the composite myself. As we reentered the room I saw that Gwyneth's eyes were closed and thought she might be asleep. But as I got nearer I realized that her eyes were closed because she was crying.

"Aww, Gwynnie, it's okay," Rice said. "It's going to be okay."

He picked up the folded paper towel again and blotted the tears on his daughter's cheeks. It was such a wrenching moment. I felt as though a scream were building in my chest. At that moment the Shrike changed from the abstract subject of a story to a flesh-and-blood villain I wanted to find. I wanted to break his neck but let him live the way this woman now had to live because of him.

"Gwyneth, I need to ask you one last thing," Rachel said. "To look at a picture—a composite sketch put together with the help of the people in the bar with you that night. I want you to tell me if it looks like the man who did this to you."

She paused. Nothing appeared on the screen.

"Is that okay, Gwyneth?"

Another pause, then:

SHOW ME

Rachel took her phone from her back pocket and opened the photo app. She pulled up the composite and held the phone a foot from Gwyneth's face. Gwyneth's eyes darted back and forth as she studied the photo of the drawing. Then her jaw started working.

YES

HIM

"The man in this composite looks like mid-thirties to me," Rachel said. "Is that what you remember?"

YES

Tears began to fall again down Gwyneth Rice's face. Her father moved in with the paper towel. Rachel stood up and stepped away, putting her phone back in her pocket.

"It's okay, Gwynnie. It's okay now," Rice consoled. "Everything's going to be all right, baby."

Rachel looked at me and then back to the bed. In that moment I saw the distress in her eyes and knew this was not any clinical interview for her either.

"Thank you, Gwyneth," she said. "You have been a wonderful help. We are going to get this man and I will come back to tell you."

After Rice stepped out of the way, Rachel returned to her position next to the bed and looked down at Gwyneth. They had bonded. Rachel reached a hand to Gwyneth's face and lightly touched her cheek.

"I promise you," she said. "We will get him."

Gwyneth's jaw went to work and she repeated the same message she had sent at the beginning of the conversation.

DON'T TAKE HIM ALIVE

36

We didn't talk until we were out of the building and walking toward the parking lot. It was dark out now.

I had seen Rachel's blue BMW when I had pulled in and parked next to it. We stopped behind our cars.

"That was intense," Rachel said.

"Yeah," I said.

"How was the dad out in the hallway?"

"Ugh. I never know what to say in that sort of situation."

"I had to do that, Jack. Get him out of the room. I wanted her to speak freely because it's important we know the details. We can assume that what happened to her happened to the other victims who we can't talk to. Gwyneth provides the template."

"And what is the template?"

"Well, for one thing. There was no rape. She invited him back to her apartment, ostensibly to show him the place for comparison since he was supposedly looking for a place to live. They had consensual sex—he used a condom—but not to completion. He couldn't keep an erection. He pulled out and that's when the nightmare began. He forced her up from the bed to stand naked in front of the bathroom mirror. He made her look at herself as he twisted her neck in a forearm lock."

"Oh, shit."

"He was naked too and she felt his erection come back against her back as he thought he was killing her."

"Fucker gets off on the act of killing them."

"All serials do. But the fact that there was no rape is important. It lends itself to why he is targeting women with the DRD4 gene. He thinks it gives him an edge in getting his victims into bed. There seems to be a psychological play in that. He doesn't want to be a rapist. Doesn't like what that says about him."

"But killing women is okay, just not raping them first."

"It's weird but not unique. Have you heard of Sam Little?"

"Yeah, the FBI's top serial."

"Caught here in L.A. and good for as many as ninety murders of women across the country. He only started confessing to the murders once the investigators stopped calling him a rapist— which in his case he was. He was okay with admitting to killing women but would never admit to a single rape."

"Weird stuff."

"But like I said, not unique. If this is part of our profile, it could be useful to strategically put something in your story or the press releases that follow to motivate the offender."

"You mean like have him come after me or Emily or *FairWarning*?"

"I was thinking more about him making contact with you. There are plenty of examples of serials reaching out to the media to sort of correct the record. But we would take safety precautions just the same."

"Well, I would have to think about that, talk to Emily and Myron for sure."

"Of course. We wouldn't do anything without everybody being on board. It's just something to think about at this stage."

I nodded.

"What else did you learn from this?" I asked. "Anything that struck you as a profiler?"

"Well, he obviously dressed her afterward," she said. "All the victims except for Portrero were dressed. All of them before Portrero were dressed and then dropped off in sometimes elaborate ways in an attempt to cover the murder. I would have to take a hard look at the other locations and where the women lived, but Portrero might show a change. He never removed her from her apartment."

"Maybe with the others the sex wasn't at their homes. They were where he was staying or in his car or something. So he had to distance them from him."

"Maybe, Jack. We'll make a profiler out of you yet."

Rachel pulled out her keys and unlocked her car.

"Now what?" I asked. "Where do you go from here? Back to the bureau?"

She pulled her phone to check the time on the screen.

"I'll call Metz—he's the agent heading this up—and tell him I talked to her and they can hold off in the morning. He probably won't be happy I jumped the gun but it will keep his people busy on the other stuff. After that, I think I'm going to call it a day. You?"

"Probably. I'll check in with Emily and see if she's still writing."

I hesitated before getting to the question I really wanted to ask.

"You coming to my place or going home?" I asked.

"You want me to come home with you, Jack?" Rachel asked. "You seem upset with me."

"I'm not upset. There are just a lot of things going on. I'm seeing this thing I started getting pulled by different people in different directions. So I get anxious."

"The story, you mean."

"Yeah, and we have that disagreement: whether to publish or wait."

"Well, the good thing is we don't have to decide that until tomorrow morning, right?"

"Right."

"So I'll see you at your place."

"Okay. Good. You should follow me so that you can get into the garage and use my second parking spot."

"You're giving me your second parking spot? Are you sure you're ready for such an important step?"

She smiled and I smiled in return.

"Hey, I'll give you a remote and a key if you want them," I said.

The ball back in her court, she nodded.

"I'll be right behind you," she said.

She moved toward the door of her car, taking her phone out of her back pocket so she could call Agent Metz. It reminded me of something.

"Hey," I said. "I couldn't see the composite when you showed it to Gwyneth. Let me see."

She walked over to me, opening the photo app on the phone. She held the screen up to me. It was a black-and-white sketch of a white man with dark bushy hair and piercing dark eyes. His jaw was square and his nose was flat and wide. His ears did not extend far from the sides of his head. The top of each ear disappeared into the hairline.

I realized he looked familiar to me.

"Wait a minute," I said.

I reached up and held Rachel's hand so she would not take the phone away.

"What?" she said.

"I think I know this guy," I said. "I mean, I think I've seen him."

"Where?"

"I don't know. But the hair…and the set of the jaw…"

"Are you sure?"

"No. I just…"

My mind raced back over my activities in recent days. I concentrated on the hours I had spent in jail. Had I seen this man in Men's Central? It was a night of intense fear and emotions. I had such clarity about what and who I had seen but I could not place the man in the drawing.

I let go of Rachel's hand.

"I don't know, I'm probably wrong," I said. "Let's go."

I turned and walked to my Jeep while Rachel got in her Beemer. I started the engine and turned to look through the passenger window to give Rachel the nod to back out first. It was then that I realized where I had seen the composite man.

I killed the engine and jumped out of the Jeep. Rachel had already backed halfway out of her spot. She stopped and lowered the window.

"What is it?" she asked.

"I know where I saw him," I said. "The guy in the composite. He was sitting in a car today at the coroner's office."

"You're sure?"

"I know it sounds far-fetched but the shape of his jaw and the pinned-back ears. I'm sure, Rachel. I mean, I guess I'm pretty sure. I thought he was there waiting for somebody inside. You know, like a family member or something. But now…I think he was following me."

That conclusion made me suddenly turn and scan the parking lot I stood in. There were only about ten cars and the lighting was poor. I would need a flashlight to determine if anyone was in one of them and watching.

Rachel put her car into park and got out.

"What kind of car was it, do you remember?"

"Uh, no, I have to think. It was dark and he had backed into his space like me. Another sign he could have been following me."

Rachel nodded.

"The quick exit," she said. "Was the car big or small?"

"I think small," I said.

"Sedan?"

"No, more like a sports car. Sleek."

"How close was he parked to you?"

"He was like across the aisle and down a couple. He had a good view of me. Tesla—it was a black Tesla."

"Good, Jack. Do you think that lot has cameras?"

"Maybe, I don't know. But if it *was* him, how would he know to follow me?"

"Hammond. Maybe they knew about you. Hammond warned the Shrike and the Shrike started eliminating threats. You are a threat, Jack."

I broke away from her and started walking down the two-row parking lot, looking for a Tesla or any car with someone sitting behind the wheel. I found nothing.

Rachel caught up to me.

"He's not here," I said. "Maybe I'm totally wrong about this. I mean, we're talking about a composite. It could be anybody."

"Yes, but you saw Gwyneth's reaction," Rachel said. "I don't usually put much stock in composites, but she thought it was dead on. Where did you go after the coroner's office?"

"Back to the office to feed everything I had to Emily."

"So he knows where *FairWarning* is. I didn't pay attention when I was there, but could he have had any sort of angle of view from the outside?"

"I think so, yes. The front door's glass."

"What could you see from the outside, looking in? Could he have seen you working with Emily?"

I thought about the times I had gotten up and gone to Emily's cubicle to confer with her. I pulled my phone.

"Shit," I said. "She should know about this."

There was no answer on Emily's cell. I next called her desk line, though I assumed she would not still be at the office.

"No answer on either of her phones," I reported.

My concern was now tipping toward fear. I could see the same apprehension in Rachel's eyes. All of it was amped up by the interview with Gwyneth Rice.

"Do you know where she lives?" Rachel asked.

I called Emily's cell again.

"I know it's Highland Park," I said. "But I don't have the exact address."

"We need to get it," Rachel said.

No answer. I disconnected and called Myron Levin's cell. He answered right away.

"Jack?"

"Myron, I'm trying to check on Emily and she's not answering her phones. Do you have her address?"

"Well, yeah, but what's going on?"

I told him of the suspicion shared by Rachel and me that I had been followed earlier in the day by the killer at the center of the story we were writing. My concern immediately transferred to Myron and he put me on hold while he searched for Emily's address.

I turned to Rachel.

"He's getting it," I said. "Let's start driving. Highland Park."

I walked to the passenger side of her car as she took the driver's seat. We were out of the parking lot by the time Myron came back on the line and read off an address.

"Call me as soon as you know something," Myron said.

"Will do," I said.

I then suddenly thought about Myron and the times Emily and I had conferred with him at the office.

"Are you home, Myron?" I asked.

"Yeah, I'm here," he said.

"Lock the doors."

"Yeah, I was just thinking that."

37

I entered the address Myron had given me into my GPS app and
muted the command voice. I gave Rachel verbal directions because the incessant commands from the app were always
annoying. The app showed we were sixteen minutes away. We
made it in twelve. Emily lived in an old brick-and-plaster apartment building on Piedmont Avenue off Figueroa Street. There
was a glass entry door with a keypad to the left with individual
buttons for eight apartments. When repeated pops on unit 8 did
not receive a response, I hit all seven other buttons.

"Come on, come on," I urged. "Somebody's gotta be waiting
for Postmates. Answer the damn door."

Rachel turned and checked the street behind her.

"Do you know what she drives?"

"A Jag but I saw a parking lane leading to the back. She
probably has a space back there."

"Maybe I should go—"

The electronic lock snapped open and we went in. I never
looked at which unit had responded and finally opened the door,
but I knew if we had gained entrance so easily then the Shrike
could have as well.

Unit 8 was on the second floor at the end of the hallway.

No one answered my heavy knocking and calling out of Emily's name. I tried the door but it was locked. I stepped back in frustration, a dread growing in me.

"What do we do?" I asked.

"Call her again," Rachel said. "Maybe we hear the phone through the door."

I walked down the hall twenty feet and called. When I heard the phone start ringing on my end, I nodded to Rachel. She leaned an ear toward the doorjamb of apartment 8, her eyes still on me. The call went to message and I disconnected. Rachel shook her head. She had heard nothing.

I walked back to Rachel and the door.

"Should we call the cops?" I asked. "Tell them we need a wellness check? Or call the landlord?"

"Looks like it's off-site management here," Rachel said. "I saw a number on an apartment-for-rent sign out front. I'll go get it and call. See if that leads to the back lot and if her car is here."

She pointed to an exit door at the end of the hallway.

"Don't get locked out," I said.

"I won't," she said.

I watched her go and then disappear down the stairs. I walked down to the exit door, wondering if an alarm would sound. I hesitated for a moment, then pushed the bar and the door swung open. No alarm sounded.

Stepping out onto an exterior landing, I saw that the stairway led down to the building's small rear parking lot. There was a mop in a bucket on the landing and a can half full of cigarette butts. Someone in the building smoked but not in their unit. I stepped farther out to look over the railing to see what was on the bottom landing. There were some empty plant pots and garden tools.

The door closed behind me. I whipped around. On the outside of the door there was a steel handle. I grabbed it and tried to turn it. I was locked out.

"Shit."

I knocked on the door but knew it was too soon to expect Rachel to be back at unit 8. I went down the stairs to the parking lot and looked around for Emily's car. It was a silver Jaguar SUV but I didn't see one. I then followed the access drive to the front. As I walked down the drive I looked up at the second-floor windows of the building to see if there were any lights on in the windows of the apartment I judged was Emily's. They were all dark.

When I got to the front of the building there was no sign of Rachel. I pulled my phone and called her but was distracted by motion in the street. I saw a car moving behind the parked cars lining Piedmont. I got only a quick glimpse of it as it passed an opening for the next driveway down.

"Jack? Where are you?"

Rachel had answered.

"I'm out front and I just saw a car drive away. It was silent."

"A Tesla?"

"I don't know. Maybe."

"Okay, I'm not waiting for this guy."

"What guy?"

"The landlord."

I heard a loud bang and a splintering of wood followed by a muffled bang. I knew she had just kicked in the door of unit 8. I moved to the front door of the building but could see it was closed.

"Rachel? Rachel, I can't get in. I'm going around—"

"I can buzz you in," she said. "Go to the front door."

I ran up the steps to the front door. The lock was buzzing when I got there and I was in.

I went up the interior stairs to the second floor and then down to apartment 8. Rachel was standing in the apartment's entranceway.

"Is she…?"

"She's not here."

I noticed that a piece of the door's wood trim was lying on the floor of the threshold. But as I fully entered the apartment, that was the only sign of disarray. I had never been there before but I saw a place that was neat and orderly. There was no sign of any sort of struggle having occurred in the living areas. A short hallway to the right led to the open door of a bathroom and a second door to the left that I assumed was the bedroom.

I walked that way, feeling odd about invading Emily's privacy.

"It's empty," Rachel said.

I checked anyway, standing on the threshold of the bedroom and leaning in. I hit a switch on the interior wall and two lamps on either side of a queen bed went on. Like the rest of the apartment, the room was neat; the bed was made and the coverlet was smoothed and had not even been sat on.

I next checked the bathroom and slapped back a plastic shower curtain to reveal an empty bathtub.

"Jack, I told you, she's not here," Rachel said. "Come out here and tell me about the car."

I stepped back into the living room.

"It drove up Piedmont," I said. "If I hadn't seen it, I would've missed it. It was a dark color and silent."

"Was it the Tesla you saw at the coroner's?" she asked.

"I don't know. I didn't get a good look."

"Okay, think now. Could you tell if it had just pulled away from the curb or was passing by?"

I took a moment and ran it through my mind again. The car was already moving down the street when it had drawn my attention.

"I couldn't tell," I said. "I didn't see it until it was already moving down the street."

"Okay, I've never been in a Tesla," Rachel said. "Do they have a trunk?"

"I think the newer ones do."

I realized she was asking whether Emily could be in the trunk of the car I saw driving away.

"Shit—we need to go after it," I said.

"It's long gone, Jack," Rachel said. "We need to—"

"What the fuck is this?"

We both turned to the front door of the apartment.

Emily stood there.

She was in the clothes I had seen her wearing at the office earlier. She carried her backpack with the *FairWarning* logo on it.

"You're okay," I blurted out.

"Why wouldn't I be?" she said. "You broke down my door?"

"We thought the Shrike had...had been here," I said.

"What?" Emily said.

"Why haven't you answered your phone?" Rachel asked.

"Because it's dead," Emily said. "I was on it all day."

"Where were you?" I asked. "I called the office."

"The Greyhound," she said.

I knew she hated to drive because she grew up driving on the other side of the road and feared making the transition. But I was confused and must have looked like it. Greyhound was for long-distance travel.

"It's a pub over on Fig," Emily said. "My local. What the hell is going on?"

"I don't know," I said. "I think I was being followed today and when—"

"By the Shrike?"

I suddenly didn't feel as sure about things.

"I don't know," I said. "Maybe. There was a guy in a Tesla I saw at the coroner's office and I—"

"How would he know to follow you?" Emily asked. "Or me, for that matter."

"Probably Hammond," I said. "He either told him or there was something in the computer or the documents taken from Hammond's lab."

I saw fear enter Emily's eyes.

"What do we do?" she said meekly.

"Look, I think we should calm down a little bit here," Rachel said. "Let's not get paranoid. We still don't know for sure that either Jack or you was being followed. And if Jack was followed, why would he jump from Jack to you?"

"Maybe because I'm a woman?" Emily said.

I was about to respond. Rachel might be right. All of this was because I thought I had matched a composite drawing to a face I had seen behind the wheel of a car in a parking lot from at least eighty feet away. It was a stretch.

"Okay," I said. "Why don't we—"

I stopped short when a man appeared in the doorway. He had a full beard and a ring of keys in his hand.

"Mr. Williams?" Rachel asked.

The man stared down at the piece of door framing on the floor, then checked the strike plate hanging by a single loose screw on the jamb.

"I thought you were going to wait for me," he said.

"I'm sorry," Rachel said. "We thought there was an emergency. Will you be able to secure the door tonight?"

Williams turned and saw that when the door had been kicked open it had swung against the side wall of Emily's entryway. The knob had put a fist-sized dent in the wall.

"I can try," he said.

"I'm not staying here if I can't lock the door," Emily said. "No way. Not if he knows where I live."

"We don't know that for sure," I said. "We saw a car driving away but—"

"Look, why don't we let Mr. Williams try to fix it and we go somewhere else to talk about this?" Rachel said. "I got more from the FBI today. I think you'll want to know it."

I looked at Rachel.

"Well, when were you going to tell me?" I asked.

"We got sidetracked when we were leaving Gwyneth Rice," Rachel said.

She pointed to the door that Williams was still examining as though that explained her delay.

"By the way, how was Gwyneth Rice?" Emily asked.

"Good stuff...but so fucking sad," I said. "He's messed her up for life."

Halfway through my answer I was afflicted with reporter's guilt. I knew that Gwyneth Rice would become the face of the story. A victim who would likely never recover, whose life path had been violently and permanently altered by the Shrike. We would use her to draw readers in, never mind that her heartbreaking injuries would last well beyond the life of the story.

"You have to ship me notes," Emily said.

"As soon as I can," I said.

"So what are we doing?" Rachel asked.

"We could go back to the Greyhound," Emily said. "It was pretty quiet in there when I left."

"Let's go," Rachel said.

We moved toward the door and Williams turned sideways so we could fit by. He looked at me.

"You kicked in the door?" he asked.

"Uh, that would be me," Rachel said.

Williams did a quick up-and-down appraisal of Rachel as she went by him.

"Strong lady," he said.

"When I need to be," she said.

38

The Greyhound was less than two minutes away and Rachel drove all three of us. I sat in the back seat, looking out the rear window for a possible tail the whole way. If the Shrike was following I saw no sign of him and my thoughts returned to the question of whether I was being vigilant or paranoid. I kept thinking about the man in the Tesla. Had I simply wanted him to look like the face on the composite or did he really look like the face on the composite?

I had never been to England but the inside of the Greyhound looked like an English pub to me, and I saw why Emily had adopted it as her local. It was all dark woods and cozy booths. A bar ran the entire length of the establishment, front to back, and there was no table service. Rachel and I ordered Ketel martinis and Emily asked them to pull the tap on a Deschutes IPA. I waited at the bar for the drinks while the women grabbed a booth in the back corner.

I took two trips to deliver the drinks so as not to spill the martinis and then settled into the U-shaped booth with Emily across from me and Rachel to my right. I took a full sip of my martini before saying a word. I needed it after the ebb and flow of adrenaline the evening had so far produced.

"So," I said, looking at Rachel. "What have you got?"

Rachel took a steady-handed draw of her martini, put the glass down, and then composed herself.

"I spent most of the day at the FO in Westwood with the ASAC," she said. "I was treated as a leper at first, but when they started going through the checkable facts of the story I was telling, they started seeing the light."

"ASAC?" Emily asked.

She said it the way Rachel had—*A-sack*.

"Assistant special agent in charge of the L.A. Field Office," Rachel said.

"You said his name is Metz?" I asked.

"Matt Metz," Rachel said. "Anyway, I already told you that they've linked at least three other cases by cause of death and then Gwyneth Rice, the only known survivor."

"Were you able to get the new names?" I asked.

"No, that's what they're holding back to trade with you for pushing the story back," Rachel said. "I didn't get them."

"That's not going to happen," I insisted. "We're going to publish tomorrow. Putting out the warning about this guy is more important than any other consideration."

"You sure that the scoop is not the most important thing to you, Jack?" Rachel shot back.

"Look, we've been over this," I said. "It's not our job to help the FBI catch this guy. Our job is to inform the public."

"Well, you might change your mind when you hear what else I got," Rachel said.

"Then tell us," Emily said.

"Okay, I was dealing with this guy Metz who I knew from when I was an agent," Rachel said. "Once they legitimized what I brought them they started putting together a war room and attacking this from all angles. They found the other cases and one team was working on that. There's also a case in Santa Fe where they're going to do an exhumation of the body tomorrow because they think AOD might have been missed at autopsy."

"How could they miss a broken neck?" I asked.

"Condition of the body," Rachel said. "I didn't get the exact details but it was left out in the mountains and animals got to it. AOD may not have been seen for what it was. Anyway, another team was looking at Hammond and the Dirty4 angle, trying to pull all of that together."

Rachel broke off there to take another sip of her martini.

"And?" Emily prompted.

"Through the site, they IDed Hammond's partner," Rachel said. "At least they think they did."

I leaned in over the table. This was getting good.

"Who is he?" I asked.

"His name is Roger Vogel," Rachel said. "Get it? *Roger Vogel* becomes *RogueVogue* in the digital universe?"

"Got it," I said. "How did they find him?"

"I think his fingerprints—digital, that is—are all over the site," she said. "They brought in a cipher team and I don't think it was that hard. I didn't get all the details but they were able to trace him to a stationary IP address. That was his mistake. He did some maintenance of the site from an unmasked computer. Got lazy and now they know who he is."

"So, what is the location?" I said. "Where is he?"

"Cedars-Sinai," Rachel said. "It looks like the guy works in Administration. That's the location of the computer he used."

At first I felt a jolt of excitement at the prospect of confronting Vogel before the FBI grabbed him. But then the reality hit me: Cedars-Sinai Medical Center was a massive, high-security complex that covered five entire blocks in Beverly Hills. It might be impossible to get to him.

"Are they picking him up?" I asked.

"Not yet," Rachel said. "They're thinking that having him loose might work to their advantage."

"As bait for the Shrike," Emily said.

"Exactly," Rachel said. "It's clear he wanted to take Vogel out and made a mistake with the guy up in Northridge. So he may try again."

"So," I said, thinking out loud. "If the bureau is watching this guy, there is nothing to stop us from going in there and confronting him. Have they traced him to his home or other locations?"

"No," Rachel said. "Thanks to you giving Vogel the warning about the Shrike, he's taking all precautions. They had a loose tail on him and lost him after he left work."

"That's not good," Emily said.

"But here's the thing," Rachel said. "He's a smoker. He is taking precautions but he still has to go outside to smoke. I saw surveillance photos of him at a smoker's bench outside the building. There was a street sign in the background. It said *George Burns Road*. That goes right through the middle of the complex."

I looked across the table at Emily. We both knew exactly what we were going to do.

"We're going to be there tomorrow," I said. "We'll get him when he comes out to smoke."

Emily turned to Rachel.

"Would you recognize this guy off the surveillance photo you saw?" she asked. "If you saw him at the bench, I mean?"

"I think so," Rachel said. "Yes."

"Okay," I said. "Then we'll need you to be there too."

"If I do that, it will burn me with the bureau," Rachel said. "I'll be like you two, on the outside looking in."

"Okay, we'll have to figure out a plan for that," I said.

I grabbed my glass and finished off my drink. We had the rough outlines of a plan and I was good to go.

39

The Cedars-Sinai Medical Center was a cluster of tall glass buildings and parking garages crowded together on a five-block parcel but still segregated by the grid of city streets passing through those blocks. At the office that morning we used the Streetview feature of Google Maps to locate the smoker's bench Rachel had seen in the FBI surveillance photo. It was at the corner of Alden Drive and George Burns Road, an intersection almost dead center in the medical complex. It was apparently centrally located to serve patients, visitors, and employees from all buildings in the complex. It consisted of two benches facing each other across a fountain in a landscaped strip that ran alongside an eight-story parking garage. There were pedestal ashtrays at the ends of each of the benches. We finalized a plan and headed there from the office at 8 a.m.—hoping to be in place before Roger Vogel would go out for his first smoking break.

We watched the smoking benches from two angles. Emily and I were in the nearby ER waiting room, where the windows gave us a full-on ground-level view of the benches, but no view of the Administration Building. Rachel was on the third level of the parking garage because it gave a commanding view of the benches plus the entrance of the Administration Building. She would be able to alert us when Vogel emerged and headed to the benches to smoke. Her position also kept her out of the view of the FBI. Using the angles she remembered from the surveillance photo she had seen the day before, she had pinpointed the FBI observation post in a medical office building across the street from Administration.

Emily Atwater was a lapsed smoker, meaning she had cut back from a pack-a-day habit to a pack-a-week dalliance, and primarily indulged herself during off-work hours. I remembered the ash can outside the second-floor exit at her apartment building.

At regular intervals she went out to the benches to smoke a cigarette, hoping that she would be in place when Vogel showed up to indulge his own habit. I had not smoked since I had moved to California but I had a prop pack of cigarettes in my shirt pocket as well, with the intention of going to the benches and using them when Vogel finally appeared.

The morning passed slowly with no sighting of Vogel. Meanwhile, the benches were a popular spot for other employees, visitors, and patients alike—one patient even walked her mobile IV pole and drip bag out to the spot for a smoke. I kept a steady text chain going with Rachel and included Emily when she was at one of the benches. That was where she was at 10:45 when I sent out a group missive suggesting we were wasting our time. I said Vogel had probably been spooked by the conversation I'd had with him the day before and blown town.

After sending it, I got distracted by a man who had entered the ER with blood on his face and demanded to be attended to immediately. He threw a clipboard he had been handed onto the floor and yelled that he had no insurance but needed help. A security guard was moving toward him when I heard my text chime go off and pulled my phone. The text was from Rachel.

He just walked out of administration, cigarettes in hand.

The text had gone to both Emily and me. I checked on Emily through the window and saw her sitting on one of the benches looking at her phone. She had gotten the alert. I headed out through the automatic doors and toward the smoking benches.

As I approached I saw a man standing by the benches. Emily was on one bench smoking and another woman was on the other. Vogel, if it was Vogel, was apparently intimidated about sharing one of the benches with the women. This was problematic. I didn't want him standing when we identified ourselves as journalists. It would be easier for him to walk away from us. I saw him light a cigarette with a flip lighter. I started to remove the prop pack of smokes from my shirt pocket. I saw Emily pretending to read a text but I knew she was opening her phone's recording app.

Just as I got there the interloping smoker stubbed out her cigarette in the ashtray and left the butt behind. She got up and walked back toward the ER. I saw Vogel take her place on the empty bench. Our plan was going to work out.

As far as I could tell, Vogel never looked at Emily or acknowledged her in any way. When I got to the spot I put a cigarette in my mouth and then patted the pocket of my shirt as if looking for matches or a lighter. I found none and looked at Vogel.

"Can I borrow a light?" I asked.

He looked up and I gestured with my unlit cigarette. Without saying a word he reached into his pocket and handed me his lighter. I studied his face as he reached the lighter out to me. I saw a look of recognition.

"Thanks," I said quickly. "You're Vogel, right?"

Vogel looked around and then back at me.

"Yeah," he said. "Are you in Admin?"

Identity confirmed. We had the right guy. I threw a quick glance at Emily and saw that her phone had been put down on her bench and angled toward Vogel. We were recording.

"No, wait a minute," Vogel said. "You're…you're the reporter."

Now I was surprised. How did he know?

"What?" I said. "What reporter?"

"I saw you in court," he said. "It's you. We talked yesterday. How the hell did you — ? Are you trying to get me killed?"

He threw his cigarette down and jumped up from the bench. He started to head back toward the Administration Building. I raised my hands as if to stop him.

"Wait a minute, wait a minute. I just want to talk."

Vogel hesitated.

"About what?"

"You said you know who the Shrike is. We need to stop him. You — "

He pushed by me.

"You need to talk to us," Emily called.

Vogel's eyes darted toward her as he realized she was with me and he was being tag-teamed.

"Help us catch him," I said. "And then you'll be safe too."

"We're your best chance," Emily said. "Talk to us. We can help you."

We had rehearsed what we would say on the ride over from the office. But the script, as it was, did not go much further than what we had just said. Vogel kept walking, yelling back at us as he went.

"I told you, none of this was supposed to happen. I'm not responsible for what that crazy person is doing. Just back the fuck off."

He started to cross George Burns Road.

"You just wanted the women to be fucked over, not killed, right?" Emily called. "Very noble of you."

She was standing now. Vogel pirouetted and strode back to us. He bent slightly to get right into Emily's face. I moved in closer in case he made a further move toward her.

"What we did was no different from any dating service out there," he said. "We matched people with what they were looking for. Supply and demand. That's it."

"Except the women didn't know they were part of that equation," Emily pressed. "Did they?"

"That didn't matter," Vogel said. "They're all whores anyway and—"

He stopped as his eyes found the cell phone Emily held up in front of her body.

"You're recording this?" he shrieked.

He turned to me.

"I told you, I want no part of this story," he yelled. "You can't use my name."

"But you are the story," I said. "You and Hammond and what you're responsible for."

"No!" Vogel cried. "This bullshit is going to get me killed."

He turned again toward the street and headed to the crosswalk.

"Wait, you want your lighter?" I called after him.

I held it up in my hand. He turned back to me but didn't slow down as he stepped into the street.

"Keep—"

Before he could say the next word, a car swooshed by and

caught him in the crosswalk. It was a black Tesla with windows tinted so dark it could have been driverless and I would not have been able to tell.

The force of the collision at the knees threw Vogel forward into the intersection and then I saw his body swallowed by the silent car as it ran over him. The Tesla bounced as it went over Vogel. His body was then dragged underneath it into the middle of the intersection before the car could finally break free of it.

I heard Emily scream behind me but there was no sound from Vogel. He was as silent as the car that took him under.

Once free of the body, the Tesla hit top takeoff speed and screamed across the intersection and down George Burns Road to Third Street. I saw the car turn left on a yellow light and disappear.

Several people ran to the crumpled and bloodied body in the intersection. It was, after all, a medical center. Two men in seafoam-green scrubs were the first to get to Vogel and I saw that one was physically repelled by what he saw. There were drag marks in blood on the street.

I checked on Emily, who was standing next to the bench she had occupied, her hand to her throat as she gazed in horror at the activity in the intersection. I then turned and joined the scrum that was gathering around Roger Vogel's unmoving body. I looked over the shoulder of one of the men in scrubs and saw that half of Vogel's face was missing. It had literally disintegrated while he had been dragged facedown under the car. Vogel's head was also misshapen and I was sure that his skull had been crushed.

"Is he alive?" I asked.

No one answered. I saw that one of the men had a cell phone up to his ear and was making a call.

"This is Dr. Bernstein," he said calmly. "I need a rescue ambulance to the intersection right outside the ER. Alden and George Burns. Somebody got hit by a car out here. We have major head and neck trauma. We'll need a backboard to move him. And we need it now."

I became aware of the sound of sirens nearby but still outside the medical complex. I hoped that those were FBI sirens and they were descending on the Shrike, running him to ground in his silent killing machine.

My cell phone buzzed and it was Rachel.

"Jack, is he dead?"

I turned and looked up at the garage. I saw her standing at the third-floor balustrade, cell phone to her ear.

"They're saying he's still alive," I asked. "What the fuck happened?"

"It was a Tesla. It was the Shrike."

"Where's the FBI? I thought they were watching this guy!"

"I don't know. They were."

"Did you get a plate?"

"No, it was too fast, unexpected. I'm coming down."

She disconnected and I put my phone away. I leaned back over the men trying to help Vogel.

I then heard Dr. Bernstein speak to the other man in scrubs.

"He's gone. I'm calling it. Ten fifty-eight. I'll call off the truck. We need to leave him here for the police."

Bernstein pulled his phone again. And I saw Rachel heading toward me. She was talking on her phone. She disconnected when she got to me.

"That was Metz," she said. "He got away."

THE SHRIKE

40

He knew it was more than likely an FBI trap but he also knew they would not be prepared for his move. They would refer to the profiles and programs they relied on like religion when it came to understanding and catching men like him. They would expect him to do what he had done before: follow his quarry and attack with stealth. And that was their mistake. Using his phone, he had watched the two reporters on the hospital's own security cameras, and knew they were staking out some kind of rendezvous spot. When he was sure they had identified the target for him, he moved quickly and boldly. Now he was gone like a blur and he was sure they were scrambling in his wake.

But they were too late.

He was pleased with himself. The last connection between him and the site and the list was surely dead and now it was time for him to fly south for the winter, maybe change plumage and prepare.

He would then come back to finish things when it was least expected.

He drove the Tesla up the ramp and into the parking garage of the Beverly Center. He drove all the way up to the fourth level. There were not many cars up here and he suspected that the mall tended to be more crowded in the later hours of the day. He parked at the southeast corner. Through the decorative steel grating that encased the structure he could see down to La Cienega Boulevard. He saw flashing lights on unmarked cars moving in the traffic. He knew the cars belonged to the feds he had just outwitted and embarrassed. Fuck them. They were searching blind and would never find him.

Soon he heard a helicopter overhead as well. Good luck with that. And good luck to the owner of every black Tesla that was about to get pulled over by feds with their guns out and anger in their eyes.

He checked himself in the rearview mirror. He had shaved his head the night before—in case they had managed to get a physical description of him. His scalp had been startling white when he was finished and he had to rub bronzer from CVS over it. It had stained his pillow while he slept but it did the trick. It now looked like he had kept the look for years. He liked it and found himself checking his look in the mirror all morning.

He lowered the windows about an inch to let air come in, then killed the engine and opened the door. Before getting out he took out a matchbook and a pack of cigarettes. He lit a cigarette with a match and drew in deeply, watching the tip glow hot in the rearview. He coughed as the smoke invaded his lungs. That always happened. He then folded the matchbook around the middle of the cigarette and put the improvised fire starter down on the center console. He adjusted it so the cigarette was tilted slightly downward and would continue to burn up toward the matches. With any luck the matches wouldn't be necessary and the cigarette would do the job.

He got out of the car, closed the driver's door, and quickly moved to the front of the car. He checked the front bumper and the plastic skirt below it to see if there was any blood or debris. He saw nothing and bent down to check beneath. He saw blood dripping onto the concrete like oil from the engine of a gas-powered car.

He smiled. He thought that was ironic.

He moved back to the side of the car and opened the rear passenger door. There was the natural-gas canister he had removed from Hammond's poolside barbecue on the back seat. He had cut the rubber-hose attachment three inches from the coupling and then bled off most of the contents. He did not want a large explosion. Just enough to do what was needed.

Now as he opened the valve he heard the hiss of the remaining gas escaping into the car. He stepped back, peeled off his gloves, and threw them into the car. The Tesla had served him well. He would miss it.

He closed the car door with his elbow and started walking toward the escalator that would take him down to the street.

On the second escalator down, he heard the unmistakable *thump* of the explosion ignite inside the Tesla. Not enough to blow out the windows but good enough to engulf the inside of the car and burn away every trace of its final user.

He was confident they would never know who he was. The car had been stolen in Miami and the current plates on it were from a duplicate Tesla in the long-term parking lot at LAX. They might have a picture of him but they would never know his name. He had taken too many precautions.

He opened the Uber app on his phone and ordered a pickup

on the La Cienega side of the mall. In the destination prompt he typed:

LAX

The app told him his driver Ahmet was on his way and that he would be at the airport in fifty-five minutes.

That was time enough to decide where to go.

THE FIRST STORY

FBI: "DNA Killer" on the Loose
By Emily Atwater and Jack McEvoy

The FBI and Los Angeles Police have begun an urgent hunt for a man suspected of killing at least 10 people in a cross-country murder spree that included breaking the necks of eight young women.

The killer, who is known as the Shrike on the Internet, targeted the women based on specific profiles from DNA they had provided to a popular genetic-analytics site. The victims' genetic profiles were downloaded by the unidentified suspect from a site on the dark web that catered to a clientele of men seeking to take sexual advantage of women.

The FBI has scheduled a major news conference tomorrow in Los Angeles to discuss the investigation.

This week the two operators of the site—which was closed down by the FBI today—were murdered by the suspect, authorities said. Marshall Hammond, 31, was found hanged in his Glendale home, where he operated a DNA lab. Roger Vogel, 31, was mowed down in the street in a hit-and-run just seconds after being confronted by reporters from *FairWarning*. A third man was also killed by the suspect earlier when authorities believe he was mistaken for Vogel.

Prior to the killing of the three men, seven women in places stretching from Fort Lauderdale to Santa Barbara were brutally murdered by a suspect who used a signature method of breaking the necks of his victims. An eighth woman survived a similar attack but was rendered quadriplegic by her injuries. The 29-year-old Pasadena woman, whom *FairWarning* is not identifying, helped provide investigators with links connecting all of the cases.

"This is one of the most vicious serial offenders we have ever encountered," said Matthew Metz, Assistant Special Agent in Charge of the FBI's Los Angeles Field Office. "We are doing all we can to identify him and run him to ground. No one is safe until we get him."

The bureau released a composite sketch of the suspect as well as a shadowy video of a man believed to be him and taken from a home-surveillance camera in Marshall Hammond's neighborhood shortly after his murder.

The bureau missed a chance to apprehend the suspect yesterday when he eluded a surveillance that was placed on Roger Vogel, who worked in the administration offices at Cedars-Sinai Medical Center. *FairWarning* reporters confronted him at a smoker's bench outside the hospital, where he denied any responsibility for the deaths.

"None of this was supposed to happen," Vogel said. "I'm not responsible for what that crazy person is doing."

Vogel then stepped into a crosswalk at the intersection of Alden Drive and George Burns Road and was immediately hit by a car believed to be driven by the murder suspect. He was dragged under the car for 30 feet and sustained fatal injuries. The car was later located by the FBI in the nearby Beverly Center parking garage, where it had been set on fire in an attempt to destroy any evidence that could lead to the identity of the killer.

The Shrike came to light after the murder a week ago of Christina Portrero, 44, who was found in her home with a broken neck after last being seen with a man at a bar on the Sunset Strip.

FairWarning began an investigation of the death after learning that Portrero had supplied her DNA to GT23, the popular online genetic-analytics company, for hereditary analysis. She had also complained to friends that she had been stalked by a stranger who knew intimate personal details about her. That man is not believed to have been the Shrike but another customer of the same dark-web site where the Shrike selected his victims according to their DNA makeup.

GT23 openly states that selling anonymized DNA to second-tier labs helps it keep costs to consumers low. Customers pay only $23 for a DNA hereditary analysis.

Among the labs the company sells DNA to is Orange Nano, a research laboratory in Irvine operated by William Orton, formerly a biochemistry professor at UC-Irvine. According to Orange County authorities, Orton left his post three years ago to start Orange Nano when he was accused of drugging and raping a student.

Orton has vehemently denied the accusations. Hammond was a graduate of UC-Irvine and had been a student of Orton's. He later started a private research lab that received hundreds of samples of female DNA from Orange Nano after they were purchased from GT23.

The *FairWarning* investigation determined that Hammond and Vogel opened a site on the dark web called Dirty4 more than two years ago. Customers of the site paid access fees of $500 annually to download the identities and locations of women whose DNA contained a chromosome pattern known as DRD4, which some genetic researchers have concluded is indicative of risky behaviors including drug and sex addiction.

"They were selling these women out," a source close to the investigation said. "These creepy guys were paying for lists of women they thought they could get an edge with. They could go pretend to meet them in a bar or someplace and they would be easy marks. It is so sick, and no wonder you end up getting a killer in the mix."

The FBI said website records indicated that Dirty4 had several hundred paying members, many of whom were solicited in online forums catering to incels—men who designate themselves as "involuntarily celibate"—and other misogynist viewpoints.

"This is a horrible day," said Andrea McKay, a Harvard University law professor and recognized expert on ethics in genetic fields. "We have reached the point where the predators now can custom-order their victims."

The DNA passed on by GT23 was anonymized, but authorities believe that Roger Vogel, a skilled hacker who used the name RogueVogue online, infiltrated the company's computers and was able to retrieve the identities of the women whose DNA was sold to Hammond by Orange Nano.

One of the Dirty4 users was the Shrike. The FBI believes he used access to the profiles provided on the site to target victims in his murder spree. Agents have identified 11 victims, including the Pasadena woman who survived her attack, and believe there may be more. An exhumation in Santa Fe was scheduled for today and could lead to the determination of a twelfth victim.

The connection between the female victims is the cause of death or injury. Each of the women suffered a devastating neck break called atlanto-occipital dislocation. Medical examiners refer to this as internal decapitation—a complete break of the neck bones and spinal cord—that occurs when the head is violently twisted more than 90 degrees past normal limits.

"This guy is strong," the FBI's Metz said. "We think he literally breaks their necks with his bare hands or in an armlock maneuver of some kind. It is a horrible and painful way to die."

The Shrike takes his online name from a bird that is known as one of nature's most brutal killers. The bird silently stalks its prey—field mice and other small animals—and attacks from behind, gripping its victim in its beak and viciously breaking its neck.

The killings and the investigation are sure to impact the quickly growing and multibillion-dollar genetic-analytics industry. A *FairWarning* investigation determined that the industry, which falls under the control of the federal Food and Drug Administration, is virtually unregulated as the agency is in the midst of a long-running effort to promulgate rules and regulations for the industry. The strong indication that measures to protect the anonymity of DNA samples have been compromised is sure to send a shock wave through the industry.

"This is a game changer," said Jennifer Schwartz, a life-sciences professor at UCLA. "The whole industry is based on the principle of anonymity. If that is compromised then what do you have? A lot of scared people and a whole industry that could start to wobble."

The FBI shut down the Dirty4 website and is actively attempting to contact women whose identities were revealed and sold by Hammond and Vogel. Metz said that there are strong indications that the suspect has multiple profiles that he retrieved from Hammond's lab computer after killing him. He said that GT23 and Orange Nano are fully cooperating with that part of the investigation.

"That's the priority at this moment," Metz said. "We have to find this guy, of course, but we need to reach all of the unsuspecting women so we can warn and protect them."

Metz said it was unclear why Hammond and Vogel were

murdered but that it is likely the two men held the keys to identifying the Shrike.

"I think he got wind of the investigation and knew that the only two people who could help identify him were these guys," Metz said. "So they had to go, and they ended up with a dose of their own medicine. There is not a lot of sympathy around here for them, I'll tell you that."

Little is known about the relationship between Hammond and Vogel but it is clear that the two men met at UC-Irvine, where they were roommates. Students from that era say the two men may have crossed paths in an informal and unsanctioned group at the school that was involved in digital bullying of female students.

"It was a forerunner of these incel groups you are seeing today," said a school official who requested anonymity. "They did all kinds of things to female students: hacked their social media, spread lies and rumors. Some girls left school because of what they did to them. But they always hid their trail. No one could prove anything."

Incels are primarily men who identify themselves as involuntarily celibate and on Internet forums blame and disparage women for their romantic problems. In recent years there has been an uptick of crimes against women attributed to incels. The FBI has listed the groups as a growing concern.

The Dirty4 website appeared to be fueled by similar attitudes and sentiments, Metz said.

"These guys were women-haters and took it to an extreme limit," he said. "And now seven or eight women are dead and another will never walk again. It's horrible."

Meanwhile, authorities fear that the hit-and-run killing of Vogel yesterday may indicate that the Shrike is changing his methods, which could make him more difficult to track.

"He knows we are on to him and the best way to avoid the net closing in on him is to either stop the killing or change his routine," Metz said. "Unfortunately, this guy has a taste for killing and I don't see him stopping. We are doing our very best to identify him and take him down."

JACK

41

One hundred days after our first story was posted, the Shrike had still not been identified or captured. In the course of that time Emily Atwater and I wrote thirty-two more stories, staying with the investigation and running out in front of the rest of the media that descended like locusts after our first dispatch. Myron Levin negotiated an exclusive partnership with the *Los Angeles Times* and most of our stories were carried on the front page above the fold. We covered the expanding investigation and the confirmation of two other victims. We posted a full take on William Orton and the rape case he beat. We wrote a piece about Gwyneth Rice and later covered a fundraiser to help meet her medical expenses. We even wrote stories that captured the sickening online deification of the Shrike by incel groups who celebrated what he had done to his female victims.

Myron Levin's concern about losing half his staff came true, but for unexpected reasons. With the Shrike still out there somewhere, Emily grew too fearful that we would become his next targets. As the story started to lose oxygen because of the lack of developments, she decided to leave *FairWarning*. We had gotten offers for a book and a podcast. We decided she would take the book deal and I would record the podcast. She moved back to England to an obscure location that even I wasn't privy to. She maintained that it was better that way because the secrecy meant that I could not be forced to reveal her location to anyone. We communicated almost every day and I emailed her the raw reporting for the final stories she would write under our names.

The one-hundred-day mark of the story was also the end point for me at *FairWarning*. I had given notice and determined that whatever updates came about I could report on the podcast. It was a new form of journalism and I enjoyed going into a sound booth and telling, rather than writing, the story.

I called it *Murder Beat*.

Myron was not too upset about having to replace us. He now had a whole drawer full of résumés from journalists who wanted to work for him. The Shrike had put *FairWarning* into the public eye big-time. Newspapers, websites, and TV news programs across the world had to give us credit for breaking the story. I made guest appearances on CNN, *Good Morning America,* and *The View. 60 Minutes* followed our reporting, and the *Washington Post* profiled Emily and me and even likened our occasionally combative partnership to that of the greatest journalism tag team in history: Woodward and Bernstein.

Readership was also up at *FairWarning* and not just on the days we posted a Shrike story. One hundred days out, we were starting to see an uptick in donations, too. Myron wasn't on the phone so much cajoling potential supporters. All was well at *FairWarning*.

The last story Emily and I wrote was one of the more fulfilling of the thirty-two. It was about the arrest of William Orton for sexual assault. Our stories on Marshall Hammond and Roger Vogel had spurred authorities in Orange County to reopen the investigation of the allegations that Orton had drugged and raped his one-time student. They determined that Hammond had taken the DNA sample submitted by Orton to the sheriff's lab and replaced it with an unknown sample, thereby creating the finding of *No match* to the swabs in the rape kit. Under the new investigation, another sample was taken from Orton and compared to the material in the rape kit. It was a match and Orton was arrested and charged.

Most of the time, journalism is simply an exercise in reporting on situations and occurrences of public interest. It is rare that it leads to the toppling of a corrupt politician, a change in the law, or the arrest of a rapist. When that does happen, the satisfaction is beyond measure. Our stories on the Shrike got a warning out to the public and may have saved lives. They also put a rapist in jail. I was proud of what we had accomplished and proud to call myself a journalist in a time when the profession was constantly under attack.

After shaking Myron's hand and leaving the office for the last time, I went to the bar at Mistral to meet Rachel and celebrate the end of one chapter in my life and the start of another. That was the plan but it didn't work out that way. For one-hundred days I had carried a question inside that I could no longer contain.

Rachel was already at the bar, sitting at the far left end where it curved to the back wall and there were two seats we always tried to occupy. The spot gave us privacy and a view of the bar and the restaurant at the same time. There was a couple sitting in the center of the long side and a man by himself at the end opposite Rachel. As with most nights, business started slow and then picked up later on.

The French Impressionist was working this night. That was what Rachel had started privately calling Elle, the bartender with the phony French accent. I signaled her over, ordered a martini, and was soon clinking glasses with Rachel.

"To new things," Rachel said.

"*Sláinte,*" I said.

"Oh, so now we have an Irish poet to go with the French Impressionist?"

"Aye, a deadline poet. Formerly, I guess. Now a podcast poet."

My Irish accent wasn't cutting it, so I dropped it and drank half the martini. Liquid courage for the big question I had to ask.

"I think Myron might have had a tear in his eye when I said goodbye today," I said.

"Ah, I'll miss Myron," Rachel said.

"We'll see him again, and he agreed to come on the podcast to give updates on the Shrike stuff. It'll plug the website."

"That's good."

I finished my martini and Elle was quick with another. Rachel and I small-talked while I worked the level down on it. I noticed she had not re-upped her own drink and had even ordered a glass of water. She kept looking down the bar at the man sitting alone at the other end.

I had my elbows on the bar and now rubbed my hands together, pushing my fingers back. As my internal alcohol level was rising, my courage was dissipating. I was deciding to let my suspicion go for another night—like the ninety-nine before it.

"Are you having second thoughts?" Rachel asked.

"No, not at all," I said. "Why?"

"Observation: you're wringing your hands. And you just seem…I don't know. Pensive? Preoccupied? Off."

"Well…I have to ask you something I've been meaning to ask you for a while."

"Sure. What?"

"That night at the Greyhound when you were acting like a source and giving me and Emily all that stuff about Vogel and describing the surveillance photo you saw…"

"I wasn't acting. I was your source, Jack. What's your question?"

"That was a setup, wasn't it? You and the FBI—that guy Metz—you wanted us to lead the Shrike to Vogel. So you told us—"

"What are you talking about, Jack?"

"I've just gotta say it. It's what I've been thinking. Just tell me. I can handle it. It was probably your allegiance to the people who kicked you out. Was it some kind of a deal to get back in, or—"

"Jack, shut the fuck up before you once again ruin something good."

"Really, I'm the one who will ruin it? You did this thing with them and I'm the one who ruins everything? That makes—"

"I don't want to talk about this right now. And stop drinking."

"What are you talking about? I can drink. I can walk home if I've had too much, but I'm not even close to that now. I want you to tell me if that was a setup with you and the FBI."

"I told you, it wasn't. And listen, we have a problem here."

"I know. You should have told me. I would've—"

"No, I'm not talking about that. We have a problem right here."

Her voice had dropped to an urgent whisper.

"What are you talking about?" I asked.

"Just play along," she said.

She turned and kissed me on the cheek and then put an arm around my neck and nuzzled in close. Public displays of affection were a rarity with her. I knew something was up. She was either going to bizarre lengths to distract me from my question or there was something terribly wrong.

"That guy across the bar," she whispered in my ear. "Be casual about it."

I reached forward for my drink and took a glance down the bar to the man sitting by himself. Nothing about him had seemed suspicious to me. He had a cocktail glass in front of him that was half filled with ice and clear liquid. There was a slice of lime in the glass as well.

I turned my stool so I was facing Rachel. We had our hands on each other.

"What about him?" I asked.

"He came in right after me and he's still nursing his first drink," she said.

"Well, maybe he's pacing himself. You're on your first, too."

"That's only because of him. He's been kind of watching us without watching us. Watching me."

"What does that mean?"

"It means he has not looked over here once since he got here. But he's using the mirrors."

There was a large mirror that ran behind the bar and another on the ceiling above it. I could see the man in question in both of them so that meant he could see us.

"You're sure?" I asked.

"Yes," she said. "And look at his shoulders."

I checked: his shoulders were large and the biceps and neck thick. In the days since the Shrike had come to light, the FBI was pursuing a theory that he was an ex-convict who had built up his body in prison and possibly perfected his neck-breaking move there as well. The investigation had zeroed in on the unsolved murder of an inmate at the Florida State Prison in Starke whose body was found stuffed behind an industrial washing machine in the laundry. His neck was broken so severely that the cause of death was listed as internal decapitation.

The case was never solved. Several convicts worked in the prison laundry or had access to it, but the surveillance cameras were fogged over by steam released by the dryers—a problem that had been noted by staff repeatedly but never addressed.

For more than a month the bureau had been looking at video from prison-yard cameras and running down data on every convict who worked in the laundry or could have had access to it on the day of the murder. Agent Metz had told me he was sure that the Shrike had killed the inmate. The murder had occurred four years earlier, well before the Shrike killings began, and it fit the pattern attributed to the Shrike starting in Florida.

"Okay," I said. "But wait a minute."

I pulled my phone and went into the photo archive. I still had a photo of the artist composite of the Shrike. I opened it and tilted the screen to Rachel.

"Doesn't really look like him," I said.

"I don't put a lot of trust in composites," she said.

"What about Gwyneth saying it was a good match?"

"She was emotional. She wanted it to be a match."

"The Unabomber composite was right on."

"One in a million. Plus the Shrike's composite has been on every TV channel in the country. He would have changed his look. That's a big thing with incels. Plastic surgery. Plus he's the right age: mid-thirties."

I nodded.

"So then what do we do?" I asked.

"Well, first, we act like we don't know he's there," Rachel said. "And I'll see if I can get Metz involved."

She pulled out her phone and opened the camera app. She held the phone out as though she was taking a selfie. We leaned close and smiled at the screen as she took a photo of the man at the other end of the bar.

She studied the shot for a moment.

"One more," she said.

We smiled and she snapped another photo, this time zooming the focus in closer on his face. Luckily Elle was leaning into a conversation with the couple in the middle so Rachel got an unobstructed shot.

I leaned over to see what she got and fake-laughed as if she had taken a bad photo.

"Delete it," I said. "I look like shit."

"No, I love it," she said.

Rachel was editing the real shot, expanding it as much as possible without clarity decay and then saving it. When she was finished she texted it to Agent Metz with this message.

This guy is watching us. I think it's him. How do we handle?

We pretended to chat while we waited for a reply.

"How would he know to follow you here?" I asked.

"That's easy," Rachel said. "I've been in your stories as well as the podcast. He could have followed me from my office. I came straight here after locking up."

That seemed plausible.

"But this flies in the face of the profile," I said. "The bureau's profilers all said he was not vengeance motivated. The story is already out. Why risk coming back to do something to us? It's behavior he hasn't shown before."

"I don't know, Jack," Rachel said. "Maybe it's something else.

You've made a lot of generalized statements about him on the podcast. Maybe you got him mad."

Her phone's screen lit up with a return text from Metz.

What's your 20? I'll send Agent Amin out in a Lyft. See if he follows and we'll lead him into a horseshoe.

Rachel sent back a text with the address and asked for an ETA on the Lyft car. Metz replied that it would be forty minutes.

"Okay, so we have to order another round and then act like neither one of us can drive," Rachel said. "We fake a request for a Lyft and then get in the car with Amin."

"What's a horseshoe?" I asked.

"They'll set up a car trap. We drive in, he follows us, they close the horseshoe behind him, and he's got nowhere to go."

"Have you ever done a horseshoe trap before?"

"Me? No. But I'm sure they have."

"Let's hope it works."

42

Forty minutes later we were in the back of the FBI's Lyft minivan with Agent Amin behind the wheel. He pulled away from Mistral and headed west on Ventura Boulevard.

"What's the plan?" Rachel asked.

"We have the horseshoe set up," Amin said. "We just have to see if you have a follower."

"Did Metz get a bird up?"

"Yes, but he had to wait until it was free from another op. It's on the way."

"And how many cars do we have?"

"Four including the Lyft."

"That's not enough. He may spot the surveillance and bug out."

"It's what we could do on short notice."

"Where's the horseshoe?"

"Tyrone Avenue on the north side of the 101. It dead-ends at the river and it's only five minutes away."

I saw Rachel nod in the darkness of the car. It did little to balance the anxiety she was exuding.

At Van Nuys Boulevard, we turned north. I could see the 101 overpass just a few blocks ahead.

Rachel pulled her phone and made a call. I only heard her side of it.

"Matt, are you running this op?"

I knew then that she had called Metz.

"Did he leave the restaurant?"

She listened and her next question seemed to confirm that the man at the bar had followed us when we left.

"Where's the airship?"

She shook her head while listening. She wasn't happy with his answer.

"Yes, I hope so."

She disconnected the call but the tone of her last words indicated she thought Metz was handling it wrong.

We crossed under the freeway and then took an immediate turn east on Riverside Drive. Four blocks later, Amin put on his right turn signal as we approached Tyrone.

Amin was monitoring radio traffic on an earpiece. He got an instruction and passed it on to us.

"All right, he's behind us," he said. "We are going down to the dead end and stopping. You two stay in the van. No matter what, you stay in the van. That understood?"

"Got it," I said.

"Understood," Rachel said.

We made the turn. The street was lined on both sides with parked cars and only dimly lit. There were single-family homes on both sides of the street. A block ahead I could see the twenty-foot wall of the raised freeway. The tops of cars and trucks were crossing up there left to right, heading west and out of the city.

"This is residential and it's too dark," Rachel said. "Who picked this street?"

"It was the best we could do on short notice," Amin said. "It'll work."

I turned to look out the back window and saw headlights sweep across the roadway as a car slowly made the turn and followed us onto Tyrone.

"There he is," I said.

Rachel glanced back and then forward, obviously better versed in this maneuver than I was.

"Where's the cutoff?" she asked.

"Coming up," Amin said.

I scanned through all the windows, wondering what *the cutoff* meant. Just as we passed an opening on our right I saw the lights of a car backed into a driveway flash on. The car then lurched into the street behind us and stopped dead in front of the tail car, creating a barrier between us and the tail. I watched it all through the back window. Simultaneously, another car pulled from a driveway behind the tail car, boxing it in.

I saw agents tumble out of the two passenger-side doors of the first car and take cover behind the front of it. I assumed the same happened with the car on the other side of the box.

Amin kept driving, putting more distance between us and the takedown operation.

"Stop here!" Rachel yelled. "Stop!"

Ignoring Rachel, Amin started to bring the van to a slow stop as we reached the terminus of the street at a fence that enclosed the concrete aqueduct known as the Los Angeles River. Rachel was reaching for the release on the side door before he brought it to a halt.

"Stay in the van," Amin said. "Stay in the van!"

"Bullshit," Rachel said. "If it's him, I want to see this."

She jumped out the door.

"Goddamn it," Amin said.

He jumped out next and pointed through his open door at me.

"You stay right there," he said.

He headed off after Rachel up the street. I waited a beat before deciding that I wasn't going to miss this either.

"Fuck that."

I climbed through the door Rachel had left open. Looking around, I saw Rachel up near the blockade. Amin was right behind her. I moved over to the right sidewalk and started up the street behind the cover of the cars parked along the curb.

The horseshoe was now lit by headlights and the spotlight of a helicopter that had swung in from over the freeway. I heard the shouts of men in the street up ahead, rising in urgency.

Then I heard one word clearly and repeated by many voices. *"Gun!"*

A volley of shots immediately followed. Too many to separate and count. All within five, maybe ten seconds. I instinctively ducked behind the line of cars on the curb but kept moving up the street.

The gunfire ended and I straightened up and kept moving, my eyes scanning now for Rachel to make sure she was safe. I didn't see her anywhere.

After an eerie silence the shouting started again and I heard the all-clear signal.

When I got to the box I cut between two cars and into the light from above.

The man from the bar was faceup on the ground next to the open door of an old Toyota. I saw gunshot wounds on his left hand and arm, his chest and neck. He was dead, his eyes open and vacantly staring up at the helicopter above. An agent in an FBI raid jacket was standing eight feet away, his feet spread on either side of a chrome-plated pistol lying on the ground.

When he turned slightly I saw it was the agent I had met after Roger Vogel had been run over by the Shrike. Metz.

And he saw me.

"Hey, McEvoy!" he yelled. "Get back! Get the fuck back!"

I raised my hands wide to show innocence. Metz signaled to another agent standing nearby.

"Get him back to the van," he ordered.

The agent moved toward me. He grabbed me by the arm, but I jerked free and looked at Metz.

"Metz, you gotta be kidding!" I yelled.

The agent moved in to grab me more aggressively. Metz left his position over the gun and moved toward me, holding his hand up to stop the agent.

"I'll handle it," Metz said. "Watch the weapon."

The agent changed direction and Metz came up to me. He did not touch me but spread his hands as if to block my view of the man on the ground behind him.

"Jack, look, you can't be here," he said. "This is a crime scene."

"What happened?" I asked. "Where's Rachel?"

"Rachel, I don't know. But Jack, you gotta move back. Let us do our job here and then we'll talk."

"He pulled a gun?"

"Jack…"

"Was it him? The Shrike didn't use a gun."

"Jack, listen to me. We are not talking about this right now. Let us work the scene and then we'll talk. Get back on the sidewalk now or we are going to have a problem. You've been warned."

"I'm media. I have a right to be here."

"You do, but not in the *middle* of the fucking crime scene. I'm really losing my patience with—"

"Jack—"

We both turned. Rachel was standing between two parked cars behind me.

"Rachel, get him out now or bail him out later," Metz said.

"Jack, come on," she said.

She waved me to her. I looked back at the dead man on the ground and then turned and walked toward her. She moved between the two cars and up onto the sidewalk. I followed.

"Did you see the shooting?" I asked.

"I just saw him go down," she said.

"He had a gun. That's not—"

"I know. We'll get answers but we have to back off and let them do their thing."

"This is crazy. Twenty minutes ago, the guy was sitting there in the bar right across from us. Now he's dead. I just realized, I've got to call Myron. I've got to tell him we have one more story to do."

"Let's just wait on that, Jack. Let them do their work and then let's see what Metz says."

"All right, all right."

I raised my hands in surrender. And then I spoke without thinking about the content or consequences of what I said.

"I'm going to ask him about that day, too. Metz. See if he denies it was a setup."

Rachel turned and looked at me. She didn't say anything at first. She just slowly shook her head.

"You idiot," she said. "You did it again."

THE LAST STORY

FBI Kills Armed Man in "Shrike" Takedown
By Myron Levin

An Ohio man stalking an investigator on the Shrike serial killer case was cut down in a volley of FBI gunfire in Sherman Oaks last night when he drew a weapon and pointed it at agents who had cornered him, federal authorities said.

Robinson Felder, 35, of Dayton, was killed at 8:30 p.m. on Tyrone Avenue just north of the 101 Freeway. Agent Matthew Metz said Felder had been following Rachel Walling, a private investigator who had played a pivotal role three months ago in revealing the killing spree of a murder suspect known as the Shrike.

Metz said that evidence collected from Felder's car indicated that he was involved in online groups that have idolized the Shrike in the months since his killing spree was revealed. Metz said the evidence, most of which was found on a laptop computer and Felder's online history, excluded him from possibly being the Shrike himself.

FBI agents stopped Felder on the dead-end street and ordered him out of his car. Metz said Felder initially complied but then pulled a gun from his waistband once he had stepped out of his car. Metz said Felder pointed the weapon at agents, provoking fire from several of them. Felder was fatally wounded and died at the scene.

In addition to the weapon recovered at the scene, agents found what they called an abduction-and-torture kit in Felder's car, Metz said. He described the kit as a duffel bag containing zip ties and duct tape as well as rope, a knife, pliers, and a small acetylene torch.

"We believe his intentions were to abduct and kill Ms. Walling," Metz said.

The federal agent said the motive for the killing plan was Walling's part in the Shrike case. Walling, a former FBI profiler, consulted with *FairWarning* on its investigation into the deaths of several women across the country who died at the hands of a killer who broke their necks in a brutal manner. The *FairWarning* investigation revealed that the women were targeted because of a specific DNA pattern they shared. All had submitted their DNA to GT23, a popular genetic-analytics provider. Their anonymized DNA was then sold in the secondary market to a genetic-research lab, which in turn provided it to the operators of a dark-web site that catered to men wishing to hurt and take sexual advantage of women.

The website has since been shuttered. The Shrike has not been identified or captured. In the weeks since the killing spree was revealed by *FairWarning,* he has become celebrated in online forums catering to the "incel" subculture. The male-dominated movement—named for a contraction of "involuntary celibate"—is characterized online by postings involving misogyny, feelings of entitlement to sex, and the endorsement of violence against women. Several physical attacks on women across the country have been ascribed by authorities to incels.

Metz said that a study of Felder's social-media history revealed that in recent weeks he had made several posts on various incel forums praising and revering the Shrike and the violence he committed against women. He ended most of these posts with #*theydeservedit,* according to Metz.

"We have no doubt that this guy came out here to abduct Ms. Walling as some kind of homage to the Shrike," Metz said. "We are lucky that she wasn't hurt."

Walling declined to comment. It was, in fact, Walling who saved her own life. In a Sherman Oaks restaurant, Walling noticed Felder watching her and acting suspiciously. She contacted the FBI and a plan was quickly formulated to determine if Felder was stalking her. Under FBI surveillance Walling left the restaurant and drove to a predetermined spot on Tyrone Avenue.

Metz said that Felder followed them in his car and drove into an FBI vehicle trap. When he was told to step out of the car with his hands visible, he complied. But then for unknown reasons, he reached to his beltline and pulled free a .45 caliber pistol. He was fired upon when he raised the weapon into firing position.

"He gave us no choice," said Metz, who was on the scene during the shooting but did not fire himself.

There were seven other agents on the scene and four of them fired at Felder. Metz said the shooting will be investigated by the bureau's Office of Professional Responsibility and the U.S. Attorney's Office.

Metz, the assistant special agent in charge of the Los Angeles Field Office, said he was concerned Felder's activities could inspire others in the incel community to act out in the same way. He said efforts are being made to safeguard Walling and others involved in the Shrike case.

Meantime, Metz acknowledged that efforts to identify the Shrike and bring about his arrest continue, but frustrations mount with each passing day.

"We are not going to be able to breathe easy until this guy is in custody," he said. "We need to find him."

JACK

43

We gathered at Sun Ray Studios on Cahuenga Boulevard to record the last episode of the podcast on the Shrike. The last, that is, until there was some sort of break in the case worthy of a new episode. I had gone through seventeen episodes. I had discussed the story from every conceivable angle and had interviewed every person associated with the case who was willing to go on the record and be taped. This even included an interview with Gwyneth Rice in her hospital room, her voice now an eerie electronic creation manifested from her laptop.

This last episode was a heavily promoted live discussion with as many of the players in the case as I could bring together. The studio had a round table in the recording room. It was Rachel Walling, Metz from the FBI, Detective Ruiz from the Anaheim Police Department, Myron Levin from *FairWarning,* and Hervé Gaspar, the lawyer who had represented Jessica Kelley, the victim in the William Orton case. I had never been able to figure out whether Ruiz or Gaspar had been my Deep Throat source. Both had denied it. But Gaspar had eagerly accepted the invitation to be part of the podcast, while Ruiz had to be cajoled.

That tipped my guess toward Gaspar. He relished the secret part he had played in the case.

Lastly, we had Emily Atwater on the phone, calling in from her unknown spot in England and ready to answer questions as well.

We had calls on hold before the scheduled hour even began. This did not surprise me. The podcast had steadily grown an audience. More than half a million people had already listened to the prior week's episode, when the live event was announced.

We gathered around the table, and Ray Stallings, the engineer and owner of the studio, handed out headsets and checked and adjusted the microphones.

The moment was awkward for me. It had been almost three months since Robinson Felder's attempted abduction. In that time, I had only seen Rachel once and that was when she had come to my apartment to collect some clothes she had left there.

We were no longer seeing each other, despite my apologizing and taking back the accusation I had made against her on that last night. As she had warned, my accusation ruined everything. We were now finished. Getting her to appear on the final podcast took an email lobbying campaign that was a digital version of begging and groveling. I could have easily proceeded without her on the episode, but I hoped that getting her into the same room with me might spark something or at least give me the chance to once more confess my sins and seek forgiveness and understanding.

It wasn't a complete shutdown of communications because we were still inextricably bound together by the Shrike. She was my source. She had access to Metz and the FBI investigation; I had access to her. Though we communicated by email only, it was still communication, and more than once I had tried to engage her in a discussion outside the bounds of the source/reporter relationship. But she had thwarted and deflected such efforts, with the request that we keep things on a professional level from now on.

I watched her as Ray positioned the microphone in front of her lips and had her say her name a few times while he checked the sound levels. She avoided eye contact with me the whole time. Looking back, I was as mystified by this turn of events as by anything else that had occurred in the case. I could not figure out what I had or didn't have inside me that would lead me to doubt a sure thing and look for the cracks in its foundation.

Once we went live, I began with the scripted intro I used at the start of every episode of the podcast:

"Death is my beat. I make my living from it. I forge my professional reputation on it…I'm Jack McEvoy and this is *Murder Beat,* the true-crime podcast that takes you beyond the headlines and on the trail of a killer with the investigators on the case.

"This episode wraps up our first season with a live discussion featuring the investigators, attorneys, and journalists who all played a part in exposing and hunting a serial killer known as the Shrike…"

And so it went. I introduced the panel members and started taking listener questions. Most of them were routine softballs. I acted as moderator and chose which participant to throw each question to. Everybody had been prepped beforehand to keep their answers short and precise. The shorter the answer, the more questions we could get to. I directed more than an equal share to Rachel, thinking that somehow it was like engaging her in conversation. But it felt hollow and embarrassing after a while.

The most unusual call came from a woman identifying herself as Charisse. She did not ask a question about the Shrike case. Instead, she said that eleven years earlier her sister Kylie had been abducted and murdered, her body left in the sand under the Venice pier. She said the police never arrested anyone for the crime and there was no active investigation she knew of.

"My question is whether you would investigate her case," Charisse said.

The question was so out-of-left-field that I struggled to answer.

"Well," I said. "I could probably look into it and check on what the police did with it, but I'm not a detective."

"What about the Shrike?" Charisse said. "You investigated him."

"The circumstances were a bit different. I was working on a story and it became a serial-murder case. I—"

I was interrupted by a dial tone. Charisse had hung up.

I got the discussion back on track after that but the episode still went long. The advertised hour stretched to ninety minutes and the only time we veered away from questions from listeners was when I had to read advertisements from our sponsors, which were mostly other true-crime podcasts.

The listeners who called in were enthusiastic about *Murder Beat* and many eagerly asked what the next season would be about and when it would start. These were questions I didn't yet have an official response to. But it was good to know that there appeared to be an audience out there waiting. It buoyed my sinking morale.

I have to admit that I secretly hoped that I would hear from *him*. The Shrike. I had hoped that he was one of the podcast's listeners and that he would feel compelled to call in to taunt or threaten the journalists or the investigators. That was why I let the session go long. I wanted to get to every caller just in case he was there waiting to speak.

But it never happened, and when we answered the last question and killed the live feed, I looked across the table at Metz. We had talked previously about the possibility of *the unsub*—FBI-speak for *the unknown subject*—calling in. He shook his head at me and I shrugged. I glanced at Rachel, who was sitting next to Metz. She was already taking her headphones off. I then saw her touch his arm and lean toward him to whisper something. The gesture looked intimate to me. My morale sagged further.

I wrapped things up with my usual thanks to those involved in the podcast: the participants, the sponsors, the studio, and the sound engineer. I promised listeners that we would be back with a new chapter in the Shrike case as soon as anything occurred. We went out with a tune from saxophonist Grace Kelly called "By the Grave."

And that was it. I took my headphones off and draped them over the microphone stand. The others did the same.

"Thanks, everybody," I said. "That was good. I was hoping the Shrike would call in but he was probably busy doing laundry today."

It was a lame and insensitive attempt at a joke. No one even smiled.

"I have to go to the restroom," Rachel said. "So I'm going to leave. Good to see everybody."

She gave me a smile as she stood up, but I couldn't hang any hope on it. I watched her leave the recording room.

Gaspar and Ruiz were the next to leave as they each had to drive all the way back to Orange County. I asked Ray if Emily was still on the line but he said she had disconnected.

Myron bailed next and then Metz. I was left with Ray, who had questions about whether I wanted him to edit the session down to an hour or post it in its entirety as the season finale. I told him to put the whole thing out. Those who hadn't listened to the live version could download the whole thing and listen to as much or as little as they liked.

I took the elevator down to the building's basement. The garage was always crowded, requiring an attendant named Rodrigo to be constantly moving double-parked cars around so people could get in and get out. When the elevator opened, I saw through the alcove that Rachel was in the garage waiting with Metz for their cars. I hung back for a moment. I wasn't sure why. I thought if Metz got his car first, I would have a chance to talk to Rachel and maybe ask for a meeting to clear the air about what was happening with us. In the last month I had used the ad revenues from the podcast both to lease a new car and rent a bigger apartment. After ten years with the ragtag Jeep I had gotten a new car: a Range Rover SUV that was the very picture of maturity and security. I thought maybe we could leave Rachel's car in the garage and go up the street to Miceli's for an afternoon glass of wine.

But I was wrong. Rodrigo brought up a car that I recognized as a fed vehicle, and both of them walked toward it, Rachel to the passenger door. That told me more than I wanted to know. Embarrassed, I waited until they were pulling away before passing through the alcove into the garage.

But I timed it wrong. Just as I stepped out, Rachel turned in her seat to reach back over her shoulder for the seat belt. Our eyes caught and she smiled as the fed car pulled away. I took it as an apology smile. And a goodbye look.

Rodrigo came up behind me.

"Mr. Jack," he said. "You're all set. First row, keys on the front tire for you."

"Thank you, Rodrigo," I said, still watching Metz's car as it turned out of the garage onto Cahuenga.

Once it was gone from sight I walked alone to my car.

44

I decided I had nowhere to go but home. I pulled out onto Cahuenga and headed north. I followed the road as it made the big bend west until it became Ventura Boulevard and I was in Studio City. My new place was a two-bedroom apartment on Vineland. I was thinking about what I had just seen in the parking garage and how I should interpret it. I wasn't paying attention to the road and didn't register the brake lights in front of me.

My new SUV's anti-collision system engaged and a sharp alarm issued from the dashboard. I came out of my reverie and slammed the brake pedal with both feet. The SUV came skidding to a halt two feet from the Prius stopped in front of me. I felt the dull thud of an impact behind me.

"Shit!"

I settled down and checked the rearview mirror, then got out to inspect the damage. I walked to the back of the car and saw that the car behind me was a good six feet away. The back of my car had no sign of damage. I looked at the other driver. His window was down.

"Did you hit me?" I asked.

"No, I didn't hit you," he said indignantly.

I checked the back of my car again. I still had a temporary tag on the car.

"Hey, buddy, how about you get in your pretty new car and keep moving?" the other driver said. "You're holding up traffic with this bullshit."

I waved him and his rudeness off and climbed back into the driver's seat, confused by the whole situation. I continued driving, thinking about what had happened. I had definitely felt some kind of heavy thud of impact when I hit the brakes. I wondered if something was wrong or loose in the new car, then thought about Ikea. My new apartment was nearly twice the size of my old one. It had dictated the need for more furniture and I had made several runs to the Ikea in Burbank since getting the new SUV, making good use of the rear storage compartment. But I was sure I had not left anything back there. The compartment was empty. Or it should have been.

Then it hit me. I checked the rearview mirror but this time was more interested in what was on my side of the back window than behind my car. The pullover cover for the rear compartment was in place. Nothing seemed amiss.

I pulled my phone and speed-dialed Rachel. The ringing came blaring out of the car stereo's surround sound. I had forgotten about the Bluetooth connection the car salesman had set up for me when I took delivery of the car.

I quickly hit the button on the dash that killed the sound system. The buzzing returned to only my phone and my ear.

But Rachel didn't answer. She was probably still with Metz and thought I was calling for some kind of maudlin let's-get-back-together conversation. It went to her voice mail and I disconnected.

I called again and while I waited I reached over to my laptop on the seat next to me and opened it. I knew I had Metz's cell number in a file on the desktop.

But this time Rachel answered.

"Jack, this is not a good time."

I slapped the laptop closed and spoke in a low voice.

"Are you with Metz?"

"Jack, I'm not going to talk about who I—"

"I don't mean that way. Are you still driving with Metz?"

I checked the rearview again and realized I had to stop talking out loud.

"Yes," Rachel said. "He's just taking me back to my office."

"Check your messages," I said.

I disconnected.

Traffic slowed again as I came to the intersection with Vineland. I used the moment to type out a text to Rachel.

I'm in my car. Strike is hiding in the back.

I realized after I sent it that autocorrect had changed *Shrike* to *Strike*. I figured, though, that she would understand.

She did and I got an almost immediate response.

Are you sure? Where are you?

I was coming up to my apartment building but drove by it. And typed in a reply.

Vineland

My phone buzzed and Rachel's name was on the screen. I connected but didn't say hello.

"Jack?"

I coughed and hoped she understood I did not want to reveal I was on the phone to the person hiding in the back.

"Okay, I get it," Rachel said. "You can't talk. So, listen, you have two choices. You get to a populated area, pull into a parking lot where there are people, and just get out and get away from the car. Give me the location and we will try to get the police there and hopefully catch him."

She waited a moment for any sort of response before going to choice two. She must have registered my continuing silence as interest in the alternate plan.

"Okay, the other thing is we make damn sure we get him. You drive to a destination and we set up a horseshoe like we did before and we finally get this guy. This choice is more risky to you, of course, but I think if you keep the car moving he's not going to make a move. He's going to wait."

She waited. I said nothing.

"So, Jack, do this. Cough once if you want the first choice. Don't cough, don't do anything if you want to go with the second."

I realized that if I took any time to consider my options, my silence would confirm that I was going with the riskier second option. But that was okay. In that moment, I flashed on a vision of Gwyneth Rice in her hospital bed surrounded by tubes and machines, and her electronic plea that we not take the Shrike alive.

I wanted the second option.

"Okay, Jack, option two," Rachel said. "Cough now if I have it wrong."

I was silent and Rachel accepted the confirmation.

"You need to get to the 101 and head south," she said. "We were just on it and it's wide open. You'll be able to get to

Hollywood and by then we'll have a plan. We're turning around and we'll be there."

I was coming up to a southbound entrance to the 170 freeway. I knew it merged with the 101 less than a mile south. Rachel continued.

"I'm going to keep the line open while Matt sets things up—he's talking to LAPD. They'll be able to mobilize quicker. You just have to stay in motion. He won't try anything while the car is moving."

I nodded even though I knew she couldn't see me.

"But if something happens and you have to stop, just get out of the car and get clear. Get safe, Jack . . . I need you . . . to be safe."

I registered the quiet, more intimate tone in her voice and wanted to respond. I hoped my silence communicated something. But just as quickly, doubt started to move into my mind. Had I left something in the storage compartment? Had the thud I felt simply come from a pothole in the road? I was mobilizing the FBI and LAPD on what amounted to a hunch. I was beginning to wish I had just coughed once and pointed the car toward the North Hollywood Police Division.

"Okay, Jack," Rachel said, her voice modulated back to a command tone. "I'll get back to you when we have it set up."

I got lucky and saw up ahead that I had a green light to turn into the freeway entrance.

Doubt aside, I made the turn. The freeway entrance looped around and then I was heading south on the 170. I took one of the 101 merge lanes and got the car up to sixty. Rachel had been right. The freeway was moderately crowded but the traffic was moving. It was pre-rush hour and most of the traffic was going northbound out of downtown to the suburbs in the Valley and beyond.

Once I merged onto the 101 I worked my way over to the fast lane and stayed in the flow, now moving at fifty miles per hour. I checked the rearview every few seconds and kept the phone to my left ear. I could hear Metz's voice as he talked on another phone in the car with Rachel. It was muffled and I couldn't make out everything he said. But I could definitely read the urgency in his tone.

Soon I was into the Cahuenga Pass and could see the Capitol Records building ahead. I was putting the picture together as I waited for Rachel to come back on the line and tell me the plan. I realized that the Shrike was a listener of the podcast after all and I had given him everything he needed. At the end of each episode I had plugged the recording studio when I thanked Ray Stallings. I had then repeatedly promoted the time and date of the live roundtable discussion that would be the final episode.

The Shrike then only had to surveil the building where Sun Ray Studios were located to figure out how he could use the parking-garage situation to his advantage. The attendant left the keys of the cars he moved around on each vehicle's front right tire. The Shrike could have snuck in while Rodrigo was shuffling cars, used the key to unlock my Range Rover, and then secreted himself in the back.

I suddenly realized there was another possibility. I had broadcast the podcast's time and location to everybody. It was possible that if someone was concealed in the back, it wasn't the Shrike. It could be another crazy incel like Robinson Felder. I took the phone from my ear to try to text this possibility to Rachel when I heard her voice again.

"Jack?"

I waited.

"We have a plan. We want you to get to Sunset Boulevard and

take the exit. It dumps you out on Van Ness at an intersection with Harold Way. Take the immediate right onto Harold Way and we'll be set up for you. LAPD has got two units there right now and more are on the way. Matt and I are two minutes out. Clear your throat if you understand and we are good to go."

I waited a beat and then cleared my throat loudly. I was good to go.

"Okay, Jack, now what I want you to do is try to text me a description of what you're driving. I know you mentioned in a recent email that you got a new car. Give me make, model, and color. Color is important, Jack. We want to know what we've got coming. Also put in what exit you last passed so we'll have a sense of timing. Go ahead, but be careful. Don't wreck while texting."

I pulled the phone away and typed the needed information into a text to her, cycling my focus repeatedly from the phone to the rearview to the road ahead.

I had just sent off the text, including the fact that I was about to pass the Highland exit, when my eyes went to the road ahead and I saw brake lights flaring across all lanes.

Traffic was stopping.

45

There was an accident ahead. My SUV gave me a view over the rooflines of several cars in front of me and I could see smoke and a car turned sideways blocking the fast lane and left shoulder of the freeway.

I knew I had to get to the right before I was stopped dead in the backup. I hit the turn signal and almost blindly started pushing across four lanes of the slowing traffic.

My moves brought a chorus of horns from angry motorists who were trying to do the same thing I was. The traffic slowed to a crawl and the spaces between cars compressed, but nobody on the road had the kind of emergency I had. I didn't care about their frustrations or horns.

"Jack?" Rachel said. "I hear the horns, what is—I know you can't talk. Try to text. We got the info you sent. Try to tell me what's going on now."

I did what most L.A. drivers do when they are alone in their cars. I cursed the traffic.

"Goddamn it! Why are we stopping?"

I had one lane left to get over to and I believed it would be the fastest way around the accident backup. I didn't trust the mirrors anymore and was turning half in my seat to check my competition through the windows, all the while keeping the phone to my ear.

"Okay, Jack, I get it," Rachel said. "But ride on the shoulder, do whatever you have to do and get down here."

I coughed once, not knowing at this point if that meant yes or no. All I knew was that I had to get around the backup. Once I got past the crash, the freeway would be wide open and I'd be flying.

I had slowly passed the Highland exit and could see that the accident scene was a couple hundred yards ahead and before the Vine Street exit. That was where traffic came to a complete halt.

Now I could see people getting out of their cars and standing in the freeway. Cars were moving inch by inch as they passed the smoking wreckage. I could hear a siren coming up behind me and knew the arrival of first responders would shut things down even further and for longer. I also knew I could go to those first responders with the deadly cargo I believed I was carrying. But would they understand what I had? Would they capture him?

I was considering these questions and the last mile I had to go to Sunset Boulevard when there was a loud *thwack* from the back of my car.

I turned around fully and saw that the spring-loaded cover to the rear storage area had been released and had snapped back into its housing like a window shade.

A figure rose from the space. A man. He looked around as if to get his bearings, then must have seen through the rear windows that the siren he had heard was from a rescue ambulance making its way to the crash site.

He then turned and looked directly at me.

"Hello, Jack," he said. "Where are we going?"

"Who the fuck are you?" I said. "What do you want?"

"I think you know who I am," he said. "And what I want."

He started climbing over the rear seats. I dropped the phone and pinned the accelerator. The car lurched forward and I yanked the wheel to the right. I clipped the right corner of the car in front of me as the SUV veered onto the freeway shoulder. The wheels spun on the loose gravel and litter before finding purchase. In the rearview I saw the intruder thrown backward into the space where he had been hiding.

But he quickly reemerged and started climbing over the seats again.

"Slow it down, Jack," he said. "What's the hurry?"

I didn't answer. My mind was racing faster than the car as I tried to think of an escape plan.

The Vine Street exit was just past the accident site. But what did that get me? My choices seemed simple in that adrenalized moment. Fight or flight. Keep moving or stop the car and get out and run.

In the back of my mind I knew one thing. Running away meant the Shrike would escape again.

I kept my foot on the pedal.

With less than a hundred yards before I would clear the traffic backup and get off the shoulder, a beat-up pickup truck filled with lawn equipment suddenly pulled onto the shoulder ahead of me—at a much slower pace.

I yanked the wheel right again and tried to squeeze by without losing speed. My car scraped sharply along a concrete sound barrier that bordered the freeway and then rebounded into the side of the pickup, pushing it into the cars to its left. A full chorus of horns and crashing metal followed, but my car kept moving. I straightened the wheel and checked the mirror. The man behind me had been thrown to the floor of the back seat.

Two seconds later I was past the traffic backup and there were five lanes of open freeway in front of me.

But I was still a half mile from the Sunset exit and knew that I could not hold off the Shrike for that long. The phone was somewhere in the car and Rachel was presumably still listening. I made what I thought might be a last call out to her.

"Rachel!" I yelled. "I —"

An arm came around my neck and choked off my voice. My head was snapped back against the headrest. I reached up with one hand and tried to pull it off my neck, but the Shrike had locked his arm and was tightening the pressure.

"Stop the car," he said in my ear.

I planted my feet and pushed back into the seat, trying to make space against his forearm. The car picked up speed.

"Stop the car," he said again.

I realized one thing: I had a seat belt on and he didn't. I remembered the salesman droning on about the safety and construction of the car. Something about *rollover protection*. But I had not been interested. I just wanted to sign the papers and drive away, not listen to things that would never matter to me.

Now they did.

I felt the car automatically lowering into its high-speed profile as the digital speedometer clicked past eighty-five. I let go of my attacker's forearm, put both hands on the wheel and yanked it to the left.

The car jerked wildly to the left and then the forces of physics took over. For a split second it held the road, then the front left wheel came off the surface and the back left followed. I believe the car became airborne by at least a few feet and then flipped side over side before impacting and continuing to rotate, tumbling down the freeway.

Everything seemed to move in slow motion, my body jolting in all directions with each crashing impact. I felt the arm that had been around my neck fall away. I heard the loud tearing of metal and the explosive shattering of glass. Debris flew around in the car and out the now glass-free windows. My laptop hit me in the ribs and at some point I blacked out.

When I came to, I was hanging upside down in my seat. I looked down at the ceiling of the car and saw that I was dripping blood on it. I reached to my face and located the source: a long gash on the top of my head.

I wondered what had happened. Had somebody hit me? Had I hit somebody?

Then I remembered.

The Shrike.

I looked around as best as I could. I didn't see him. The rear seats of the car had broken loose in the accident and were now tilted down to the ceiling, obstructing my view.

"Shit," I said.

I could taste blood in my mouth.

I became aware of a sharp pain in my side and remembered my laptop. It had hit me in the ribs.

I put my left hand down on the ceiling to brace myself and used the other to release my seat belt. My arm wasn't strong enough and I crashed down to the ceiling, my legs still tangled with the steering column. I slowly lowered myself the rest of the way. As I did, I became aware of a tinny voice calling my name.

I looked around and saw my cell phone on the asphalt about four feet outside the front window. The screen was spider-webbed with cracks but I could read the name "Rachel" on it. The call was still active.

Once my legs were free I crawled through the space where the windshield had been and reached for my phone.

"Rachel?"

"Jack, are you all right? What happened?"

"Uh…we crashed. I'm bleeding."

"We're on our way. Where is the unsub?"

"The…what?"

"The Shrike, Jack. Do you see him?"

Now I remembered the arm around my neck. The Shrike. He was going to kill me.

I crawled all the way out of the wreck and unsteadily stood up by the front end of the upside-down Range Rover. I saw people running down the shoulder of the freeway toward me. There was a car with flashing blue lights working its way down as well.

I took a few uneasy steps and realized there was something wrong with one of my feet. Every step sent a jolt of pain from my left ankle up to my hip. Nevertheless I kept moving around the wreckage and looking through the windows into the back.

There was no sign of anyone else. But the car was canted unevenly on the ground. When the people got to the car, I heard shrieks of panic.

"We have to move this! He's underneath!"

I limped around to their side and saw what they saw. The car was resting unevenly on the roadway because the Shrike was underneath it. I could see his hand extending out from the edge of the roof. I carefully lowered myself to the asphalt and looked under the wreck.

The Shrike was crushed under the car. His face was turned

toward me and his eyes were open, one of them staring lifelessly, the other in a broken orbit and at an off-angle.

"Help me push this off him!" somebody yelled to the others running to the scene.

I started to get up.

"Don't bother," I said. "It's too late."

THE END

46

As of now, they don't know the identity of the man who was crushed under my car. We can't put a true name to him. There was no identification in the gray hoodie he wore or the pockets of his pants. His fingerprints and DNA were submitted by the FBI to every available database in the world and produced no match. An extensive and thorough search of a mile-wide grid around the Sun Ray Studios building found no abandoned vehicle and only a gas-station camera that captured an out-of-focus angle on a man in a gray hoodie crossing east to west over the 101 freeway on the Barham Boulevard overpass. He was moving in the direction of the studio an hour before the live podcast. But a new grid search on the east side of the freeway produced no vehicle and no record of a drop-off by any car service.

Examination of the body during autopsy revealed a prior surgery to repair a broken arm bone called the radius. It appeared to have been a childhood injury, a spiral fracture, which is an indication of abuse. There was limited dental work. What there was appeared to be distinctly American, but not enough to successfully trace X-rays to a specific dentist or patient.

As of now the Shrike remains a cipher in death.

Most likely it will remain that way. In the parlance of the

newspaper business, he is now off the front page. The public's moment of grim fascination with him dissipated like smoke curling away from a cigarette as the focus of the media moved on. The Shrike had flown beneath the radar for most of his existence. He returned there after his run was over.

With the Shrike no longer a threat, Emily Atwater returned from the UK, having found that she missed Los Angeles. And with the ending to the story I had provided on the 101 freeway, she was able to complete the book. She then returned to *FairWarning* as its senior staff writer, and I know Myron was happy about that.

Still, I remained haunted by not knowing who the Shrike was and what made him a killer of women. To me, that left the story unfinished. It was a question that would remain in my mind forever.

The whole story changed me. I wondered often about what might have been if I had not happened to go on a date with Christina Portrero. If my name had not come up in the LAPD investigation and Mattson and Sakai had not followed me into the garage that night. Would the Shrike still be out there below the radar? Would Hammond and Vogel still be operating Dirty4 on the dark web? And would William Orton still be selling the DNA of unsuspecting women to them?

These were scary thoughts but also inspiring ones. They made me think about all the unsolved cases out there. All the failures of justice and all of the mothers, fathers, and families who had lost loved ones. I thought about Charisse, who had called the podcast, and wished there was a way to reach out to her.

I knew then that I could no longer be an observer, a journalist who wrote about these things or talked about them in a podcast.

I knew that I could not be a sideline reporter. I needed to be in the game.

On the first working day of the new year I drove downtown in my replacement Range Rover, found parking, and walked into the offices of RAW Data in the Mercantile Bank building. I asked to speak to Rachel and soon enough was directed back to her office. We had not spoken since the day the Shrike had been killed. I didn't bother to sit down. I expected this to be quick.

"What's up?" she asked tentatively.

"I have an idea and I want you to hear me out," I said.

"I'm listening."

"I don't want to just tell murder stories on the podcast. I want to solve them."

"What do you mean?"

"What I said. I want to work murders on the podcast. We bring in a case, a cold case, discuss it, work it, solve it. I want you to be part of it. You profile the cases, then we go to work on them."

"Jack, you're not—"

"It doesn't matter that I'm not police. We live in digital times. The police are analog. We can put things together. Remember that woman who called the podcast? Charisse? She said nobody's working that case. We could."

"You're talking about being amateur detectives."

"You're not an amateur, and I know when we were working on the Shrike you loved it. You were back doing what you were meant to do. I took that away from you but now I'm offering it back."

"It's not the same, Jack."

"No, it's better. Because we have no rules."

She said nothing.

"Anybody can run background checks," I said. "But you have a gift. I saw it with the Shrike."

"And you're saying this would be a podcast?" she asked.

"We meet, talk about the case, record and post it. The advertising will fund the investigations."

"It seems kind of crazy."

"There's a podcast out there about a housewife who got a serial killer to confess. Nothing is crazy. This could work."

"And where do these cases come from?"

"Anywhere, everywhere. Google. I'm going to find the case Charisse called about. Her sister's case."

Rachel was silent for a long moment before responding.

"Jack, is this…"

"No, it's not a lame attempt to get back with you. I know I ruined it. I accept that. This is exactly what I just said it is. A podcast. We go after those who think they got away with it."

She didn't respond at first, but I thought I saw her almost nod when I had spoken.

"I'll think about it," she finally said.

"Okay, that's all I ask," I said. "Just don't think too long."

Having made the pitch, I turned and left the office without a further word. I walked out of the elegant old building and onto Main Street. There was a chill in the January air but the sun was out and it was going to be a good year. I headed down the street to my car. My phone buzzed before I got to it.

It was Rachel.

AUTHOR'S NOTE

This book is a work of fiction, but *FairWarning* is a real news site offering tough watchdog reporting on consumer issues. It is a nonprofit founded and edited by Myron Levin. The author is a member of *FairWarning*'s board of directors. *FairWarning* and Myron Levin's name were used with permission. Go to FairWarning.org for further information and to consider making a donation to support its important work.

The genetic research explored in this novel is based on fact and current understanding of the human genome. The reporting regarding government oversight of the genetic-analytics industry is also based on current standards. Any errors or omissions are strictly the fault of the author.

ACKNOWLEDGMENTS

The author gratefully acknowledges the help of many in the research, writing, and editing of this book. They include Asya Muchnick, Emad Akhtar, Bill Massey, Heather Rizzo, Jane Davis, Linda Connelly, Paul Connelly, Justin Hysler, David Vasil, Terrill Lee Lankford, Dennis Wojciechowski, Shannon Byrne, Henrik Bastin, John Houghton, Pamela Marshall, and Allan Fallow.

The author also acknowledges the book *Our Genes, Our Choices: How Genotype and Gene Interactions Affect Human Behavior* by Dr. David Goldman, founder of the Laboratory of Neurogenetics at the National Institutes of Health.

ABOUT THE AUTHOR

Michael Connelly is the author of thirty-three previous novels, including the #1 *New York Times* bestsellers *The Night Fire, Dark Sacred Night, Two Kinds of Truth,* and *The Late Show.* His books, which include the Harry Bosch series and Lincoln Lawyer series, have sold more than seventy-four million copies worldwide. Connelly is a former newspaper reporter who has won numerous awards for his journalism and his novels. He is the executive producer of *Bosch,* starring Titus Welliver, and the creator and host of the podcast *Murder Book.* He spends his time in California and Florida.

WHEN MICKEY HALLER IS ARRESTED FOR THE
MURDER OF A CLIENT, HE KNOWS HE'S BEEN
FRAMED. WITH THE HELP OF HIS TRUSTED
TEAM, HE MUST FIGURE OUT WHO HAS
PLOTTED TO DESTROY HIS LIFE AND WHY.

THE LAW OF INNOCENCE

AVAILABLE NOW

PLEASE TURN THE PAGE FOR AN EXCERPT

A murder case is like a tree. A tall tree. An oak tree. It has been carefully planted and cared for by the state. Watered and trimmed when needed, examined for disease and parasites of any kind. Its root system is constantly monitored as it flourishes underground and its tendrils cling tightly to the earth. No money is spared in the protection of the tree and its caretakers are many. Its branches eventually grow and spread wide in splendor. They provide deep shade for those who seek true justice.

The tree's branches spring from a thick and sturdy trunk. Direct evidence, circumstantial evidence, forensic sciences, motive and opportunity. They must stand strong against the fiercest winds.

And that's where I come in. I'm the man with the ax. My job is to cut that tree down at the ground and carry its wood to the chipper.

PART ONE

ECHOES AND IRON

1

It had been a good day for the defense. I had walked a man right out of the courtroom. I had turned a felony battery charge into a righteous case of self-defense in front of the jury. The alleged victim had a bad reputation and a history of violence that both prosecution and defense witnesses, including an ex-wife, were eager to describe on cross-examination. I delivered the knockout punch when I recalled him to the witness stand and led him down a path of questioning that put him over the edge. He lost his cool and threatened me, said he'd like to meet me out in the street where it would be just him and me.

"Would you then claim I attacked you like you have in this case?" I asked.

The prosecutor objected and the judge sustained. But that was all it took. The judge knew it. The prosecutor knew it. Everybody in the courtroom knew it. I notched the NG after less than half an hour of jury deliberation. It might have been my quickest verdict ever, guilty or not.

Within the informal downtown defense bar there is a sacred duty to celebrate a not-guilty verdict in the way a golfer celebrates a hole in one at the clubhouse. That is, drinks all around. My celebration took place at the Redwood on Second Street, just a few blocks from the civic center, where there were no fewer than three courthouses to draw celebrants from. It started early and ended late and when Moira, the heavily tattooed bartender who had been keeping the tab, handed me the damage, let's just say I put more on my credit card than I would be receiving from the client I had just set free.

I had parked in a lot on Broadway. I got behind the wheel, took a left out of the lot and then another to put me back on Second Street. The traffic lights were with me and I followed the street into the tunnel that went under Bunker Hill and the Harbor Freeway. I was halfway through when I saw the reflection of blue lights on the tunnel's sea-foam-green tiles. I checked the mirror and saw an LAPD cruiser was behind me. I hit the blinker and pulled into the slow lane to let him pass. But the cruiser followed my lead into the same lane and came up six feet behind me. I got the picture then. I was being pulled over.

I waited until I was out of the tunnel and took the first right onto Beaudry. I pulled to a stop, killed the engine, and lowered the window. In the Lincoln's side-view mirror I saw a uniformed officer walking up to my door. I saw no one else in the patrol car behind him.

"Can I see your license, car registration, and proof of insurance, sir?" he asked.

I turned to look at him. His nametag said Milton.

"You sure can, Officer Milton," I said. "But can I ask why you pulled me over? I know I wasn't speeding and all the lights were green."

"License," Milton said. "Registration. Insurance."

"Well, I guess you'll eventually tell me. My license is in my pocket inside my coat. The other stuff is in the glove box. Which you want me to go for first?"

"Let's start with your license."

"You got it."

As I pulled my wallet and worked the license out of one of its slots, I reviewed my situation and wondered if Milton had been watching the Redwood for lawyers exiting my party and possibly too tipsy to drive. There had been rumors about patrol cops doing that on nights when there was an NG party going on and defense lawyers could be picked off for a variety of moving-vehicle infractions.

I handed Milton my license and then went for the glove box. Soon enough the officer had all he had asked for.

"Now, are you going to tell me what this is about?" I asked. "I know I didn't—"

"Step out of the car, sir," Milton said.

"Oh, come on, man. Really?"

"Please step out of the car."

"Whatever."

I threw the door open, forcing Milton to take a step back.

"Just so you know," I said. "I spent the last four hours in the Redwood but I didn't have a drop of alcohol. I haven't had a drink in more than five years."

"Good for you. Please step to the back of your vehicle."

"Make sure your car camera is on because this is going to be embarrassing."

I walked past him to the back of the Lincoln and stepped into the lights of the patrol car behind it.

"You want me to walk a line?" I said. "Count backward, touch my nose with my finger, what? I'm a lawyer. I know all the games and this one is bullshit."

Milton followed me to the back of the car. He was tall and lean, white with a high and tight haircut. I saw the Metro Division badge on his shoulder and four chevrons on his long sleeves. I knew they gave them out for five years of service each. He was a veteran Metro bullethead.

"You see why I stopped you, sir?" he said. "Your car has no plate."

I looked down at the rear bumper of the Lincoln. Milton was right. There was no plate.

"Goddamn it," I said. "Uh…this is some kind of prank. We were celebrating—I won a case today and walked my client. The plate says IWALKEM and one of those guys must've thought it was a joke to steal the plate."

I tried to think about who left the Redwood before I did, and who would have thought this was a funny thing to do. Daly, Mills, Bernardo…it could have been anyone.

"Check the trunk," Milton said. "Maybe it's in there."

"No, they would need a key to put it in the trunk," I said. "I'm going to make a call, see if I can—"

"Sir, you're not making a call until we're finished here."

"That's bullshit. I know the law. I'm not in custody—I can make a call."

I paused there to see if Milton had any further challenge. I noticed the camera on his chest.

"My phone's in the car," I said.

I started moving back to the open door.

"Sir, stop right there," Milton said from behind me.

I turned around.

"What?"

He snapped on a flashlight and pointed the beam at the ground behind the car.

"Is that blood?" he asked.

I stepped back and looked down at the cracked asphalt. The

officer's light was centered on a blotch of liquid beneath the bumper of my car. It was dark maroon at the center and almost translucent at its edges.

"I don't know," I said. "But whatever it is, it was already there. I'm—"

Just as I said it we both saw another drop come down from the bumper and hit the asphalt.

"Sir, open the trunk, please," Milton demanded as he put the flashlight into a belt holster.

A variety of questions cascaded through my mind, starting with what was in the trunk and ending with whether Milton had probable cause to open it if I refused to.

Another drop of what I now assumed to be bodily fluid of some sort hit the asphalt.

"Write me the ticket for the plate, Officer Milton," I said. "But I am not opening the trunk."

"Sir, then I am placing you under arrest," Milton said. "Put your hands on the trunk."

"Arrest? For what? I'm not—"

Milton moved in on me, grabbing me and spinning me toward my car. He threw all of his weight into me and doubled me over the trunk.

"Hey! You can't—"

One by one my arms were roughly pulled behind my back and I was handcuffed. Milton then put his hand into the back collar of my shirt and jacket and yanked me up off the car.

"You're under arrest," he said.

"For what?" I said. "You can't just—"

"For your safety and mine I'm putting you into the back of the patrol car."

He roughly turned me again and walked me to the rear

passenger door of his car. He put his hand on top of my head as he pushed me into the plastic seat in the back.

"You know you can't open the trunk," I said. "You have no probable cause. You don't know if that's blood and you don't know if it's coming from the interior of the car. I could've driven through whatever it is."

Milton pulled back out of the car and looked down at me.

"Exigent circumstances," he said. "Someone in there might need help."

He slammed the door. I watched him go back to my Lincoln and study the trunk lid for some sort of release mechanism. Finding none, he went to the open driver's door and reached in to remove the keys.

He used the key fob to pop the trunk, standing off to the side should someone come up out of the trunk shooting. The lid went up and there was an interior light. Milton supplemented it with his own flashlight. He moved from left to right, stepping sideways and keeping his eyes and the beam on the contents of the trunk. From my angle in the back of the patrol car, I could not see into the trunk but could tell by the way Milton was maneuvering and bending down for a closer look that there was something in there.

Milton tilted his head to talk into the radio mic on his shoulder and made a call. Probably for backup. Probably for a homicide unit. I didn't have to see into the trunk to know that Milton had found a body.

2

Edgar Quesada sat next to me at a dayroom table as I read the last pages of the transcript from his trial. He had asked me to review his case files as a favor, hoping there was something I could see or do to help his situation. We were in the high-power module in the Twin Towers Correctional Facility in downtown Los Angeles. This was where they housed inmates on keep-away status as they waited for trial or, as in Quesada's case, sentencing to state prison. It was a Sunday evening in February and the jail was cold. Quesada wore white long johns under his orange jumpsuit, the sleeves all the way down to his wrists.

Quesada was in familiar surroundings. He had been down this path before and had the tattoos to prove it. A third-generation White Fence gang member from Boyle Heights with lots of inked allegiance to the gang and the Mexican Mafia, which was the largest and most powerful gang in California's jail and prison systems.

According to the documents I had been reading, Quesada had been the driver of a car that carried two other members of White Fence as they fired automatic weapons through the plate-glass windows of a bodega on East First Street where the owner had fallen two weeks behind on the gang tax White Fence had been extorting from him for almost twenty-five years. The shooters had aimed high, the attack intended to be a warning. But a ricochet went low and hit the bodega owner's granddaughter in the top of the head as she crouched behind the counter. Her name was Marisol Serrano. She died instantly, according to testimony I read from the deputy coroner.

No witnesses to the crime identified the shooters. That would have been a fatal exercise in bravery. But a traffic cam caught the license plate on the getaway car. It was traced to a car stolen from the long-term parking garage at nearby Union Station. And cameras there caught a glimpse of the thief: Edgar Quesada. His trial lasted only four days and he was convicted of conspiracy to commit murder. His sentencing was in a week and he was looking at a minimum of fifteen years in prison, with the likelihood of many more beyond that.

"So?" Quesada said, as I flipped the last page over.

"Well, Edgar," I said. "I think you're kind of fucked."

"Don't tell me that. There's nothing? Nothing at all?"

"There's always things you can do. But they're long shots, Edgar. I'd say you have more than enough here for a 2254 motion but—"

"What's that?"

"Ineffective assistance of counsel. Your lawyer sat on his hands the whole trial. He let objection after objection pass. He just let the prosecutor—well, here, you see this page?"

I moved back through the transcript to a page where I had folded a corner over.

"Here the judge even says, *Are you going to object, Mr. Seguin, or do I have to keep doing it for you?* That is not good trial work, Edgar, and you may have a shot at proving that, but here is the thing: at best you win the motion and get a do-over, but that doesn't change the evidence. It's still the same evidence and with the next jury you'll go down again, even if you have a new lawyer who knows how to keep the prosecutor inside the lines."

Quesada shook his head. He was not my client so I didn't know all the details of his life, but he was about thirty-five and looking at a lot of hard time.

"How many convictions do you have?" I asked.

"Two," he said.

"Felonies?"

He nodded and I didn't have to say anything else. My original assessment stood. He was fucked. He was probably going away forever. Unless…

"You know why they got you here in high power instead of the gang module, right?" I said. "Any day now they're going to pull you out of here and put you in a room and ask you the big question. Who was in the car with you that day?"

I gestured to the thick transcript.

"There's nothing here that will help you," I said. "The only thing you can do is deal the time down by giving up names."

I said the last part in a whisper. But Quesada didn't respond as quietly.

"That's *bullshit*!" he yelled.

I checked the mirrored window of the control room overhead even though I knew I could see nothing behind it. I then looked down at Quesada and saw the veins in his neck start to pulse—even beneath the inked necklace of cemetery stones that circled it.

"Cool down, Edgar," I said. "You asked me to look at your file and that's all I'm doing. I'm not your lawyer. You should really talk to him about—"

"I can't go to him," Quesada said. "Haller, you don't know shit!"

I stared at him and finally understood. His lawyer was controlled by the very people he would need to inform on: White Fence. Going to him would almost assuredly result in a Mexican Mafia–hired snitch shanking, whether he was in the high-power module or not. It was said that the *eMe,* as it was more formally known, could get to anybody anywhere in a California lockdown.

I was literally saved by the bell. The five-minute warning horn before bed check sounded. Quesada reached across the table and roughly grabbed up his documents. He was through with me. He got up while still smoothing all the loose pages into a neat stack. Without a *thank you* or a *fuck you,* he headed off to his cell.

And I headed to mine.

3

At 8 p.m. the steel door of my cell automatically slid closed with a metallic *bang* that jolted my entire being. I had been in lockup for five weeks and it was something I couldn't and didn't want to ever get used to. I sat down on the three-inch-thin mattress and closed my eyes. I knew the overhead light would stay on another hour and I needed to use that time, but this was my ritual. To try to blank out all the harsh sounds and fears. To remind myself of who I still was. A father, a lawyer—but not a murderer.

"You got Q all hot and bothered out there."

I opened my eyes. It was Bishop in the next cell over. There was an air-vent grate high up on the wall that separated our cells.

"Didn't mean to," I said. "I guess next time somebody needs a jailhouse lawyer in here I'll just pass."

"Good plan," Bishop said.

"And where were you, by the way? It was about to become kill-the-messenger time with him. I looked around, no Bishop."

"Don't worry, Homes, I had you covered. I was watching from up on the rail."

I was paying Bishop $400 a week for protection, the payment delivered in cash by my investigator to his girlfriend and mother of his son in Inglewood. His protection extended throughout the quarter of the high-power octagon where we were housed: two tiers, twenty-four cells, with twenty-two other inmates presenting varying levels of known and unknown threat to me.

On my first night Bishop had offered to protect me or hurt me. I didn't negotiate. He usually stuck close when I was in the dayroom but I had not seen him on the second-tier walkway rail when I had given Quesada the bad news about his case.

I reached under the bed for the cardboard file box that held my own case docs. I checked the rubber bands first. I had wrapped each of the four stacks of documents with two bands each, horizontal and vertical, with the bands crossing at a specific spot on the top sheet. This told me if Bishop or anyone else had snuck in and started pawing through my papers. I had a client once who almost went down on a first-degree murder because a jailhouse snitch had gotten to the files in his cell and was able to read enough discovery material to concoct a convincing but phony confession he claimed my client had made to him. Lesson learned. I set rubber-band traps and would know if someone had looked through my stuff.

I was now facing a first-degree murder charge myself and was going *pro se,* meaning I was defending myself. I know what Lincoln said and probably many wise men before him. Maybe I did have a fool for a client, but I couldn't see putting my future in any hands other than my own. So, in the matter of the State of California versus Michael Haller, the defense's war room was cell 13, level K-10 at Twin Towers.

I pulled my motions packet out of the box and snapped off the rubber bands after confirming that the documents had not been tampered with. A motions hearing was scheduled for the following morning and I wanted to prep. I had three requests before the court, beginning with a motion to lower bail. It had been set at my arraignment at $5 million, with the prosecution successfully arguing that I was not only a flight risk but a threat to witnesses in the case because I knew the inner workings of the local justice system like the back of my hand. It didn't help that the judge handling the arraignment was the honorable Richard Rollins Hagan, whose rulings in prior cases I had twice gotten overturned on appeal. He got some payback on me, agreeing with the prosecution request to more than double down on the schedule that recommended a $2 million bail for first-degree murder.

At the time, the difference between $2 and $5 million didn't matter. I had to decide if I wanted to put everything I had into my freedom or into my defense. I decided on the latter and took up residence in the Twin Towers, qualifying for keep-away status as an officer of the court who had potential enemies in all of the gen-pop dorms.

But tomorrow I would stand before a different judge—one I believed I had never crossed—and ask for a reduction in bail. I had two other motions to argue as well and now reviewed my notes so I could stand and argue before the judge instead of read.

More important than the bail motion was the discovery motion that accused the prosecution of withholding information and evidence I was entitled to, and the challenge to the probable cause of the police stop that led to my arrest.

I had to assume that Judge Violet Warfield, who had drawn the case on rotation, would put a time cap on arguments on all the motions. I would need to be ready—succinct and on point.

"Hey, Bishop?" I said. "You still awake?"

"I'm awake," Bishop said. "What's up?"

"I want to practice on you."

"Practice what?"

"My arguments, Bishop."

"That ain't part of our deal, man."

"I know but the lights are about to go out and I'm not ready. I want you to listen and tell me what you think."

At that moment the lights on the tier went out.

"Okay," Bishop said. "Let's hear it. But you pay extra for this."

4

In the morning I was on the first bus to the courthouse, having dined on a baloney sandwich and a bruised red apple for breakfast. It was the same breakfast every morning and it was served again at lunch for good measure. I was long past any revulsion with it. It was the routine and now I put it away easily. I estimated I had already lost between ten and twenty pounds during my incarceration and I looked at it as getting down to fighting weight for what would surely be the bout of my life.

On the bus I was with thirty-five other inmates, most of whom were heading to morning arraignment court. I had seen the wide-eyed look of fear in clients when I met them for the first time at first appearances. But that was always in court and always with me calming and preparing them for what lay ahead. On the buses I was always surrounded by it. Men facing their first experience of incarceration. Men who had been in lockup many times before. There was a desperation to it whether you were a rookie or a recidivist.

I found the bus rides to and from court to be my own moments of biggest fear. It was random selection when you were loaded on. I had no Bishop, no bodyguard. Should anything happen to me, the deputies were behind an iron grate at the front: Driver and Shotgun. Their role would simply be to sort out the dead and dying when whatever happened was over. They weren't there to protect and serve. Just to move people along in the underbelly of the justice system.

The bus pulled into the cavernous garage beneath the Clara Shortridge Foltz Criminal Justice Center and we were offloaded and escorted into the vertical maze of holding cells that served the building's twenty-four courtrooms.

As a *pro se* I was entitled to some legal niceties not afforded most of the men and women who came off the buses. I was taken to a private holding cell where I could confer with my investigator and stand-in attorney—the lawyer assigned as my backup to handle the printing, filing, and in some cases fine-tuning of motions and other documents produced as part of the case. My investigator was Dennis "Cisco" Wojciechowski and the stand-in was my law partner, Jennifer Aronson.

Everything moves slowly in incarceration. My 4 a.m. wakeup at Twin Towers resulted in getting to my private conference room at 8:40 a.m., a total travel distance of four blocks. I had brought one rubber-banded stack of documents with me— the motions—and was spreading them on the metal table when my team was escorted in by a detention deputy at nine sharp.

Cisco and Jennifer were required to sit across the table from me. No handshakes or hugs. The meeting fell under attorney-client privilege and was private. But there was a camera in one corner of the ceiling. We would be watched but the camera carried no audio back to the deputy who monitored it. I wasn't sure I fully believed this and during prior team meetings I would occasionally make a remark or issue an order designed to send the prosecution off on a wild-goose chase, if they happened to be illegally listening in. I used a code in each statement to alert my team to the ruse.

I was in dark blue scrubs with LAC DETENTION stenciled across the front and back of my shirt. Like Edgar Quesada the evening before, I wore long johns underneath. I had learned quickly during my stay with the county that the early-morning bus rides and courthouse holding cells were unheated and I dressed accordingly.

Jennifer was dressed for court in a charcoal suit and cream-colored blouse. Cisco, as was his routine, was dressed for a sunset ride down the Pacific Coast Highway on his classic Harley panhead: black jeans, boots, and T-shirt. It appeared that his skin was impervious to the cold, damp air of the conference cell. That he was from Wisconsin might have had something to do with it.

"How's my team this fine morning?" I said cheerily.

Although I was the one incarcerated and wearing the jailhouse scrubs, I knew it was important to keep my team engaged and not worried about my predicament. *Act like a winner and you will become a winner*—as Legal Siegel, my late mentor, used to say.

"All good, Boss," Cisco said.

"How are you doing?" Jennifer asked.

"Better to be in the courthouse than the jail," I said. "Which suit did Lorna pick out?"

Lorna Taylor was my case manager as well as my sartorial consultant. This second duty extended from when she had been my wife—my second wife, in a union that lasted only a year. Though I would not be appearing this day before a jury, I had previously secured Judge Warfield's approval of a motion allowing me to dress in my professional clothes during all appearances in open court. My case had drawn considerable attention from the media and I didn't want a photo of me in convict garb going viral. It was act like a winner and the potential jury pool out there would think you were a winner. My carefully curated selection of suits added to my confidence when I stood before the court to argue my case.

"The blue Hugo Boss with pink shirt and gray tie," Jennifer said. "The courtroom deputy has it."

"Perfect," I said.

Cisco rolled his eyes at my vanity. I ignored it.

"What about the time?" I asked. "You talk to the clerk?"

"Yes, the judge slotted an hour," Jennifer said. "Will that be enough?"

"Probably not with argument from Dana. I might have to drop something if Warfield sticks to the schedule."

Dana was Dana Berg, the Major Crimes Unit star prosecutor assigned to convicting me and sending me off to prison for the rest of my life. Among members of the informal downtown defense bar, she was alternately known as Death Row Dana because of her propensity to seek maximum penalties or as Ice Berg because of her demeanor when it came to negotiating pleas. The fact was that her resolve couldn't be melted and she was most often assigned cases where trial was inevitable.

And that was the situation with me. The day after my arrest I put out a media statement through Jennifer that forcefully denied the allegations against me and promised vindication at trial. It was most likely this statement that got the case assigned to Dana Berg.

"Then what do we drop?" Jennifer asked.

"Let's put bail on the back burner," I said.

"Wait, no," Cisco said.

"What? I wanted to go with that right out of the gate," Jennifer said. "We need to get you out of there and into unrestricted strategy sessions in an office, not a cell."

Jennifer raised her hands to take in the cell we were sitting in. I knew that they would both protest my decision on bail. But I intended to make better use of today's time in front of the judge.

"Look, it's not like I'm having a great time over there," I said. "It's not the Ritz. But there are things that are more important to accomplish today. I want to get a full hearing on the probable-cause challenge. That's number one. And then I want to argue the discovery issues. You ready on that, Bullocks?"

It had been a long time since I had called Jennifer by her baby-lawyer nickname. I had hired her right out of Southwestern Law School, which was housed in a former Bullock's department store. I had wanted somebody with a working-class law degree and an underdog's drive and fierceness. In the years since, she had proved me a genius, rising from an associate counsel to whom I handed off low-money cases to a full partner and trusted confidante who could hold her own and win in any courtroom in the county. I wasn't interested in using her as a mere filer of documents. I wanted her going toe to toe with Dana Berg on the prosecution's delays in discovery. This was the most important case of my career and I wanted her side by side with me at the defense table.

"I'm ready," she said. "But I'm also ready to argue bail. You need to be out so you can prepare for trial without needing a bodyguard watching your back while you're eating baloney fucking sandwiches."

I laughed. I guess I had complained a little too often about the Twin Towers menu.

"Look, I get that," I said. "And I don't mean to laugh. But [I] need to keep payroll going and I don't want to come out of th[is] thing bankrupt and with nothing left for my daughter. Some[-] body's got to pay for law school and it's not going to be Maggi[e] McFierce."

My first ex-wife and the mother of my child was a lifer in th[e] District Attorney's Office. Real name: Maggie McPherson. Sh[e] made a comfortable living and had raised our daughter, Hayle[y,] in a clean and safe neighborhood in Sherman Oaks. I had pai[d] for private schools all the way and now Hayley was looking a[t] USC law after graduating from Chapman this year. That woul[d] carry a steep price tag that would fall to me to pay. I had planne[d] for it and had it covered in savings, but not if I pulled the cas[h] and put it into a nonrefundable bond just to spring myself loo[se] to prep for trial.

I had done the math and it wasn't worth it. Even if w[e] persuaded Judge Warfield to cut bail in half, I was still looking [at] needing $250,000 to buy a bond that really only amounted to tw[o] months of freedom. After all, I had refused to waive my rig[ht] to a speedy trial and had the state on a clock. The trial was on[ly] six weeks away and the verdict would either give me back m[y] freedom or permanently suspend it. On many previous occasio[ns] I had counseled clients to save their bond money and nut it o[ut] in Twin Towers.

Now that was the counsel I gave myself.

"Look, you know that Lorna, Cisco, and I have all said we ca[n] defer paychecks till this is over," Jennifer said. "I really think y[ou] need to reconsider — for the sake of the case."

I nodded.

"Duly noted," I said. "Let's see if there's time to get to [it] today. If not, we'll take it up in the next round. Let's move [on past the motions. Cisco, what's happening with the review of previous cases?"

"Me and Lorna are through about half the files," Cisco said. "So far nothing stands out. But we're working on it and making a list of possibles."

He was talking about a list of former clients and enemies who might have the motive and wherewithal to pin a murder case on me.

"Okay, I need that," I said. "I can't just go into court and say I was framed. A third-party culpability case requires a third party."

"We're on it," Cisco said. "If it's there, we'll find it."

"If?" I asked.

"I didn't mean it like that, Boss," Cisco said. "I just meant—"

"Listen," I said. "I've spent the last twenty-five years of my life telling clients that it didn't matter to me whether they did it, because my job was to defend them, not judge them. Guilty or innocent, you get the same deal and the same effort. But now that I'm on the other side of it, I know that's bullshit. I need you two and Lorna to believe in me on this."

"Of course we do," Jennifer said.

"Goes without saying," Cisco added.

"Don't be so quick to answer," I said. "You must have questions about it. The state's case is more than persuasive. So if at any point Death Row Dana turns you into a believer, I need you to step up and step out. I don't want you on the team."

"Not going to happen," Cisco said.

"Never," added Jennifer.

"Good," I said. "Then let's go to war. Jennifer, can you go get my suit and bring it in so I can get ready?"

"Be right back," she said.

She got up and hammered on the steel door with one hand while waving to the overhead camera with the other. Soon heard the sharp metal *crack* of the door unlocking. A deput opened it to let her out.

"So," I said once Cisco and I were alone. "What's the wate temp these days down in Baja?"

"Oh, it's nice," Cisco said. "I talked to my guy down there and he said high eighties."

"Too warm for me. Tell him to let me know when it get down to about seventy-five. That would be perfect for me."

"I'll tell him."

I nodded to Cisco and tried not to smile for the overhea camera. Hopefully, this last bit of conversation was intriguin enough to any illegal listeners to send them fishing for a re herring down in Mexico.

"So, what about our victim?" I said.

"Not a lot so far," Cisco said hesitantly. "I'm hoping Jennife gets discovery going today so I can run down his movements an how and when he ended up in your trunk."

"Sam Scales was a slippery guy. Nailing him down is going t be tough, but I'm going to need that."

"Don't worry. You'll have it."

I nodded. I liked Cisco's confidence. I hoped it would pay of I thought for a moment about my former client Sam Scales. Th ultimate con man who had even conned me. Now the victim i the biggest con of all, I was set up for a murder that I knew wa going to be a hard frame to break.

"Hey, Boss, you okay?" Cisco asked.

I looked at him.

"Yeah, fine," I said. "Just thinking about things. This is goin to be fun."

Now Cisco nodded. He knew it was going to be anything but fun, but he understood the sentiment. *Act like a winner and you'll become a winner.*

The cell door slid open again and Jennifer came back in carrying my court clothes on two hangers. I usually reserved the pink oxford for appearances before a jury, but that was okay. Just seeing the sharp cut of the suit on its hanger kicked my mood up to a new level. I started getting ready for battle.

5

M y suit fit me loosely. I felt like I was swimming in it. The first thing I told Jennifer when they moved me into court and took off the chains was to ask Lorna to go to my house, pick out two of my suits, and take them to the tailor to be refitted before my trial started.

"That's going to be kind of hard without you there to be measured," she said.

"I don't care, it's important," I said. "I don't want to look like a guy in a borrowed suit in front of the jury."

"Okay, I get it."

"I'll probably lose another five pounds by jury selection. Tell her to have them take them in a full size all around."

"What are they feeding you in that place?"

"Apples. I mostly eat apples. I trade baloney sandwiches for apples."

"You'd better start eating the baloney."

Before I could respond, Dana Berg stepped over to the defense table and put down a set of documents.

"Our answers to your motions," she said. "I'm sure it will all come out in oral."

"Timely," Jennifer said, meaning it was anything but.

She started reading. I didn't bother. Berg seemed to hesitate, as if expecting a retort from me. I just looked up and smiled.

"Good morning, Dana," I said. "How was your weekend?"

"Better than yours, I'm sure," she said.

"I think that would be a given," I said.

She smirked and returned to the prosecution table.

"No surprise, she's objecting to everything," Jennifer said. "Including bail reduction."

"Par for the course," I said. "Like I said, don't worry about bail today. We'll—"

I was silenced by the booming voice of the courtroom deputy announcing the arrival of Judge Warfield. We were instructed to remain seated and come to order.

I had believed I got lucky when we drew Warfield on the case. She was a tough law-and-order firebrand, but she was also a former member of the defense bar. Oftentimes defense lawyers who become judges seem to go out of their way to show impartiality by favoring the prosecution. That was not what I knew about Warfield. While I had never had a case before her, I had checked with Daly, Mills, and some of the other defense pros who were regulars at the Redwood and Four Green Fields, and they all told me that Warfield threw her pitches right down the middle. That was good with me. In addition, she was black and that made her an underdog in society. Coming up, she had had to be better than the other lawyers to make her way. That demanded a mindset I liked. She knew full well the disadvantages I faced in trying to defend myself. My guess was that she would include that knowledge in her decisions.

"We're on the record in *California versus Haller* and we have a series of motions to consider," the judge said. "Mr. Haller, you are *pro se* in this matter. Will you be offering argument, or will it be your co-counsel, Ms. Aronson?"

I stood to reply.

"May it please the court," I began, "we would like to tag-team a little bit today. I would like to start with the motion to suppress."

"Very well," Warfield said. "Proceed."

Here is where it got tricky. I had filed what was technically a motion *in limine* to exclude evidence that had been unconstitutionally obtained. I was challenging the traffic stop that led to the discovery of the body of Sam Scales in the trunk of my car. If I won the motion, the case against me would probably be DOA. But it was a long shot to believe that a judge, even as impartial as I had heard Warfield to be, would throw such a wrench into the state's case. And that was what I was counting on. Because I didn't want that to happen either. With any other client I would want that ruling. But this was my own case. I did not want to win on a technicality. I needed to be exonerated. The trick here was to have a full-blown hearing on the constitutionality of the traffic stop that put me in jail. But I only wanted it in order to get Officer Milton on the stand so that I could draw out his story and lock it down under oath. Because I believed I was set up for this and that setup had to have included Milton in some way.

Carrying the printout of the motion, I walked to the lectern between the prosecution and defense tables. On the way I casually checked the gallery and saw at least two people I recognized as journalists covering the hearing. I knew I had a conduit to get my defense out into the world through them.

I also saw my daughter, Hayley, in the back row. She was spending her summer before law school shadowing her mother in the D.A.'s office. But since it was an unpaid internship, she was granted the freedom to attend all hearings that brought me into court. I had forbidden her from visiting me in jail. I didn't want her ever to see me in jail scrubs.

I threw her a nod and a smile, but seeing her now reminded me how ill-fitting my suit was. It looked borrowed and announced *CONVICT!* to all courtroom observers. I might as well have been wearing the scrubs. I tried to shake off these thoughts when I got to the lectern and turned my attention to the judge.

"Your Honor," I said. "As the motion before the court states, the defense contends that I was set up and framed in this case. And that setup came into play with the illegal and unconstitutional stop by the police on the night I was arrested. I have re—"

"Set up by whom, Mr. Haller?" the judge asked.

I was thrown by the question. As valid as it may have been, it was unexpected from the judge, especially before I finished my argument.

"Judge, that is irrelevant at this hearing," I said. "This is about the traffic stop and whether it was constitutional. It—"

"But you are saying you were framed. Do you know who framed you?"

"Again, Your Honor, that is irrelevant. In six weeks it will be very relevant, but I don't see why I have to reveal my case to the prosecution while challenging the validity of the traffic stop."

"Then continue."

"Thank you, Your Honor, I will. The—"

"Is that a shot?"

"Excuse me?"

"What you just said, is that a shot at me, Mr. Haller?"

I shook my head as though confused. I couldn't even remember what I had said.

"Uh, no, not a shot, Judge," I said. "I don't remember what I said but it was in no way intended to—"

"Very well, let's move on," the judge said.

"Okay, well, I apologize if anything was misinterpreted. As I was saying, I've filed a motion to suppress, challenging the probable cause to stop and the probable cause supporting a warrantless search of the trunk of the vehicle I was driving. An evidentiary hearing is required on the issues raised with the attendance of the officer who stopped me and searched my vehicle. I would like to schedule a time for the hearing. But before we can do that, I have other matters that need to be addressed. My investigator has been trying for two weeks, Your Honor, to talk to the officer who stopped me—Officer Roy Milton—and has been unsuccessful despite numerous requests to him and the police department. I know we will be discussing our discovery motion later but, same thing, no cooperation from the D.A.'s office in regard to the arrest. Officer Milton was clearly wearing a body camera, in keeping with LAPD regulations, and we have not been given the video. There was a video camera in the police car as well and we have not been given that either."

"Your Honor?" Dana Berg said. "The state objects to defense's argument. He is turning a motion to suppress evidence in the case into a request *for* evidence. I'm confused."

"So am I," Warfield said. "Mr. Haller, I allowed you to defend yourself because you are an experienced lawyer, but you are sounding more and more like an amateur. Please stay on point."

"Well then, I too am confused, Your Honor," I said. "I filed a legally sufficient motion to suppress the fruits of a warrantless search. Ms. Berg bears the burden of demonstrating the justification for the search. Yet I don't see Officer Milton in the courtroom. So unless the prosecution is about to announce a concession, Ms. Berg is not ready to defend against the motion. Yet Ms. Berg acts as if I'm supposed to merely argue and be done with it.

"Judge, the point is that I request an evidentiary hearing and an opportunity to prepare for that hearing after receiving the discovery I am entitled to. I can't properly and fully argue the motion to suppress because the prosecution is violating the rules of discovery. I ask the court to table this for today, order the prosecution to fulfill its discovery obligations, and schedule a full evidentiary hearing on the motion at a time when witnesses, including Officer Milton, may appear."

The judge looked at Berg.

"I know we have a discovery motion in Mr. Haller's stack," Warfield said, "but where are we on those items just mentioned? The video from the officer and the car. Those should have been turned over by now."

"Judge," Berg said. "We have had technical issues with the transfer of—"

"Your Honor," I roared, "they can't be pulling this *technical difficulty* excuse. I was arrested five weeks ago. My freedom is on the line here and for them to say technical issues have delayed my due process rights is patently unfair, Judge."

"I agree," Warfield said. "We are going to continue this motion to Thursday morning, when we will have a full hearing. Ms. Berg, my first question at that hearing will be to ask you if full discovery has been shared. I am talking about every frame of film or video. Is that understood?"

"Yes, Your Honor," Berg said humbly.

"Your Honor?" I interrupted. "Witnesses?"

The judge nodded her thanks for the reminder.

"I want Officer Milton here Thursday to tell us about the traffic stop of Mr. Haller," she said. "If he does not appear, I'll be inclined to either grant the motion or hold you in contempt."

"Yes, Your Honor," Berg said.

"Very well, let's move on to the next motion," Warfield said. "I have to leave the courthouse at eleven for an outside meeting. Let's press on."

"Your Honor, my co-counsel Jennifer Aronson will discuss the motion to compel discovery."

Jennifer got up and approached the lectern. I went back to the defense table and we lightly touched arms as we passed each other.

"Go get 'em," I whispered.

6

The perks I received as a *pro se* inmate extended to the detention center, where I was afforded space and time for daily meetings with my legal team. I set these meetings Monday through Friday at 3 p.m. whether or not there were issues or strategy to discuss. I needed the connection to the outside, if only for the mental-health maintenance.

The meetings were a hardship for Cisco and Jennifer because they and whatever belongings they had were searched coming in and going out, and the rule was that they had to be in place in the attorney-client room before I was even pulled from the pod where I was housed. Everything in the jail moved at an indifferent pace set by the deputies running the show. The last thing afforded an inmate, even a *pro se,* was punctuality. It was the same reason why my wake-ups were at 4 a.m. for a hearing six hours later and only four blocks away. These delays and harassments meant that my team usually had to present themselves at the jail's attorneys' entrance at 2 p.m. so that I might see them for an hour beginning at 3 p.m.

The meeting that followed the court hearing was more important than a mental-health hour. The hearing had resulted in a major gain for the defense when Judge Warfield, perhaps remembering her days as a defense attorney, came down hard on the prosecution for delays in discovery. And Dana Berg, perhaps anticipating the judge's ruling on the motion, revealed she had come to court with many of the materials we had been requesting for weeks, including the videos from Officer Milton's body and car cams. The judge then signed an order allowing Jennifer Aronson to bring a disc player into the jail for the legal-team conference so that I could view the videos.

I was late to the meeting because it had taken nearly four hours to bus me the four blocks back from the courthouse to the jail. By the time they put me in the lawyer room, Jennifer and Cisco had been waiting nearly an hour.

"Sorry, guys," I said as I was ushered in by a deputy. "I don't control things around here."

"Yeah, no kidding," said Cisco.

It was the same setup as with the attorney room in the courthouse. They sat across from me. There was a camera that supposedly had no audio feed. The difference here was that I was allowed to use a pen when I was in the room to keep notes or handwrite motions to the court. I was not allowed to take the pen back to my cell because it could be used as a weapon, a pipe, or a source for tattoo ink. In fact, I was only allowed a pen with red ink because it was considered an undesirable tattoo ink should I somehow smuggle it back to my pod.

"Have you looked at the videos yet?" I asked.

"Only about ten times while we were waiting," Cisco said.

"And?"

I looked at Jennifer with the question. She was the lawyer.

"Your recall of what was said and done was excellent," she said.

"Good," I said. "Can you stand to watch it again? I want to take notes for the Q&A with Officer Milton."

"Do you think that's the best way to go?" Jennifer asked.

I looked at her.

"You mean my asking the guy who arrested me the questions?"

"Yeah. Might look vindictive to the jury."

I nodded.

"It could. I'm still going to write questions and we'll make it a game-time decision. You should write up what you would ask and we'll compare tomorrow or Wednesday."

I was not allowed to touch the computer. Cisco turned the screen toward me. He played the video from Milton's body cam first. The camera was attached to his uniform at chest height. It began with a view of the steering wheel of his car and quickly moved to him exiting the car and walking up the shoulder of the road toward a car I recognized as my Lincoln.

"Stop it," I said. "This is bullshit."

Cisco hit the stop button.

"What is bullshit?" Jennifer asked.

"The video," I said. "Berg knows what I want and she's fucking with us even though she made the grand gesture of compliance in court today. I want you to go back to the judge tomorrow with a motion requesting the full video. I want to see where this guy was and what he was doing before I supposedly crossed his path. Tell the judge we want to go back half an hour minimum on the body cam. And do it tomorrow because we want the full video before we go in for the hearing Thursday."

"Got it."

"Okay, go ahead with what they gave us."

Cisco hit the play button and I watched. There was a time code in the corner of the screen and I immediately started writing down times and notes to go with them. The traffic stop and what happened afterward was pretty much how I had remembered it.

I saw several places where I thought I could score points during the questioning of Milton, and a few others where I thought I might be able to lead him into a lie trap.

Where I saw new stuff on the video was when Milton opened the trunk of the Lincoln and looked down to examine Sam Scales for any sign of life. I had been in the back seat of Milton's patrol car at that point, my view of the trunk limited and from a low angle. Now I was looking at Sam's body on its side, knees pulled up toward the chest and arms behind his back, secured with several wraps of duct tape. There were bullet wounds in the chest and shoulder areas, and what looked like an entrance wound on the left temple and an exit through the right eye.

Sam Scales in life had deserved no sympathy but in death he looked pitiful. Blood from his wounds had spread across the floor of the trunk and dripped out through a hole created by the bullet that exited his eye.

"Oh, shit," Milton could be heard saying.

And then he followed his exclamation with a low humming that sounded like a stifled laugh.

"Play that part again," I said. "After Milton says *Oh, shit.*"

Cisco replayed the sequence and I listened again to the sound Milton had made. It was almost like he was gloating. I thought it might be useful for a jury to hear.

"Okay, freeze it," I said.

The image on the screen froze. I looked at Sam Scales. I had represented him for several years and through different charges and had somehow liked him even as I privately joined the public in their outrage at the scams he pulled. A weekly newspaper had once labeled him *the most hated man in America* and it wasn't hyperbole. He was a disaster con artist. Without showing a scintilla of guilt or conscience, he set up websites to take donations for survivors of earthquakes, tsunamis, mudslides, and school shootings. Wherever there was a tragedy that caught up the rest of the world in horror, Sam Scales was there with the quickly built website, the false testimonials, and the button that said DONATE NOW!

Though truly believing in the ideal that everybody charged with a crime deserves the best defense possible, even I could not take Sam Scales for very long. The final straw came with his arrest for soliciting donations to pay for coffins for children killed in a childcare-center massacre in Chicago. Donations poured into a website Scales had built, but the money went right into his pocket. He called me from jail after his arrest. When I heard the details of the scam, I told Sam our relationship was over. I got a request for his files from a lawyer with the Public Defender's Office and that had been the last I had heard about Sam Scales — until he ended up dead in the trunk of my car.

"Anything unique on the car cam?" I asked.

"Not really," Cisco said. "Same stuff, different angle."

"Okay, then let's skip that for now, we're running out of time. What else was in the discovery package from Death Row Dana?"

My attempt to inject a little levity into the discussion fell on deaf ears. The stakes were too high for these two for humor. Cisco answered my question in the full-on professional tone that contradicted his look and demeanor.

"We also got video from the black hole," he said. "I haven't had time to go through it all but it will be my priority once I get out of here."

The black hole was what regular downtown commuters called the massive underground parking garage beneath the civic center. It spiraled down into the earth seven stories deep. I had parked there on the day of the Sam Scales murder, giving my driver the day off because I expected to be in trial all day. The prosecution's theory was that I had abducted Sam Scales the night before, put him in the trunk, and shot him—leaving his body there overnight and then the next day while I was in court. To me that theory defied common sense and I was confident I could convince a jury of that. But there was still time between now and the trial for the prosecution to change theories and come up with something better.

Time of death had been set at approximately twenty-four hours before the body's discovery by Officer Milton. This also accounted for the leakage under the car that had supposedly alerted Milton and led to the grim discovery of the trunk's contents. The body was beginning to break down and decompose, and fluids were leaking through the bullet hole in the floor of the trunk.

"Any theory on why the prosecution wanted those angles in the garage?" I asked.

"I think they want to be able to say nobody tampered with your car all day," Jennifer said. "And if the camera angles are clear enough to show the dripping of bodily fluids under the car, then they have that, too."

"We'll know more when I can get a look," Cisco added.

A sudden chill went through me as I thought about how someone had murdered Sam Scales in my car, most likely while it was parked in my garage, and then how I had driven around with the body for a day.

"Okay, what else?" I asked.

"This is new," Cisco said. "We have a witness report from your next-door neighbor, who heard the voices of two men arguing at your house the night before."

I shook my head.

"Didn't happen," I said. "Who was it, Mrs. Shogren or that idiot Chasen who lives downhill from me?"

Cisco looked at the report.

"Millicent Shogren," he read. "Couldn't make out the words. Just angry voices."

"Okay, you need to interview her—and don't scare her," I said. "Then you talk to Gary Chasen on the other side of the house. He's always picking up strays in West Hollywood and then they get into arguments. If Millie heard an argument it was from Chasen's. It's a stepped neighborhood and she's at the top of the hill. She hears everything."

"What about you?" Jennifer asked. "What did you hear?"

"Nothing," I said. "I told you about that night. I went to bed early and didn't hear a thing."

"And you went to bed alone," Jennifer confirmed.

"Unfortunately," I said. "If I knew I was going to be tagged with a murder, maybe I would have picked up a stray myself."

Again, stakes too high. Nobody cracked a smile. But the discussion of what Millie Shogren had heard and from where she heard it prompted a question.

"Millie didn't tell them she heard the shots, right?" I asked.

"Doesn't say it here," Cisco said.

"Then make sure you ask her," I said. "We might be able to turn their witness into ours."

Cisco shook his head.

"What?" I asked.

"No go, Boss," he said. "We also got the ballistics report in the discovery package and it doesn't look good."

Now I realized why they had been so somber, with me trying to cheer them up instead of the other way around. They had buried the lede and now I was about to hear it.

"Tell me," I said.

"Okay, well, the examination of the two slugs removed from the body were indicative of double spiraling."

I knew that when a bullet is fired from a gun it spins as it moves down the barrel, leaving a distinctive spiral pattern on the soft lead. The spiraling pattern, called *rifling,* can then be used to identify the make of gun that fired the bullet and match the slug to a specific weapon. I wasn't sure, however, what double spiraling indicated.

"What's that mean?" I asked.

"A sound suppressor was used," Cisco said. "A silencer would leave its own mark on a slug, just like the gun barrel."

"Okay, so no noise," I said. "We can deal with that."

"It gets worse," Cisco said.

"Worse how?" I asked.

"The one shot that was through and through the victim's head and then punctured the floor of the trunk," Cisco said. "They found it. On the floor of your garage. Along with blood. It hit the concrete and flattened, so matching of the rifling was no good. But they did metal-alloy tests and matched it to the other bullets. According to what we got in the package, the DNA is still out on the blood, but we can assume that will be matched to Sam Scales as well."

I nodded. This meant the state could prove that Sam Scales was murdered in my home's garage at a time I had just confirmed I was at home. I thought about the legal conclusion I had offered Edgar Quesada the night before. I was now in the same sinking boat. Legally speaking, I was fucked.

"Okay," I finally said. "I need to sit with this and think. If you two have no more surprises, then you can get out of this place and I'll do some strategizing. This doesn't change anything. It's still a setup. It's just a fucking good one and I need to close my eyes and figure things out."

"You sure, Boss?" Cisco asked.

"We can work it with you," Jennifer offered.

"No, I need to be alone with this," I said. "You two go."

Cisco got up and went to the door, where he knocked hard on the metal with the side of his meaty fist.

"Same time tomorrow?" Jennifer asked.

"Yes," I said. "Same time. At some point we have to stop trying to figure out their case and start building ours."

The door opened and a deputy collected my colleagues for exit processing. The door was closed and I was left alone. I closed my eyes and waited for them to come get me next.

visual ping

play your vaccine

CAT

All posters -